THE OSSUARY TREE

LONG GAP

Gap Br.

COYOTE WARREN

NORTH WOOD

THE LONG ROAD

THE COUNCIL TREE

WILDWOOD

THE

DEERSKULL DRAGONFIGHTER

WASTES

Ghost Br.

THE BLUFF

WILLAMETTE RIVER

St. JOHNS

TO THE CRAG

PRUE'S HOUSE

WILDWOOD
IMPERIUM

WILDWOOD
IMPERIUM

THE WILDWOOD CHRONICLES, BOOK III

COLIN MELOY

Illustrations by
CARSON ELLIS

BALZER + BRAY
An Imprint of HarperCollins*Publishers*

Library of Congress catalog card number: 2013953784
ISBN 978-0-06-202474-9

Typography by Dana Fritts
13 14 15 16 17 LP/CG/RRDH 10 9 8 7 6 5 4 3 2 1
❖
First Edition

For Milo

CONTENTS

PART THREE

LIST OF COLOR PLATES

❧

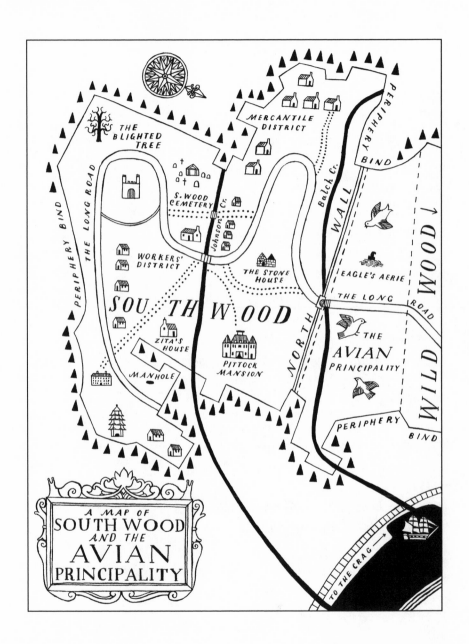

PART ONE

The May Queen

First, the explosion of life. Then came the celebration.

    Such had it been for generations and generations, as long as the eldest of the eldest could remember; as long as the record books had kept steady score. By the time the first buds were edging their green shoots from the dirt, the parade grounds had been cleared and the maypole had been pulled from its exile in the basement of the Mansion. The board had met and the Queen decided; all that was left was the wait. The wait for May.

    And when it came, it came wearing a bright white gown: the May

Queen. She appeared on horseback, as was tradition, wearing a blinding white gown and her hair sprouting garlands of flowers. Her name was Zita and she was the daughter of a stenographer for the courts, a proud man who stood beaming in the stands—a person of honor—with the Interim Governor-Regent-elect and his flushed, fat wife and his three children looking bored and bemused, stuffed as they were into their little ill-fitting suits that they only wore for weddings.

But the May Queen was radiant in her long brown braids and white, white gown, and everyone in the town flocked to see her and the procession that followed. In the center square, a brass band, having performed "The Storming of the Prison" to satisfy the powers that be, launched into a familiar set list of seasonal favorites, led by a mustachioed tenor who played up the bawdiest bits to the delight of the audience. A traditional dance was endured by the younger set among the audience, while the elders cooed their appreciation and waxed nostalgic about their own time, when they wore those selfsame striped trousers and danced the May Fair. The Queen reigned all the while, smiling down from her flower-laden dais; she must've been only fifteen. All the boys blushed to make eye contact with her. Even the Spokes, the hard-liners of the Bicycle Revolution, seemed to drop their ever-present steeliness in favor of an easy gait, and today there were no words of anger exchanged between them and the few in the crowd who might question their fervor. And when the Synod arrived to rasp the benediction on the day, the crowd suffered them quietly.

The rite was a strange insistence, considering the fact that the May Fair's celebration had long predated the sect's fixation on the Blighted Tree; indeed, the May Fair had been a long-standing tradition, it was told, even when the tree's boughs were full with green buds, before it earned its present name, before the strange parasite had rendered the tree in a kind of suspended animation. But such was the spirit that day: Even the spoilers were allowed their separate peace.

By the time the festivities, the beribboned maypole their axis, had spiraled out into the surrounding crowd and the light had faded and the men gathered around the barrels of poppy beer and the women sipped politely at blackberry wine and the dancing had begun in earnest, the May Queen had long since been hoisted on the shoulders of a crowd of local boys and brought with much fanfare to her home, where, her now-tipsy father assumed, she was peacefully asleep, her white gown toppled in a corner, her braids a tattered mess, and her pillow strewn with flowers.

But this was not the case.

Zita, the May Queen, was climbing down the trellis from her second-floor room, still wearing her white gown, and her wreath of flowers still atop her braided hair. A thorn from the climbing rose made a thin incision in the taffeta as she reached the ground. She stopped and studied her surroundings. She could hear the muffled, distant sounds of the celebrations in the town square; a few straggling partygoers, homeward bound, laughed over some joke on the street. She whistled, twice.

Nothing.

Again, she pursed her lips and gave two shrill whistles. A rustle sounded in the nearby junipers. Zita froze.

"Alice?" she asked to the dark. "Is that you?"

Suddenly, the bushes parted to reveal a girl, dressed in a dark over-coat. Remnant pieces of juniper stuck obstinately to her short blond hair. Zita frowned.

"You didn't have to come that way," said Zita.

Alice looked back at her improvised path: a hole in the bushes. "You said to come secret."

Another noise. This time, from the street side. It was Kendra, a girl with wiry, close-cropped hair. She was carrying something in her hands.

"Good," said Zita, seeing her. "You brought the censer."

Kendra nodded, proffering the thing in her hands. It was made of worn brass, discolored from decades of use. Tear-shaped holes dotted the vessel; strands of gold chain clung to its side, like hair. "I need to get this back tonight," she said. "It's serious. If my dad knew this was missing. He's got some weird thing he has to do tomorrow." Kendra's dad was a recent recruit to the rising Synod, an apostle to the Blighted Tree. She clearly wasn't very happy about his newfound religiosity.

Zita nodded. She turned to Alice, who was still brushing needles from her coat. "You have the sage?"

Alice nodded gravely and pulled a handful of green leaves, bundled by twine, from a bag slung over her back. The earthy smell of the herbs perfumed the air.

"Good," said Zita.

"Is that all we need?" asked Alice, stuffing the herb bouquet back in her bag.

Zita shook her head and produced a small blue bottle. The two other girls squinted and tried, in the half-light, to make out what was inside.

"What is it?" asked Kendra.

"I don't know," said Zita. "But we need it."

"And isn't there something about a mirror?" Again, this was Kendra.

Zita had it: a picture mirror, the size of a tall book. The glass sat in an ornate gold frame.

"Are you sure you know what you're doing?" This was Alice, fidgeting uncomfortably in her too-large coat.

Zita flashed her a smile. "No," she said. "But that's half the fun, right?" She shoved the bottle back in her pocket, the mirror in a knapsack at her feet. "C'mon," she said. "We don't have a ton of time."

The threesome marched quietly through the alleyways of the town, carefully avoiding the crowds of festivalgoers on their weaving ways homeward. The red brick of the buildings and houses gave way to the low, wooden hovels of the outer ring, and they climbed a forested hill, listening to the last of the brass bands echo away in the distance. A trail snaked through the trees here; Zita stopped by a fallen cedar and looked behind them. The lit windows of the Mansion could be seen winking some ways off, little starfalls in the narrow gaps between the crowding trees. She was carrying a red kerosene lantern, and she lit it with a match; they were about to continue when a noise startled them: more footsteps in the underbrush.

"Who's there?" demanded Zita, swinging the lantern toward the sound.

A young girl appeared, an overcoat hastily thrown over flannel pajamas.

"Becca!" shouted Alice. "So help me gods, I'm going to kill you."

The girl look appropriately shamed; her cheeks flared red and her eyes were downcast. "Sorry," she muttered.

Zita looked directly at Alice. "What is she doing here?"

"I'd ask her the same thing," said Alice, her eyes not leaving the young girl.

"I know what *you're* doing," said the young girl.

"Oh yeah?" asked Zita.

"Becca, go home," said Alice. "Do Mom and Dad know you're gone?"

The young girl ignored her sister's question. "You're calling the Empress."

Zita's eyes flashed to Alice's. "What did you tell her?"

"N-nothing," stammered Alice. She glanced around at the gathered girls, hoping for some rescue. Finally, she frowned and said, "She heard us talking. Last night. She said she'd tell Mom and Dad if I didn't let her in on it."

"I wanna come," said Becca, still staring at Zita. "I want to see you do it. I want to see what happens."

"You're too young," said Zita.

"Who says?" said Becca.

"I do," said Zita. "And I'm the May Queen."

This seemed to silence the little girl.

"Go home, Becca," said Alice. "And I won't make you rue the day you were born."

Becca rounded on her sister. "I'll tell Mom and Dad. I swear to the trees. I'll tell 'em. And then you won't be able to go out for a week. You'll have to miss the school Spring Pageant."

Alice gave Zita a pleading, desperate look that seemed to say, *Little sisters: What can you do?* The May Queen gave in, saying to Becca, "How much do you know?"

The young girl gave a deep, relieved breath and said, "I heard about it before, but I didn't know anyone who'd done it. At the old stone house. Off Macleay Road. They say she died there." She looked from girl to girl, judging by their silence that there was truth in her telling. "You say something? A chant? In the center of the house. And turn around three times. To wake her. Her ghost."

Zita listened to the girl in silence. When she'd finished, Zita nodded. "Okay," she said. "You can come. But you've got to swear you'll
not tell a soul what you see. You swear?"

"I swear."

"Follow me," said Zita, and she continued walking. Alice, cuffing
her sister on her head, took up the rear of the procession.

A clock struck the half hour, somewhere in the distance, and Zita
quickened her pace. "Not long now," she said.

"Why the rush?" asked Kendra.

"After midnight, it won't work. It's got to start before the hour.
The first of May, *too loo too ray.*"

Kendra looked to Alice for some sort of explanation, but Alice
only shrugged. Zita had long been a mysterious force in their lives:
Since they were little, she'd always had a kind of peculiar magnetism.
An imaginative girl, she'd captivated her friends with strange draw-
ings and poetry, with her long-standing fascination with the occult.

The forest grew wilder as they moved away from the populous
part of South Wood and into the mangy scrub that bordered the
Avian Principality. A path led through the undergrowth; before long,
the girls arrived at the house, or what was left of it.

It was a ruin, its stone walls worn down by the elements and nearly
consumed by a thick blanket of winding ivy. Branches invaded the
house where the roof had been, and thick swatches of moss lay in the
chinks of the stone. The four girls walked cautiously into the center of

the house, its floor long overtaken by the forest's greenery: a carpet of ivy fighting for dominion of the small enclosure. Whoever had lived here before had made do with very little: The house amounted to a single, small room. Two breaks in the rock walls suggested windows; a door, its keystone long collapsed, led out into a dark, empty expanse. Which is not to say that the house had remained entirely uninhabited all these years: Empty tins of food, their labels sunbleached indecipherable, littered the corners of the house, and the names and exploits of past explorers made a kind of diary on the inner walls: BIG RED SLEPT HERE SOME. TRAVIS LOVES ISABEL. NOT REALLY NOW NOT ANYMORE. LONG LIVE THE EMPRESS! were all scrawled in chalk and paint or chiseled into the stone.

Zita looked at her watch. She nodded to the other girls. "Let's do this," she said.

As she'd been told, as she'd heard from the older girls in her class (who whispered around her in the back of the small schoolhouse classroom, who smoked illicit cigarettes in the schoolyard and who sneered when she approached), as she'd finally learned when she'd got older: The Verdant Empress was a ghost who inhabited the house, who'd lived in the house, centuries before, when the Wood was an empire. She'd run afoul of the old government and they had sent knives to exact their final revenge. But rather than take her life, the assassins went after something more precious to her: her son. They stole into her garden one afternoon and cut the child down in front of his mother. To greaten her suffering, they let the woman live. The Empress, it was said, lost her mind over her murdered child and spent the rest of her many years wandering the Wood asking after his whereabouts, her addled mind having ceased to believe that he was dead. It was said she died of a broken heart, a forgotten and embittered old woman. Her gray hair became so filled with leaves and twigs in her wanderings that the locals coined a new name for her: the Verdant Empress. It was almost as if she was becoming a part of the forest itself. It was said her body was never found, that her corpse had simply decayed into the earthen ground of the house. And it was common knowledge, at least among the village teenagers, that when someone does not receive a proper burial, her soul is cursed to wander the world of the living for eternity.

Learning the story was like a coming-of-age benchmark for teenagers in South Wood; everyone knew it. However, very few acted on the promise of the story, the dark epilogue: With the right incantation, at the right time of the month, when the moon was full and the sky bright with stars, the Empress's soul could be called from her hellish purgatory to be witnessed by the living. Once she'd been called, though, there was very little information about what she would do: Some said she would do your bidding for seven days. Others swore she would administer revenge on whomever you named. Still others claimed only her shade appeared and wept for her murdered son, keening like a banshee. In any case, it was enough to drive the macabre fantasies of Zita and make her determined to bring the woman's ghost from the ether.

At Zita's instruction, the three other girls gathered around her in a tight circle in the center of the structure. She set the mirror at her feet. Taking the censer from Kendra, she opened it and filled the chamber with the sage leaves Alice had brought. The girls were silent as they followed Zita's instructions, staring at their friend with the quiet expressions of parishioners before a solemn clergyman. Finally, she produced the blue bottle from her pocket and proceeded to pour its contents into the censer: By the light of the lantern, held by Kendra, the stuff appeared to be a grainy, gray powder.

"Match," said Zita.

Alice brought out a small box labeled THE HORSE AND HIND PUBLIC HOUSE. Pulling a match from within, she struck it against the side and the thing flickered alight. Zita took it from Alice and held the flame to the now-closed censer.

A light exploded from the object.

Kendra shrieked; Alice threw her hand to her face. Only Zita and little Becca remained calm as an eerie illumination blew from the holes in the censer and flooded the ruined house like someone had tripped a floodlight. The smell of sage filled the air, sage and another scent that none of them could properly identify: Perhaps it was the smell of water. Or the smell of air released from an attic room long closed off.

"Okay," said Zita calmly. "Everyone join hands around me."

The girls did as they were told. Zita stood in the center with the glowing censer, thick tendrils of smoke now pouring from the teardrop-shaped holes in the brass. Taking a deep breath, she began her recitation:

>*On the first of May*
>*Too loo too ray*
>*Before the dark succumbs to day*
>*When sparrows cry*
>*Too loo too rye*
>*We call the Verdant Empress*

She looked at the small circle of girls surrounding her. Their eyes were tightly shut. The littlest, Becca, furrowed her brow in deep concentration. "Now you all repeat," said Zita, "after me."

And they did:

> *We call you*
> *Verdant Empress*
> *We call you*
> *Verdant Empress*
> *Verdant Empress*
> *Verdant Empress*

Then Zita spoke alone. "Now count off. I'm going to turn."

The girls hummed the count as Zita made slow pirouettes in the center of the circle.

> *ONE*
> *TWO*
> *THREE*

Suddenly, the light from the censer was snuffed out, like an extinguished candle flame.

The ivy rustled at their feet, though no breeze disturbed the air.

And then, issuing from the ground came the distinct sound of a woman's low, gravelly moan.

Kendra screamed and fell backward; Alice grabbed Becca and, in a state of absolute panic, threw her sister over her shoulder and stumbled for the house's doorway. Within a flash, three of the four girls had made a hasty exit from the house and were sprinting, screaming, through the encircling woods. Only Zita remained, transfixed, the extinguished censer swinging in her hand.

All was silent. The moaning had ceased; the ivy had stopped writhing. Zita looked down at the mirror at her feet. The glass was fogged.

Slowly, words began to scrawl across the glass, as if drawn there by a finger.

GIRL, they read.

Zita's breath caught in her throat.

I AM AWAKE.

A Difficult Houseguest

"**P**ancakes, pancakes, pancakes," Prue's dad announced in a cheerful singsong as he stuck his head around the kitchen door. "Who wants some more pancakes?"

Prue politely demurred, saying, "None for me, thanks." She'd already had two. Her mother and baby brother, Mac, didn't say anything, as if they hadn't heard a word the pancake chef had said. Instead, they were staring intently at their houseguest, who was taking up most of one side of the dining room table.

"I'd go for a few more," said the guest. "If you insist."

Prue's mother's eyes went wide, and the color vanished from her face.

"That's what I like," said Prue's dad, undeterred. "A guy with an appetite." He disappeared back into the kitchen, whistling some unidentifiable pop song.

"W-would you like some m-more o-orange juice?" managed Prue's mother.

The guest looked at the three empty jugs of juice on the table. He suddenly seemed embarrassed. "Oh, no thanks, Mrs. McKeel," he said. "I think I've probably had enough."

Just then, Prue's dad reappeared from the kitchen and heaped another five pancakes on the guest's plate, steam hissing from the blueberries in the cooked batter. By Prue's count, these would bring the guest's pancake intake up to thirty-seven.

"Hope you don't want any more," said Prue's dad, smiling, "'cause we're cleaned out of flour. And milk. And butter."

The guest smiled appreciatively at Prue's dad, saying, "Oh, thanks very much. This'll do just fine." He reached across the table for the pitcher of syrup but stopped, daunted by the task of fitting a golden hook, which stood in place of his hand, through the pitcher's handle.

"Here," said Prue. "Let me help." She picked up the syrup pitcher and proceeded to pour the thick brown liquid over the guest's heap of pancakes. "Say when."

"When," said the guest.

"Your friend sure has an appetite," said Mrs. McKeel.

Prue looked at her mom and sighed. "He *is* a bear, Mom," she said.

That much was true: the McKeels' breakfast guest was a very large brown bear. What's more, he was a bear with shiny hooks in place of his claws. He could also talk. But the McKeel household had, by this time, become somewhat used to strange phenomena in their lives.

Only last fall, the youngest of the clan, Mac, barely a year old, had been abducted by a flock of crows (or, as Prue had corrected them: a murder of crows), and their daughter, unbeknownst to her parents, had gone after him, putting not only her own life in very serious danger, but also the life of her schoolmate, Curtis Mehlberg, who'd followed her. And it wasn't as if the crows had simply deposited the babe in a nest somewhere; rather, they'd brought him to the Impassable Wilderness, a deep, vast stretch of woods that bordered the city of Portland, Oregon. It was a forbidden place—stories were traded about unlucky people becoming lost and walking into the woods, never to return. Apparently, this wasn't the entire truth: Prue and Curtis had discovered a thriving world inside the boundary of these woods, a world of wise Mystics, savage bandits, warring moles, bird princes, and a Dowager Governess, consumed by living ivy. They'd become inextricably entwined with the events in this land, and now it seemed like the very fate of the place relied on their actions.

In normal households, a child coming to his or her parents reporting such things would mean immediate psychiatric evaluation, or, if the parent were particularly gullible, a call to the local authorities at the very least. The McKeels, having had their son Mac returned to them, did neither. In fact, it could be argued that they had themselves brought the whole episode down on their unsuspecting children. You see, in order to have children, they'd had to make a deal with a strange woman who'd emerged from the Impassable Wilderness, crossing a bridge that had appeared out of the very mist. So it didn't strike them as being overly strange, this world inside the forest. They'd mostly just been happy to get their kids back safely.

After that, things just got weirder; Prue had disappeared some months before on her way to get naan bread from the local Indian take-out joint. They'd both, Lincoln and Anne McKeel, suffered a kind of instinctual shudder of fear when she hadn't returned, but they both knew, deep down, that there were likely stranger things afoot. Their instincts had been proven right when, later that evening, an egret had landed on their front porch and knocked on their door with his beak. He announced, somewhat nonchalantly, that their daughter had been taken back into the Impassable Wilderness—more specifically, an area of the I.W. that this bird had called Wildwood—for her own safety. Apparently, she was someone of importance in this strange world, and an enemy had dispatched a shape-shifting assassin to end her short, preteen life. It made perfect sense to them at the time, and they immediately set about writing the requisite letters to her middle school, informing them that she had mono and would be missing class for the foreseeable future. They waited patiently for her return, knowing she was in very good hands.

And now this: Prue had arrived at their home some few weeks prior walking with a slight limp, her arm in a makeshift sling and a very large, very English-speaking brown bear in tow. They'd done their best to accommodate the new guest, setting up their giant car camping tent in Prue's room so that the bear, whose name was Esben, could best achieve his preferred cavelike habitat. They'd made extra trips to the grocery store, procuring economy-size bags of flour and vats of milk to keep up with his ursine appetite. When seen by curious neighbors while making such excursions, the back of their station wagon riding low under the weight of thirty pounds of ground beef, Anne had said that they were stocking up for the end-times. (She'd even gotten used to making a kind of secretive, winking gesture at her husband for the neighbors' benefit, as if to say, *He's the crazy one.* Lincoln, for his part, played it up and peppered his daily exchanges with folks around town with conspiracy theories that he'd literally made up just moments before, e.g., "The Department of Transportation is hoarding avocados for use in avocado-fueled rocket ships that will take only DOT employees to a terraformed resort/theme park on the dark side of the moon, where they will engineer the eradication of Earth's something-billion people in favor of genetically modified offspring of moon-living DOT employees. I'm not making this up.") The novelty of the adventure had soon worn off, leading the family to be politely curious about the bear's departure date. The only concern: He was bound to take their daughter with him.

Lincoln McKeel, de-aproned, joined them at the table, nursing a smoothie and a single fried egg. He smiled at the table while he tucked into his meager meal.

"Any idea when, you know, you'll be . . . ," began Prue's mom. She trailed off, unsure of her footing, not wishing to be a rude host.

"What my wife is trying to say, Esben," took up Lincoln, his mouth full of yolk, "is we were just curious about, you know . . . Well, it does seem that we're out of flour. And butter. And eggs."

"And while we're perfectly happy to go out and get some more," interjected Anne, "it would be maybe helpful to know . . . to know . . ."

Prue couldn't take it anymore. "We'll be out of here tomorrow, promise," she said.

"We?" her parents said simultaneously.

"WEEEEEE!" shouted Mac, who swung his fork around his small, lightly furred head like a pike. The half-eaten piece of pancake that had been speared on the tines went flying across the room. "WEEEEE ANNND BEARRRR!"

"I told you guys the plan," said Prue, watching the arc of the projectile. "This was always part of the plan."

Esben, his mouth full of pancakes, grunted in agreement.

Prue continued, "As soon as my ankle and my arm got better, we had to get back to the Wood. We're needed. We can't waste any

They were staring intently at their houseguest, who was taking up
most of one side of the dining room table.

more time. We have to find——"

"The other 'maker,' sure," finished her mother. "Whoever that is. I just thought that, well, maybe Esben could go. Work it out himself. You've missed a lot of school, Pruey. I don't want to see you have to repeat the seventh grade."

Prue stared at her mother. A silence filled the space between them. "I don't care," she said finally. "I don't care about seventh grade anymore. I belong in there, in the Wood. They need me."

Esben stopped chewing momentarily to grunt his agreement again. "It's true, Mrs. McKeel," said the bear. "This is very important. She's needed."

"You're a *talking bear*," pointed out Anne McKeel angrily. "Don't tell me about parenting."

Esben, a hookful of pancake nearly to his jaws, froze.

"Honey," said Prue's dad, reaching across the table to rest his hand on his wife's, "I think we have to listen to them here. This is bigger than us."

Just then, as the quiet descended over the dining room table and each person, even little Mac with his tuft of hair crusty with errant pancake, breathed in the silence like it was a calming gas and the periodic hum of cars on the street in front of the house punctuated their unsaid sentences, Anne McKeel burst into tears. Esben the bear was the first to react, saying "Aww, there now, Mrs. McKeel," like the kind, embarrassed houseguest he was, witnessing something very

21

private and perhaps very human.

Was that all that was needed to be said? For a time, the sound of Prue's mother crying was all there was in the room until she sniffled the tears away and the bear finished his pancakes and everyone cleaned up the table, bringing the dirty dishes to the sink. The spring day unfolded in front of them, and before long the morning's drama had been forgotten. Anne McKeel swallowed her tears.

That night, as the rest of the house was sleeping, Prue remained awake, her head reclined against her pillow. The bear snored fitfully in the houselike tent by her bed. When she heard a prolonged pause in the sawing, she ventured, "Esben?"

"Hmm?" grumbled the bear.

"Can't sleep."

"Again?"

"I don't know how you can. There's so much to think about."

"Try not to."

Prue pursed her lips and tried to do what the bear advised. Somehow, trying was making the whole endeavor more unlikely.

"Esben?" she said, after a while.

"Hmmm?"

"What's he going to think? It's the one thing that keeps bothering me."

A shuffling noise followed: an immense body rolling over in a too-small fleece sleeping bag. "What's who going to think?"

"Alexei."

"Oh. Not entirely sure."

"But the tree has to have, like, thought this through, right?"

"I suppose it has." A pause. "Prue?"

"Yeah?"

"Try to get some sleep. Big day tomorrow."

And so she tried, listening with amazement as Esben fell instantaneously into deep, clamorous sleep. But the thoughts continued to collide in her head: What *would* Alexei think of his own resurrection? It was something that had been bothering her, in the recesses of her mind, since she'd been given the message from the Council Tree: that the automaton child prince needed to be revived. Hadn't the prince himself been responsible for his own death after his mother had re-created him? What sort of offense were they committing by making him live that same inconsideration—his resurrection—all over again? And yet the directive had come from the spiritual heart of the Wood itself, the Council Tree: *Peace can only be gained by bringing back the boy prince.* Wouldn't he forgive them this imposition, for the greater good? What *was* the greater good? What sort of situation would be dispelled by simply bringing a single soul back from the ether?

The morning sun was brightening her bedroom window long before any sort of solution presented itself; Prue admitted defeat and pulled herself from her blankets, underslept and overwrought.

She set about packing her bag full of supplies for the trip, the pain in her ankle now nearly vanished and her arm only aching when she pulled it too taut. Esben played with Mac in the living room, letting the two-year-old climb over his furry back and tumble into his lap; he spun twin Frisbees on his golden hooks, a trick perfected during his tenure in the circus, and Mac cooed with appreciative laughter. When Prue appeared at the bottom of the stairs with her packed bag slung over her shoulder, her parents were sitting in their respective chairs in the living room, her father reading a book and her mother attempting to coax a shape out of some new tangle of knitting.

Esben set Mac down and looked at Prue. "Ready?" he said.

Prue nodded.

Anne didn't look up from her knitting; Lincoln stood and walked to his daughter. "Okay," he said. "Let's hit it."

Anne remained in her chair, tussling with yarn.

"Bye, Mom," said Prue.

Anne didn't look up. Prue looked to her dad for guidance, but Lincoln only shrugged. Together they proceeded to wrap a threadbare quilt around Esben's massive frame and enshroud his head with the giant knitted cap that Anne had made him. The bear, thus disguised, sidled out the door, and the three of them made their way to the family Subaru, parked out in front of the house.

They drove in silence, Esben huddled down in the back: An

amorphous pile of blankets and yarn, he could easily be mistaken for one family's Goodwill donation haul. The car speakers burbled a public radio pledge drive.

"Are we going to get another message-by-egret?" asked Prue's dad.

His daughter smiled. "Only good news, promise."

"And this assassin—that's all taken care of?"

Prue briefly shuddered at the mention of Darla Thennis, the shape-shifting fox. She recalled the ungracious *THUNK*s that sounded her demise. "Yeah, she's gone. Though there might be more. We don't know. So that's why we're staying underground till we get to South Wood."

"And you're going to be greeted like a hero, right? That's what you've said."

"Yeah, if our hunch is right."

"Unless things have changed," pointed out Esben.

"There's that," said Prue, though she'd not wanted to consider the potentially darker side of their plan. She ran her finger along the car's window, feeling the sun beat against it. They'd pulled up alongside a sedan at a stoplight, and the toddler in the backseat craned his neck. A light in his eyes suggested he'd seen Esben, and he began frantically hitting the window, trying to point out the anomaly to his parents. The light changed and they'd taken a right turn before the bear had been made by the adults in the car, leaving the toddler, Prue assumed, to an afternoon filled with ignored proclamations.

They arrived at the junk heap after a time, and Esben ditched his disguise: The place was empty of any other soul that might be thrown by the appearance of a talking bear. He breathed a deep sigh of relief and stretched his thick arms skyward. "No offense," he said to Lincoln, "but that blanket smelled like cat drool and moldy carpeting."

"None taken," said Lincoln.

The bear did, however, keep the knit cap on his head. He'd said, when he was given it, that he always had a hard time finding suitably fitting headwear. He nestled it close over his small ears as he walked down toward the shack in the middle of the trash heap, its door hanging on its loose hinges; clearly, whoever was responsible for the upkeep of this tunnel access had been negligent in their maintenance. The shack covered a concrete conduit leading into the belowground. Esben stopped at the entrance and turned to the McKeels, who were still standing by the car.

Prue and her father shared a long hug. A flurry of plastic bags floated around them like revenant angels. "Careful out there," said Lincoln McKeel.

"I will, promise," said his daughter. She walked down the hill of trash to join the bear at the doorway to the underground.

CHAPTER 3

The Forgotten Place

Either the flash or the boom from the explosion—she couldn't know which—startled Elsie from her sleep. Thing is: She hadn't realized she was sleeping; she'd only begun telling herself she was simply resting her eyes and the world dropped away and she was transported, weightless, to some other place, some other world, when the sound of the explosion anchored her rudely back to her present circumstances. She rubbed her eyes and squinted against the dark of the night; somewhere, a fire was raging, a flickering glow on the distant horizon. A few months ago, such a sound would've set her heart racing, but now, two months into her newfound life, it served only to remind her that she was neglecting her duty.

Answering a pleading ache from her crisscrossed legs, she stood up and stretched, her hand holding tight to the broken brick wall. It was a long fall from this distance, she judged. She kicked at the ground; a piece of rock flew from her perch and sounded, some seconds later, on the ground below.

Another explosion lit up the dark; this time she saw it happen. Some chemical silo, miles distant. Flames erupted skyward and showered the surrounding buildings with light and stray metal. The fire smoldered a little but soon became indistinguishable from the gas flares and yellow electric lights that dotted the landscape of the Industrial Wastes. They were curious, these explosions. They happened fairly regularly, enough that it was clear they weren't part of the normal workings of the Wastes. The older kids said there was a war going on, but between whom, they couldn't say. They'd all grown accustomed to the noise—the flash and the boom—and treated it as you would the sound of the garbage truck appearing at your curb, or the mailman knocking on your door.

She was tempted to press the voice-box button of the doll she held in the crook of her arm—it was an Intrepid Tina toy and so came preprogrammed with every manner of confidence-building aphorism—but held off, having been forbidden by the older kids to do so for fear of alerting anyone to their presence in the warehouse. Instead she pulled the doll's face close to hers and gave it a quick pat on the shoulder with her fingertip.

"It's okay, Tina," said Elsie. "No explosions here."

The dark was taking on a tinge of blue, heralding the coming sunrise. To Elsie's left, just below her, a light winked. She looked at it; a voice came in a loud whisper: "Elsie!"

"Michael?"

"It's five. Hit the hay."

"Got it." Elsie grabbed the small bag at her feet. Opening it, a burlap bag one might carry onions or potatoes in, she stowed the provisions she'd packed for the evening: a flashlight, a bag of raisins, and a yellowed pamphlet on earthquake safety (her only reading material). By the time she'd finished, Michael appeared at the top of the stairs that led from the perch. For a moment, they shared the narrow space that was the warehouse's stairwell, the brick wall that had once hidden it long broken away.

"How'd it go?" he said.

"Fine," said Elsie. "Nothing special. Couple explosions, just now. One after another, real quick. Otherwise, normal stuff." She paused, remembering. "Oh. And I saw him."

"Him. The Weirdo?"

"Yeah, but it was a ways off."

The boy sniffed a few times, looking out at the vista. They'd called the figure the Weirdo, or at least that's what Carl had called it—he was the first one to have spotted the figure—and it had first made its appearance a few weeks prior. They couldn't tell if the Weirdo was a he or she—it was too shrouded in clothing and blankets to be discernible. They'd quickly deduced that this person—whoever it was—was mostly harmless, as it rarely strayed very close to their hideout and when it did, a well-placed rock seemed to scare the thing away handily, like a sad, stray dog.

Clearly, Michael was unalarmed, saying to Elsie, "Well, Sandra's got some oats on the stove. If you're quick, you could be first in line."

"Okay, thanks," said Elsie. She handed Michael the rusty machete she'd propped against a pile of bricks at her side. He accepted it with a grunt of thanks. It was the only weapon the Unadoptables carried—they'd found it nearly a week into their residency in the Wastes, lodged amid a thicket of half-hacked blackberry brambles. She took a few careful steps down the wooden stairs before lighting the flashlight, as she'd been taught. It was one of many precautions they took; the more invisible they remained, the less likely they were to be found out. Even in this farthest redoubt of the lonely Industrial Wastes, a vast wilderness of burned-out warehouses and buildings, which the Unadoptables had taken to calling the Forgotten Place.

The light was growing as Elsie made her way down the twisting stairway, lighting the path ahead through the great breaks in the brick walls and the emptied window frames. By the time she'd made it back to the floor of the abandoned warehouse, the place was filled with a dim light and a fire was raging in a metal barrel in the center of the massive room. A few pigeons darted between the eaves and the rafters, high above her head, and the sleeping forms of the other children were like the peaks of little waves on the weathered wooden floor. Sandra was stirring something in a black metal pot, and she greeted Elsie as she arrived.

"Morning," said Sandra.

"Morning," said Elsie. "Whatcha cooking?"

"Gruel. I think," the cook said, smiling. She scooped up a ladleful of the pot's contents by way of demonstration: It looked like phlegm.

"Yum," said Elsie. "I love gruel."

"That's the spirit," said Sandra. She grabbed a tin bowl and, filling it with the pasty stuff, handed it to Elsie. "Dig in."

Elsie could feel her stomach growling as she made her way over to the children's dining area: an old cafeteria table, rotted by weather and disuse. By now, the rest of the kids were rousing and pulling themselves from their salvaged blankets. A familiar mop of black hair appeared from one such blanket and proceeded to shake itself out: It was Elsie's sister, Rachel, fifteen years old as of this morning. She sat in her pile of blankets as if marinating in them, clearly mourning inwardly about having a birthday in such desperate circumstances. Elsie put a spoonful of gruel in her mouth and let the warmth descend into her chest and fan out across her shoulders and into her arms. She watched her sister stare into space until she couldn't take it anymore. "Rach!" she said.

Rachel looked in her direction; her eyes were sad, quiet.

"Happy birthday," said Elsie, stirring her gruel.

Her sister smiled and pushed herself up. Many of her fellow sleepers had made their way over to Sandra's pot of morning mush. Rachel walked over and sat across the table from Elsie.

"Thanks, sis," said Rachel.

Elsie spoke around a mouthful of food. "Get some gruel. It's good. Sandra made it."

Rachel looked into Elsie's bowl and attempted a meager smile. "Guess I'm not hungry. You had lookout last night, right? How'd it go?"

"Fine," Elsie said. "I saw him. The Weirdo."

"Get a better look?"

"Nah. He didn't come close or anything. I think Michael's right. He's just some lost hobo."

"Anything else?"

"Nothing special," said Elsie. "Couple explosions. Pretty far off."

"Oh yeah?" This came from Carl Rehnquist, a boy about Elsie's age, who'd come and joined them at the table. Steam rose from his bowl of breakfast. "What kind?"

"What do you mean, what kind?"

"Like, big explosions? Or little ones? What blew up?"

"I don't know," said Elsie. "Just some buildings. A ways off."

"Cool," said Carl.

Elsie shrugged and took another spoonful of gruel. "It's just the Wastes, right? Seems like it's just industrial . . . stuff."

"Michael said that it's happening more often, the explosions," said Carl.

"Really? He didn't say anything to me about that," replied Elsie.

"I overheard him, just yesterday. He said that they're happening a lot more. And they're closer."

"Yeah, don't trust everything that kids tell you," said Rachel.

Carl took a big bite of his breakfast. "Next thing you know, right here: *boom!*" Bits of wet, white oats flew from his lips; whether he did this on purpose for effect or accidentally, the girls couldn't know. "Whole place goes up. Doesn't matter to you guys, though. Aren't you out of here in a bit? I mean, didn't you say your parents would be back from their trip soon?"

The two sisters didn't say anything. Rachel toyed with the strands of her hair; Elsie stirred her gruel in silence.

Carl sensed he had overstepped. "They *are* coming back, right?"

What Carl couldn't know was that the two girls had received another postcard from their parents, the second since their adoptive orphanage had gone up in flames in the winter's violent uprising. The first had arrived just after their discovery of the abandoned warehouse in this, the children's new home in the Forgotten Place. It was postmarked February 20 from Iğdır, Turkey: Their parents wished them well and reported briefly that their attempts to find their son, Curtis, in the slums of Istanbul had been a dead end; however, they now had actionable intelligence that the boy had been smuggled over the border into Armenia by a group of gypsy circus performers, and the elder Mehlbergs were likely to stay abroad for a further two weeks (a check, payable to the Joffrey Unthank Home for Wayward Youth, would be on its way, presently, to the orphanage's address). The second postcard, received only the day before, had their intrepid parents now in the farthest-flung reaches of the Russian continent: a black-and-white photo of a ship frozen in thick, jagged ice, with their mother's clean handwriting on the flip side saying, *"Greetings from Archangel'sk! Ignore that bit about the Armenian circus; was a red herring. Good news: A young American boy was spotted near here, on an island off the north coast. Nearly the Arctic Circle! Brrrr! Back in two weeks, promise! Check en route to Mr. Unthank; tell him sorry for delay."* Rachel, the unofficial archivist of the two Mehlberg sisters, kept both cards folded neatly in the pocket of her jumper.

Elsie deftly changed the subject. "You know it's Rachel's birthday today?"

"Really?" Carl's eyes had lit up. "No kidding?"

Rachel grumbled an affirmative.

"May ninth," said Elsie. "Nineteen . . ."

"Ninety-eight," finished Rachel. "Yup."

"Well, we'll have to have a party or something," said Carl.

"That's okay," said Rachel.

"No, really," continued the boy. "When Michael gets back, we'll have to do something, you know, special."

"Like what?" asked Rachel. "Fry up an oatcake? Pop the cork on some rat pee champagne?"

Elsie gave her sister a withering look. "C'mon, Rach. He just wants to be nice."

"Suit yourself, grump," said Carl, unaffected. He shoveled more breakfast into his wide mouth.

It was true: Any kind of celebration they threw in their new home would have to be a fairly scanty one. In the two months since they'd been there, a few of the orphans' birthdays passed by uncounted save for a few cheers from their fellows and an extra ration of bread for the birthday boy or girl at dinner. Anything beyond that was deemed an extravagance. And so most of the kids kept their celebrations to themselves, not wishing to somehow highlight their destitute circumstances just when they were all trying to get their feet under them. They still had faith in Martha Song's clear vision for their future: They would build their own insulated world here, free of the strictures of either the Periphery, their previous prison within the boundary of the Impassable Wilderness, or the world of the adults, which loomed beyond the Industrial Wastes like a disapproving parent. Here, they were Living Free. So far, they had the freedom part down pretty well; the "living" side of the equation was proving to be a challenge.

Food was scarce; every day, a scavenging party set out into the occupied areas of the Wastes, pulling half-eaten apples and sandwich scraps from Dumpsters and trash barrels. The stevedores, the maroon-beanie-wearing hulks who populated the silos and warehouses of this industrial zone, congregated for lunch on the stoops and staircases of their factories after the noon whistle; whatever they left behind was quarry for the orphans. While modest, it was enough to eke out a subsistence.

Protection was another matter; not only did they have to thwart the occasional stevedore sentry, still bitter from the hiding they'd received during the Unthank Home uprising, but packs of wild dogs were known to inhabit this reach of the Wastes, putting the children's lives, if not just their food stores, at risk. Hence the nightly vigil at the perch in the warehouse's bombed-out stairwell. They all took turns, trading shifts. They'd established a simple system: One

whistle meant stevedores. Two meant dogs. They'd gotten it down to a science: In the case of the stevedores, they'd send out a decoy party to lure the sentries farther away from the warehouse. At the sound of a second whistle, they knew to batten down the hatches, secure all the doors, and wait for the marauding dogs to find some other place to terrorize. The rusty machete, which the kids had taken to calling Excalibur, seemed to serve only as a bravery totem: They were all emboldened by it but were a little afraid of what it would mean to actually use it. But with every invasion scare, with every drill, they became more and more proud of the home they were defending. The home that Martha Song had envisioned; just without Martha herself.

That was the thing that still stuck in Elsie's craw: the fact that two of their family—Martha and Carol Grod—were still, as far as they knew, in the grip of the stevedores. They'd been captured by the stevedores during the orphanage rebellion; their whereabouts

were anyone's guess. This fact had become even more important to Rachel, something she was keen to remind the rest of the kids anytime they felt like they'd become more acclimated to their new situation.

And so, that evening, when the nightly meeting was called to order, Rachel was poised for confrontation. Michael, holding the machete, hushed the crowd: Seventy-three children, varying in age from eight to eighteen, sat around the burning steel drum fire and squirmed to attention. "Unadoptables," he said. "Gather round." Even though most of the kids hadn't earned the title of Unadoptable, they'd all taken it on as a show of solidarity to those who'd been sent off by Joffrey Unthank to molder in the Periphery.

"First off," said Michael, "we should all wish one of our family a happy birthday. Rachel Mehlberg is—what—fifteen today?"

The crowd murmured their congratulations.

Rachel seized the opportunity. "Thanks. So what about Martha and Carol?"

Michael gave her a weary smile. "We're going to get to that."

"When?" challenged Rachel. "We've been 'going to get to that' for two months now."

"Well, it will take time. . . ."

"Time enough. We've been sitting here like a bunch of, I don't know, *whatevers* while our friends—our family!—are out there, being who-knows-whated by those clods. I think it's pretty simple:

We just—" She was interrupted by Michael, who was waving the machete, Excalibur.

"I've got the sword," said Michael. "So you're talking out of turn."

"It's not technically a sword," one of the boys at Michael's feet said. "It's more like a machete."

"Whatever," Michael shot back. "Whoever has it does the talking."

This seemed to quiet the room. Michael cleared his throat and continued.

"Carol and Martha, believe me, are really important to me. Martha was a good friend. She was one of the first people I met at the Unthank Home." Here he turned to Rachel. "And I remember it was me who introduced you to Carol, Rachel." He paused, soaking in the silence of the dead room. "You might even say we wouldn't be in this situation if I'd had my way. We'd still be happy and safe, all of us, in the cottage in the Periphery."

"And I wouldn't be having a birthday," pointed out Rachel. A few of the other kids nodded sagely; time was literally stopped in the Periphery, the protective boundary around the Impassable Wilderness, and none of the children aged while they lived there. It was part of Martha's pitch to leave: She, astutely, questioned the benefits of not growing old.

"We're still getting on our feet here," said Michael, ignoring Rachel's riposte. "It's going to take some time. As soon as we're strong, that's when we'll act."

"We're strong now," said Rachel. "We've waited long enough as it is."

Michael began to interject, to insist to the girl that he was still the one holding the machete, when the rest of group began to howl in support of Rachel: "Give her Excalibur!" "Give it up, Michael!" "Give her a chance!" With a begrudging grimace, Michael walked over to Rachel and handed her the machete, hilt first.

Elsie watched as her sister took the grip of the blade in her hand, weighing it, and walked to the front of the assembly. Change comes over people slowly, gradually, Elsie reasoned. But ever since their exit from the Periphery, along with the revelation that the Mehlberg sisters were able to walk through the boundary itself unaffected, Rachel had become a new person, a stronger person. Gone was the cross-armed girl who seemed to vanish beneath her long, straight hair, her chin burrowing ever farther into her threadbare black T-shirt. The fact that it was Rachel's birthday today only seemed to underscore how much Elsie's sister was in the process of some grand transformation that she, Elsie, could barely comprehend.

"Listen up," said Rachel as she arrived in front of the group. "We've got a good thing here, we've got a system down. But as far as I'm concerned, the longer we wait to go after Martha and Carol, the more we're seriously letting them down. The stevedores have them. Who knows what they're doing to them right now. We owe it to them to be devoting every waking hour to finding where they are and rescuing them. It's super simple. We've been here two months. We can't afford to wait another two."

Several of the kids in the audience nodded. Michael stood with his hands in his pockets, alternately watching the girl as she spoke and surveying the crowd.

"I say we do a show of hands. Who wants to start organizing a search-and-rescue party now? Huh? No more waiting." Rachel's head was held high as she spoke, the machete sitting comfortably in her hand as if she'd been born to wield it.

Elsie was about to raise her hand in agreement—she had the sense that she would be in the majority, weighing in—when the alarm was sounded: a single, shrill whistle from the perch above the warehouse. It was the unmistakable whistle of Cynthia Schmidt, who was a practiced whistler; it came like a wren's call. The room was seized with a sudden, palpable fear.

The stevedores were coming.

The Spiral in the Trees;
A Finger on a Windowpane

They'd traveled for days, over mountain passes still stuck with snow, through craggy valleys where trees grew in the most unreachable places. They traversed hillsides and crossed grand plantations, where the farmers' children ran from their work in the fields to meet the small, yet immediately recognizable procession. There were four travelers: two humans, a fox, and a coyote. One of the humans was a middle-aged woman, the other a boy of perhaps ten. They were all Mystics, of the North Wood. They wore identical sackcloth robes. They were on a journey that would bring them into the very heart of Wildwood.

The youngest, the boy, carried a small, bright flag in his hands.

They didn't speak as they walked, choosing instead to pass the long spans of time in meditation, absorbing the spectrum of languages they received from the plants and trees that surrounded them on their journey. It was their gift: the ability to commune with the mute flora of the forest. They wore this incredible ability with solemnity, using it not so much as one might flourish some crass magic trick, but in a reserved and mindful way, so that their relationship with the plants and trees would be a model to the rest of the citizens of the Wood, that they might live in more perfect harmony with the organic world around them. For this reason, the people of North Wood revered them.

As they came down from the mountains, their surroundings began to change; gone were the little hovels by the road and the farmhouses and inns. Instead, the vegetation by the side of the single, curving road they followed grew heavy and cluttered with thick, wild greenery, fighting for supremacy on the uneven ground. Even the language of the plants and trees shifted; it became uneven and scattered, a white noise of garbled shouting, barraging the quiet minds of the Mystics as they traveled. They found they needed to stop and rest more often; carrying the weight of the forest's belligerent voices was burden enough.

They broke camp early and traveled all day. As the final morning of their journey dawned, the young boy sat on the cracked stump of a storm-fallen hemlock and stared into space. The older woman came over to him and put her hand consolingly on his shoulder.

"Not long now," she said. "We're not far off."

He acknowledged her with a wan smile. "I can feel it," he said. "But there's something else. . . ."

The woman looked at him curiously. "What is it?"

"I don't know," the boy said. His finger, lazing at his side, began drawing a looping spiral on the grain of the tree trunk. "I've been having dreams."

"About the tree?"

The boy cleared his throat; his finger continued to trace the pattern. "No," he said. "I can't say. I can't quite see it."

The other two Mystics had risen and were busily pulling down their canvas tents. The early morning sun was breaking through the tangle of trees; a mist had settled on the lower branches. The boy's finger had finally traced to the center of the spiral he'd been creating, and it stopped there. He looked down at his fingertip and watched it, like someone monitoring an unmoving spider in the center of an elaborate web.

"Let's go," he said.

The other three Mystics followed him wordlessly. They knew not to question his leadership, even though his selection as the Elder Mystic, a role once reserved, as its name would suggest, for the eldest of the sect, was wholly unprecedented. After the death of the prior

Elder Mystic, Iphigenia, the tree surprised everyone by selecting the young boy—a Yearling—as the old woman's successor. As long as anyone remembered, as long as the histories had been written, there was no record of anyone but the eldest being selected for this highest responsibility; the change was enough to cause confusion among even the most sage and learned of the robed sect. But, as was clear in the teachings of the tree, all was flux; nothing was determined or permanent. Change was the only certainty of life. Perhaps, they decided, the descriptor *Elder* did not so much refer to the individual's physical age as their *spiritual* age. And so the boy was raised from Yearling to Elder Mystic; the boy himself seemed neither surprised nor flattered by the election. He seemed suited to the calling.

And this was their first task: to make the pilgrimage to the Ossuary Tree, in deepest Wildwood, where vicious animals lived freely and bandits made easy prey of the unwary traveler. There to hang a flag on a bough in remembrance of the departed Elder Mystic, Iphigenia. Because the journey was only made on the occasion of an Elder Mystic's death, each generation of acolytes and Mystics were forced to relearn the journey from the writings of the Ancients and their guidance from the trees. They could follow the road for only so long; eventually they would need to break away and traverse Wildwood itself.

Here there were no roads, no paths. Occasionally a game trail would open up to them, but often they chose instead to follow the guidance of the trees and the plants, ferreting what information they could from the jumble of voices they produced, snaking carefully through the maze of branches and brambles made by the forest.

Now, on the eighth day of the pilgrimage, they arrived at their goal, having broken through a ring of blackberry bushes into a wide, sweeping glade. In the center of the clearing stood the Ossuary Tree.

The Ossuary Tree, one of the three Trees of the Wood, was neither living nor dead. It seemed to hover in some in-between place; it had no leaves, though its bark was a deep, lively brown and its boughs strived skyward and it stood taller by several lengths than any of the other trees in its proximity. Fastened to the ends of its long, gnarled limbs were little colorful flags; each one had been tied there in remembrance of Elder Mystics past. Some of the fluttering scraps of fabric were centuries old, and while they all endured the ravages of the seasons, they remained as perfectly intact as when they first were tied. They became, essentially, the leaves of the Ossuary Tree and were imbued with its life.

Wordlessly, the four Mystics sloughed off their bags. They sat for a moment at the base of the tree, wondering at its height and sharing a few good-natured handshakes in celebration of a successful journey. The sun was shining now; it was clear the season was ebbing into the next, and the May day felt fresh and alive. The young boy, the Elder Mystic, had elected to do the tying himself, though this was unprecedented as well; typically the Elder Mystic, often infirm from age, deferred such a challenging duty to the young and agile. The boy, without saying a word, his face still etched with a strange, contemplative stillness, took the little red flag, the flag that would hang for Iphigenia, in his teeth and began scaling the trunk of the great tree.

The others stood at the base of the wide trunk and watched him climb. Like most of the citizens of North Wood, he had a deep connection with his natural surroundings, his nonhuman neighbors, and he scaled the tree's rough bark with the agility of an ocelot. Before long, he'd disappeared from the sight of the spectators on the ground.

In the higher boughs, bedecked with snapping pendants, the view was breathtaking. The world splayed out before the boy like a dappled carpet of green and brown and blue. A tussock of clouds migrated slowly eastward, across the distant horizon. The Cathedral Mountains, which they'd crossed only days prior, presented themselves like magnificent knuckles of earth, all snowcapped and tall. The boy found a bare branch and, pulling the flag from his teeth, tied the memorial to the deceased Elder Mystic Iphigenia on the stalk of one of the branch's thin fingers. It joined its fellow pieces of fabric on the tree, rippling unanimously in the wind.

Watching his footing as he prepared to make his way down the tree, the boy noticed a change in the forest; it was something he couldn't have seen from ground level. It was as if the texture of the wood changed very slightly in a distinct block of the greenery. Looking closer, he noticed that the pattern repeated itself in a slow, lazy curve away from the base of the Ossuary Tree. As he followed the pattern outward, it began to take the form of a very familiar shape.

The boy was greeted with uncertain smiles when he arrived back at the ground. They still found him unknowable. He barely spoke, and when he did, his speech patterns were stilted and strange and he never made eye contact. It was unnerving to the personable Mystics; they waited for the boy to speak now and he did not.

"How was the climb?" the woman ventured finally.

The boy was staring somewhere, just beyond her shoulder.

"Was it comfortable? Did you get very high?" The woman was keen on making a connection.

"There," said the boy. "Just there."

The woman looked over her shoulder. The other two Mystics followed his pointing finger.

"What?" asked the woman. "What's there?"

The boy ignored her question, but instead began moving into the thick of the bushes, clambering over the bowed saplings that stood in his way. The other Mystics went to follow the boy but he moved too quickly; before they could even cross the threshold of bushes, the boy was gone.

⚘

The mirror rested against the wall on top of the girl's dresser. She sat across the room from it, staring at it with her arms crossed. She was sitting upright in bed. Her bedside table light was on; the windows had gone dark. A gaslight flickered into life outside her window and she blinked at it, suddenly aware of the passage of time. How long had she been staring at the mirror? Long enough to have lost track of the hours; she could hear her father in the hall outside her door, shuffling his way toward bed. She could hear the wheeze of a wind gust. She could hear the absence of the songbirds. She could hear the rattle of a single, lonely coal cart.

The mirror, on the dresser, was not speaking. She was thankful for this. But she knew, when the tall grandfather clock in the sitting room chimed midnight, the words would appear on the glass.

It'd been this way for several days. Ever since the séance at the old stone house.

She'd already dismissed the first time she'd seen the letters, the scrawled writing, on the mirror's surface as being something she'd dreamed up, something her overactive imagination had conjured out of her own desperate need to see the thing happen. It was a hallucination, pure and simple. It appeared that her friends, the ones who had been there that night, had taken a similar course—it was as if the incident hadn't even occurred. No one spoke about it; in school, when they met before class, the conversation swirled around other topics, normal topics. No one dared broach the bit about the glowing aura, the distinct moan, the woman's moan, that rose from the ground.

But they hadn't seen the writing. The fogged-up mirror, the scrawl across the glass in the shape of a thin fingertip. The words: *I AM AWAKE*.

And that hadn't been the last of it.

Every midnight, shortly after the chime of the grandfather clock in the sitting room, a strange mist would overtake the simple mirror sitting propped on her dresser, and the glass would become cloudy, as if someone had breathed over it, and the sound would come: the sound of a hand drawing over a wet surface, a sort of gasping scrape; and then the words would appear.

The first time it'd happened in her room, Zita had only seen the word *GIRL* appear before she'd dashed from her bed in a panic and slammed the mirror down on the top of the dresser. After she'd taken several pacing spins around her room, she was relieved to see, when lifting the heavy glass again, that the word was not there. A single hairline crack had crawled across the top left corner of the mirror, but the writing was definitely gone.

The next night, though, it happened again. Zita was an insomniac, had been since she was a toddler, and the second night after the séance found her trying a new braiding pattern in the mirror very late at night when the grandfather clock in the hallway chimed its chime and her face, lit by the kerosene lamp on the dresser, grew suddenly dim and fogged. To her terror, the writing came again: *GIRL*.

This time, she was frozen in horror, her fingers still tangled in her braid. The writing continued: *BRING* came next. Before the specter had a chance to write a third word, Zita had slammed the mirror down flat again and had leapt, shivering, into her bed. She lay tossing in fitful sleep the rest of the night. The morning came cold and a new realization dawned on Zita, the May Queen, and she ate her cereal in silence, reflecting on the change.

That night, she lay in wait for the chime of the grandfather clock, determined to hear out the spirit that haunted her. She had decided that however she might resist this encroachment on her life by the supernatural, it would likely be no use. Better to give in, to not tempt the anger of the spiritual world.

And when the grandfather clock chimed, when midnight struck, she watched with halting breath as the disembodied finger scraped the word in the fog across the glass.

GIRL, it read.

BRING, it continued. But that wasn't all.

❧

The boy walked through the woods like it was second nature. He spoke to the plants and the trees as he walked, continuing an ongoing conversation with his mind, sorting through a vast snarl of disparate voices for a common thread. He followed the pattern that he saw in the green, a slight change in color and the timbre of the voices. It led him in a wide circle that steadily crept inward, as if affixed to a central point. It soon became clear that he was following a spiral. The voices of the other Mystics disappeared behind him, lost in the shroud of voices and the trees and the ivy and the trilliums, white and blooming.

As he grew closer to the center of the spiral, he felt the voices of the forest begin to soften, to arrive at a decided consensus: A hush overtook the warring voices and suddenly conjoined into a steady, meditative hum. The circle was tighter now, and it was as if he were retracing his own winding steps until he found the center of the spiral, the heart of the thing.

There, in a small womblike tuft of moss, a single green sprout grew. The sapling sported three identical branches; only one, however, bore a leaf.

A new tree was being born.

The boy reached out to touch the single downy leaf of the shoot, and the ground promptly opened up below his feet and he was swallowed by the earth.

⚶

The noise was unbearable: The friction of a finger against a windowpane, damp with dew, amplified a thousand times over in Zita's mind, and she pressed her fingers to her ears in an effort to shut out the sound.

BRING ME, the words read. The noise continued.

BRING ME THREE THINGS

BRING ME THREE THINGS BY THE CHIME OF MIDNIGHT IN TEN DAYS.

Zita rasped with fear: "What? What should I bring?"

There was room only for two more words, scrawled on the bottom of the glass:

EAGLE FEATHER.

The glass went clear. The words were gone.

C H A P T E R   5

Return to the Wood;
A Fugitive of the Wastes

"WE ARE DOING WHAT WE CAN, WITH WHAT TOOLS ARE AVAILABLE TO US. THE WORKERS ARE SAYING THAT THE RECONSTRUCTION SHOULD ONLY TAKE A FEW MORE MONTHS, BUT I'LL BELIEVE THAT WHEN I SEE IT." The inflection of the voice could only come from one species, the moles of the Underwood, and Prue had a hard time containing the happiness she felt to hear it once again. Besides, the despotic rule of Dennis the Usurper had long been washed away, and what had been left in its wake resembled nothing if not a peaceable and just society—something that Prue herself had helped bring into existence. She felt like she had a stake in the well-being of this strange subterranean civilization.

The speaker of the words had been the Sibyl Gwendolyn, the de facto queen of the Underwood, and she was describing the lengthy rehabilitation underway to bring the City of Moles back from the near rubble it had been reduced to during the Great Siege that had removed Dennis from power. The walls had been reconstructed, and the neighborhoods of houses and buildings, razed by a torrent of fire arrows, were in the process of regaining their old shapes. The Fortress of Fanggg itself, Gwendolyn said, was to be repurposed as a city park and public space—renamed the Fortress of Prurtimus after the city's trio of saviors. "THE VIEW FROM THE TOP IS SAID TO BE EXTRAORDINARY." The Sibyl smiled ironically; the moles of the Underwood were, of course, quite sightless.

Prue and Esben had been received with great pomp and clamor—it was Esben, after all, who had rebuilt the massive underground city the time before, after the destruction of the Seven Pool Emptyings War (it was clear that the moles of the Underwood lived their lives in a constant shuttling between states of war and peace). The bear's return was welcomed with all the display that would befit a hero of state. In fact, he was currently helping rebuild a particularly complex suspension bridge while Gwendolyn gave Prue a tour of the scaffolding-laced city under construction.

"I wish we could be here for the great unveiling," said Prue. "I'm sure the party will be spectacular."

"OH, IT WILL," said Gwendolyn. "WITHIN REASON. WE CAN ONLY AFFORD SO MUCH CELEBRATION THESE DAYS." She paused, as if scanning the middle distance from the balustrade she stood on, just below Prue's eye level. "BUT YOU HAVE BIGGER THINGS TO ATTEND TO."

"Yep," said Prue.

"I TRUST YOU KNOW WHAT YOU'RE DOING." Gwendolyn turned to face the area of the city where Esben, towering over his fellow engineers, was holding up the suspension cables of the bridge, while the moles at his feet were busily erecting the twin towers that would support the roadway.

"We have a plan," said Prue. "I think."

It was only later, the following day, after Esben and Prue had bid farewell to the moles, that they started to reckon with the great tangle that

was this master plan. They'd just arrived at the long, dark passage that would lead to what the moles called the Overworld, under the guidance of Gwendolyn.

"I'd prefer not to do *that* again," said Esben, finishing a long harangue about violence and his particular squeamishness toward it. His attack on Darla, it turned out, had been the only time he'd ever used his hooks to harm another soul; they'd been designed by the moles to help him and those around him, not to hurt them.

"Right," responded Prue, her hands running absently along the ancient brickwork that lined the tunnel walls. "I'd prefer you didn't do that again too." Still, the idea of parading Esben, the exiled machinist, around South Wood brought concerns for their safety—not just from those elements who were supposedly out to revive Alexei for their own gain, but perhaps the old allies of the Dowager herself, who might not take kindly to this scofflaw returning to freedom.

"PERHAPS HE SHOULD WEAR A DISGUISE," put in Gwendolyn. The diminutive mole was leading the way, some few feet in front of them, navigating the endless forks and intersections that interrupted their path like it was no more than a casual morning commute.

Prue craned her head over her shoulder to take in the towering form of the brown bear, illuminated behind her by Esben's lantern light, and tried to imagine a mustache or a hobo costume rendering the creature unrecognizable. "I don't know if that would work so much."

"I could put on an accent," suggested the bear. "Something foreign." He then began a string of sentences in what might've been the most bizarre and unrecognizable attempts at a dialect that Prue had ever heard; one part German and another part southern belle, the bear's voice seemed to straddle continents, and Prue erupted into laughter before he'd even finished his display.

"What?" Esben himself was stifling a laugh. "It's transatlantic."

"WHAT IS TRANSATLANTIC?"

"Do you even know what the Atlantic is?" Prue asked Esben.

"Yes," said Esben, playing affronted. "It's in the Outside. Somewhere." He paused, thinking, reviewing geography. "Ships sail on it."

"Not going to work," said Prue.

"BUT IF HE IS OUT IN THE OPEN, HE WILL BE FOUND," said Gwendolyn.

"That's the trick," said Prue, chewing on her lip in thought. "The tree said others would be trying to rebuild Alexei for their own devices. We have to keep Esben safe from them."

"AND TO WALTZ HIM AROUND THE OVERWORLD WOULD BE AKIN TO SIMPLY FLASHING THE WORLD YOUR POKER HAND." Gwendolyn turned and smiled at Prue, clearly proud of her Overworldian analogy; she was a well-traveled and worldly mole, this Sibyl.

"Right, Gwendolyn," said Prue. "We need to keep those cards hidden."

"Until we find Carol," put in Esben.

"Yep," said Prue.

"Then let's keep them hidden," said the bear. "I'll find some out-of-the-way place to hide myself while you run reconnaissance in South Wood."

Prue thought about the idea for a moment before saying, "And you won't mind? I'm not sure how long it'll take me. Hopefully I'll get some help once I get to the Mansion."

"Will I mind?" asked the bear. "Camping in the woods? Prue, my friend, I wouldn't hesitate to remind you that I am, in fact, a bear. After all."

And so it was settled. Esben would be secreted away in the trees, safe from those who might thwart their quest, while Prue hunted out the whereabouts of the bear's old machining partner.

After several days of walking, the unusual traveling party (a mole, a human, and a bear; each more than double their neighbor in size) arrived at a workaday iron ladder, which Gwendolyn gestured to with her tiny paw. "HERE IT IS," she said. "THE PATH TO THE OVERWORLD."

They bid their farewells to the Sibyl, promising another visit once their task had been completed, and wished her luck on her city's reconstruction. Then Esben and Prue began the long climb up the ladder, which ended after some distance at the bottom side of a manhole cover. It was slightly ajar, and a shaft of light poured into the dark chamber.

Prue, at the top, squinted at the light. With one arm braced against the ladder, she pushed at the cover, widening the sliver of daylight. She caught a whiff of the forest air, and it rushed into her lungs as she breathed deeply. After so many days breathing stale air in the dark vacuum of the Underwood, it was brisk and refreshing. Esben was just below her, and he nudged her shoe with his hook, saying, "What do you see?"

"Light," said Prue. "Lots of it." She heaved again at the iron disc and grunted under the weight. "I can't quite . . . ," she started.

"Here," said the bear at her feet. "Let me."

A bit of acrobatic reorganization occurred as the twelve-year-old girl shifted to one side of the ladder to let the one-ton brown bear overtake her. The bear, with the slightest flick of his arms, threw the manhole cover aside, and the long chamber was filled with light and air.

The bear breathed deep. "That's more like it," he said.

"Is it clear?" asked Prue.

The bear crept his snout a few inches above the lip of the hole. "Seems like."

They crawled into the sunlight, finding themselves in a deep, dappled forest. Light fell in ribbons between the branches, newly

bedecked in the buds of spring. Shadows were everywhere, though compared to the dun of the underground tunnels and chambers, it was as if they'd stepped into the sun itself.

"Any idea where we are?" asked the bear. A simple dirt path cleaved its way through the dense forest; having climbed from the manhole, they found themselves standing to one side of this road.

"You're the Woodian here," said Prue. "I don't have a clue."

They'd not stood there long before a quiet jingle could be heard in the distance.

"Shhh," said Esben. "I think something's coming."

Prue frantically waved her arms at the bear. "Get hidden!"

Esben, flustered, was about to leap behind an obliging shield of evergreen huckleberries when a badger appeared from around a corner, towing a bright spangling rickshaw. When he arrived at where Prue and Esben stood, he came up short and stared at them. A little radio sitting in the plush red seat of the rickshaw blared some frenetic sitar music, and the purple baubles dangling in a fringe around the canopy almost seemed to dance to the beat.

"Of course," whispered Prue to herself.

The badger stared confusedly at the mysterious girl and the hook-handed bear in the knitted cap. He looked down at the open manhole. "Did you both just climb out of there?" he asked.

"Yep," she said, smiling. "Do you know where we are?"

The badger looked shell-shocked. He answered, "Just this side of South Wood." He paused, looking back at the manhole. Then back at Prue. "Do I know you from somewhere?"

"Maybe," said Prue. "Don't suppose you could give me a ride into town."

The badger swallowed loudly, eyeing the bear's twin hooks. "Just you? What about your bear friend?"

"I don't actually exist," said Esben, improvising.

The badger raised his eyebrow.

"Right," said Prue. She then turned to Esben. "I think this is where we part ways. This seems like as good a spot as any for a hiding place. Lots of cover, middle of nowhere. And you'll have the manhole for a quick escape if you need to."

"Got it," said Esben.

She handed him her shoulder bag. "Take this. I'll be back with more supplies. That should hold you for a few days. Just keep your head down, right?"

"Will do," said the bear. He then looked over at the badger. "What about that one? Think he'll keep quiet about me? How do we keep him from talking?"

The badger seemed to visually startle; the color had drained from his black-and-white-furred face.

"Leave it to me," said Prue. Walking back over to the badger, she stood in front of him with her feet planted wide and her hands on her hips. She looked down at the brooch the badger was wearing: a single bicycle gear.

"Nice gear," said Prue.

"I'm a patriot," said the badger, still very clearly uncomfortable.

"That's what I like to hear," said Prue. "You'll keep your mouth shut about this bear, right?"

The badger swallowed loudly. "I suppose I could. But I don't want to get wrapped up in anything illegal—I'm an honest badger, making an honest living here."

"How about if I said you were under instruction of the Bicycle Maiden?" asked Prue.

The badger blanched. "You?"

Prue nodded.

The handles of the rickshaw fell from the badger's grasp, and he dropped to his knees. "I can't believe it!" he said, his voice breaking with excitement. "I knew it was you! The moment you showed up. I knew it!" Tears had appeared in his eyes. "What are you doing back in the Wood?"

"I'm here to fix things," said Prue. She said the words with certainty, with purpose. The feeling of power flooded over her; she reveled in it. She felt like she was, at long last, standing on solid ground. She knew now what to do.

❧

They knew the drill; they'd been practicing it for weeks. The fire in the tin drum was immediately smothered; their store of foodstuffs covered by the waxed canvas tarp. Without a word, Michael appeared by the trapdoor in the worn wooden floor and began ushering the children—the youngest first—down the ladder into the building's dark subbasement. Rachel pulled up the rear, ushering the stragglers quickly toward the hole in the floor, all the while casting a careful eye over her shoulder at the rumblings on the outside.

Cynthia came dashing down the staircase and arrived breathless at Michael's side. "A whole mess of 'em!" she said, petrified. "They were all coming out of nowhere, like they'd just appeared. Tons of 'em. Never seen so many in one place!"

She was referring, of course, to the stevedores, the beanie-clad shock troopers of the Industrial Wastes. Bending to the whim and

will of Brad Wigman, Chief Titan of the Quintet, they were tasked
to investigate, root out, and put down any insurrection or uprising
inside the boundaries of their empire. The Unadoptables had managed to elude the stevedores so far, staying quiet in their hidden home
in this Forgotten Place—until now.

"Get in!" hissed Michael, and the girl promptly disappeared down
the hole. Michael nodded to Rachel, who began to take her first steps
down the ladder when a noise startled them both.

The iron lattice of one of the ground-level windows had been
forcibly kicked apart, and through the obliging hole climbed a
very haggard and desperate-looking man. He was not a stevedore:
Notably absent were the de rigueur maroon beanie and coveralls.
Instead, he was dressed entirely in black: black slacks, black shoes,
black turtleneck. On his head was perched a prim black beret. His
eyes widened when he saw the two kids, standing frozen above the
open trapdoor.

"Help me!" he said in a rasped whisper.

Rachel looked up at Michael; Michael's face went blank.

The man ran up to them, his face lined with anguish. "You've got
to hide me! They're coming!"

The sound of a multitude of heavy-booted footsteps could be
heard just outside the warehouse walls; bulky silhouettes could be
seen darting about through the dirty windows. There was no time to
ask questions.

"Get in," said Michael. Rachel hurried down the steps and the man followed, clambering down the ladder rungs above her.

Michael had just hopped into the hole, the trapdoor slamming down behind him, when the doors of the warehouse were broken in and the sound of the footsteps—perhaps dozens—came thundering into the room.

The three of them froze in the narrow stairwell, terrified to make a move lest they give away their hiding place. A pair of boots landed heavily on the trapdoor; they shuffled as their owner pivoted, searching the room. Rachel, at the bottom rung of the stepladder, turned to the huddled mass of kids behind her and raised her finger to her lips in a frantic mime: *shhhhh.*

"Where'd he go?" shouted a voice from through the floor. More boot steps sounded; the stevedores were wandering the length and breadth of the warehouse, searching for their prey.

"Dunno. Swear to God he came in 'ere. Saw 'im with my own eyes."

"Well, find 'im then."

"What is this place, anyway?"

"Aw, some old warehouse, from the old days. These ain't been used since the days of the Sextet."

"Good place to hide out in."

"Yeah, that's for sure."

"C'mon, keep lookin' for 'im."

Rachel glanced up at the man between her and Michael; he was staring into open space, a look of abject horror on his face. His hands, held firmly at his sides, were trembling, and his breath came in quiet, quick pulses of his chest.

"I see a bunch of old cans here, like old soup cans," said one of the stevedores.

"Some hobo livin' 'ere or somethin'?"

"Nah. Ain't nobody livin' out 'ere. We'da seen 'em comin' and goin'. Plus, them dogs'd get 'em before we ever did."

A voice came from some distance off; the other voices quieted to listen. "Let's move it! 'E must've gotten past us. We got other places to check."

One of the voices above the trapdoor grumbled audibly. "Boss ain't gonna be happy 'bout this."

"Well, we tell 'em the dogs got to 'im. Nothin' left to bring back."

"Yeah, good idea."

Another symphony of footsteps rang out above the Unadoptables' heads, and before long, the room descended back to its usual silence.

The subbasement, a modest concrete box that smelled of damp moss, barely contained the seventy-five anxious children, and when Michael signaled the all clear, the room burst abuzz with frantic voices. The black-bereted man on the middle of the step-ladder, his attention drawn for the first time away from what was happening above him, followed the sound of the kids' voices, a stunned look coming over his face.

"W-who are you?" he stammered.

"Good question," said Michael. "Maybe I'd ask you the same thing."

The man looked down at Rachel, who was staring at him intently. "We've been here for two months. That was the first time any stevedore set foot in this place," she said. She pushed him, jostling his foot on his ladder rung. "Not. Remotely. Cool."

The man fidgeted nervously. "It's a little, I don't know, stifling in here. Is the coast clear? Can we climb out now?"

"One second," said Michael. He propped open the trapdoor, gave a quick survey of the warehouse, and climbed out, letting the door fall back closed behind him. He returned some short moments later with a long spool of rope, which he tossed casually down to Rachel. "Tie him up," he instructed. "Then we'll climb out of here."

After the last Unadoptable had been ushered from the hidden room below the warehouse floor and the last child had been given an opportunity to walk by the hog-tied form of their intruder, bound as he was to a rickety wooden chair, the room grew quiet as the interrogation began. A young girl was standing off to the side, wearing the man's black beret and entertaining the crowd with a kind of jackbooted dance; a boy sat at the man's side, holding the machete Excalibur and doing his best to sneer menacingly. The man in the chair wore a very chagrined expression as Michael, standing in front of him, began to pepper him with questions.

"Who are you?" the boy said. "And what were you doing all the way out here?"

"Listen," the man said. "I'm not a threat to you guys. I'm on your side!"

"Quiet," said Michael. "Answer the question."

The man took a deep breath and said: "Name's Nico. Nico Posholsky." He glanced at the children, as if weighing the discretion of saying the next words. "I'm part of the Chapeaux Noirs."

"The *what?*" asked Elsie, who'd pushed up to the front of the crowd and was standing at her sister's side. She looked at her neighbors, saying, "What did he say?"

"I think it's Polish," said one of the Unadoptables.

"It's *French*," corrected Rachel, who'd taken first-year French in high school.

"Aaaaaah," sighed the impressed crowd.

"It means black cake," Rachel continued, smiling knowingly.

"*Hats*," said the man in the chair. "It means black hats."

"Whatever," said Rachel. "It's a weird name for a . . . what is it, exactly?"

Swallowing his annoyance, Nico Posholsky said, "We're a radical anarcho-syndicalist collective. Saboteurs. Our one aim is to free the proletariat from the yoke of the industrialist state."

Elsie looked to her sister, her brow knitted. "Is that French?"

"That might be English," said her sister.

Michael, being the oldest boy of the group, nodded knowingly, though it was unclear whether he'd been able to unpack the man's language any better than the other kids. "Fair enough. But what are you doing here? Why were the stevedores after you?" he asked.

The man spat angrily. "It was a stupid mistake. The wires got tied. I couldn't get the explosive rigged in time, so I couldn't get far enough away. By the time they'd come running, I was cut off from my escape route. They trapped me. Managed to set a few decoy explosions, but in the end, it was just *chat et souris*." He eyes scanned the room before he added: "Cat and mouse."

Elsie spoke up. "You make those explosions?"

"We do," the man said proudly. "The Chapeaux Noirs. We're gaining strength. Soon, we'll have the whole Quintet by the ankles." He cast his eyes around the room, studying the children. Elsie suddenly became aware of their desperate circumstances, their greasy hair, their unwashed clothes. She hadn't seen an adult in a full two months; as the man's look fell on the destitute mass of parentless children, Elsie knew her own poverty.

"That's how you do it," the man said. "When you're fighting with a giant. Get 'em by the ankles and see how quickly they're on their knees."

Michael was silent.

The confined man took a deep breath and spoke again. "I've told you who I am. Now, it might be helpful if I knew who you are and what you're doing here."

"The Unadoptables," said Michael, attempting the same tone of pride the man had taken. "We live here."

"The Una—" Nico began, before realizing: "Are you the orphans from Unthank's slave shop? Escaped after the fire?"

Michael was quick to correct: "We *started* the fire."

The room hummed in agreement.

"Wow," said Nico. "Nice work. I'd applaud if my hands weren't tied tightly around my back."

Rachel and Michael exchanged a glance. The boy next to Nico with the machete waited for instruction. "We can't let you go yet," said Michael. "Not till we're sure you're not an enemy."

"We all thought that fire had been an accident, like maybe Joffrey had overextended himself," said Nico. "Pushed you tykes a little too hard and some mechanical slipup caused the whole thing. That was the word, anyway."

"You're right about the pushing us too hard bit," came a voice from the crowd. It was Angela Frye, a longtime belt operator who'd survived five years at the Unthank Home with only a single demerit to her name. "But there weren't no mechanical slipup. We rebelled."

"Well, I'm very impressed," said the man. "You managed to do something in an evening that we'd been trying to do for years. Knocked out one of the arms of the Quintet. Very nice work."

"I see what you're doing," said Michael. "Don't think I don't. Nice words aren't going to win you any friends here."

"Hey," said Nico. "Don't get all riled up. I'm not trying to make friends. I'm a saboteur. I destroy things for a living. I don't need friends."

Elsie tugged on Rachel's jumper; the entire room was fixated on the man in the chair. She could feel the tension in the room growing and wanted to somehow dispel it; to her, it exuded danger and violence. It didn't feel right.

Just then, Michael looked at Cynthia Schmidt, his fellow elder among the Unadoptables, and said, "What do we do?"

"I say we kill him," said Cynthia.

Nico Posholsky turned very suddenly and very dramatically pale. Elsie stared in disbelief at the elder children.

Michael, unfazed, looked back at the man. "She thinks we should kill you," said Michael. "And I might just agree with her. We can't afford for any adult to know our whereabouts. This is *our* territory. You are a trespasser. Trespassers are dealt with harshly."

"Michael," Rachel whispered, attempting a tone of conciliation. "Let's not get too carried away. Maybe he can help us find Martha—"

"Quiet," said Michael. "Let me deal with this one."

Elsie tugged on Rachel's hem again, whispering, "I'm scared." Her sister brushed her hand away, transfixed by the tense standoff between the bound man and the older kids.

At a loss for another solution, Elsie hit the button nub on the back of her Intrepid Tina doll, a thing she reserved for only the direst of situations. More often than not, the prerecorded maxims from the plastic doll had no bearing whatsoever on the situation at hand, though Elsie had become practiced at applying them creatively to her present circumstances. The charged silence of the room was filled with the doll's chirpy, mechanical voice: "THE JUNGLE IS A DANGEROUS PLACE. TRUSTWORTHY PARTNERS ARE A MUST!"

The attention of everyone in the room swiveled to Elsie, who was standing slack-jawed by her sister. Never had one of Tina's suggestions been more apt.

The man in the chair seized his opportunity: "We're in this together, kids. You hate the stevedores? We hate the stevedores. You hate the Quintet? We hate the Quintet. No need for senseless violence, unless it's directed at our mutual enemies, right?"

Michael's intensity seemed to soften. "I suppose . . . ," he began.

"If we can't be friends, let's be partners," said the man. "The jungle is, after all, a dangerous place."

Elsie smiled at the man. Nico Posholsky smiled back.

CHAPTER 6

The Maiden Returns
to the Mansion; For the Sake
of a Single Feather

P rue, faced with returning for the first time to the southern-most region of the Wood, to a place she hadn't seen since the triumphant coup that she herself had set in motion—with the worrisome question of how she would be received hanging low over her head—could only think of her friend Curtis.

They'd parted ways in February, on that cold, rainy night when their goal of reuniting the two machinists had seemed hopelessly dashed and the rain had poured down on them, a humiliating and heavy rain. He'd left her angry and ashamed; he'd also left her to weather the final attack of Darla Thennis, the Kitsune assassin, alone. If it hadn't been for Esben, Prue would undoubtedly be dead right now (sitting nestled into the plush velvet seat of the bouncing rickshaw, her mind briefly touched the void: If she'd been killed, where *would* she be? She shook the thought away). Not that she blamed Curtis; their task did seem at a complete dead end and he'd been intent, ever since they'd escaped the underground, to discover what had happened to his fellow Wildwood bandits. Reviving Alexei had been Prue's revelation; Curtis had only been dragged into the debacle out of loyalty to his friend.

The little radio at her side chimed tunefully, and she found herself willing the best to her friend Curtis, hoping he was finding success in his journey; she couldn't help but wish that he could be here now, witnessing her return to South Wood. And perhaps there was a little needling insecurity in her mind—a concern that she'd been forgotten or that she wouldn't necessarily be as safe from harm as she supposed.

The rickshaw hit a pothole in the gravel arterial road; the badger apologized. "How are you sitting back there?"

"Just fine, thanks," said Prue. The trees flew by like telephone poles. The sky appeared in fits and starts above the conifers' boughs. Houses were appearing between the trunks, little hovels and homes that seemed to be made of the earth itself, with earthen roofs and white stucco walls and dogwood wattle fences surrounding well-tended gardens. From where she sat, Prue could see the back of the badger's head; he shook it and gave another glance over his shoulder. She'd lost count of how many times he'd done that since their short journey began. "My wife is not going to believe this. Me giving the Bicycle Maiden a ride on my humble rickshaw."

Prue blushed. "It's not a big deal. I'm just a girl."

"A girl?" shouted the badger, in disbelief. "You're the one who single-handedly brought down the Svik regime; saved all us common folk from that evil, evil man and all his cronies. Released all those folks from the prison!" He repeated her words: "'Just a girl.' *Pfft!*"

"What's it like there now?" she asked, her mind still in turmoil over what was to come. "I've been away so long."

"Oh, you'll find it very much changed, milady," said the badger. "I'm just a lowly rickshaw driver—I try not to meddle in politics. I'll say this much: We're better off than we were under Lars Svik and his lot."

"That's good news. Still a little nervous, though. Me showing up after being away so long," she said.

"Oh, milady. I suspect you'll be pleasantly surprised. You're a bit of a folk hero in these parts. You're immortalized in song, you know."

"In song?" asked Prue, her curiosity piqued.

"You mean to tell me you've never heard 'The Storming of the Prison'?"

"I haven't, no."

"I'd sing it myself, but I can barely carry a tune. Should be on the radio, though. It's on every hour," said the badger.

"That's helpful."

The badger continued, "I suppose the Caliphs are the only ones you won't find singing those songs. They say it's just nostalgia."

"Caliphs?"

"You've got a lot of catching up to do," said the badger. "Caliphs: members of the Synod, Mystics who meditate at the Blighted Tree. Wasn't much of a thing during the Svik regime; Lars followed in the footsteps of his uncle, Grigor, and made much of keeping South Wood a secular place. Free from the taint of religion, you see. But it's out with the old and in with the new. With the Sviks gone, the Synod came roaring back and all these folks come out of the woodwork, having secretly been praying to the Blighted Tree all along, in the privacy of their own homes. Way I see it, gives people hope when they didn't have it before. And what with the hard winter, they've needed it."

They lapsed into silence, with Prue watching the trees feathering by and the badger politely humming along with the music on the radio. When the song break came up, he was pleased to hear the trumpet fanfare that introduced the next number. "Here it is!" he said. "Like I said, played on the hour, every hour: 'The Storming of the Prison.'"

Prue listened closely as the words came flowing in a river of static through the radio's single speaker:

O the storming of the prison
On the evening of the day
When the maiden came a-riding
And we cast the bums away

And we all came out to meet her
With the wagon and the babe
And we all marched to the prison
For to free the poor enslaved

The badger chimed in on the third verse:

O the storming of the prison
At the end of our despair
Give the Avians their freedom
As they rise into the air

Let the fascists die and wither
All the retinue demands!
Let their children hear them suffer
At the Maiden's stiff command

And the blood of all the martyrs
Will not be shed in vain
At the storming of the prison
We will all be free again.

The triumphant melody was taken up by the brass ensemble and was blatted out ad nauseam until the song slowly faded into silence. The badger looked back at Prue, smiling. "See?" he said. "You're a hero!"

Prue was still processing the lyrics. "I didn't *command* anything."

"Well, no," said the badger. "It's metaphorical. Figurative. You didn't *literally* command that the children of the fascists see their parents suffer. Poetic license." He paused, breathing in through his snout deeply. "Stirs the heart, it does."

"I actually don't like the idea of children's parents suffering at all—or anybody, for that matter," said Prue, now gathering steam. "I think it's pretty awful, actually."

The badger laughed nervously. "It's the fascists who are suffering, though. I mean, that's who we overthrew, right?"

"Even fascists," said Prue. "Whatever a fascist is."

The badger didn't have a response to this; he seemed genuinely confused. Up ahead, a small group of teenage boys in the road stalled his progress.

"'Ey," shouted one of the boys. "Not so fast, there, Citizen Badger."

There were four of them, ranging in age from what looked to be fourteen to nineteen. They had typical teenage complexions—flushed and spotty—and they all wore identical caps with the visor knocked back. Cycling casquettes, Prue realized. Tricolored sashes—blue, yellow, and green—were draped across their chests, and on the lapels of their natty plaid vests they wore brooches similar to the one the badger wore: a single metal sprocket.

"Hello, lads, citizens," said the badger cheerily—though Prue could detect a wariness beneath his happy tone. "You'll be amazed to see—"

He was cut short; the youngest boy stepped forward and approached the rickshaw. "Where's your brooch, citizen? You ain't forgot to wear the badge, now have you?"

"N-no!" sputtered the badger. "Of course, I always wear the sprocket. With pride!" This accusation seemed to have put him off finishing his previous, interrupted proclamation.

"I see it, there," said one of the other boys, chewing on a too-large bite of apple. "It's on his coat, there."

"Good," said the youngest one, now within a few feet of the badger. "Nice to see the guy's a patriot. Might want to wear it a little more conspicuously, though. You're not ashamed of the sprocket, now are you?"

"Not in the least!" the badger complained. "The very opposite, in fact. I—"

"Shhh," said the boy. "Don't want to upset your passenger." The boys had now taken an interest in Prue and were beginning to study her, hidden as she was beneath the drapery of the rickshaw's dangling baubles.

"Actually, you'd be surprised to find—" began the badger, before he was again rudely interrupted.

"Citizen, stand down," said one of the other boys. Prue looked closely and saw that he was swinging a bicycle chain.

Another observed, "A citizen in servitude. Carryin' around some bourgeois too lazy to walk. I believe that's a symptom of the old order, don't you think?"

"Citizen," responded the boy, referring to the other, "I believe you are right."

"We all threw off the bonds of servitude," said the boy with the apple in his mouth, "when the Bicycle Coup came." He then referred back to the badger. "You may be a patriot, but you sure ain't no revolutionary."

Prue couldn't stand it any longer; she was appalled by the boys' bullying behavior. "Leave him alone!"

The boys froze; they stared at the figure in the back of the rickshaw. "Says who?" said one of the boys.

"Says the Bicycle Maiden," said Prue, and she hopped from her seat to the road.

The boy eating the apple promptly spat out the white, globby contents of his mouth; the young boy by the rickshaw fell backward into the chest of his friend, and they both spilled out into the road, toppling comically to the gravelly ground. The fourth boy, who'd remained silent during the whole exchange, stumbled forward and addressed Prue in a startled and aghast tone: "You're . . . her?"

"Yep," said Prue definitively. "And I don't really like how you're talking to my friend the badger here."

"Sorry, ma'am," said the boy, swiping the casquette from his head and squashing it reverently to his chest. "It's just that, these days . . ." His voice faltered. "You really are her? Like, from the songs? The *real* Bicycle Maiden?"

"It was a LeMond, actually. Red single speeder. My dad bought it for me for my eleventh birthday. Towed a wagon behind it. My brother, Mac, if you remember, started it all." She waved her hand at the sky, as if to say: all of this.

The two boys who'd fallen had by now stood up and were approaching the rickshaw as if it were wired with explosives. They'd followed the example of the other boy and had removed their caps, holding them ceremoniously at their chests. "We had . . . ," said one. "We had no idea!"

The badger stayed quiet, seemingly pleased by the turn of events.

"Now, if you don't mind," said Prue, "let this badger get on with his day; we've got some very sensitive information to deliver to the

Mansion." The words seemed to roll from her tongue. She liked being in this position: four boys trembling in her presence.

The oldest boy spoke up: "In fact, would you do us the honor of allowing us to escort you, personally, to the Mansion?"

"We're Spoke Cadre Twenty-Four," said one of the other boys. "Sworn to serve the revolution."

It occurred to Prue that the boys had changed their attitude fairly quickly—what once was a ragtag group of snotty teenagers had suddenly transformed into a fawning clique; it was not becoming of a group of kids who were supposed to be representing the radical change that she herself had set in motion. "I've got a better idea," she said.

And that was how four boys in bicycle caps and woolen vests ended up parading into the more populous part of South Wood as the yoked-up carriage horses to a brightly colored rickshaw with a girl and a badger as passengers.

"A little faster, you on the right," shouted Prue from her seat. "You're not really keeping up." She nudged the badger. "Try it," she said. "It's very gratifying."

"Oh, I couldn't," said the badger, clearly uncomfortable at being the driven and not the driver.

"C'mon!" pressured the girl at his side.

"Oh, all right," he said, caving. He then addressed the huffing quartet at the front of the vehicle. "Not so herky-jerky, citizens! A true rickshaw driver measures his steps!"

A grumble arose from the four boys, the Spokes, but the ride did improve somewhat. "That was very satisfying, you're right," said the badger, smiling.

By the time they'd left the ramshackle houses of the drowsy suburbs and had entered the pell-mell of the town, the road now a cobbled thoroughfare, a modest procession had grown up around the rickshaw. Word was spreading fast that this particular carriage, one of many in the bustling town, was carrying none other than the Bicycle Maiden herself, she of song and story. Children, human and animal alike, came running after the carriage, offering to help carry the coach toward its awaiting goal: Pittock Mansion.

The streets wound up through the familiar tangle of brick buildings, though South Wood seemed changed since Prue had been here last. Many of the storefronts were boarded up, with indecipherable slogans scrawled across the plywood in angry red paint. A few beggars stumbled up to the rickshaw, desperately clawing at the dangling baubles at an effort to get at the passengers within. The boys at the yoke shooed them off, citing something about them being parasites; Prue watched them, disturbed by the beggars' presence. It was a jarring sight and something she hadn't remembered being present in the old South Wood.

With every block they traveled, they gathered more followers. Foxes, humans, bears, and mice—all clambering to get close to the growing procession. "The Maiden!" came shouts from the throng. "She's here!" "Returned! She's finally returned!" An impromptu chorus among the crowd started singing "The Storming of the Prison," adding more verses than the ones Prue had heard; their inclusion did not lessen her discomfort with the song:

> *We will search out all the Svikists*
> *We will tear them from their beds*
> *We will drag them to the Mansion*
> *And remove their sorry heads*

> *O the blood of all the fascists*
> *Will flow freely in the drains*
> *Like a pair of moldy trousers*
> *We will wash away the stains*

More self-proclaimed Spokes, men and women wearing what appeared to be biking gear from a bygone era—pleated knickers, woolen vests, and short-billed casquettes—began falling in line with the parade, becoming a kind of cavalcade of like-dressed humans and animals, bright sprocket brooches pinned to their chests. When they crested the hill and broke free of the knot of buildings to arrive at the Mansion's front gardens, the crowd was now hundreds strong, a tide of humanity, waving pennants and singing songs and blowing horns and shouting slogans and stamping feet and dancing on the margins and crying out and clapping hands. All in all, the passage bore very little similarity to her first time making the trip, when she'd been a passenger of the charitable postmaster general, Richard, and the fantastic world had opened up to her like an unbelievably beautiful flower, strange and alien.

"The Maiden returns to the Mansion!" yelled a man at her side. "There's a song in that!"

Prue had long since lost her ability to process everything that was happening; everything was coming too quickly for true inspection. The roar of the crowd was like a symphony of cymbals in her ears, and she truly felt like she was being carried along on a wave of unbridled enthusiasm. It was intoxicating.

That is, until they'd rounded the corner and come across a great contraption that loomed over the central square before the Mansion's front doors. The crowd paid it no mind, fixed as they were on conveying the triumphantly returning Bicycle Maiden through the doors to confront the Mansion's leadership, there to do whatever it was she'd come to do (expectations were raised very high). But Prue froze as she stepped down from the rickshaw, just as her right foot touched the fabric of some chivalrous young man's proffered coat, and studied the apparatus.

It was, undoubtedly, a guillotine.

The silhouette of the gruesome thing stuck in her mind, like the blot left behind in the dark of one's closed eyelids after looking at a lightbulb or the sun, and stayed there as she was transported by the rush of the mob into the foyer of the Mansion.

✹

Zita had never been this far into the forest; she'd never left the safe confines of the North Wall, that wide stone edifice that stretched east to west through the vast woods and separated, as her father had described it, the civilized world and the world of the birds.

She'd known a few birds; she'd been a small child when the partition had been agreed on, and she still remembered when South Wood had been filled with birds, before their diaspora to the newly founded Avian Principality. They'd been kind, the birds she'd met, but she knew there'd been strife. When the partition had been decided and the lines drawn, it seemed to release some of the built-up pressure. Naturally, some Avians decided to stay on in South Wood and they were welcome by most quarters. It wasn't until the Night of Broken Doors, the night that the SWORD began rounding up and imprisoning the remaining birds, that it became clear that there were still differences that could not be erased. Tensions had eased since the Revolution, but most of the birds of the Wood tended to keep to themselves and more than a few had left for the Principality, in search of a kinder community. Notably, all the eagles had left South Wood; none remained. This surprising exodus went unnoted by most people, out of fear of insulting the legacy of the Bicycle Coup—after all, there was a new dawn breaking in relations between ground dwellers and tree nesters—but the Avians, shortly after the Storming of the Prison, could be seen beefing up the security on their border with South Wood. In answer to this, a larger detachment of South Wood soldiers was assigned to the guarding of the North Gate. It was a quiet escalation, all done in the name of the old maxim "Good fences make good neighbors."

Which was why Zita was forced to blaze a trail through the tangled vegetation of the forest, rather than tramp openly on the cobbled Long Road. She knew if she was caught, out this late and so close to the border, questions would be asked. And how would she possibly answer? She ran the conversation in her mind: "What are you doing here, miss?" comes the authoritarian voice. "Oh, just sneaking into the Avian Principality," she would answer. "And why?" "To steal a feather from an eagle." "And why would you need to do that?" "To satisfy the Verdant Empress, who's leaving me notes in writing on the mirror in my bedroom." She had to stifle a laugh; it was perfectly ludicrous, the whole situation, and she was undoubtedly going completely insane. But there was something about it—something about following the will of the spectral Empress—that seemed to save her from going completely, willy-nilly, over the cliff of sanity. Being a gofer for a ghost—it had a kind of purpose to it.

There was another reason, a deeper reason, for her giving in to the spirit's whims, but she hadn't allowed herself to consider it too closely.

Every time it surfaced in her mind, she pushed it away. Best to focus on the task at hand, she reasoned.

A task that was now bringing her close to the wall—the darkness seemed to lighten as the flickers of gas lamps illuminated the tree boughs. Through a break in the bushes, she could see a small gathering of soldiers on the road: talking among themselves, calmly pulling on cigarettes. Four had settled down around a battered tree stump for a game of cards. Just beyond them, Zita could see the wide gate in the wall itself: the North Gate, the only passage between South Wood and the Avian Principality.

She counted the soldiers: ten in all. They swarmed like khaki-clad mice around the gate; there would be no getting through this exit. She watched as one of the soldiers, his bayonet-topped rifle slung over his shoulder, began walking idly toward her hiding place. Before he got too close, she ducked back into the bushes and began moving her way eastward, away from the road and the gate.

The light dwindled here, away from the gas lamps, and she waited until she was a safe distance from the road before she struck a match and held it to the wick of the lantern she carried. Holding it aloft with her left hand, she walked along the base of the wall, her right hand feeling the rough, weathered stone and the mossy chinks in the rock. The wall itself was easily twice her height, but the stone was uneven and she soon found a spot, some fifty or sixty feet from the road, that she thought she could scale without too much difficulty.

She tied the lantern to the bottom of her knapsack and tested the first jutting stone; the soles of her moccasins held fast and she began to climb.

No sooner had she arrived at the top when she heard a crunching in the vegetation below her; a soldier had stepped away from his cohorts and had begun a solitary walk up the perimeter of the wall. She pressed her body flat to the stones and slowly, achingly dragged the lit lantern toward her face, so she might extinguish the flame. The thing glanced against the rock, and a metallic *ting* echoed out into the night. The soldier below her swung his flashlight toward her position, shouting, "Who's there?"

Panicked, she threw her weight toward the Principality side of the wall and tried to make quick purchase on the stones of the other side; she found the surface to be not so obliging as the one she'd just climbed, and the rough-hewn stone tore at her skin and her clothing as she slid the distance of the wall to the ground.

By this time, the soldier's comrades had been alerted and the gate had been thrown open. "There's an intruder on the wall!" came the shout. Zita barely had a moment to consider her injuries from falling before she was bounding through the forest, a host of angry soldiers giving chase.

"Stop!" Zita heard one soldier shout. "You are a trespasser in the Avian Principality!"

A wild flapping of wings alerted her to the fact that several Avians had taken up the chase from the air; the unmistakable voice of a bird sounded from the tree boughs. "Human! You must surrender immediately!"

Zita's heartbeat slammed in her chest; her breathing came in frenzied gasps. She ducked under bent saplings and leapt over fallen tree trunks, the spindly bracken of the forest whipping at her skin like a million tiny fingers. Just as she felt her pursuers were about to overtake her, she found herself within feet of a mighty hemlock, as big around as a small house, and she dove into the protection of its gnarled roots. There, she found she could winnow her way deep into the tree's inner recesses, and soon she was completely concealed.

Within seconds the soldiers' footsteps were beating down the brush outside her hiding place; they circled up in a glade just beyond the hemlock and could be heard speaking loudly to the hovering Avians.

"She hopped the wall—east of the gate," explained one. "A girl. I swear it was a young girl."

A bird responded, "You have no authority beyond the wall, soldier. Please return to your post. This is a matter for the Principality."

"But she's j-just—" was the stammered response.

"Soldier, you are in direct violation of the Border Treaty. Return to your post before I have you arrested."

This threat, barked from the air, seemed to silence the South Wood soldiers, and Zita heard their slow footsteps retreat through the woods toward the gate. The girl stayed huddled in the nook of the massive tree for a while longer, listening as the wing beats of the birds cycled farther away until it became clear that she'd been given up for lost. Breathing a sigh of relief, she extracted herself from her tight hiding spot and continued on her way.

She knew from her father's tutoring that eagles built their nests high in the exposed limbs of trees; great confusions of salvaged wood called aeries. As the night gave way to a bright morning and her breath stained the air in a cloud of fog, she searched the high branches for such creations. She kept an eye out for any bird sentries, though as she traveled farther, she knew that she had eluded them. It wasn't entirely uncommon for a human to be in the Principality; a few non-avian settlers, South Wood expats, made their homes among the ground cover. If she were to be caught, she could merely explain that she was out foraging, a daughter of the Principality's few human citizens.

Finally, after a few hours of searching, she found what she'd been looking for: Cresting a small hill, she got a view through the trees and saw the wide, woody bowl of an eagle aerie perched in the top of an ancient cedar tree. An adult had just disrupted the branches around it as it came in for a landing, bearing some bit of food in its mouth for the awaiting juvenile who lay in the cavity of the nest. No sooner had the bird done this than it was off again, presumably in search of more forage. Zita prowled her way to the base of the tree and began searching the ground for a feather, hoping that one might've fallen during molting. Admittedly, she wasn't sure if eagles molted.

Her search was interrupted when she heard a voice in the air above her. "What are you doing down there?"

She jerked her head up; she couldn't find the speaker.

"Up here," came the voice again. "In the nest."

Shielding the rising sun with her hand, she saw the beak of the juvenile eagle pointing out from the lip of the aerie. "I'm . . . ," she responded, unsure how to answer. "I'm looking for a feather."

"A feather? Why would you do that? What, are you making a pen or something?"

"Yes," said Zita quickly. "I'm making a pen. A quill pen."

"Well, I don't think you'll find any feathers down there," said the eagle. "I haven't molted yet."

"Oh," said Zita.

"But tell you what," said the eagle. "If you can get up here, I'd be happy to give you one."

Zita eyed the height of the tall tree. "Really?" she asked.

"Sure thing. Got plenty of 'em."

The girl grabbed hold of the lowest reachable branch. It was solid, rippled with bark. She looked back up at the distant aerie. "This is going to be hard."

The eagle answered, "I'd fly it down, but I don't think I could get back up."

And so Zita began to climb, limb by limb. She heaved her midsection over the lower, solitary boughs and stepped gingerly on those that presented themselves in series like woody stairs. Occasionally she would stop on a wider branch and gauge her position in the tree. The eagle in the nest egged her on, saying, "Almost there! Don't give up now!"

"I'm not going to," was her reply.

"My dad'll be back soon," said the eagle, when she'd stopped again. "I don't think he'll take too kindly to a human climbing up to our aerie."

Zita grimaced at the bird, still some thirty feet above her head. "That's news," she said.

"Hmmm," said the bird. "I should've mentioned that earlier."

With renewed vigor, Zita scrambled the rest of the distance between her and the nest, weaving her way through the branches. When she arrived at the aerie, her hair was as tangled with cedar tree detritus as the nest itself; she heaved a sigh of relief to see that the juvenile eagle was still alone.

"Hi," said the eagle. "So what do you *really* need a feather for? I don't buy the quill bit."

"Long story," said Zita, catching her breath.

"I'm patient."

"Really? You're going to make me go into all this?"

"C'mon, I'm bored. All I do is sit up here and wait for my dad to bring me little bits of food. I can't even really fly that well," said the eagle.

"Okay," said Zita. "But I'm warning you, it's sort of weird."

"Weird? Curiosity: piqued."

"It's part of a charm. From, like, a spirit. The Verdant Empress. I'm supposed to bring her three things. She's commanded me."

The eagle looked at her, his head cocked sideways. "And then what happens?"

"I honestly don't know," said Zita.

The eagle paused, considering what the girl had said. "That doesn't seem very smart," he said finally. "I mean, what's she going to do with these three things? What's so important that she needs you to do all this?"

Zita stared at the eagle, perplexed. In all honesty, she hadn't really considered all the implications that thoroughly. She'd been lost in a haze, following the instructions that had miraculously appeared on her bedroom mirror. "I guess I don't know," said Zita.

"Well, it smells funny to me," said the eagle. "But whatever. You do your thing."

"Can I have that feather now?" asked Zita.

"Oh, yeah," said the bird. "What color?"

"What?" Zita thought she felt the air near her disrupted; she heard a loud cawing in the distance.

"What color, like, the plumage?" asked the bird. "And quick: My

dad's coming back right now. He'll probably pick you up and drop you from the air."

"I don't know," said Zita, petrified. "Silver?"

The eagle rolled his eyes. "We don't *have* silver feathers. What do you think I am, a griffin or something?"

"Whatever color you've got, I really don't care," said the girl, hastily, as the eagle's father approached. The massive bird had made a great arc in the air and was beginning a winding descent toward the nest, something large and furry and very dead in its talons.

The juvenile in the nest began rummaging around in the cavity of the aerie. "Dark brown? No, too pedestrian. Something mottled would be nice. Like, a little spackle of white on tan. That'd be very pleasing, I think."

"Yeah, sure," said Zita, watching the eagle's father approach. "That's fine." The adult eagle had spotted her, and she saw a look of affronted anger cross his brow. He screeched loudly as he zeroed in on his approach.

"No, maybe you do want plain brown. Sometimes simple really is the best."

Zita lost her patience. "Whatever! Just please! I just need that feather!"

The father eagle began his furious descent; his talons, having already dropped their furry cargo in preference to this trespassing human, began to extend like sharpened knives. The juvenile tossed

Zita a simple brown feather with its beak, and the girl shoved it in her pocket and scurried desperately down the topmost branches of the tree. She'd barely reached the nearest branches below the nest when the eagle made contact with the aerie, and the treetop swayed under his enormous weight. Zita practically threw herself down the first twenty feet of the tree trunk, diving from one bough to the next like a loosed monkey, the eagle's screaming echoing behind her, and she didn't stop until she'd reached the ground, eagle feather safely nestled in the pocket of her jacket.

The first item had been won.

In the Realm of the Black Hats

Nico, the man dressed in black, rubbed his wrists and winced. Edwin Peach, nine years old with a penchant for knots, had bound his hands so tight that it took well over a quarter of an hour to free the man from his bonds; the ropes had left wide red welts crisscrossing his wrists. The man looked around the room, sizing up the children who had gathered around him, all observing him with a decidedly suspicious gaze. The boy with the machete who stood at his side held it threateningly, waiting for the strange man to make any sudden move.

"Can I have my hat back?" was the first thing Nico said.

The black beret was swiped from the head of a child and passed through the crowd to the owner. Elsie walked up to him with the hat; Nico bowed and Elsie set it back on his head.

"Thank you," said Nico.

Elsie blushed.

The man adjusted the beret so it sat slightly askew on his balding head with its strawlike hair, which he tucked up into the back of the hat. He was a handsome man, possibly in his midthirties, and wore the frame of someone who likely followed a sensible diet. He reminded Elsie of a cashier at their family's local co-op, the kind of guy who would look down his nose a bit if you hadn't brought in your own bag. A bit of mustache colored his upper lip.

"So," said Nico Posholsky, "you're the Unadoptables, huh?"

"Yep," said Michael. "And this is our home."

"Nice place," said Nico. "Could use some cleaning up."

"We do our best."

The man began to amble about the large room, studying the salvaged pieces of furniture, the ratty bedding, and the sad remains of the children's meager breakfast. "Surprised the stevedores haven't rooted you out yet." He pulled away a waxed cotton tarp, revealing a portion of the Unadoptables' food stores: a few greasy bags of sandwich crusts, what was to be their lunch for the day. "Maybe they know you're here and they just don't care." He pivoted on his heels, gracefully, and glanced up at the high rafters, the light angling in through the tall leaded windows. "Good hiding spot, though. Can't think of why they'd come out here."

Rachel was the one who finally interjected, sounding annoyed by the man's musings. "So we let you go. Now you have to help us. Two of our family. An old man and a girl. They were caught by the stevedores. We don't know where they are."

Nico stopped and chewed on this information for a moment before replying. "Old man? Was he blind?"

"Yes!" spouted Elsie.

"And the girl—she's Asian?"

Rachel nodded. "Do you know where they are?"

"No," said the man. "And yes. We caught word. There was some serious to-do, not long ago, at Titan Tower. We get intel, occasionally, from inside the Shipping Division. Something about a couple of hostages—a blind man and a little girl. Seemed weird that they were so high priority."

"Intel, huh?" asked Michael, remaining suspicious of the newcomer's intentions. "How do we know you're not working for them—for the stevedores?"

Nico glared at Michael. "This'd be a pretty elaborate ruse, don't you think? A bunch of angry stevedores chasing me down out here, just to get me talking to a bunch of ragamuffin orphans?"

"Ex-orphans!" one of the children exclaimed.

"Sorry," said Nico. "Ex-orphans. Unadoptables." He continued talking to Michael: "A good man died to bring us that information. It's not easy infiltrating Wigman's Division."

"What's a Division?" asked one of the younger children.

Nico frowned. "You guys are pretty new to these parts, huh? They didn't tell you much at the orphanage, I imagine."

"Only how to work," said another Unadoptable.

"I'd heard that," said the man. "That Unthank was using his orphans in his machine-parts shop. *Pitoyable*. There was a plan in place to free you guys, you'll be pleased to know. Within the Chapeaux Noirs. One of the senior members suggested it—an action to liberate the child proletariat. Operation: Mass Adoption, I think it was called. But other, more pressing actions came up. Got put off. I'm happy to see you guys managed it for yourself."

The room rustled proudly at Nico's statement.

"You're in the Industrial Wastes," continued Nico. "That much you know. This used to be the old Science and Research Division, back when the Wastes were a sextet. Got pushed aside by the other Titans. Now it's just a no-man's-land. The Industrial Wastes was a Quintet for a long time after that, run by the five Titans of Industry, until a couple months ago. You guys brought down the fifth Titan, Unthank, in your little sabotage action. Knocked out a whole Division, something we've never come close to achieving. You worked from the inside, though. Brilliant."

"So what've you got against the Titans, then?" asked Michael.

"Everything," said Nico. "They're the real evil that needs to be rooted out. This place needs to be leveled, brought down to its foundations. That's what the Chapeaux Noirs are all about: a clean slate for the Industrial Wastes. Wipe out the oppressors, the wreckers, the looters. *Finis*."

"Good for you," pressed Rachel. "But where are our friends? The blind man and the girl. You didn't answer that question."

"Somewhere," said Nico, sounding unperturbed by Rachel's impatience. "Somewhere deep in Titan Tower, would be my guess. Seems like Wigman has a keen interest in your friends. That is, if they're still alive."

A few kids gasped at this. Michael waved his hands dismissively. "I think you're just trying to scare us," he said. "Why would this guy want to kill them?"

"Oh, believe me," said Nico. "Brad Wigman? He's done worse things. Much worse things."

"Say they are alive," said Rachel, "and they're in the tower. How do we get to them?"

"Well, that's the trick, isn't it? The place is impregnable. Ringed by an ever-changing phalanx of guards, an uncrackable security system. *Il est impossible*." The man did this, peppered his speech with little French phrases, causing the younger among the Unadoptables to look confusedly at their elders. He didn't seem remotely French.

"Are you, like, the boss of your—whatever you call it?" asked one of the children.

Nico laughed. "No. The Chapeaux Noirs have no leaders. Like I said, we're an anarcho-syndicalist collective. Decisions are made by committee."

"But can you help us get Carol and Martha back?" Rachel said, ignoring the man's jargon. "I don't care about your committee, your collective."

"Rachel," said Elsie, frowning at her sister. "Don't be rude."

"We're all getting ahead of ourselves here, I think," said Nico. "You guys look hungry. Are you hungry?"

A few of the younger kids nodded. It was true: They'd been living off grainy mush and table scraps for weeks now. Elsie's stomach rumbled at the mention of food.

"Why don't you come with me, back to our place?" said Nico. "Let's see if we can't get some food in these bellies. What do you say, champ?" This last question he directed to Michael, who, in the interim, had sat down in the chair where the black-clad man had so recently been restrained. The teenaged boy held his forehead in his hand, as if grappling with some bigger concern, like the weight of adulthood was pushing into him like the squeezing of a vise.

✌

The following morning, once they'd determined that the stevedores were well and truly gone, Nico led a contingent of Unadoptables out of their warehouse and into the light of the graying sun, filtered through the seemingly permanent cloud of haze in this cold, clamorous region. The Forgotten Place had returned to its normal level of quietude, with only the faraway noises of industry coloring the air. Most of the children elected to stay behind, to mind the warehouse against any further intrusions, with the promise that the voyaging party would bring back food, preferably sweets too, to nourish their empty stomachs.

The man in the black hat led them through a boxy labyrinth of burned-out structures, areas with which the children were familiar from their scavenging expeditions. Soon, however, they traveled past the pale of their territory and into the heart of the inhabited Wastes themselves. Here they traveled carefully, with Nico scouting the horizon while the children remained behind cover, waiting for the man's all clear. They arrived after a time at a dip in the ground where a giant concrete pipe belched effluent into a stagnant green pond.

"Let me guess," said Michael, coming up behind Nico. "We go that way."

"*Intelligent*," said Nico, dipping into French again.

Elsie blanched. She'd joined Rachel on the trip, despite her older sister's objections. She wanted to see the meeting place of this strange organization, the Chapeaux Noirs, and the comrades of the mysterious man who'd stumbled into their lives. Five other kids, including Cynthia Schmidt, rounded out the party. The youngest Mehlberg watched the brownish-green liquid pouring from the tall pipe and stifled a gag.

"Hold your noses, *mes enfants*," said Nico.

One by one, they followed the man into the pipe, straddling the torrent of filth and holding their breath until they'd passed a branch that came in from the right, the source of the fast-flowing stuff. Beyond that point, the going was relatively dry, though the smell remained ever-present. Shafts of light played across the dirty surface, shining down from conduits in the ceiling of the pipe every fifty feet or so. The pipe broke away in many directions, and Elsie felt dizzied by the number of times they'd changed directions in the maze of the sewers. Finally, the channel they were following ended abruptly and the party found themselves high on a wall overlooking a large, subterranean chamber; the room was cold but dry and lit by small, caged electric lights affixed to the brick walls. A few rusted pieces of machinery stood at one end of the room, suggesting some sort of long-abandoned water treatment plant. Nico led the children down a tall ladder to the floor of the room; he stretched mightily after having been forced to walk stooped for so long. He then ambled over to an iron door in the wall and rapped out an elaborate knocking pattern on the surface.

Within moments, a voice sounded from behind the door.

"*Qui* is it?" asked the voice. "*Qu'est-ce que c'est* the password?"

"*Je t'aime, Brigitte Bardot*," answered Nico.

"*Bon*," said the voice. A pause followed, and then the door was pulled noisily open by the person within. He was a skinny soul, dressed identically to Nico in black turtleneck and beret, and he fixed Nico with a look of amazement. "We gave you up for dead!" he exclaimed, sizing up his comrade as if he were a risen spirit. "They said the stevedores had you cornered!"

Nico laughed. "I'm not that easy of a catch, Augustin." He gestured to the seven children behind him, crowding in to see whom he was talking to. "These are the Unadoptables. Or some of them, at any rate. I'd be dead if it weren't for them. They're living in a warehouse in the old Science and Research Division. Living off scraps. They escaped Unthank's last February. They were the ones who burned the place to the ground. *Carbonisé.*"

The Unadoptables looked at one another uncertainly, curious as to how this sort of news would be received. They were happy to see a wide smile break across Augustin's face. "*C'est bon,*" he said. "Born saboteurs."

"They saved my life," continued Nico. "I owe them a decent meal, at the very least."

"And some to bring home to the others," interjected Elsie, who couldn't help but think of the hungry lot they'd left behind.

"Anything for friends of Nico's," said Augustin, standing back from the doorway. "Come on in, Unadoptables. Welcome to *chez* Chapeaux Noirs. Don't mind wiping your feet, it's plenty dirty in here."

They crossed over the threshold, all seven of the Unadoptables, following Nico and Augustin. The door let onto a hallway, which itself was broken up by narrow black doorways that branched off to either side every ten feet or so. As they walked, Elsie peered into the open doors and saw an incredible variety of activity taking place within them: black-bereted men standing at a table, poring over a large map held flat by empty green wine bottles; a man wearing a strange pair of goggles, carefully appending wires to a cannonball-like object; a group of men piling those selfsame bomblike objects in a box for storage; a long room filled with the black-clad men, drinking wine and throwing knives at the wall. When Elsie passed this latter scene, the men paused and watched as the congregation in the hall-way walked by; they stared at Elsie with suspicious eyes.

The hallway ended at a large room, similar to the one they'd entered from the pipe; it seemed to have been intended at some point to contain a large amount of water. Massive bladed turbines were stacked against one of the walls, somewhat haphazardly, rusted in their discarded state, long-lying evidence of the room's formerly intended function. A simple round table was set up in the center of the room, and several other members of the Chapeaux Noirs—near-identical in their uniform of black slacks, black turtlenecks, and black berets—sat around it, talking. When they saw Nico and the Unadoptables enter, they stood up, amazed.

"Nico Posholsky," exclaimed one of the men. "As I'm standing here. I thought you were *mort*."

"That means dead," whispered Rachel to her sister.

"Quite the opposite," replied Nico, "thanks to my friends here. Committee, meet the Unadoptables."

One of the men, a tall man with a shaved head and a little downward-pointing arrow of a graying beard gracing his long chin, pushed himself away from the table and walked toward Nico, his arms extended. "Comrade Posholsky. You *diable*," he swore under his breath.

The two men embraced mightily.

"How could you escape?" asked the older man. "You were cornered."

"I blasted my way out, Jacques," said Nico. "I still had two explosives. Managed to make a screen and I was able to open up an escape route. They chased me to the old S & R Division, where I found these kids, holed up in one of the old warehouses. They hid me. Saved my life."

The man, Jacques, slowly shifted his gaze to fall on the children who surrounded Nico. "Children?" he said. "In that wasteland?"

"They were Unthank's kids, Jacques," said Nico. "The ones who overthrew the machine-parts factory. The ones who burned it to the ground."

"*Incroyable*," the man mused. And then: "Please, children," he said, waving his long hands out in front of him. "Sit. If you've come from the old Science and Research Division, you've traveled a long way."

Several benches lining the brick walls of the room were soon filled with tired Unadoptables, sitting and studying the strange layout of the room: the rusty turbines, the vast arched ceiling, the unused piping jutting in from some outside source. Jacques returned to his chair and, reclining, waited for the children to get comfortable before he began talking again. "It's funny, *drôle*, that Nico should find you— or, rather, you should find Nico—in the S & R Division, of all places. I don't suppose you know what that area is, do you?"

"The Forgotten Place," said Elsie.

Michael interjected, "That's what we started calling it. It's our new home."

Jacques smiled. "As it was once mine."

"Yours?" asked Cynthia Schmidt.

"My name is Jacques Chruschiel, proud founding member of the Chapeaux Noirs. Sworn and committed to the destruction of the oppressive industrial state. But before I took on that name, my nom de guerre, I was Jack Kressel, head of development for the Science and Research Division of the Industrial Wastes. I was a Titan of Industry, as they say."

Michael gasped. "You were a Titan?" As one of the older orphans, he'd been partially aware of the structure of the Wastes.

The man nodded. "Back when it was the Sextet: Shipping, Petrochemical, Nuclear, Mining, Machine Parts, and Science and Research. This"—here he gestured to the large, strange room—"this was my

111

work. I designed this refinery, among many other things."

Several other members of the Chapeaux Noirs had left their grottos in the hallway and had joined the growing crowd in the brick room, quietly watching the new arrivals.

"But you must be hungry, *mes amis*," said Jacques.

"I did promise them food," said Nico. "It's the least of what I owe them."

"And eat you shall," said Jacques. "Comrade Posholsky, why don't you bring some food for the children? I believe there's some chocolate cake left over from the party last night, don't you think?" He winked at Elsie, saying, "It was Xavier's birthday."

At the mention of chocolate cake, Elsie's mouth began to water. She hadn't had chocolate in months, not since her parents had left and she and her sister had been entrusted to the guardianship of the Unthank Home for Wayward Youth. The idea of it alone was enough to make her heartbeat quicken. She looked over at Rachel, expecting to share a celebratory smile, but Rachel's attention was fixed on Jacques.

"We want more than chocolate cake," said Rachel. "We need your help."

Jacques seemed unflustered by the girl's sudden impatience. "But chocolate cake is a good starting point, *oui*?"

The other six children on the benches muttered in agreement. Rachel stayed silent.

An incredible array of food was fetched and laid out on the table in the center of the room: veggie shepherd's pie, mashed potatoes, seitan sandwiches ("The Chapeaux Noirs are strictly vegetarian," explained one of the crew. "Explosive experts and animal lovers."), and the promised chocolate cake, layered and luscious and coated in a thick shellac of creamy frosting. The children dug in with enthusiasm, heaping their plates with the food and filling their mouths with combinations of the available ingredients that they would have found repulsive before this, their most desperate time of life. Jacques spoke in his sonorous voice while they ate:

"Six Titans for six Divisions. We divided up this country, this stretch of land along the wide river. The six of us. The scions of our respective families, destined for greatness among men. For Peter Higgs, the control of the minerals below the earth. For Joffrey Unthank, the control of machine-part manufacture. Reginald Dubek, nuclear power, and Linus Tumson, the enriching and divining of fossil fuels. And then there was Bradley Wigman, a school friend of mine, who excelled in managerial organization, the eldest of a family born to an empire in the shipping industry. Together, we made the Industrial Wastes an efficient and cogent whole, all six Titans of Industry working for the betterment of the industrial state. I, like my father and his father before him, had a mind for science and, as was my birthright, the Science and Research Division became my jurisdiction. We worked in synergy, we six, and soon became very respected, powerful, and wealthy men in our own rights."

The children had polished off their cake and were happily being given second helpings as Jacques continued:

"But Bradley Wigman changed. The promise of wealth and power, to work with his fellow industrialists for the good of all, transformed him. He wanted more. He wanted to crush his competitors; and once they were crushed, he turned on his fellow industrialists. He reorganized the Sextet so that it answered only to him, that his Division should control the other five. He oversaw the streamlining of the various products the Wastes produced and made it clear in no uncertain terms that dissent would not be suffered.

"It had long been my desire to develop an alternative energy, something that did not require the destruction of the land and that did not release harmful matter into the atmosphere. I devoted my entire team to the discovery of this elusive ideal, and soon we had managed to create a small batch of highly combustible, zero-emission fuel that was made from vegetal compost and sewer waste. And we did it all there, in what you call the Forgotten Place, a place once thrumming with the excitement and energy of a fleet of the nation's best scientific minds. This fuel—it was a major breakthrough, the kind that happens only once in a generation. We threw our shoulders into the work and built this, an underground treatment center near the heart of the Industrial Wastes, where we would turn the world's garbage into gold."

Elsie forked a fresh chunk of cake and stared with renewed

understanding at the abandoned machinery in the room.

"At first," Jacques continued, "Wigman supported our efforts, as long as the work wasn't interfering with our normal day-to-day responsibilities. But as soon as it became clear that what we were making was, in fact, the sort of breakthrough material that would make entire swaths of industry obsolete—including his beloved Petrochemical and Nuclear Divisions, to say nothing of Mining—he was petitioned on all sides to put us out of business. And put us out of business he did."

The tenor of the room seemed to darken as Jacques described, in detail, how Wigman had sent in his army of stevedores and sabotaged the entire operation. The thugs chased the scientists from the warehouses and proceeded to burn the entire place to the ground. "All my research," said Jacques, solemnly, "gone. All my prototypes, my samples, my great library—turned to ash and smoke."

The collective noisy masticating of the seven Unadoptables in the room quieted as they listened to the man's story. A few of the Chapeaux Noirs played a game of mumblety-peg in the corner; Nico traced some sigil on the grain of the table. An echoey drip from a far-off chamber could be heard; Jacques continued.

"In a way, it was an epiphany for me—do you know what an epiphany is?" he asked.

"Yes," said Michael. Then, when the eyes of the room turned on him, he recanted. "No, actually."

"It's a realization. A sudden confrontation with the self. Predicating a sea change. A clarity. This is what happened to me. In that great conflagration, in the detonation that brought my precious research laboratories and life's work literally to dust, I saw my life anew. I saw the hypocrisy, the cynicism, the poison of the industrial mind-set. The destructive power of capitalism. It all became very clear. And so, that very day, as I escaped with my cohort into the very sewers that we had built for our creation, I swore that I would devote the rest of my life to the tearing down of the institutions that built me. That day, Jack Kressel died. Jacques Chruschiel was born."

A silence followed this dramatic telling. Elsie paused in the chewing of her last mouthful of chocolate cake, swallowing it down with a loud gulp in the quietness of the moment. Out of the corner of her eye, she saw her sister set an emptied plate down and cross her arms. Elsie could tell she was getting impatient.

"So that's how all this started?" asked Michael, wiping a cake crumb from the specter of his teenage mustache. "The Shadow Nawr?" He reddened a little as he fumbled his pronunciation. "Or whatever."

Nico spoke: "Chapeaux Noirs. Yes. Jacques found us, other discarded and alienated workers of the Industrial Wastes, and united us around this common goal."

"So what do you do?" asked Michael.

"Blow stuff up," said Nico. "Eventually, everything here will be

Jacques Chruschiel

Nico Posholsky

The Chapeaux Noirs

"That's what the Chapeaux Noirs are all about: a clean slate for the Industrial Wastes. Wipe out the oppressors, the wreckers, the looters. Finis."

flattened. Then, and only then, we'll be satisfied."

"Seems like you've got a long way to go." This was Rachel, still sitting against the brick wall with her arms across her chest. "Doesn't seem like you've made much of a dent. Except for Unthank's place. Oh wait. That was us." She cracked a wry smile.

Nico wagged a finger at her, grinning. "I like this one, Jacques," he said. "She's a pistol."

Jacques leaned back in his chair, watching the girl. "Actually, you've made a good point. We can only attack from the outside, but Wigman has built a strong empire. His walls are tall and thick. It's a long game. A war of attrition."

"We're getting them by the ankles. That's how you—" began Nico.

"Bring down a giant, by the ankles," finished Rachel. "We got that part. But you're not going to be able to help get our friends back by biting at some giant's ankles."

"Their friends?" asked Jacques, looking at Nico.

"Right," responded the other man. "That's sort of part of the deal. They helped me escape the stevedores, so I said we'd help them get two of their . . . club back."

"Their names are Martha Song and Carol Grod," said Rachel. "Martha's an Asian girl, a little younger than me. Carol's an old man. He's blind."

Jacques made a kind of punctuated hum at the mention of the

two abductees. "Sounds familiar. Old blind man, Asian girl. Weren't they . . ."

"The two people the stevedores took into custody," said Nico.

"Refresh my memory, comrade. These were the two they brought into the tower?"

Nico seemed abashed. "The same."

Jacques then turned to the Unadoptables. "I'm afraid our Comrade Posholsky made a bargain he cannot, in good conscience, keep. Your colleagues are in the tower. They're as good as gone, my friends. No one could bring them back."

"Liar!" shouted Rachel suddenly. She leapt up from her bench and threw herself at Nico, who scrambled backward to avoid the girl's attack. Elsie let out a shrill yelp of surprise and Michael dove forward, grabbing Rachel by the shoulders.

"Rachel!" he shouted, pulling her back. "Easy!"

"We would've killed him," yelled Rachel, her voice breaking with anger. "But we let him go. He promised us!"

Nico had scuttled over behind several other members of the Chapeaux Noirs and was laughing embarrassedly, having been so spooked by the teenager's sudden attack. Jacques watched him calmly, his eyes jumping the distance between him and the black-haired girl. He sighed heavily before speaking.

"Oh, Nico," he said. "It is a sad man indeed who makes a promise he cannot keep. Even if it's only to save his life."

"Apologies, Jacques," said Nico, smiling. "*Excuse-moi*. I did what I had to do."

"The Chapeaux Noirs keep their promises, children," said Jacques. "But I tell you, this thing you want, the rescue of your friends, it is an impossible task. Titan Tower is impregnable. Full stop."

"Then give us Nico back," said Rachel calmly. "That's the deal, right?" A mischievous smile cracked across her lips. She shook free of Michael's restraints.

"Yeah," said Cynthia Schmidt, rising to stand by Rachel's side. "Give us our prisoner back."

Nico's face went pale. "Jacques," he said desperately. "You can't do that. These kids are . . . these kids are savages."

Jacques seemed to be considering the exchange. He remained quiet, his hand gently stroking the little gray triangle of his beard. "A deal is a deal . . . ," he mused.

"Wait a second, Jacques," pleaded Nico. He shook his finger at the elder man, buying the time he needed to conjure the right words. "Operation: Urban Renewal. Remember? We could do it, with the right guys."

Jacques cocked an eyebrow. "That wouldn't work on several levels. I assume these children want their friends back alive and not vaporized?"

"With a little rejiggering—couldn't we make it work? I mean, it's about time we went for the big guy, isn't it?" Nico's voice was trembling in its desperate sincerity.

Jacques folded one leg neatly over the other, as someone whose sinewy joints had seen years of careful exercise, and continued to stroke the fur on his chin. "I apologize for my associate's irresponsible behavior, children," he said. "He made a gambit knowing that it was an unlikely bet. However: We do have a similar goal, the two of our, shall we say, organizations. It might be that our aims are not mutually exclusive. In fact, they might dovetail in a very satisfactory manner." He looked around the room, at the other black-clad saboteurs present, and said, "Call Le Poignard. Clear the table. Let's see what sort of plan we can hatch."

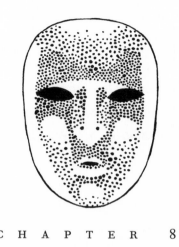

C H A P T E R   8

The Interim Governor-Regent-Elect

It had been nearly seven months since Prue had last set foot in the Pittock Mansion, the seat of power of South Wood, with its opulent twin towers and ivy-laden facade. It was no longer the pristine, whitewashed edifice she remembered; the interior seemed to have suffered the effects of a weeklong party that no one was too keen to clean up. The portraits in the foyer, the walls of which she only had a moment to scan as the throng of celebrants carried her on their shoulders through the doors, hung badly askew. One of them, of a corpulent general in dashing fatigues, had been defaced with a giant, black-marker mustache below the general's regal nose. The red velvet bunting that had hung along the central staircase's banister and along the first-floor balcony had been torn out in favor of a ream of fabric striped blue, white, and green that looked like it had been hung by a person with poor spatial coordination.

A smell of smoke and possibly cheese that had gone bad was on the air. Prue tried to organize her thoughts as the crowd, with some difficulty, managed to navigate the looping central staircase toward, she supposed, the Interim Governor-Regent's office. There, she thought, she would present her plan. Out in the open, as Curtis had said. Announce the tree's call for the resurrection of Alexei; damn the skeptics. Get the entire populace to fall in line and help in the search for Carol Grod, the other maker. Who would dare assassinate a child while surrounded by her staunchest fanatics? Still, the sight of the guillotine, something she recognized from a book she'd been shown once by a friend, was deeply troubling to her. And was that blood on the blade? She'd only had a moment to see it, but the image haunted her.

"What is this racket?" shouted a man at the top of the stairs. Prue looked up and immediately recognized him: the attaché who'd presented her to Lars Svik, back when she'd first set foot on the Mansion's parquet floors in search of news of her brother's disappearance. "No more mobs in the Mansion! I thought we'd come to an agreement!"

The crowd paused on the steps, awkwardly juggling their twelve-year-old cargo in place.

"Put me down," said Prue calmly. Her carriers did as she asked. She pushed her way to the top of the stairs, to the head of the crowd. The attaché peered through his spectacles at her.

"I know you," he said.

"I don't s'pose I'll need to make an appointment this time," said Prue.

The attaché smiled nervously at the crowd behind the girl. "Not that you did last time, if I recall correctly."

"In fact," said Prue, emboldened, "I think that I will be making a general announcement right here." She gestured to the bowed lip of the second-floor railing, a balcony that overlooked the whole of the foyer. "If the Governor-Regent would like to be here for that, it would be fine with me."

"I will ask the Interim Governor-Regent-elect himself," said the attaché, and he ran off toward a pair of doors down the hall.

A young man in bicycle britches at her elbow said, "What are you going to say?" He spoke in a breathless, excited voice that seemed to match the general tenor of the entire crowd.

"Well . . . ," began Prue.

"Is she going to make an announcement?" someone asked from farther down the stairwell.

"I think so!" shouted another.

"Excuse me," said an older man who'd pushed his way to the front of the crowd. "Are you going to say something about taxes?"

"*Pfft!*" said another, a rabbit. "The Bicycle Maiden's got more on her mind than taxes. She's here to start another revolution!" The rabbit then looked up at Prue. "Aren't you?"

"No, I'm not," corrected Prue, though in truth, she really didn't know what she was going to say, and the noise of the crowd made it difficult to compose her thoughts.

"Perhaps you could spare a word or two about water quality," said someone who Prue couldn't see. "Or public transportation."

The crowd murmured approval. "It has gone a bit messy, the bus system," someone conjectured.

"What about street repair? There's a pothole on my street that's the size of a bear's fat belly," said another.

"Hey!" shouted an offended bear.

"The firemen haven't been paid since March, Maiden," said someone else.

"The fire marshal had his head chopped off in April, so no surprise there."

"Didn't improve the service much."

"The tariffs on poppy beer imports are outrageous!"

"The food in your tavern is outrageous, Citizen Fox, that's what."

"Shhhh! She's about to speak."

"No, she isn't."

"She just said something, listen carefully."

"What did she say?"

"Are we to teach the writings of the Synod in schools, Maiden?"

"She'll get to that, citizen. Haven't seen you in the chapel lately."

"I thought the revolution freed us of all that stuff."

"Watch it, or the Spokes will free you of your head."

At this point, Prue was completely paralyzed by the noise, and her hands moved instinctively to her head, cupping her temples in the way she'd seen her mother do when Mac had torn apart some precious craft project. She was also paralyzed by indecision. She felt like she was on the cusp of some major action, the consequence of which she still couldn't quite see.

"Maiden?" came a voice at her heel. She looked down. It was a mouse, tugging gently at her pant leg. "Are you going to speak?"

"Yes," whispered Prue.

She then realized what must be done: She needed to get away from these people. She pushed her way through the teeming mob, which had now surpassed the top of the stairs and was encircling her. Arriving at the balcony overlooking the crowded foyer—following the commotion, many more onlookers had crushed into the building— she raised her hands out in front of her, willing silence.

"QUIET!" she yelled. "PLEASE!"

The crowd, after some shushing between one another, did as she requested. Every eye in the room swiveled to fall on her.

She smoothed the front of her peacoat. "Thank you," she said. In her peripheral vision, she saw the double doors to the Interim Governor-Regent's office thrown open; several figures emerged. They stopped on the threshold and watched as the speaker addressed the crowd.

"People of South Wood," said Prue. It was as good a way to start as any, she decided. It seemed like the sort of thing returning heroes always said to their slavish army of followers—"people of such-and-such." Now that she had that out of the way, she tried to divine exactly what would come next. She stalled for time by scanning the room with the gravitas of a Roman emperor surveying his people. She felt the surge of something inside her, similar to what she'd felt when the badger rickshaw driver had prostrated himself in front of her.

"I have . . . *returned*," she said, drawing out each word in a slow, deep-voiced cadence. Too cheesy? she wondered. Too much?

The room erupted in cheers. She looked over to her right, to where the attaché stood with someone who she guessed to be the Interim Governor-Regent. To her surprise, he was a possum with a bleach-white face and a long, sinewy tail. He wore a tousled suit coat, and his fur was all disheveled. The air in the foyer and the staircase and the balcony was ripe with unbridled excitement; they waited for her next words.

"First off," she said, "I don't appreciate people treating other people badly, like, if they were for this revolution or not. That's not cool." She found that the Roman-emperor mode, which was great for making grandiose, crowd-silencing announcements, was not very sustainable when one got into the nitty-gritty. It fell away from her very twelve-year-old voice like the protective covering of some sad, dumpy Buick, when one expected a Porsche to be beneath.

The crowd became very quiet; whether they were internalizing what she'd said or casting silent judgment, she couldn't say.

"Seriously," continued Prue, "what's with the thing out front? The guillotine."

The crowd now seemed genuinely confused.

"Why," offered a shrew with a surprisingly deep and loud voice, some ways down the staircase, "that's for chopping people's heads off." The crowd around him nodded as he qualified the explanation by saying, "Those that aren't patriotic, anyway."

"Chopping people's . . . ," Prue hiccuped, echoing the words back in disbelief. "That's not what this was all about! I mean, when we came and freed the birds from the prison."

"But weren't they the enemies, the Svikists?"

A Svikist—someone who supported the old regime, she figured. "No," she said. "And yes. I mean, I didn't think they'd be treated *that* way."

"What were we supposed to do with them?" shouted someone.

"How did we know they weren't going to just come and oppress us all over again?" shouted another.

"How about we just cut off their hands?" suggested another voice, and his neighbors nodded, as if understanding the wisdom of such a proposal.

"Or maybe just their little toes? The pinkie ones?"

"NO!" shouted Prue. "Don't cut off anything!" She took a deep breath, commanding all her inner strength. "As Bicycle Maiden, I *order* that you—"

"Oh, order, huh?" said one of the onlookers. He was human, but he did not wear the uniform of the Spokes—the bicycle cap and knickers. "What are you, an empress now?"

"Careful!" shouted one of his neighbors, a Spoke. "That's the Bicycle Maiden you're talking to!" He gestured to some of his pals, who were dressed in the requisite riding gear, and they began to sidle toward the naysayer.

"No, I'm not a queen or an empress or anything," said Prue. "And I don't really mean to order you to do anything. No one should order you around. But I'm just saying, I mean, the spirit of the, you know, time that we, like, did all that stuff. Last fall. I just don't think . . ." She found she was losing her audience. Indeed, she felt like she was losing herself.

Meanwhile, the immediate neighbors of the man who'd made the snide comment were now pointing frantically at the perpetrator while the Spokes made their way to his position. "That's him," said one of the Spokes. "He's not even wearing a sprocket."

"Svikist!" someone shouted, and suddenly the man was tackled and hauled away toward the door.

"Please!" Prue yelled, her voice now growing hoarse. "Just listen for a second. I've got something really important to tell everyone."

The room hushed again; the Spokes halted their movement toward the door, their captive squirming in their arms.

Prue took a deep breath. "I've been instructed. By the Council Tree. To bring together the two makers who made Alexei, the heir apparent. The tree wants Alexei brought back to life."

A great pause followed as the members of Prue's audience looked at one another, perplexed. Prue heard someone clear their throat; it was the possum, to her right. She shifted her feet a little and continued in the quiet:

"I'll need your help," she said, "in finding one of his makers. The man's name is Carol Grod. He's a blind man, an old man."

One of the older members of the crowd spoke up. "Alexei. You mean Alexandra and Grigor's son, the young Svik? The one that the Governess brought back with the black magic?"

"I do," said Prue.

They all stood and stared at her, and the air in the building began to collect and build upon itself like the air in a balloon stretched to its very limits. The following shout, coming from a man in the back of the room, acted as the pin for this balloon:

"SHE'S A SVIKIST!" it came.

At that very moment, the crowd descended into absolute chaos. Which is not to say it hadn't been chaotic before; it had. It was just that now all of that chaotic energy, which had been, up to that point, directed toward a very particular subject, began to suddenly turn in on itself as every closely held belief of those present flipped inside out and became as unclear to those who held them as a ship navigating a foggy sea. It began in ripples: little exclamations of confusion, followed by rebuttals of those very exclamations, which led to recriminations, which led to someone getting hit squarely in the nose. The man the Spokes had been roughly escorting to the door, presumably to his death, was just as roughly dropped as his captors began sparring angrily with one another, arguing over whether the Bicycle Maiden was truly who she said she was, considering the sort of antipatriotic, Svikist, antirevolution thing she'd just said. The entire scene soon escalated to an out-and-out brawl, easily two hundred humans and animals in the giant, collective scrape.

"Oh boy," was all Prue could say.

"Ms. McKeel," came a voice, managing to cut through the din: It was being spoken directly into her right ear. She looked over and saw that the voice was coming from the small, furry frame of the possum she'd seen earlier, held to a human's height by the attaché. "I'd say you should come with me, immediately."

The battle raged below the balcony; the combatants on the staircase seemed to flow like a wave upward, flattening all in its path.

They had crested the second floor; the riot seemed to be making its way toward Prue. Judging from the curses coming from within the scrum, Prue could tell she had as many defenders as detractors, but still: She blathered something to the possum and then wordlessly followed him and the attaché toward the double doors in a crouched run with her hands over her head.

When they'd arrived at the safety of the Interim Governor-Regent's office, the attaché slammed the door behind him as the battle waged loudly without.

"So that couldn't have gone worse," said the possum.

"I didn't know it would be taken so badly," said Prue, still reeling. Her entire body felt like one of those plastic horse puppets, the ones with the elastic in the joints, atop their plastic pedestals with the button underneath that makes the thing collapse.

"Then you don't know this crowd," said the attaché.

Promptly, some celestial being pushed in the button on Prue's pedestal, and her elastic joints gave way and she slid down the wainscoting of the wall until she was a crumpled mass on the floor.

"Easy, easy," said the possum, walking to her side. "It'll pass. They get fired up fairly easily. They'll likely simmer down in a short matter of time."

"Who are you?" asked Prue blearily.

"I'm Ambrose Pupkin, Interim Governor-Regent-elect," said the possum, bowing a little. He, too, wore a brass sprocket brooch on his vest. "Now you see what I've had to deal with."

"What happened out there? Why'd they react that way?" asked Prue.

"I could've warned you," said Ambrose. "Had you taken a moment."

"I thought I knew. I thought they worshipped me."

"They do, to a degree," said the possum. "But you don't understand what we've gone through, over the last many months, since you were here."

Prue rubbed her eyes a little. The animal wavered in her vision. "Have we met before?" she asked.

"No," said Ambrose. "Though I've watched you. I was around when you first arrived here at the Mansion. I was a lowly janitor then. And look what the revolution's done for me. Me, the Interim Governor-Regent-elect."

"Why not just Governor-Regent?" asked Prue, wiping a strand of hair from her brow. "Why the long title?"

"Better to stay this way," he said. "The last Governor-Regent-elect lost his head."

"Oh," said Prue, thinking she understood what Ambrose had said, but then realized she hadn't, not entirely. "Oh!" she said again, with a renewed understanding.

The possum went on, "*Interim* doesn't quite suggest accountability, if you get my meaning. The buck doesn't stop here, not yet. I'm just passing through." He scissored his little fingers in the air, miming a walking figure.

"I see why they gave the job to the janitor," said Prue.

The possum winked at her. "You catch on fast," he said. "Now what's all this business about Alexei? The boy's been dead five years. Not only that, but his tomb is graffitied with anti-Svik slogans."

Prue shook her head. "I don't know," she said. "It's what the tree told me."

"You see?" said Ambrose, snapping his little fingers. "That's one place you went wrong. You're a tree-talker, aren't you? North Wood mysticism. Doesn't necessarily fly in the South."

"But still . . ."

"But still nothing. You'd have been better off saying you received it from a vision in your dreams. A dappled goddess, or some such nonsense, bearing a crystal staff et cetera, et cetera. You start talking the Council Tree to a bunch of red-blooded South Wooders, you're sunk."

"Okay," was Prue's only reply.

"And more importantly: What the devil do you intend to do with a reanimated mechanical boy?"

"The tree said it would bring peace. To the Wood."

The possum exchanged a glance with the attaché. "Oh, did it? It'll erase the infighting? The strife among the lower classes? The ruined harvest? It'll refill the empty coffers of the Mansion?"

"The tree didn't really go into detail," said Prue.

"I suppose trees rarely do," added the attaché snidely.

"It's madness," said Ambrose. "But I've got too much on my plate to run interference for an Outsider on an inane quest. One thing: When you decided to announce your intentions to that bloodthirsty rabble, did you take a moment to consider that these were the very people who exiled the old Governess to begin with—for the precise thing that you're trying to reenact?"

"I had, I mean I did. I just didn't think . . ."

The possum shook his head. "That's the trouble with you Outsiders. So impetuous. Well, you've cooked yourself up a real stew, haven't you, Bicycle Maiden?"

"What do I do?"

"Oh, they'll calm down," said the attaché. "Riots are a weekly occasion. Surprising, this happening on a Wednesday. Typically, they only riot on Thursdays and occasionally Monday afternoons. Extenuating circumstances, I suppose." He had picked up a stack of papers from the desk and was busy thumbing through it. "Svikists, Spokes, Caliphs. It's the new world here. This is what revolution looks like."

"Can you send in guards?" asked Prue. "To, you know, get things under control?"

"We tried that," said the attaché. "Only gets them more riled up. They start getting oppressed when you do that."

"So how do you keep order?"

"We wait for them to move on, after they've done whatever damage they plan on doing." This was Ambrose, who'd moved to the office's window and was carefully pushing the curtain away to see the outside. "These days, the Synod has been nice enough to handle the crowd control." He paused. "See? They're already starting to disperse."

Prue crawled her way to the window, a captive wary of a sniper shot, and peeked her head above the sill. Sure enough, the crowd was scattering away from the Mansion across the deep-green pitch of the grounds. Several figures, wearing long gray hooded robes, seemed to be guiding the figures away.

"Who needs to pay for security when you've got a religious sect keeping things organized?" Ambrose said. "Certainly makes things easier for us."

"So that's the Synod? The Caliphs?" asked Prue, watching as the robed figures seemed to wordlessly corral the agitated crowd away from the Mansion. They wore masks over their faces, shiny human masks that caught and reflected the sun when they turned their covered heads. A few of them swung pendulum-like things on chains that puffed smoke with every swing.

"Basically, these are the Mystics of the South Wood, just like the North Wood has theirs," explained Ambrose. "They'd been outlawed by the old regimes. Decades ago it was a crime to have any kind of Caliphate iconography around. Once the sect had been routed, folks in the Mansion started getting lax about enforcing the laws. And once the revolution hit, and the old Svik dynasty was torn down for good, it made a window for a revival. The Blighted Revival, they called it."

"After the Blighted Tree," explained the attaché, "the first living tree of the Wood."

"I thought the Council Tree was the first living tree of the Wood," said Prue.

"And that's how you're going to run into problems," said Ambrose. "The North Wood's just a bunch of cultists and bumpkins. According to the Southerners."

The attaché had moved to the desk and was sorting through the massive pile of papers that lay heaped there. "Now if you wouldn't mind, Ms. McKeel," he said. "We have a lot of work to do here. Those Svikist collaborators' heads are not going to chop themselves off."

Prue blanched. "But is it safe?" she asked, bewildered. "For me to go out there?"

"Oh, I'm sure you'll still find support," Ambrose said. "You are the Bicycle Maiden, after all. Go out there and show them what you're made of."

"But they called me a Savi-, a Svikist!" She had some difficulty pronouncing the word. It was a silly thing. She qualified: "Which I'm not."

"Oh, I'm sure you're not. And it's unlikely that you'll be beheaded, anyway. You'll have enough defenders to save you that fate."

Ambrose had moved over to the attaché's side and was helping him sort through the stack of papers on the desk. Prue had paused by the door, thinking.

"Please," she said. "Can you help me? I just need to find out what happened to the other maker," she said.

The possum glared at Prue. "If you take my advice, you'd drop the whole affair. Grave robbing is a capital offense, you know. You're on your own, Bicycle Maiden. We've got enough trouble as it is. We've got executions to decree, censures to sign. An angry, violent people to appease. Don't drag us into your little quest."

"What about, like, a paper trail?" asked Prue desperately. "There's got to be some record, somewhere. Of the exile."

The attaché pushed a stack of papers in front of Ambrose, who'd taken his seat behind the desk. The Interim Governor-Regent-elect began signing the papers as the attaché slid them under his pen, like a practiced casino card dealer laying out a blackjack hand.

"I suppose," said the attaché in the midst of this action, "you could go to the archives."

"The archives," repeated Ambrose, his arm a blur above the pages he was gracing with his scribble. "Oh yes, the archives."

"The archives?" asked Prue.

"I suppose," said the attaché, "there might be a record in the archives."

Prue waited for more information, but the two figures were silent,

lost in their work. "So . . . ," she prompted.

"What?" asked Ambrose, looking up from the papers.

"Where are the archives?" asked Prue.

"Oh," said Ambrose. "Here, in the Mansion. Ask one of the staff; they can direct you. But first you'll need a request, signed, dated, and notarized by the Interim Governor-Regent-elect." He said that as if it were an obstacle too high to hurdle.

"That's you," said Prue.

"Oh," said the possum, seemingly surprised by the suggestion. "Right. Sorry. Fairly new to the job." He continued signing papers.

"I'd like to do that," said Prue. "Get access to the archives."

"Very well," said Ambrose. "Mr. Secretary, if you wouldn't mind getting the girl a . . . what's the bloody name of the form?"

"A 651-C-5, I believe, sir," said the attaché. "I have one right here." He reached into a filing cabinet off to one side of the desk and retrieved the document. Setting it down on the only clear space on the desk, he spun it around so that it was facing Prue. "You'll need to sign here," he said, pointing to a series of empty blanks on the page. "Here. And here. And initial here. And sign here. And fill in your intent here, e.g., looking for a record of two exiled toy makers."

"Only one," said Prue. "I need to find only one. Carol Grod."

Ambrose looked up from his signing. "But you'll need both makers," he said. "Isn't that what you said?"

"No. Just the one. I've found one. I just need to find the other." She said this as she scanned the very small print on the piece of paper she was presently signing and initialing, distracted by its very complicated layout. "Only the two of them can make the thing, the cog that will bring him back to life."

"Oh," said Ambrose. She didn't see that he'd stopped in his labors and was making eye contact with the attaché. "Where is he, this other maker—the one that you've found?"

Prue, in her distracted state, had quite forgotten the plan, that Esben's location remain secret until she found Carol and could reunite them. "He's safe," she said. And that was all.

The Interim Governor-Regent-elect shrugged and continued scribbling away at the pages that the attaché slid in front of him in a shushed conveyor-belt-like activity. Prue finished signing the form she'd been given and handed it back to the attaché, who promptly slid it in front of the possum.

"For the girl, sir," said the attaché.

Ambrose signed it and handed it back to Prue, saying, "Good luck with this one, Bicycle Maiden. May the Blighted Tree light your way."

"Thank you," said Prue hesitantly. She took the piece of paper and wheeled about, heading for the double doors on the opposite side of the room. Halfway across the carpet, she paused. "Okay. Wish me luck."

The possum looked up from his paperwork to say, "If you stood up to the SWORD and stormed the South Wood Prison, I suppose a few harmless revolutionaries could hardly stand in your way."

"Right," said Prue, taking a deep breath. "Here we go."

And she stepped out of the office and back into the heart of the Mansion.

Where the Air Comes From; The Second Thing

They cleared the table in the center of the room with a flourish; a heavyset man who'd been introduced as "Le Poignard" unfurled a large blueprint map and stretched it out on the table's wooden surface. A host of Chapeaux Noirs gathered there like priests unveiling a holy writ. The glow of a single lightbulb, from above, illuminated the blue ink on the waxy paper: an incredibly detailed architectural diagram of what appeared to be a very tall and very fortified building. On the bottom of the sheet was written TITAN TOWER in the perfect symmetry of architectural script. The Unadoptables all crowded around one edge of the table and peered down at the blueprint, their eyes wide. Jacques Chruschiel loomed over them, his hand tracing little imaginary lines on the paper.

"An outer wall, made of five-foot-thick concrete and topped with concertina wire," said Jacques. "Guarded *tout le temps* by the tower's best-trained stevedores." His finger, unrestricted by the tower's defenses, made its way past the gridded outline of the wall and into the square that was the building's ground floor. "A state-of-the-art security system, linked to a closed-circuit video surveillance package on every floor. Stevedores here, here, and here," he said, his finger tapping on each corner of the box. "And here. Access to the top floor is only viable through the elevator *ici*, here." Tap. "Which is security-locked, accessible to only those whose handprints have clearance."

"How do you know all this stuff?" asked Michael.

"I told you," said Nico Posholsky, who was cast in the bulb's dim light on the opposite side of the table. "A good man died to bring us this intel."

"The blueprint we've had since December. The rest is stuff we've learned over months of hard recon work," said Jacques.

"Who was it?" asked Elsie, Intrepid Tina held tight to her chest.

"What?" asked Jacques, surprised to hear the little girl speak up.

"Who died?" She looked at each man in turn, each black-bereted man who stood around the table staring at the stolen plans. She'd been thinking of the man who'd died bringing the "intel" ever since Nico had mentioned it back at the Forgotten Place, and it bothered her. She couldn't help but imagine him, this man who wore a black beret too and was once as alive as the men who were now crowded around this table, talking espionage.

"Michel," said Jacques, finally. "Michel Blatsky. A good man. *Vraiment un bon homme*." He smiled at Elsie warmly. "It's good you asked. Too soon we forget."

"He'd posed as a stevedore, infiltrated their ranks. He had to gain seventy-five pounds to do it," said Nico. "Ten weeks of work, reporting back to us every other night on the sly. In the end, it was too much. He slipped up, dropped some French into a casual conversation, and he was made." He stopped talking here, as if overcome by the memory. "All that we found later was his maroon beanie."

"Since then, our hopes of staging an attack on the tower itself have been abandoned," said Jacques, still staring at the blueprint. "It was too risky. We've been hitting smaller jobs ever since."

"How can you be sure that Carol and Martha are in there?" asked Rachel.

"Michel was there when the stevedores brought them in. They were escorted into the tower under heavy security. More than likely, they're here." He threw back the blueprint, revealing a stack of pages beneath. Flipping through, he found what he was looking for and spread it flat. It was labeled TITAN TOWER: TOP FLOOR DETAIL. His finger stabbed down on a small, closetlike room that branched off a rectangular space that dominated the surface area of the floor. "Wigman's safe room, connected by a secret door to his office and trophy room. The man's a paranoid, deep down. He had this room built as a safe harbor were the tower to come under attack. It's the hardest room in the building to crack. In a building that's impossible to crack. If he really cared about these two—and it appears he does—this would be the best place to keep them."

"So how do you get in?" asked Michael.

"You don't," said Jacques. "Before Michel was nabbed, we were in the midst of an action called Operation: Urban Renewal. It was to be the biggest action in the history of the Chapeaux. A full-scale attack on the tower, detonations set at every floor. The whole thing—the tower, the stevedores, Wigman and his cronies—would all come toppling down in a glorious explosion. Needless to say, that wouldn't necessarily work in a search-and-rescue mission."

"The only way is to blow our way in," said Nico. "Put enough C-4 on the outer wall to make a hole and hope that a few more guys can get through to blow the doors."

"Security system then puts the whole building on lockdown," said Jacques. "Elevators lock, doors lock. Alarms everywhere. And then you've got the entire stevedore security detail to wrangle with."

Nico rubbed his chin. "But if you threw some decoy detonation on the east and north corners, just to throw 'em off . . ."

"So you've scattered the stevedores," Jacques interrupted. "You've still got the lockdown *and* a stevedore threat that's bigger than our team could handle, especially if we've got technicians on the east and north wall, laying bombs."

"Say one of the bombs is lobbed at a generator," said Nico. "Knock the power out."

"Have you been listening at all during the council meetings?" asked Jacques disdainfully. "Generator's underground. And there's backup in the building." A group of men began arguing these points across the table from Jacques and Nico; soon, the entire room became lost in a buzz of anarchist saboteurs, all heatedly discussing the minutiae of storming Titan Tower.

Elsie, standing next to Jacques, her arms folded on the lip of the table, was stroking the cropped hair of Intrepid Tina and trying to think how she could be of help. She'd been so accustomed, in her former life, before her parents' abandonment, to sitting back and letting the adults handle the big decisions. But things had changed. She was now a parent to herself, her own mother and father, and the adult world now appeared to her less fortified than it had seemed prior to life as an Unadoptable. She now saw adults as incredibly fallible people, just like children. Their adulthood did not necessarily save them from constantly making bad decisions—in fact, she speculated, they were more likely to make bad decisions. Surely, Elsie herself should be able to come up with a reasonable plan to snag Martha and Carol from Wigman's clutches. She was a nine-year-old girl, after all.

She bit her lip and thought. And thought. The swarm of voices around her became like a distant hum as she meditated on the circumstances. It seemed awfully familiar, the scene: There were two captives in a tall tower, surrounded by guards and a vengeful overlord. She realized that it was exactly the setup for the season finale of *Intrepid Tina: Danger's Foil,* in which Sailor Steve, Tina's sometime love interest, had been captured by the Robot Fiend and was being held prisoner on the Island of Doom, at the top of the Robot Fiend's hideout, which was very towerlike. Elsie searched her memory, trying to recall how it was that Steve was eventually freed. Very suddenly, it came to her.

"Where does the air come from?" asked Elsie quietly.

Rachel looked askance at her sister. "What did you say?"

"Can you ask them where the air comes from?"

The noise in the room had become nearly deafening. No one had heard her; they were all much too busy arguing their own points, gesturing wildly at the plans on the table.

"Excuse me!" shouted Rachel, who had a deeper and louder voice than her sister.

No response.

"EXCUSE ME!" she screamed, and this time, everyone stopped talking. In the silence, Rachel cleared her throat. "My sister would like to know where the air comes from."

"What?" asked Nico, perplexed. "What does that mean?"

"Good question," said Rachel. She turned to Elsie. "What does that mean?"

Elsie spoke up. "There's little tunnels, right? Metal tunnels. That run through buildings. It's where the air goes, where it comes from."

"Metal tunnels," repeated Jacques. "Where the air comes from."

"Ductwork," said Nico, a light coming over his face. "She means ductwork. The HVAC system." He spun the blueprints around and began thumbing the pages. "Runs through the whole building. Access points at each floor."

"We've gone over that," said Jacques, realizing now what the girl had meant. "They're too small for a man to get through."

Rachel had caught on. She beamed at her sister. "Too small for a man to get through, yeah," she said. "But not an Unadoptable."

Jacques looked at Elsie, surprised, before he suddenly began laughing. Laughing loudly. The sort of laughing that racks the body and seems to ripple from its core. He held his hands over his stomach in an almost comical depiction of someone laughing hard and gasped for breath. His friends, the black-clad saboteurs in the room, all stared at him with little smiles pinpricking their faces. They'd never seen the man so jubilant, it was clear. The laugh was contagious; soon everyone in the room was laughing with Jacques, some more timidly than others, not entirely sure why they should be sharing in one man's strange reaction to what amounted to a very good suggestion from a very small girl.

"We were lucky indeed to have crossed paths with you," said Jacques. Nico had peeled aside the first pages of the stack of plans and was studying, with new eyes, the intricate ductwork that wove around Wigman's fortified structure like veins around a heart. His finger tapped at each intersection, each access point where the renderings showed the HVAC tunnels connecting with the interior walls.

"Brilliant," said Nico. "But flawed."

Elsie frowned; it had been so simple on the Intrepid Tina episode.

Nico continued, "We'll still need to get beyond the outer wall, to even get the kids into the ducts. And that security system is going to be a thorn in our side. Not to mention the fact that the vents likely end in vent coverings, impossible to remove from *inside* the ductwork. They'll have to kick them out, and that's just going to draw attention."

"But still," said Jacques. "It's a good place to start."

"There's something to it," Nico said. The saboteur continued to frown, though he nodded in agreement.

Michael had moved to Nico's side and was hovering over the plans, searching them. He pointed to a ghostlike shaft that fell away from Wigman's safe room. "What's that?" he asked.

Nico squinted his eyes, trying to make sense of the splayed lines. "An elevator," he said. He tapped his finger on it, twice. "Must be some kind of secret elevator, an escape route from the safe room.

Leads down to the ground floor—doesn't stop anywhere else."

"So if we can get into there," said Michael, "through the ducts, with the smaller kids, we can get them out the elevator. Wigman'd never know."

Nico chewed on his lip before replying, "But the ducts don't connect directly to the safe room. There's a route we could map, but you'd still have to transfer a few times. Meaning you'd have to kick out the vent coverings and reenter the ducts at another place. Meaning you'd create an awful lot of clamber *and* likely set off the alarm—not to mention the fact that you kids'd be out in the open until they found the other access point." He shook his head. "Too risky," he said.

"That's where your decoy detonations come in," said Jacques, having recovered from his jubilant laughing fit. He was still smiling, and the tone of his voice suggested that he still very much liked the cut of Elsie's idea. "We stage an attack—a real brazen one. Draw the stevedores away from their stations. Time the explosions so they happen right when the vent coverings are kicked."

"What about the security system?" asked Nico. "I hate to rain on everybody's fun parade here, but I seriously doubt that a state-of-the-art security system is not going to go off when you're getting pieces of the wall kicked out from inside the ductwork."

"Blow up the security center," said Jacques. "Take it all down with explosives. Level the thing." A mad gleam had appeared in his eyes.

Nico watched him warily. "That brings us back to Operation:

Urban Renewal, Jacques. The whole place comes down and the kids get buried."

"That's not going to happen," said Rachel. "You're losing the plot here, guys."

But before any reasonable alternative could be aired, loud noises suddenly came from the hallway: the sounds of shouting voices and heavy doors being thrown back violently. Everyone in the room turned to watch three members of the Chapeaux Noirs rudely drag a very sad figure into the room and throw him, even more rudely, onto the floor in front of the table.

"Jacques!" shouted one of the men. "We got ourselves an intruder."

Elsie craned her neck around the bodies of the men in her sight radius to catch a glimpse of the person who'd just been thrown to the floor. She saw not so much a human being as a pile of greasy rags, lumped messily in a heap like a pile of bedding en route to the washing machine. She recognized the figure immediately—she'd seen him only the night before, wandering the Wastes. It was the mysterious Weirdo, the figure that was always loitering at the perimeter of the Forgotten Place. As the figure settled, a face appeared amid the heap: a tired, grizzled face, more unkempt facial hair than flesh, and a pair of sad, gray eyes, lined deeply in red. She immediately felt very sorry for the poor soul.

"The Weirdo!" hissed Michael, making the same connection Elsie had.

"Who?" barked one of the saboteurs, kicking absently at the man's side.

"Easy," chided Jacques, looking as much surprised by the stranger's sudden appearance as his treatment at the hands of his fellow saboteurs. "He's clearly no threat. He's just some homeless man, found a way into the sewers for shelter."

"We found him in the main pipe," said one of the men. "He must've followed Nico and the kids in here."

Jacques moved forward, splitting the sea of men, to look into the stranger's eyes. "You're safe here, friend," he said.

The man in the heap of clothes looked up to see Jacques approach, and a look of terror came over his dirty face. He threw himself backward, and the men behind him wrangled him down to constrain him. "You!" shouted the man in a voice hoarse as a whisper. He then began to quietly laugh.

"Careful, Jacques," said Nico. "He's a madman. No telling what he'll do."

"Friend," said Jacques consolingly to the Weirdo. "Why have you come here?"

"Where? Am I anywhere?" asked the man, between fits of high-pitched laughter.

Someone from the back of the room said, "He's crazy. Listen to him."

"Quiet!" Jacques shouted to the room. "We are the Chapeaux Noirs, comrades. Enemies of the elite, friends to the downtrodden.

Allow this man to speak."

But the man didn't so much speak as mumble in a syntax that seemed nearly alien, graced as it was with quick fits of laughter and strings of melody. "Yes, yes," said the man. "Let the man speak, yes, yes. Tra la tra la. To speak of old times. To speak of new times and old times."

"How did you get in here?" asked Jacques through this burble of nonsense.

"Through the under, under through. By way of the night and the light. To find my children. To find my long-lost children, tra la tra la," said the man.

"See?" said one of the men behind him. "He's followed the kids in. We've given away our location."

Elsie edged forward; for all the dirt and matted hair clinging to the Weirdo's face, for all the pile of clothes he had huddled about him, for all the smell that was emanating from the poor, wretched thing, there was something vaguely familiar about him.

"Please," continued Jacques, stepping closer to the quivering man. "We mean you no harm." He reached out and pushed aside a wisp of the man's long, oily hair to get a better look at his eyes; just then, Elsie could see that the same vague recognition had overcome the elder Chapeau Noir as well.

"Hello, Joffrey," said Jacques.

It was true: Crouched there, held fast by the men around him, was

none other than Joffrey Unthank himself, the proprietor of the Unthank Home for Wayward Youth and the children's former guardian and overseer. Elsie could see that his goatee still outgrew the rest of his beard, bereft of its once well-trimmed shape. The pile of scavenged bedding he had collected over his shoulders fell back to reveal a dirty argyle sweater-vest below. "It's him?" asked Nico.

Michael and Cynthia both wormed their way through the crowd and looked down on the sad man with surprise. "It's him, all right," said Michael, barely containing the anger and disgust in his voice.

"A serendipitous day, indeed," said Jacques. He watched the huddled figure of Joffrey Unthank as one would a frightened animal.

Michael knelt down by Jacques's side and stared at Joffrey. He took a deep breath and said, "You stink, Mr. Unthank. Do you remember me, Mr. Unthank? Michael Denison. My parents were killed in a plane crash, and I ended up in your little home. I manned the steam furnace. Do you remember?"

Joffrey's dazed eyes became dewy, and they darted back and forth, searching Michael's face. "Yes, yes, yes," he said in a whisper. "How do you do again. Tra la la."

"I broke the nozzle on the furnace and you made me Unadoptable, do you remember? Took me into your office and stuck a needle in me and sent me out into the woods." Michael's voice was overcome with emotion, and it quavered as he spoke. "I swore that if ever I saw you again, I'd tear you limb from limb."

"Oh yes, child," blubbered Unthank. "Oh yes, oh yes."

Michael's hands reached out and touched the cheek of his former boss, his former captor, and his hands shook.

"Don't do it, Michael," said Cynthia Schmidt, coming up from behind and laying a hand on his shoulder.

Instead, Michael pursed his lips and spat a bright glob of phlegm at the sad man, hitting him directly below his right eye. A stain of white skin appeared, the moisture having cleaned away a spot of the filth that covered the man's face.

Just then, Joffrey began to cry. Deep heaves of sobbing, punctuated by more weird laughter, came from the man, and tears dripped down from his nose. Michael stepped away from him, a look of revulsion on his face.

"What's happened to him?" asked Elsie, who was standing at her sister's side. She'd only once seen an adult man cry who wasn't on the TV; it had been her dad, after her brother's disappearance. This was different, though. This bout of crying seemed to come from a further-off place, a stranger place.

"I don't know," responded Rachel. "He's crazy, I guess."

"Serves him right," said Cynthia. "That place was like a prison. It's a crime what he did to us."

Jacques had put his arm around Unthank and pulled his sobbing head into the crook of his shoulder. "There, there," said Jacques, a consoling parent. "Cry it out, Joffrey. It's true, my old friend. My old partner. You've done terrible, terrible things. Not just to these children: Oh, no—though that was a very serious misstep—worse, you've corrupted yourself and your own mind in your search for satisfaction, despite the costs. You've lost track of the man inside in your restless need to create *things*, to amass *stuff*, to have *power*. It is the disease of desire, my friend. And it has rotted your soul to the very core."

Joffrey, smothered in the fabric of Jacques's turtleneck, could only mumble a weird, "Hmm hmm tra la. Tra la." The tears continued to fall, and they wet Jacques's shirt.

"But you can redeem yourself, Joffrey," continued the saboteur. "You can rise, like the phoenix, from the flames of your destroyed creation. You have arrived here, at my home, at your former fellow Titan's home, to come face-to-face with your past and all the terrible decisions that you've made and that have led you, inexorably, to the place you currently, sadly, desperately inhabit. Look at your failed life, Joffrey: It is standing right in front of you."

At this, Unthank pushed himself away from Jacques's embrace and stared, teary-eyed, at the figures that surrounded him: the Chapeaux Noirs, the Unadoptables. Elsie, standing frozen by her sister, saw that Jacques, too, had started weeping.

Planting an affectionate kiss on Joffrey's forehead, Jacques spoke again. "But you, like the rest of us, are a victim. You are ultimately not to blame. You were set up by a cruel and unfeeling master. You are not bad, not at the core. And fate has deposited you here to be a part of a great rebirth, a grand destruction of an empire of which you yourself have been its most recent victim."

"Wiggggg...," mumbled Joffrey through his sobs. "Wiggggg..."

"Yes," prompted Jacques. "Yes, speak his name. Speak his name as a soul newly hatched."

"Wigmannnnn!" shouted Joffrey.

Just then, Jacques abruptly yanked Unthank from the floor and dragged him, stumbling, to the table. He held him by the scruff of his neck, as a mother cat would hold its litter, and pointed to the sheaf of pages on the table. "Here is your Babel, Joffrey. Here is your pillar of salt. Here is the beacon that has brought you to us, that has brought us all together. Look on it and laugh. For you are now free."

And Joffrey Unthank began to laugh.

She'd placed the eagle feather on her dresser, right next to the framed mirror, in a little brass bowl. She wasn't quite sure how the spirit wanted the things presented to her, but she figured a little bit of ceremony couldn't hurt. It was a little disappointing to have the mirror do nothing when she'd arrived home, her hair a snag of twigs and moss, to present the feather she'd labored so hard to retrieve. True, the spirit only visited at night, when the clock chimed twelve—but she thought that maybe the ghost would make an exception now, when she'd brought the first thing the spirit had requested. When she got no response, Zita grabbed the little brass bowl, the one she herself had chosen from her mother's belongings, the one her mother had kept her rings in at night, and set it in front of the mirror, placing the newly won feather in the dish. Still, nothing. She waited out the clock, waiting for the night to come.

When it did come, when the chime rang out in the hallway and her father was silently asleep in his room, she was prepared for the spirit's return.

GOOD was written in the fog on the pane of glass of the mirror.

"Thank you," said Zita, getting over her initial chill to see the words appear. What's more, she found herself to be ever so slightly more comfortable with the fact that she was in the presence of a disembodied soul, one who was communicating with her through the mist on a mirror. "What's next?" asked Zita timidly, her hands clutching her duvet.

The mirror cleared and again a mist, unseen in the room, clouded the surface. *PEBBLE* was scrawled.

Easy enough, thought Zita. A pebble could be gotten from just about anywhere.

ROCKING CHAIR CREEK. The words had taken up all the remaining real estate on the mirror. Zita's face fell. She had never heard of Rocking Chair Creek, let alone where it might be. "I don't have to go to the Avian Principality again, do I?" she asked to the ether.

But there came no response from the mirror. The fog disappeared. The mirror again reflected the small, dark room and the glow of the candle at Zita's bedside. A moon, half-full, shone through the window and cast its light across the room as Zita contemplated her next move. Her father's atlas would have an answer, she decided. Retrieving it from the hallway, she opened its cracked and dusty spine and smoothed the pages that showed the Wood in its entirety. Optimistically, she searched the area directly around her house, in the mercantile district, for the Empress's words: *ROCKING CHAIR CREEK.* As she'd sadly expected, she found nothing. Moving farther afield, she crossed with her eyes the boundary of the Avian Principality and scanned the area's many squiggly blue lines for the words—still nothing. It wasn't until she'd glanced even farther north that she saw what she was looking for. Rocking Chair Creek did exist.

It was a creek that was deep in the heart of Wildwood.

The Empty Folder;
Unthank Reborn

Prue cracked the door open carefully, slowly. The sounds of the angry crowd had receded, but she couldn't be sure if there weren't some desperate souls directly outside the door to the Interim Governor-Regent-elect's office, waiting in secret for her inevitable escape. Through the small crack, she saw nothing; the bunting had been torn on the balcony and a few mismatched pairs of cycling shoes—evidently having been used as missiles—lay strewn about the landing.

Taking a deep breath, she pushed the heavy oak door open and saw that she was very much alone, aside from a rather disgruntled-looking janitor who was sweeping up the torn clothing, broken teeth, and casquettes that littered the granite floor. Seeing Prue, the man glowered at her and continued on with his work, mumbling something denigrating about bicycles and maidens and revolutions.

Prue walked to the top of the staircase and was surprised to see a group of people still holding vigil in the foyer; fearing they would attack, she edged backward, her heart racing. It wasn't until she saw the crowd's expressions turn into ecstatic smiles that she knew she was safe.

"Maiden!" called one, a teenaged girl. "You've come back!"

"We were waiting for you," announced another, a man with a bushy brown beard.

"What are we to do now?" called another—it was the badger rickshaw driver.

Prue edged apprehensively to the first step of the staircase. "You guys aren't mad at me?" she asked.

A collective look of surprise came over the gathered faithful; there were at least fifteen of them. "No, of course not," came the response, chimed in unison.

"You're the Bicycle Maiden, the hero of the revolution," said a fox. "We'd never abandon you."

"Those others, those were just pretenders. Poseurs," said the teenager. "They aren't the true believers."

The bearded man suggested, "We'll apply to have their heads chopped off, Maiden, assuming that's what you'd wish."

Someone shushed him, saying loudly, "The Maiden clearly said there were to be no more decapitations." The speaker turned to Prue for confirmation. "Right?"

"Right," said Prue, walking unsteadily down the stairs. She was still a little shaken by the near riot she'd escaped. "No more of that."

"But what should we do with the people who oppose you?" asked a young man with short, dark hair wearing riding pants.

"Let them believe whatever they want," said Prue. "Who cares? That's the beauty of things, right? People should be able to believe what they want to, follow who they want to."

The crowd seemed to be impressed by this pearl of wisdom, and they all said, "Ahhhh" simultaneously.

"Where to now?" asked the badger.

Prue chewed on her lip, thinking. She took a deep breath, her heart still beating fast. "Okay. Everyone," she said as she climbed down the stairs. "Fan out. Talk to people. Spread the word about Alexei. Tell them the Council Tree wants him brought back to life and in order to do that, we need his two makers. We need to find out what happened to Carol Grod. Tell them the other maker has been found. Follow any leads you can. Find his family, find his friends. He was exiled somewhere; we need to find out where."

The small crowd murmured their understanding and made for the doors, their steps energized with a kind of newfound bounce. Before the man with the beard could depart, however, she called out to him, "Wait!"

The man turned around. He was perhaps in his twenties, and he wore a pair of bib overalls with a sprocket brooch pinned to the right suspender. "Me?" he asked.

"I need someone to keep me protected," she said.

The man smiled widely. "I can do that, ma'am," he said. He walked back toward the center of the foyer.

"I'll just wait by the rickshaw, then," said the badger, making his way to the front doors.

"Actually," said Prue, "stick with me. A third pair of hands couldn't hurt."

When she arrived at the checkerboard parquet of the foyer floor, she extended her hand out to the lumbering, bearded man, saying, "I'm Prue. What's your name?"

"Charlie," said the man. He was blushing; the skin above the hair of his brown beard was flushed red. "Very nice to meet the Bicycle Maiden, in person."

"You can just call me Prue," she said.

"I'll do my best," said the man. "But you're still the Bicycle Maiden to me."

"I'll need you guys to stick by me," she said. "There was an attempt on my life, not so long ago. Someone sent an assassin. Still don't know who. I thought by coming here, I'd be safe. But I see I'm not quite as loved as I thought I'd be."

The man, Charlie, frowned. "Oh, you're still very loved. Anyone who don't can expect to be missing their head, quick snap."

"No more of that," said Prue quickly.

"Sorry," said the man.

"Unless they actually attack us. Then . . ." She paused in speaking. "Then, do whatever you want."

"With pleasure, Bicycle Maiden," said Charlie.

"Prue."

"Prue, sorry."

She'd noticed, ever since she'd left the safety of the Interim Governor-Regent-elect's office, that a kind of fog of anxiety had come over her. She felt like the supporting foundation of her plan, the plan she'd devised with Curtis and with Esben, had eroded: She didn't necessarily feel safe in the wide open now. She should've foreseen it, the crowd's displeasure with her ultimate goal, but now it was too late. She still had these few supporters, and perhaps that would be enough to save her life. In any case, she decided, the quicker she found this mysterious blind Carol Grod, the better.

"We're going to the archives," said Prue. "Follow me."

It became clear that in the intervening months since Prue's last time at the Mansion, the place had been stripped of its staff as it had been stripped of its influence and importance in day-to-day affairs. It was a sad shadow of the bustling place it had been prior to the revolution. Gone were the attendants and the secretaries, the butlers and the maids (Prue wondered what had happened to Penny in the time between; she hoped she was safe). Instead, a few grumpy bureaucrats tried to do what the veritable army of staff had worked to achieve, and the deficit was clear. Each room had the same look of the foyer: The day-after-an-apocalyptic-party decoration scheme was carried over throughout the building. The three of them, Prue, Charlie, and the badger (whose name was Neil), wandered the massive building, asking directions when they could from the harried staff. No one seemed to know where the archives were; they were continually being sent in the wrong direction, ending up in strange dead ends and janitor's cupboards. They lost about half an hour in a larder they'd stumbled on because Charlie was hungry. Replenished, they continued their search, which finally led them up a steep, winding staircase in a far-flung wing of the building. They found themselves at a wide wooden door with the sign ARCHIVES hanging over it.

"I'm guessing this is it," said Neil helpfully.

Prue pressed the door's iron handle and watched it slowly, creakily open into a giant, circular room that appeared to occupy the entire top floor of one of the Mansion's towers. The windows were set high on the curved walls, walls that seemed to be built entirely of bookcases.

Made of a dark, marbled wood, the bookcases towered over the room and were filled with a staggering number of binder spines, all colored the same bland off-white. Several ladders, attached at a high rail, provided access to the higher shelves, and it looked to Prue that someone would risk a very serious injury if they needed to consult any of those volumes. A few lecterns were scattered about the carpeted floor of the room, and a small desk presented itself directly in front of the open doorway. There was someone, or something, cowering underneath the desk, Prue could see. The round feathered cap that peeked above the desk's leather-covered surface gave him away.

"Hello?" asked Prue.

No answer came.

"Hello?" she repeated. "I can see you, you know. I can see your hat."

A shuffling sounded, echoing in the high, vaulted chamber. The hat disappeared below the desk.

"I have a form here," said Prue, undeterred. "Signed by the Interim Governor-Regent-elect. I need to look something up."

Finally, a voice replied, "No one here!"

Prue and Charlie exchanged a confused glance. "I can hear you," said Prue. "You're talking to me."

A silence followed as the speaker apparently considered this oversight on his part. The hat appeared again, above the lip of the desk. "Well," said the speaker, the whoever-it-was under the desk, "make it quick, then."

"Why are you hiding?" asked Prue.

"Is that your question? Is that what you've come here for? Will you leave if I answer?"

Prue knitted her brow. "No," she said. "That's just me being curious. That's what a normal person would ask."

"So what's your form for, then? What are you here to look up?"

"I need to find a record of someone who was exiled, five years ago. Think you'd have that somewhere?"

"No," came the definitive answer.

"You didn't even look," said Prue.

"I did."

"You didn't move. I can still see your hat."

The speaker behind the desk let out a loud, importuned sigh, as if cursing his telltale headwear. "I don't have to look. The records aren't there."

Prue's stomach dropped. "What do you mean, they're not there?"

"They're not there. That's what I mean."

"Can you look again? How can you be sure?"

"I just looked. You're the second person today who's had me look."

"Second? Who was the first?"

"Listen, I know you're angry about this and I can understand your frustrations, to a certain degree. You've come looking for something and it isn't here. I apologize. As the keeper of the archives, it is as dismaying to me as it is to you, rest assured. Perhaps more. Dismaying. To me. However, there's little I can do, and it is likely only a matter of hours before the next riot comes through, and I've just finished this morning putting the place back to order." During this recitation, the hat began to float upward, and soon the speaker's brow was revealed. Prue was surprised to see it was a rather large tortoise who'd been speaking. "Now if you'd kindly let me be, I can better protect myself."

"Just, please," said Prue, now more uncertain about her next step than she'd been in the past many weeks. "I need to know. He could be anywhere. Maybe the record is misplaced somewhere. Did you look anywhere else?"

Now the tortoise's head appeared in its completeness above the cover of the desk. It was green, scaly, and fairly mushroomlike and sported as frightened a look as Prue had seen grace any human's head. She immediately felt sorry for the thing.

"Fine!" he shouted. "Fine! Fine, fine, fine." The tortoise then stood up fully from behind the desk (he wasn't much taller than the structure he'd been hiding behind) and waddled over to the wall of bookshelves. "No need to look it up in the card catalog," the tortoise fumed, having suddenly become almost manically fearless. "I just put it back. That's helpful!" He laughed, once, madly. "The whole file's up here. Institutional Punishment, Exile, years 340–345, Common Era. Ha, ha! Look at the memory on the turtle!" Arriving at one of the bookshelves' ladders, he began climbing it. His journey took him to the very topmost rung, where he splayed a single flipper out to the limit of his reach and there grabbed one of the yellowing white binders. "Here, catch!" he howled.

Luckily, Charlie and Prue had both followed the tortoise over to the bookshelf and were there to catch the binder as it fell from its great height. Two more followed, the binder's direct neighbors, with a fourth and fifth tagging along for good measure. The tortoise on the ladder cackled as he dropped the binders, muttering things that were thankfully just out of hearing of the two humans on the floor— they didn't seem quite cleared for twelve-year-old ears.

"Satisfied?" shouted the tortoise once both Charlie's and Prue's arms were full.

The two staggered with their loads over to a long table and dumped the binders on the surface. They quickly set about arranging them in some semblance of order and began their search. The binders were filled with manila folders, three-hole punched, and were labeled on the top right corner in an orderly script with the names of the convicted.

It was a sad odyssey, searching through the records of the long-exiled convicts of South Wood, and strange. Charlie, who'd never so much as left his garage, where he'd worked on salvaged automobile parts and old cassette machines, fell into his role as co-researcher with gusto. Both he and Neil tore through the manila folders and

translated much of the language for Prue when it proved too arcane.

"'WW': I assume that means Wildwood," she said, leafing through the pages.

"Must be," responded Charlie, peering over at her stack. "I'm seeing a lot of that too. Pretty common, looks like. Do you think Carol ended up in Wildwood?"

"He's from the Outside, like me," said Prue. "I'm not sure if there's a particular punishment for Outsiders."

"Don't know that there's been many Outsiders in the Wood. You're the first I ever met," said Charlie.

"And what's this?" asked Prue, returning to her folders. "Something about the Crag—'imprisonment on the Crag,' it says. Some poor guy named Lucky. Doesn't sound lucky."

Neil nodded. "You never heard of that? I guess, how would you?"

"What is it?"

Charlie put in, "My mother used to warn me when I was a kid—I think a lot of folks in South Wood got the same warning. 'If you don't shape up, I'll put you on the Crag.' Get you into order quick, that would. It's off somewhere, in the middle of the ocean. A rock in the ocean where they built a prison. If you end up on the Crag, it's over."

"Suppose Carol ended up there?" wondered Prue.

"Could be," said Charlie, licking his finger and flipping through more of the pages. "But that's imprisonment, not exile." He paused for a moment in his searching, watching as the tortoise returned, muttering, to his desk. "You say this guy was an Outsider?"

"Yeah," said Prue.

"There was talk—when I was a kid—I remember asking about the Outside, the place beyond the boundary. There was rumor about that world and what went on. Didn't ever sound like the sorta place I'd want to visit, but we'd all get worried that some Outsider was gonna come in and terrorize the Wood, you know. But I remember my parents telling me, 'Nah, quiet down. The Periphery would stop 'em.' And they said that if ever they caught an Outsider, say he somehow got walked through—you know, like escorted by a Woodian—well, they'd throw him in there, into the Periphery, and he'd live out his days stuck in a kind of nowhere forever. Wonder if they'd do that sort of thing to your Carol Grod."

Prue was struck by the idea. "How would we ever find him then?"

"We wouldn't, I don't guess," said Charlie. "So our best bet is just to hope that didn't happen."

"Not much of a strategy," said Prue, and she continued shuffling papers. Before long, she came across a folder that bore the name ESBEN CLAMPETT written in the selfsame black script. Opening it, she was bemused to find its contents missing.

"Someone's taken Esben's too," she said, showing it to Charlie and Neil. "This is not helpful."

"Do you suppose they were after the information themselves?" asked the badger.

"Yeah. Either that or they didn't want me finding out."

Charlie continued his search; only a few moments passed before he let out a little yelp. "Here's your man, Carol Grod!" He held up the folder—Carol's name was there, written on the top corner.

The tortoise at the desk must've overheard the exclamation. "Empty," he said. "You'll see."

Charlie smirked at the grumpy tortoise; as if to appease his own curiosity, he opened the folder and peered inside. "Yep," he said. "Gone." He paused, cocking an eyebrow, before saying, "Though not quite."

"What's up?" asked Prue.

The bearded man reached into the folder and retrieved a small, folded-up piece of paper. He held it up between his thumb and forefinger; the name PRUE had been written on the surface. He tossed it across the table.

Unfolding the paper, Prue read the following message, scrawled in a delicate hand:

We are of the same mind. Come to the Tree.
Tonight.

Prue flipped it around and showed it to her partners in sleuthery, who each squinted to read the writing. "Lots of trees around here," Neil said.

"Who did you say had come here this morning?" Prue called out to the tortoise. "The one who asked for this same file?"

"Couldn't tell," responded the turtle, bent over his work. "He was hooded. One of them Caliphs."

"Ah," said Neil, sitting back in his chair. "I know which tree it means."

🍃

Rachel and Elsie sat together on the bench, watching the activity that was unfolding across the room. A gang of Chapeaux Noirs were attending to the harried form of Joffrey Unthank like he was the subject of some trashy reality show in which a poor, downtrodden soul gets the makeover of a lifetime and they were the disdainful, metropolitan hairdressers tasked to bring off this impossible feat. Clippers whirred, scissors clacked, and Joffrey's dirt-smeared skin was toweled off bit by bit, revealing the bright whiteness below.

Elsie felt at her own scalp. "I could use a haircut," she said. "You could use one too," she said to her sister.

Rachel scoffed. "I'm growing it out."

"What, to the floor?" The long, thin black strands were already touching the middle of her back.

"I don't know," said Rachel. "Whatever."

Elsie thought for a moment. "I'm growing mine out, too."

Looking at her sister sideways, Rachel said, "You'll just get a Jewfro."

"That's what I want. A Jewfro." Elsie wasn't sure what that was.

173

Rachel smiled. It was the first time Elsie had seen her smile all week, it felt like. She chalked it up to this recent turn of events. They were closer now to getting Carol and Martha back than they'd ever been, and all of them, the Unadoptables here in the Chapeaux Noirs' lair, shared a kind of surge of excitement at the prospect, Rachel in particular. Elsie didn't quite know why, but Rachel was the one most bent on getting the two of them back safely. She thought maybe it was because she'd been there when the stevedores captured them, with the Unthank Home burning in the background. At Martha's urging, Rachel had abandoned Carol's side and let the stevedores capture her instead. And why? Because Rachel had a gift: She could pass through the boundary of the Impassable Wilderness without getting caught in the magic. Martha had wanted to protect her from falling into the stevedores' hands. Elsie had this gift too. She didn't know what it meant or why she and her sister were blessed with this ability but not the other kids. It was all so confusing.

"Clippy clippy, snippy snippy, tra la, tra lee," came the voice from inside the huddle of black-clad men. It was Unthank's chirpy singing voice. He'd been singing all afternoon, providing the soundtrack to his dramatic makeover. Rachel glowered.

"I don't know how this is going to work," she said. "He's so obviously lost it completely."

"What happened to him?" asked Elsie, smoothing Intrepid Tina's hair.

"I guess he saw his life kind of fall apart. I suppose that's what happens," said her sister. "People just go crazy."

"What about Miss Mudrak?"

"Who knows? Maybe she's gone crazy, too, somewhere."

Elsie thought for a moment before saying, "Do you think I'm crazy?"

Rachel looked down at her sister. "No," she said. "I don't think so. Why would you be crazy?"

"Well, my life is really weird and is sort of falling apart."

"Yeah, well, you're tough. You can take it."

"I can?"

"Of course you can, Els." Rachel paused before saying, "Do you think I'm crazy?"

"No," said Elsie. "You're just crazy in the normal ways."

Rachel made a face at her sister. "I take that back. I think you're totally crazy."

The two girls laughed, and Rachel pushed her shoulder into Elsie's. As they were sharing this rare moment of levity, Michael approached them.

"Hey, you two," he said. "You guys should come over here. We need to learn these vent plans."

"Right," said Rachel. "C'mon, Els."

"What about him?" asked Elsie, nodding toward the singing Unthank.

Michael frowned. "He'll get it together," he said. "He has to." As if punctuating what Michael had said, Unthank let out a loud, harried yelp and then began reciting what sounded like the technical manual to some obscure apparatus. "Come on," said Michael, and the three of them made their way to the table in the center of the room.

Nico was briefing the children on the ductwork of Titan Tower, carefully drawing in a navigable route in red ink on the plans. It was complex: a snaking line that moved in and out of the little corridors on the blueprints at fixed points. The route had to be amended several times, apparently, as there were dead ends that had been scratched out and new routes appended like a particularly challenging maze in an activity book. He'd finally arrived at a usable path, but it was going to require the children to become fluent in the ductwork's crazy patterns and movements.

"Okay," said Nico, breathing deeply. "You'll enter here, through the subterranean ducts. There's a security gate in the ventilation here. Should be disabled when you get to it. Crossing through that, you'll be in the system."

"Who's disabling the security gate?" asked Michael.

Nico made eye contact with Michael, as if to say, *You know who.* He looked over at the crowd of Chapeaux Noirs swarming Joffrey Unthank. "After he's disabled the tower's security system."

Joffrey was now loudly quoting warranty information over the hum of his barber's clippers. "FAILURE to HEED the INSTRUCTIONS will result in VOID of WARRANTY. Tra la! Tra la! USE ONLY as DIRECTED!"

"After he's disabled the security system," repeated Michael. "And how's he going to do that?"

"By going inside the front gates, just like he's always done."

"DO not UNDER any CIRCUMSTANCES use THIS PRODUCT as a HEAT SOURCE! Tra la!" came the shouting voice. The black-bereted men around him swore as they tried to keep their subject in his seat.

"He's one of their fellow Titans," said Nico, swallowing hard. "Now, once you've—"

Michael interrupted him. "Wait, wait, wait. He *was* one of their fellow Titans. He's been kicked out, hasn't he?"

"Our sources suggest he's just been suspended," answered Nico. "They've absorbed his Division into Shipping. So it shouldn't be that big of a hurdle. He shows up, tells them he's ready to come back into the fold. They let him in."

"Excuse me, gentlemen," sang Unthank in a faux-Slavic accent on the other side of the room. "We must get back on the chicken!" He then began laughing uproariously. "Tra la! Tra la!"

Michael stared at Nico.

Nico looked back down at the plans.

"You were saying?" prompted Elsie.

"Right," said Nico. "You'll need to pick a team—the smallest of the kids. Judging from the plans, they'll all need to be about your height, Elsie. The shafts get fairly narrow at points."

"Wait a second," said Rachel. "Elsie's not going. Not without me."

"You wouldn't fit," said Nico. "And Elsie's here. We'll still need a few more of your kids. She can get them up to speed."

Rachel looked down at her sister, wide-eyed. "I can do it, Rach," said Elsie. "I can fit."

"I want to be there," said Rachel. "I want to be close."

"We'll get you close," said Nico. "You can be on the demolitions team, if you'd like."

"I would like."

"A teenager?" asked a voice from behind them. It was Jacques, who'd just left the circle around Joffrey. He frowned at Rachel, studying her, before saying, "You know, your typical Chapeau trains for months before his first deployment."

"Come on, Jacques," replied Nico. "Trust me. She's a natural-born saboteur. She's got the guts for it."

"What about him?" asked Michael, still staring at Unthank. "I don't understand how he's going to pull off his part of the plan."

Jacques seemed to ignore this question. Instead, he addressed the entire room in a booming, proud voice. "Comrades, Unadoptables, I would like to introduce you to our old friend Joffrey Unthank. Those of you who have met him before, I kindly suggest you reacquaint yourself and look upon a man reborn." With that, he turned around and waved his hands, a magician revealing his final trick of the evening. The black turtlenecks parted and there sat Joffrey Unthank, his hair shorn to its usual cropped length, his face cleaned of the grime and filth. His blankets had been cast aside and his argyle sweater-vest and pleated slacks had been laundered and pressed. He looked, to Elsie's estimation, as close a facsimile of the man who had been her employer and captor as you could imagine.

Jacques, the master of ceremonies, addressed the man. "Joffrey Unthank," he said, "introduce yourself."

Joffrey stood, somewhat unsteadily, and looked at the man who'd spoken. Finally, he said, "My name is Joffrey. Joffrey Unthank. Former Titan of Industry. Machine Parts."

"Very good," said Jacques, proud of his protégé. "Permit me this illusion. I am a stevedore, and I am standing guard at the front gate of Titan Tower. I will say this to you: 'Mr. Unthank, what are you doing here?'" He adopted a low, gravelly voice for his stevedore impression.

Unthank paused, an actor calculating his lines. Finally, he spoke. "I've come to see my old friend Bradley Wigman." That was it.

Jacques frowned. "And . . . ," he said in the stevedore voice.

"I'm sorry for my transgressions. I would like to come back, to be a part of the Quin—the Quartet once more."

"Very well," said Jacques, smiling. "You may come in."

"The Quin-Quar," continued Joffrey, unabated, his voice

becoming a singsong again. "The Quin-Quar and the humidor, bill-abore, dillabore. Tra la!" His formerly rigid posture dropped and his head slumped comically to one side. His feet began to shuffle in a kind of clownish dance.

"That's enough, Joffrey," said Jacques.

But Joffrey continued: "It was a Quintet, now it's a Quartet, soon to be a trio and a duo and a solo and what comes after that? Tra la tra la!" sang the silly man, dancing his steps.

"Are you kidding me?" said Michael. "*That's* how you're getting in?"

"Yes," said Jacques, rounding on the teenager. "If you have a better idea for bypassing a guarded, fortified wall and an encrypted security system that requires *handprint* and *retinal* identification, I'm happy to entertain it. For now, this is the best option we have." He then walked over to Joffrey and grabbed him by the shoulders and looked him directly in the eye.

"Listen to me, Joffrey," he said. "Listen close. I know you're in there. We need your help. We can't do this without you. If you want to bring Wigman down, if you want to rattle his chains, you've got to pull it together and help. It's the only way."

Joffrey had stopped dancing and was listening closely to what the man had to say. "Yes, Jack," he whispered after a time.

"Why don't you and me go find a place to talk, quiet. Titan to Titan," said Jacques.

"Yes, Jack," said Joffrey.

Jacques threw his spindly arm over Unthank's shoulder and led him, silently, through the crowd of watching saboteurs, past the table with the plans, and through the iron-belted door to the hallway, which, once they'd passed out of sight, slammed shut behind them.

Elsie watched this all proceed, quietly. The whole room retained a kind of wondering silence before Nico broke it by saying, "Okay, back to the plans."

Into Wildwood

Z ita the May Queen sat quietly at the kitchen table and stirred her oatmeal. Her father sat in his usual spot, just to her right, his fingers threaded through the handle of his coffee mug. He was reading the paper, as he often did in the mornings, and grumbled beneath his white-flecked mustache as if he were conducting a moderated dialogue with the morning's news. Zita brought her spoon to her mouth, blew the steam from the oatmeal, then set it back down into the bowl.

"No school today," she said.

"Hmmm," said her father.

"Headmaster said we should celebrate the return of the Bicycle Maiden."

"Hmmm."

"I was thinking I'd go over to Kendra's. She's doing flower pressing. The trilliums are in bloom."

"Mm-hmmm."

Zita stirred the oatmeal some more, the cream making a tight spiral into the center of the bowl. "I was wondering . . ." She paused here, measuring her words. "If I could take the motorcycle."

Her father looked up from the paper. His mustache twitched a little. "What do you need that for?"

"All the good flowers are farther off," said Zita, sitting up straight. "We can't get to them by foot. It'll take all day."

"It needs a tune-up. I've barely started the thing since . . ." He paused, clearing his throat. "And it'll need gas."

"I'll fill it," said Zita. "And you can help me with the tune-up. Would you?"

Her father looked at the grandfather clock on the wall, the clock that chimed midnight when the spirit of the Verdant Empress visited, and nodded. "Seems like a good project."

Zita smiled. She was thrilled to see her father emerge from his quiet, stormy stupor. They cleared the table quietly, father and daughter, and washed the dishes in the sink. They went out to the garage where the old motorcycle sat, its mismatched sidecar a receptacle for whatever junk in the garage had not found a proper home. Zita and her father collected this stuff, a pile of blankets, a spare tire, and a box of spent candles, and set it on the nearby workbench. Her father undid a tethered pouch, revealing a set of worn tools, and the two of them, together, began tinkering with the engine of the machine. Soon enough, the thing had been started and was growling in a healthy way, spewing its usual vapor into the atmosphere. Zita's father wiped his hands clean of grease, watching his daughter, now astride the bike, shrug a silver-sparkle helmet over her head and a pair of riding goggles over her eyes.

"Thanks, Dad," she said.

He smiled warmly, looking at the whole ensemble: his daughter, the motorcycle, the sidecar, and Zita could guess what he was thinking. He was thinking about the one thing missing: her mother, his wife.

Zita chose not to let him dwell on the image for too long: the fact that her mother had often been the passenger, the helmeted head sprouting from the sidecar, while he gripped the handlebars and rode them from hamlet to hamlet. Instead, she spoke. "I'll be back sometime tomorrow." (She'd furnished camping gear to complete the ruse that she'd be sleeping with Kendra in the woods.) "I love you," she said.

"I love you too," said her father, momentarily disarmed. She could see: His eyes brimmed with tears, but none fell.

Zita curled the grip, and the engine sputtered and roared. She walked it backward, out into the sunlight, and without giving a further look at her father, she kicked it into gear, the old thing, and wheeled out into the road.

She was an old hand at riding the ancient motorcycle, its gas tank all dented and scored; her father had taught her to ride it when she was barely seven—much to the consternation of her mother. It felt good to be back in the saddle again, feeling the air beat at her cheeks and whip at her coat. She raced through the Mercantile District, her home district, down its narrow cobblestone alleyways, which she knew like the veins on the back of her hand. Whipping past an old beaver trawling a hay cart, she nearly upset a card-trick grifter's table and caused a black-clad nanny to anxiously yank her charges (two human toddlers) out of the road and onto the sidewalk. "Sorry!" shouted Zita above the cooing roar of the motorcycle.

She swerved out onto the Long Road and into the flow of traffic: Automobiles and bicyclists, rickshaws and lumbering palanquins all vied for real estate on the cluttered roadway. She zipped around a horse-drawn cart and into the slipstream of a clattering roadster until the exhaust became too unbearable and she zipped around it, nearly running headlong into a fleet of rickshaws.

"Watch it!" cried one of the drivers.

But Zita sped on, watching as the Mercantile District, the tightly knit rows of brick houses and shops, began to fall away and the road became lined with towering trees and wide fern glades. Here the traffic let up, and she was able to really open up the motorcycle's throttle and the scenery blew by in a fading blur. She girded herself for what was to come.

It had been one thing to climb the North Wall and sneak like a thief into the Avian Principality; it was another to have to blow the gate on a sidecar-dragging motorcycle. There was no way she'd be able to get to Wildwood on foot—it was too far—and right now there was no available transport to North Wood that would let her climb out in the middle of the wildest part of the Wood, not to mention that the

next bus wouldn't be leaving for another three days. So she'd decided she'd just make a run at the gate.

She'd heard, since her early morning escapade in search of the eagle feather, that many of the soldiers who manned the North Gate had abandoned their posts, that a kind of chaos had come over the security infrastructure of South Wood. The word was that the soldiers weren't getting paid, there was no money left in the coffers, and it was a resilient guardsman indeed who stayed at his post when he hadn't received a paycheck in three weeks. The Synod had been quickly forthcoming about taking their place, providing security

where there was none, but she hoped that transition had yet to reach the North Gate.

The world sped by; the needle quivered on the motorcycle speedometer, and she fell behind a mail truck that was, she assumed, bound for the North Gate. She caught sight of the driver in the truck's sideview mirror: An old, grizzled man, he wore the visored cap of a postmaster general. After a time, the wall came into view, and she eased up on the throttle, following the truck as it rolled to a slow halt.

Only one soldier, dressed in dirty khakis, appeared to be manning the gate, and he seemed to be none too pleased with the responsibility. Seeing the mail truck, he slowly stepped away from his prior position leaning against the stone wall, and sauntered toward the vehicle. He didn't ask for papers; he merely looked in the front of the truck and made a visual ID of the subject, nodding. He then walked over to the gate and, after some wrangling, threw the giant double doors open.

That was when Zita made her move.

Letting go the clutch, she cranked the throttle and peeled out from behind the mail truck, spraying a rooster tail of gravel behind her. The soldier, shocked, fell backward and impotently raised his hand in objection. Zita flew through the gate and, quickly shifting, was soon well beyond sight of the soldier's objecting cries.

It was shocking how easy it was. She threw a glance over her shoulder in time to see a pair of golden eagles swoop down from their perches and fall in behind her, squawking loudly.

"HALT, HUMAN!" one shouted.

Lowering her brow against the headwind, Zita twisted the hand-grip, and she felt the bike leap forward at her command; soon the shouts of the pursuing eagles grew quiet and distant behind her. There was little they could do—within an hour she'd be on the other side of the Principality. She was bent on her task, the retrieval of a single pebble from some obscure creek in the middle of Wildwood.

Now that she'd cleared the gate, she had a moment to reflect on the craziness of the thing she'd just done. Where, in what remote part of her, had she managed to distill that kind of courage? She'd never been a particularly courageous kid—not any more so than her schoolmates, though perhaps a little more headstrong and curious—and yet here she was, riding her father's motorcycle at a breakneck pace through the North Gate and toward the most inhospitable and dangerous province of the Wood. There were stories that were told around fireplaces and banquet halls, stories of wights and wyverns that lived in the depths of Wildwood; stories of the Wildwood bandits, who'd strip you clean of your possessions and leave you tied to a tree in the middle of the wilderness, an easy lunch for any number of wights or wyverns who might happen to be passing by.

All for the strange calling of this woman, this Verdant Empress.

Who was the Verdant Empress? It was one thing she'd had a lot of time to consider. The origin story she had learned (though admittedly there were many) went that she was a bereaved mother, one of the Ancients, a woman whose own child had been violently and horrifically taken from her. It was said she'd died of sadness. And so: She visited the living, children especially, in search of her departed child. If these stories were true, Zita had to think she was doing the spirit world a tremendous service by carrying out these errands.

But there was something else; something else dug at her insides as she went about these tasks, something that had very much to do with the empty sidecar that she tugged alongside the speeding motorcycle.

Zita knew what it was like to lose, to feel loss. She'd felt that incredible incision when her mother had been taken from her.

But her loss hadn't been violent, not like the Verdant Empress's— if anything it had been the very opposite: drawn out and slow, the woman's passing marked by silence and fog. It'd been some kind of illness; that's what the doctors had said. Some seven months ago, she'd taken to bed at the beginning of the week, complaining of pain in her chest, and by Friday she was gone. And it felt like the foundation that held up Zita's life had been promptly taken apart, stone by stone, and she was left with a weird, empty space. She felt like a person without legs, like a car without wheels. Like some very integral part of her was missing and yet here she was: keeping going.

So she understood the Verdant Empress's pain. She understood her loss. And in many ways it felt like she owed this service to a mother, a mother who very well could be much like her own, as a way of completing some kind of circle.

These were the thoughts that occupied Zita the May Queen as she sped farther into the Avian Principality.

There was no wall marking the boundary between the Avians' province and Wildwood—the birds had no need for walls. Instead, a series of signs had been posted, one after another, along the side of the road:

YOU ARE LEAVING THE AVIAN PRINCIPALITY.

YOU ARE ENTERING WILDWOOD.

WILDWOOD APPROACHING; TRAVELERS BE WARY.

JUST BEYOND THIS SIGN IS WILDWOOD.

ACTUALLY, THIS SIGN.

THERE ARE BANDITS AFOOT.

YOU ARE NOW IN WILDWOOD.

A final sign, tipped over on its post, read GOOD LUCK.

Zita cranked the throttle and rode her motorcycle and sidecar across the border and left civilization behind.

She rode for the better part of the day. The rattle of the front forks and the roar of the engine began to turn her arms into rubber, and she finally stopped at what appeared to be an old way station. There was little there: just a stone front stoop and a gnarled tree guarding what would have been the entrance, but the ground was flat and relatively free of brambles; she laid out her sleeping bag in the crook of a large hemlock, shielding herself and the motorcycle from the road. The dark came on quickly, casting the deep-green surroundings in a gray haze. Zita ate her dinner: a peanut-butter-banana sandwich and a box of raisins, washed down with stale-tasting water. She curled up in the nook of the tree's roots and looked up at the sky, the pinpricks of stars appearing between the arrowlike treetops. An owl hooted; the wind rustled the leaves of the surrounding bushes. She fell into a deep, powerful sleep.

She started early, struggling against the aching of her limbs. The motorcycle was old but reliable, and the engine ignited without much trouble. Straddling the bike, she studied the map she'd brought, a pencil sketch she'd traced over the map in her father's atlas. Rocking Chair Creek was not far off, she guessed: another day's ride. Judging from how far she'd gone in the first day, she supposed she could be there by nightfall. The squiggly line of the creek bed wound its way, three tines of a fork, through a section the map had called the Ancients' Grove.

The sky grew cloudy and the forest took on an ominous aspect as she stepped the motorcycle into gear and made her way down the rough gravel of the Long Road. She kept a keen eye on the roadside, wary of bandits or other dangerous characters. She'd never seen a bandit herself; she'd only heard about them. Apparently, they'd come to South Wood during the Bicycle Coup—the Bicycle Maiden had managed to tame their wildness and win them to her side. But once they'd left, many citizens of South Wood breathed a sigh of relief. They were known to be a vicious lot, and Zita, for one, was dearly afraid of them.

Before long, in fact right around lunchtime, she arrived at the first of the three bridges that, according to her map, crossed the three forks of Rocking Chair Creek. The water here cut a deep gulf into the hillside, and Zita stopped the motorcycle at the edge of the bridge to look down into the gorge. The snowmelt had turned the creek into a raging torrent, and while she assumed that there'd be many pebbles to be had in that particular creek bed, the chance that she'd break her neck in the trying was a little too off-putting. Looking back at her map, she decided she'd check out the middle fork of the creek, to see if there wasn't a place where a pebble could be easier got.

She was there within the hour; a rough wooden bridge, layered in moss, allowed precarious travel over the rushing creek bed below. Again, the seasonal rains and melted snow had turned what she assumed would be a placid trickle of a creek into a small river, and the idea of climbing down the bracken-covered bank to retrieve a pebble seemed awfully dangerous. Looking farther eastward, up the hillside, she saw that the ravine grew shallower; she decided she would try her luck off the road. Letting the motorcycle laze on its kickstand, she stepped off the path and into the trees.

The going was hard, the terrain unkind. As she climbed higher, she found herself crawling into a bank of clouds that obscured her vision ahead. The trees took on strange shapes, like giants with spindly heads, and she thought she saw movements in the trees, spectral movements, and she wondered if the stories were true: that spirits and sprites haunted these woods. Suddenly, a shape came into view, through the shroud of mist: It was a toppled white column, its fluted shape covered in a web of ivy. Zita's jaw dropped to see it; she hadn't expected to see any sign of civilization in these woods, let alone a shape that suggested a former, carefully wrought structure. As she walked, more of these objects presented themselves until she saw that she was standing in the middle of a wide courtyard, surrounded by these white columns, all in various states of decay.

She could hear the rushing of Rocking Chair Creek, and she followed the sound up a worn stone stairway that let onto a man-made pool, where the creek spilled down a white stone sluice to feed a bubbling cistern. Looking inside the bowl of the object, she saw a single, opaline stone.

"There you are, pebble," said Zita, aloud, like some crazy person.

She reached in and grabbed it; it was smooth to the touch. The water was frigid, and it sent a violent shiver through her body. Shoving the pebble in her pocket, she turned to head back to the motorcycle when the world around her seemed to shift.

The mist had grown closer, like a blanket smothering a fire, and even the closest trees and columns grew hazy. She thought she saw lights flicker through the fog: firefly-like flickers, like starfalls. A howl erupted, not far off, followed by a series of whiny yips. She recognized that call: coyotes.

She'd heard that the coyotes that had fought in the Battle for the Plinth, now returned to their natural state, were a lawless and savage kind. She chose not to wait and find out if this was true. She bolted back down the hill, following a winding stone path that led away from the cistern.

She'd lost track of which direction the road was in; the mist consumed everything. It seemed to fall on her, to enshroud her. She leapt over trickling brooks and under fallen marble columns. She threw herself through a clutch of thistles, the thorns tearing at her coat. The sounds of the coyotes' braying grew louder; the lights flickered on all sides. A noise like a whisper suddenly shushed at her ear and she screamed, once, loudly. She fell into a wide glade, like a sea of ivy, and there she saw the Plinth.

A feeling of horror overtook her to see this thing, this stone thing that she'd only heard about. It was here that all those good folk died, the Wildwood Irregulars, when they fought the Dowager Governess's coyote army. It was here, the stories told, that the Governess nearly conducted her horrible conjuration. Zita stood, transfixed, and very suddenly she was stripped of her fear—even though the fairy lights continued to flash around her and the braying of the coyotes sounded as if they were growing closer and closer—she suddenly felt an incredibly placid wave come over her.

She reached into her pocket and pulled out the pebble she'd stored there. The size of a walnut, it had a surface as smooth as glass and as white as an ivory tusk.

The ivy rustled at her feet, as if it were alive.

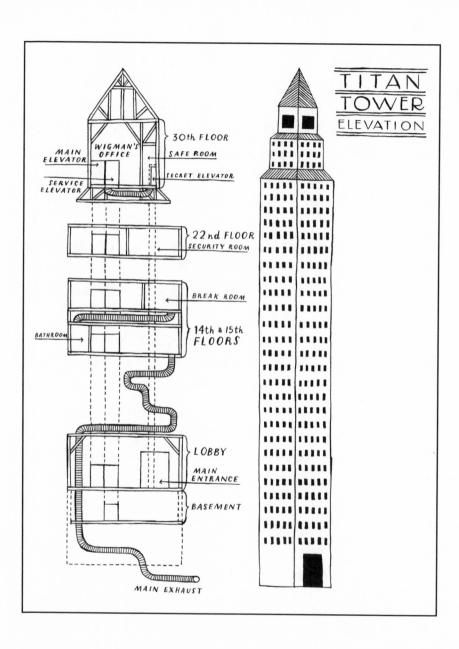

TITAN TOWER ELEVATION

30th FLOOR

MAIN ELEVATOR
WIGMAN'S OFFICE
SAFE ROOM
SERVICE ELEVATOR
SECRET ELEVATOR

22nd FLOOR
SECURITY ROOM

BREAK ROOM

14th & 15th FLOORS

BATHROOM

LOBBY

MAIN ENTRANCE

BASEMENT

MAIN EXHAUST

PART TWO

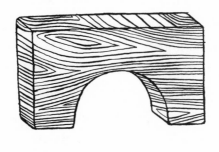

CHAPTER 12

Fifteen Summers

S he hadn't known what it was, at first, when she stepped on it. Some discarded thing that the gardener had dropped. Some trinket or tool. Her ankle twisted when she stepped on it, and she momentarily lost her balance. She cursed, once, quietly.

It was one of those summer days that seemed to stretch on into eternity, and the heat was such that you couldn't believe that the grass, yellow in patches where the gardener's watering can had been remiss, didn't just erupt into flames. She'd been standing in the garden, the chinks in her sun hat dappling her skin with bright, light freckles, weeding the wildflower beds. Or she thought she had. Instead, she'd been taken by her thoughts and her mind had become clouded over by the heat and the light and she'd dropped her spade and swooned. Deciding she needed a glass of water, she'd carefully walked back toward the Mansion, excusing herself to the staff who had stood up from their labors, concerned about their mistress's health.

"I'm okay," she'd said. "Just the heat."

And then she stepped on the thing and cursed and lifted her foot to see what it was: It was not some mislaid tool. It was a toy block.

A wooden thing—perhaps the missing crenellation of some battlement or the capstone of a pyramid—it suddenly and shockingly made her realize how quickly time had passed; that this little block, once a beloved and necessary thing to her child, was no more missed now than a piece of clothing that had long outlived the time of its fashion. She picked it up and studied it, turning it over in the light of the bright sun.

Just then, she heard his voice. "Mama!" called her son, the boy who'd, at some point in the distant past, mislaid this crucial block. His voice was deepened now, showing the first sign of his father's husky baritone, but she found it was still inflected with the tone of a child, a boy. She waited to answer; she wanted to hear it again.

"Mama! Where are you?" A little louder now. It was coming from the other side of the Mansion, where the shade fell and covered the crocuses and the yellowed blossoms of the sunburnt rhododendrons.

"Alexei!" she yelled in response, her gloved hands at her mouth. "Just here!"

And then, her son appeared from the curtain of shadow: a boy of fifteen summers, fourteen winters. He wore a smart suit, newly tailored, which clung to his thin, handsome frame. His hair was a color that only came on in the summer, a kind of reddish brown, which would return to brown once the season had ebbed. She knew him well enough; she'd known him through every season of his life.

The garlands of ribbon had only just been taken down the day before; a banner, thirty feet wide, had proclaimed HAPPY 15TH BIRTHDAY ALEXEI! and it had stretched between the twin spires of the Mansion's gabled roof. Gifts had arrived in droves. Emissaries from far-flung provinces had been announced every quarter hour, it seemed, bearing presents of blackberry cordial and hand-carved wooden toys the boy had long outgrown; they came with quiet entreaties as well, which Grigor received stoically, leading the requester away with a patient arm around a shoulder. A parade had been arranged by the townsfolk, and a band played a marshaling tune while the family sat on a raised platform and witnessed it all, an out-pouring of love for the heir apparent to the Mansion's seat. Alexei had sat through it with such resolute patience, with such enduring focus, that Alexandra found herself looking to her son every time she felt the spark of boredom flourish in her gut; his sweet, handsome face with its direct gaze and relaxed brow renewed her. He would make an excellent Governor-Regent. Of this there was no doubt.

And once the parade grounds had been cleared and the July sun had passed its apex and was beginning to arc toward the far, green hills to the west, then came the coup de grâce. Back at the Mansion, the staff all a-tizzy in preparation for the evening's feast, Grigor had enticed his son to follow him to the carriage house to help, ostensibly, with some trivial chore. Alexei, his voice already betraying a weariness for the day, gamely bore his father's request, and the two of them exited the front doors. Alexandra had heard her son's tremendous shout—hadn't a bit of his childhood shown there? a squeak at the top of his range, despite his age?—and she walked quickly to the window to see Grigor standing proudly while the stable master presented the boy with his own horse, his first horse: a pitch-black mare with a brilliant white diamond between her brown eyes.

And now: Here he was. The fifteen-year-old boy. No longer a child. A boy. A growing boy. Soon to be a grown man. A politician. A statesman. A husband. A father. Her son.

"Mama!" said the boy again. "I wanted to ride Blackie, but Papa said I should ask you first."

"Oh?" she said, toying with him. The heat had dissipated. The glass of water seemed a distant need. The boy's arrival had quenched her. "Did he say that?"

Alexei knew the game. "Yes, he did. And I said I would. So here I am."

"And?"

"And . . . ," said Alexei, his smile growing. "Can I?"

"Did you speak to Mr. Cooper?" The stable master.

"No, but Papa said I could ask him if he wasn't too busy."

"And have you finished your algebra?"

The smile disappeared; he became astute. "Yes, Mama. Miss Brighton said I did well enough."

"Well enough?"

"That's what she said." He paused, searching his mother's expression. "That's good, right?"

Alexandra strove to retain her motherly concern. "And your father said it was okay?"

"Yes," said Alexei, loosening a bit, knowing that the prospects had suddenly turned for the better. "He said it was okay, but I should ask you."

"Very well," said Alexandra. "Speak to Mr. Cooper. As long as he's not too busy."

The boy beamed. "Yes, Mama!" A sudden energy then overtook him, and he practically leapt from where he stood and bolted for the other side of the Mansion.

Alexandra called out her son's name. The boy stopped, just in the shade of the house. She said something then, something she couldn't later recall, later when she replayed the entire exchange in her mind, over and over again, like a film taped in a tight loop, always stopping when the boy had reached the shelter of the building's shade, connecting smoothly and flawlessly with the image that had preceded it, with him approaching, there in the same rhombus of dark. She said something: perhaps a word of caution. A token of motherly concern, in the hopes he might carry it with him, like a guarding charm. Or was it something unimportant? An impotent demand, a suggestion that these sorts of privileges were conditional, dependent on his good works. It never was clear. She tried, later, to conjure from that mist, that long patch of shade, a simple declaration. That she had told him that she loved him. That he was everything to her. But then he was gone, and the film replayed: the heat, the light, the block beneath her foot, the sound of his voice.

Because what came next was nothing.

It almost seems pointless to recount it.

She is in the gardening shed, peeling the gloves from her hands. She is hanging the sun hat on a hook. She is speaking to the master gardener, briefly. She is remembering the glass of water. She is walking through the back door, through the glassed-in sunroom. Across the checkerboard of the foyer; she is greeting a staff member bent at some task. She is entering the kitchen, acknowledging the kitchen staff quietly, trying to be unseen. An empty glass under the tap. And then: a shout from the courtyard, loud, through the window. Looking up to see a wild black horse, rearing. Mr. Cooper struggling to hold the bridle.

Her son, Alexei, fifteen summers, lying on the ground.

She dropped the glass in the sink, its crystalline shatter a tiny explosion, and ran for the front doors. She threw them open, her thin limbs imbued with a new strength, and tore out into the courtyard, her every heartbeat a fresh tremor in her ears. Mr. Cooper was shouting, wrangling the horse as it kicked and whinnied. No obstacle could stop Alexandra from getting to her son, and she felt the air the horse moved all around her and felt the pebbles spat by the horse's hooves shower her.

There was blood. A lot of blood. The boy was pale and still as a stone, as still and pale as a white stone. The red blood seeped onto the courtyard and welled about his head. His hair was matted with fresh blood, and his eyes were closed.

She grabbed him by the shoulders and held him to her chest. She shouted his name. She threw her arms around his limp body and embraced it with all the energy and love she could muster. She thought, maybe, she felt the last few thrums of his heart. Little phantoms. Little wisps of smoke: gone as quickly as they'd appeared.

She felt him disappear. Fourteen winters, gone.

The horse had been spooked, they said. A flash of light from the bright summer sun against a leaded pane of glass. A thrush startled from its hiding. His little body had been thrown from the horse's back like a doll. He'd hit the cobbles headfirst and was gone before he could utter a cry. The boy couldn't have felt a thing, they reasoned, they reassured. But no amount of reassurance could placate the demon inside Alexandra's breast. She stayed by the lifeless body of her son for days; she bade the funeral director teach her how to clean the body. She performed the ablutions lovingly, as she had when the boy had been alive: A sallow yellow sponge carefully ran along his abalone skin. He had put up such a fuss, hadn't he, when she'd done the same thing when he was alive? She'd practically had to wrestle him down, in a torrent of water and bath suds, to wash his feet, his shoulders, his little fingers: him laughing ecstatically, she trying to keep her composure, the placid mother. The picture of calm. But now he lay still and raised no objection to her washings.

Maybe it was then that she decided that this was not her son. This still thing. That there was something else, something elusive, that had animated this dead vessel. They interred the boy with full honors, the same band that played for his birthday playing for his funeral. Grigor, of course, was in bed, having heaped enough blame on himself for his son's death that he could barely rise under the weight. She became disgusted with her husband as the demon inside her breast grew larger and noisier. She stood silently as the casket was entombed and ignored the hushed words of sympathy from the surrounding mourners.

She'd had an idea. Something that occurred to her one night, as she lay beside the sleeping body of her idle, bedridden husband. The film unspooled in her head, the loop of film that ran from Alexei's arrival to his departure in that same piece of shade by the Mansion wall. It was as if, suddenly, after reviewing the same piece of film for the hundredth time, without an inkling that anything new would reveal itself, she'd caught a glimpse of something. Something only she could see.

She had a plan.

Grigor died, the fool. Shortly after the funeral. She woke up one day to find him dead, and that was that. Poor Grigor. His heart simply became too heavy, there in the cavity of his chest. She loathed him for his cowardice. The funeral players had barely been disbanded when they were called again for the Governor-Regent's burial, to be laid in state in a tomb not far from his departed son. The government was thrown into confusion; no sooner had the man been put in the ground than his silent, seething wife was crowned the Dowager Governess, to reign over South Wood in her husband's stead; but this new ruler had different concerns on her mind.

She consulted ancient texts, sought the teachings of market conjurers, reviled necromancers. She invited them into the Mansion, braving the scorning eyes of her staff. Soon, the air in the stuffy place breathed with the smell of sandalwood and sage. She started with simple conjures: a piece of red tissue, flourished correctly, could become a songbird; a table could be set to dance on its legs. They taught her the magic sigils to ease rain from a threatening cloud, they showed her which mushrooms provoked the greatest visions—they even taught her the steps required to gain command over the ivy. But she always pressed her teachers for the ultimate incantation: to call a soul back from the land of the dead.

An itinerant herbalist who claimed Wildwood as his home province was sought and retained. He was thought to be the greatest sorcerer in the whole of the Wood, more powerful than the Mystics of the North, all of whom had spurned her when she sought their counsel.

Savages, she thought. *Witch doctors and savages.* They would soon know true power.

The herbalist sat quietly in the Dowager's study, glancing about the room with a disinterested air. He wore little more than rags, and a conical felt hat was perched on the crown of his head. A tremendous beard grew down to his knees, a white and stringy thing in which it seemed all manner of living things had taken up residence.

"No," he'd said finally, once he'd had his fill of the Mansion's poppy beer and cleaned his plate of the stew he'd been served. "This thing can't be done. To return a soul to a body long dead idn't possible. P'raps if I'd a-gotten to him right after 'is time of passin'. Maybes then. Now, no. Y'need a vessel to contain th' soul. Not no rotted carcass."

"What kind of *vessel*?" she asked, leaning in from her chair, smarting at this ugly man's description of her son as a rotten thing. She couldn't stand the image it summoned.

"A seed," said the man slowly: a mentor doling out his wisdom.

"Can be taken from th' fruit and when its flesh is gone, be trick'd into life when placed in a simple glass o' water."

"You're saying my son's soul can be brought back in a glass of water?" asked the Governess in disbelief.

The man grumbled. "No," he said. "I mean to say that th' spark o' life remains in the tiny bits o' the body and can be *tricked*, with th' right conjuries, into comin' afresh if the right sort o' en-*vir*-onment is provided."

"But how? What do you mean, environment?"

"Y' must build a new body for the boy. One that matches all th' intricacies of the flesh-and-blood machine. Plant the seed there. Only then can the living thing grow again."

She'd known toy makers who could build things of staggering complexity: little automaton dolls she'd been given on her own birthdays as a child. Surely such a thing could be built. "But what is the seed?" she asked.

The old man smiled, revealing an astonishingly ugly row of brownish-yellow nubs. "The teeth," he said. "Y' must retrieve th' teeth."

And so she did; the body was exhumed secretly—present were only herself and a short, muscular grave digger named Ned. She watched him break the seal and pull back the door of the mausoleum; she held the lantern for him to see. At long last, the body was recovered. Alexandra, by this point, was indifferent to the condition of the body, of her deceased son. She knew that it was simply his disused husk, a banana peel thrown on the compost heap. She removed his teeth one after another, methodically, as if she were plucking feathers from a chicken bound for the oven.

The grave digger, Ned, was exiled promptly the next day.

But to make the boy again, a machine replica of the living, breathing thing, special expertise would need to be engaged. This was no simple automaton, no blinking ceramic doll that wet itself when its left arm was raised. The task before her was to imitate the workings of the Maker, the Divine Being. For this, she consulted blacksmiths and machinists, toy makers and engineers. A bear, living in seclusion in the farthest reaches of South Wood, was known for his intricate metalwork. His family had repaired the Mansion's clocks for generations; the bear himself was known for the construction of little trinkets: mechanical waxwings that aped the behaviors of their flesh-and-blood models and bellowed about in thick flocks, clouding the air of the market where he sold the things to ecstatic children. But he alone could not re-create a human child. To do so, he needed the aid of an Outsider machinist, a man who existed in legend only among the toy makers and tinkerers of the Wood. He explained this to the Governess in quaking tones while she stared at him from behind her desk in the Mansion's office.

"His name is Carol Grod," said the bear. "I believe together we could make such a thing."

A pair of eagles was dispatched to fetch this machinist from some lonely hovel in the Outside. How easy it seemed, the Governess reckoned, to simply have a thing, a person, *carried* to oneself at one's bidding. The man's story was uninteresting to her, the demon having bloomed fully in her breast: how his creations had astonished and wowed Outsider children and adults alike for decades, little contraptions made of brass and copper with intricate inner workings that clicked and whirred. But his abilities became overshadowed by the wondrous worlds available by screen, by computer, and his inventions were forgotten and ignored and he disappeared into anonymity.

He had use here, though, here in the world his kind called the Impassable Wilderness. And so the two of them, the old man and the bear, working in seclusion, began to create the body that would house the soul of Alexei. The soul of her son.

A Meeting at the Tree

Esben the bear stirred at the fire with the hooks of his hands and breathed in the dark around him. The night had come on quickly, here in the woods, where the tall shroud of trees acted as a kind of curtain to the sun. An owl hooted, somewhere, far off. He shivered, a reflexive shiver, as a slight uneasiness came over him. It'd been many hours since he and the girl parted ways; he'd expected her back before sundown. What's more, he was getting a little peckish. He'd eaten through what food they'd had in her bag fairly quickly; his appetite did tend to get the best of him from time to time. Prue had promised to bring more food—she'd said that, hadn't she?

And then, her son appeared from the curtain of shadow:
a boy of fifteen summers, fourteen winters.

He knocked over one of the burning branches in the fire, sending sparks in the air, and stabbed his hooks into a fresh log just to the side of the pit. It was one thing, he reflected, he was particularly good at now—fire tending. The hooks were kind of a godsend in that way: If he ever had to tend fires for the rest of his life, it'd be something he'd do well at. It'd been—what—thirteen years now, right? Since he'd had his paws roughly removed—a surgeon's scalpel had done the job in a scant few minutes. He grimaced a little now, here at the fire, remembering the pain. The searing pain.

A noise startled him: a scratching somewhere beyond the throw of the firelight. "Who's there?" he shouted. No response came. The scratching stopped. Esben adjusted the rake of his knitted cap and grumbled a little, there, angry at the invisible thing for disturbing his peace. "Fine," he said to the darkness. "Don't show yourself."

Probably a squirrel, he reasoned. He hoped it wasn't some spy for the Mansion—some holdout from the old days who might catch him, accuse him of breaking his parole. He was supposed to be dead, exiled away to the deepest reaches of the Underwood. Even though Prue seemed convinced that he'd be safe—that the people responsible for his mutilation and exile were long gone, washed away in the flood of revolution—he still couldn't fight the residual fear that he'd be thrown back into that dark world. Or worse. Surely, seeing he'd survived the most horrific disfigurement and exile they could devise, they'd want to try something more severe. He shivered, again, at the thought.

Another sound came from the surrounding woods, this time

louder: It was indescribable to the poor bear; it was both airy and watery, if such a thing could be said to exist. It called to mind the angered battle cry of some terrible creature, something that perhaps had the body of a squid, all slippery tentacles and ooze, and the head of an owl. The noise came again: a kind of bubbling *WHOOOO*. A drowned ghost, perhaps, called to Esben's position by the promise of a warming fire, where the wandering spirit might dry his soggy, moss-covered clothes.

"Who's th-there?" managed Esben, staring off into the dark, his hooks held in a defensive position.

There came a pause, then the words: "Oh, forget it." It was, unmistakably, Prue's voice.

The bear let out a breath of relief when he saw the girl's figure appear from out of the forest's dark. She set her hands on her hips in a show of frustration and said, "I can't whistle. I forgot."

That was, after all, to be their signal that a friend was approaching.

The bear smiled. "No matter," he said. "Takes some practice."

Two other figures appeared behind the girl, a short-statured badger and a lumbering hulk of a man sporting a nappy brown beard.

"This is Neil, who you met earlier," said Prue, gesturing to the badger. "And this is Charlie. They're going to help us."

"How do you do?" said Esben.

"Very well, thanks," said Charlie. "Nice fire you got there."

"We have a moment, anyway," said Prue. "If you want to take a load off. It's been a long day."

"What happened?" asked the bear.

The man, Charlie, put in enthusiastically before Prue could answer, "Oh, you wouldn't have believed it, if you'd 'a been there. A glorious return, it was. The Bicycle Maiden, come back to the Mansion. I'll be tellin' my grandkids about that."

"Oh, please," demurred Prue, her cheeks showing their blush by the light of the campfire.

"It's true!" continued Charlie. "Quite a show. Even those Caliphs were quakin' in their boots to see her show up."

"Charlie's a fan," said Prue, by way of explanation. Remembering herself, she shrugged her bag from her shoulder and let it fall with a thump to the ground. "I got you some more food. A little dried fruit and some bread. Some jerky and potted meat, too. It was all I could grab."

"That'll do very nicely, thanks," said Esben. He easily unpeeled the top of one of the cans of meat and began dishing the pink stuff into his mouth. "How'd it go?" he asked between bites.

"As well as you could expect, I guess."

"And it was a big deal, you coming back?"

Again, the bearded man answered before Prue had a chance. "As big a deal as you could—"

Prue waved him off. "At first, yeah," she said. "But things got a little ugly. It turns out a lot of those people don't really like the idea of bringing Alexei back from the dead."

"Didn't I say that?" said Esben, looking back and forth between all the figures present around the campfire. "I said that. I said that would be tough. Alexei himself wasn't too keen on the idea. I mean, he removed the cog himself once he found out he'd been remade. I've said it before and I'll say it again: Even I have some ethical quandaries about what we're supposed to do."

"Well, maybe you're right," said Prue. "But I still can't ignore what the tree said. There must be a reason."

"Did you find out what happened to Carol?" asked the bear.

"No," she said. "But I have a clue." She pulled from her pocket the note that had been left in Carol Grod's file and handed it to the bear. He set his tin down and fumbled with it, his twin hook-hands clanging together until Prue had the good sense to reach over and just stab the paper through his right hook like it was a spike file.

"Thanks," he said. He peered at the piece of paper, at the writing on the paper, in the light of the campfire. "Meet tonight, huh? What *tree*?"

"The Blighted Tree," said Neil, the badger. "It must be."

"That old relic?" asked Esben, shocked. "I though people had given up on that thing long ago."

"The Synod's back," said Prue. "And seems pretty strong from what I saw."

The bear scratched at his chin with the point of his left hook for a moment before saying, "My grandpa had a thing for the Blighted Tree. Still had a shrine in his house when he died."

"Oh, yes," said Neil. "It's a regular revival. Unfortunately, and I say this as a true patriot and supporter of the revolution"—he said this with some deference toward Prue—"the Spokes haven't done that good a job of running the place."

Charlie frowned a little at this statement before saying, "Those are strong words, Citizen Badger. But true. The revolution's all about freedom, personal freedom. That works great as a jumping-off point, but it's no good at making for a safe and just society."

The badger nodded, now fanning his little hands in front of the crackling fire. "I have to say, I'm getting a little tired myself of being harangued by the hard-line Spokes." Saying this, his head suddenly darted side to side, scanning the immediate vicinity for secret listeners.

"It's okay," said Prue, noticing this. "You're safe here."

"It's the kind of talk that could get you written up," said the badger. "I mean no disrespect to the revolution, Maiden, you know that."

Prue nodded.

"I gave up my casquette," said Charlie, "after I saw what was happening. Those hard-liners were taking the idea of the revolution and turning it into just another reason to justify gang vigilantism. At least the Synod's looking out for the people, not just their own selves."

"That much is true," said Neil.

"But can you trust them? The Caliphs?" asked Esben, now

masticating a particularly tough hunk of beef jerky. "Assuming that's who you're going to meet."

"I suppose I'll have to," said Prue. "They've got Carol. Or know where he is, anyway."

"Well, I think you ought to be careful," said the bear. "We still don't know who sent those Kitsunes, for one. Could've been them, the Synod."

"But they want to help," said Prue, frowning. "Why would they want me, you know, out of the picture?"

"Complicated times, Maiden," said Charlie, stroking his beard. "Everyone's a friend and everyone's an enemy."

The four individuals around the fire lapsed into a kind of contemplative silence as the flames crackled and leapt from the pit and a bag of dried mangoes was passed from badger to bear to human. Finally, Prue took a deep breath and said, "Shall we?"

"I think we shall," said the badger.

Esben stood up to see Prue off, giving her a protective pat on the shoulder. "Careful," he said. "Keep your wits about you."

"Will do," was her reply.

"And work on your whistle a bit," he said.

She smiled and turned away from the campfire. The three of them, the badger, the bearded human, and the Bicycle Maiden, all walked off into the gloom of the forest.

The bear returned to his position, gamely stirring the fire with his hooks, and his mind drifted, his belly somewhat sated by the rations Prue had brought him. After a time, he lay back with his head against a log and watched the wheeling stars above his head, trying to pick out Ursa Major, the Big Bear—it was his favorite constellation. Finding it, he followed the tail toward the bright point just above it—it was the belt buckle of the Toy Soldier, a constellation his father had shown him as a cub. His father said it was a guiding light for the makers of things, for the tinkerers and the riveters. The bear felt himself drift off as he began to imagine the task before him: the re-creation of his greatest achievement, the mechanical boy prince. It would be hard, granted, but he was up for the task. He only needed hands, gifted hands, and he guessed that the girl Prue was bound to find them for him. Sleep stole over him as he recalled his old compatriot Carol Grod, the Outsider machinist; their hours of toiling in the Mansion garret. He recalled the old man's complexion, the cadence of his voice; a kindred spirit.

The bear had only been asleep a few hours when he heard the whistle. It was shrill, practiced. *Impressive,* he thought. *A little woodshedding goes a long way.* By the time he'd gained enough consciousness to realize how faulty this logic seemed, it was too late.

🌿

They kept to the road; that was the strategy. Staying out in the open. Still: The wrought-iron gaslights that began appearing along the side of the road did little to dispel the gloom that seemed to hover just beyond the trees. Prue found herself darting quick glances out into the dark, imagining an army of shape-shifting life science teachers emerging, claws bared, shifting interminably between human and fox.

Reflexively, she focused her mind and *listened*.

The plants and trees, the bushes and the shrubs, all spoke in a collective rattle. It'd been something she'd been able to do for a while now: Prue could hear the voices of the living vegetation around her. Only once had the voices codified into any kind of language she could understand, and that happened at a moment of extreme duress. On the other hand, it seemed that they were able to understand *her*, which was something, anyway. But she'd heard a word—a clear, concise holler of *GO!*—when Darla, the assassin, had been in hiding, preparing her attack. Prue had been waiting, these many months since that occurrence, to hear another word, another English word, spoken. But nothing had come—just more humming and whispering. It had something to do with the intensity of the situation, she assumed. Something in her had clicked; she guessed she didn't quite have the discipline to make it happen again. And now: Could the rattling of the surrounding forest be a kind of warning in its own right? Was another assassin, bound to her task, waiting for the precise moment to attack?

No answer was forthcoming.

The fox-women of her imagination continued their advance.

She blinked the image away and faced forward in the seat of the rickshaw, watching Neil the badger's bobbing head as he skillfully piloted the little vehicle over the cobblestones of the Long Road. Charlie gamely trotted alongside, keeping a guarded watch on their surroundings as they traveled.

"How's it going up there?" she asked Neil, trying to drive the fear from her mind.

"Oh, fine," said the badger between labored breaths.

"Are you sure you want to drive me? I could easily walk."

"No, no, no." The badger shook his head vehemently. "The road is rough, Maiden. You might throw your ankle. And then where would we be?"

"I've actually done that before and—"

"Besides," Neil continued, "no one knows these roads like me. I can get you there in half the time."

"Okay," said Prue. She knew better than to argue with the badger. In any case, riding in a rickshaw did give her a kind of aura of importance—they seemed to collect hangers-on wherever they went. Riding from the Mansion, after the debacle in the Archives, had been like wading naked through a cloud of mosquitoes: No sooner had the mob been dispersed by the Synod when a new congregation of admirers appeared, previously hard-liner Spokes who now adopted the slogans: "REANIMATE THE PRINCE ALEXEI!" and "BRING THE ROBOT BACK!" The boy's last name, Svik, was conspicuously absent from these shouted mantras; Prue suspected there was a kind of cognitive dissonance going on—a phrase her dad had once defined for her as being the ability to believe in two radically conflicting beliefs at the same time, despite the illogic of it all. She could see how these political movements got their steam.

And now: She'd barely finished flipping through these series of thoughts and recollections when she found that the rickshaw was once again surrounded by a small crowd of Spokes and admirers, citizens roused from their beds when Prue's arrival had been announced by some overexcited witness. They came teeming about the rickshaw, some still wearing their pajamas, climbing on top of its canopy and dragging along the back. Initially, Charlie made an effort to keep the carriage free of hangers-on, but soon the collective momentum of the crowd was so great that Neil didn't even have to pull the cart—it was carried along like a paper boat in a swiftly flowing stream. Needless to say, the specter of Kitsunes creeping in the bushes seemed a concern of the past.

"We're with you, Maiden!" shouted some from the crowd. "It's time to bring back the mechanical boy prince!"

"Peace! Peace in our time!"

The crowd carved their way into the populated districts of South Wood, past the storefronts and the houses, around the wide path that bowed away from the glow of the Mansion's lit windows. Here, the forest grew darker. The canopy of the trees seemed to hang lower over the road, and the gas lamps were fewer and fewer. Many of the crowd that followed the rickshaw seemed to stray, and the throng grew thinner.

"Where are you going, Maiden?" one follower, a teenaged bear in a bicycle cap, inquired.

"To the Blighted Tree. I'm supposed to meet someone there."

"Who would want to meet you there?"

"Gonna find out, I guess," said Prue.

"Ooh," said someone at Prue's left. She turned to see it was a middle-aged woman, dressed in a kind of flowery-patterned dress. "They speak to the trees, you know. They can hear the plants talk."

Prue smiled, though the idea made her all the more confused: Were these Synod members simply the South Wood's answer to the Mystics of the North? She thought of Iphigenia, the dear departed Elder Mystic, and wished she could be here now to guide her. She didn't know who to trust, what to believe. She listened for the trees, again, and noticed a marked change in their tone: The noises were lower and almost throatier. What's more, she could now discern a kind of hum occurring just on the fringes of her hearing. Something big, like the lowing of somebody's car stereo, just down the street and out of view.

"Here we are," said Neil, drawing up at the top of a little rise in the road where two gnarled and ancient hemlocks made a kind of gateway. "The Blighted Tree's just beyond there."

"Will you come with?" asked Prue.

"Only those who are called can cross the threshold to the Blighted Glade," said Charlie. He nodded his head, gesturing to the road ahead, and Prue saw two figures appear from behind the hemlocks. They wore identical gray hooded robes that covered their bodies entirely. As they came closer, a bright spark of light, a reflection from a nearby gas lamp, revealed that their faces were covered in silvery mirrored masks. The look was alarming, and Prue stared in disbelief at the two approaching figures.

The few stragglers of the crowd around the rickshaw fell away, bowing reverentially to these strange newcomers. Prue stepped down to the road and greeted the figures, saying, "Hi." When there came no response, she said, "I'm Prue. I'm supposed to meet someone? At the tree?"

The figures, their shiny silver masks obscuring their faces, their long gray cowls covering their heads, said nothing. Instead, they waved the way forward, beneath the boughs of the twin hemlocks. Prue gave a quick look over her shoulder: All that remained of her former retinue was the tall bearded man, the badger, and his bright, baubled rickshaw. "Go ahead," said Charlie. "Be safe."

The road became rough here, its cobbles all buckled and broken from years of use with few, if any, repairs. Clumps of grass and moss defaced the surface, and the roots of trees plowed up great sections in lumpy furrows. Prue walked between her two chaperones as they led her down the hill. Having received no response to her last few questions, she decided it would be rude to keep asking more. Perhaps some vow of silence was involved here; she hated the idea that she might be somehow offending their sensibilities.

She couldn't tell if they were animal or human, male or female. Their shrouding getup all but erased any kind of distinction. One was a little shorter than the other; that was really the only discernible difference between her two chaperones. She turned her attention to the greenery around her, wanting to suss out some kind of guiding information, but she was, as before, unable to coax anything but humming murmurs from the surrounding forest. Still, the hum, the low hum, remained. It pulsated somewhere off in the distance, a sound without a knowable source, and it seemed to be growing louder as they approached. Another sound presented itself, suddenly, to Prue: some kind of needling *tick* from the two Caliphs at her side. *Strange,* she thought. It was no sound a human would produce; what's more, it seemed to be originating *in her mind,* which would lead her to believe that some kind of vegetation was the source. She didn't have much time to contemplate what this meant when the three of them arrived at a point in the road where the trees fell away and an immense meadow presented itself, bathed a glowing white by the rising moon.

The scene was eerily familiar: A group of hooded, robed figures stood in a wide circle in the center of the meadow around a gigantic tree. Behind them, making a larger circle, was a ring of burning torches. The shadows of the robed figures cast by these torches grew distorted and tall, clambering at the tree's raw and twisted trunk. Prue could now see why the tree was called blighted; it was as if someone had taken a healthy, thriving tree of immense proportions and proceeded to mangle it, deform it, shedding it of its leaves and twisting its hulking trunk into a contorted, knuckly thing. The tree's bark folded and gaped like ancient flesh and its branches corkscrewed skyward, reaching higher than any other tree in the vicinity. Prue caught her breath; she suddenly realized that this was where the lowing, the distant hum, was coming from. It was coming from the Blighted Tree. It was calling her.

Seeing the approaching three, one of the figures in the circle broke away and walked toward them. He, too, was entirely covered in the gray robes and gray cowl, but his face mask was a shiny, brilliant gold instead of silver. The masks themselves were unremarkable—a neutral human face, nondescript. When the robed figure drew closer, Prue could see the shadows of the man's eyes, catching the torchlight in the twin cavities of the mask.

"Prue McKeel," said the figure once he reached them. "I've long desired to meet you. This day has been in the making for some time now. Surely, you know this as well."

A man's voice, it was slightly muffled by the presence of the gold mask. He nodded to the two figures at Prue's side, who silently stepped away and walked toward the circle around the tree.

Prue watched them go. "They don't speak? Is it a vow or something?"

"They choose not to speak," said the man. Prue felt strangely comfortable in his presence, and his tone of voice was almost fatherly, despite the filter of his mask. "The teachings of the Blighted Tree are enough language for their contemplation. The noise of people is merely a distraction."

"Why do you talk, then?" She hoped the question didn't seem

rude; the man's aura invited a certain level of familiarity. In fact, she could swear she'd met the man before, somewhere.

"I've ascended beyond acolyte. I'm the Elder Caliph. My name is Elgen. Welcome to the Blighted Glade. Your path has been long, Prue McKeel of the Outside, but it has inevitably led you here. It has been leading you here from the moment you set foot in the Wood." The lights of the torches gave a sparkling glow to the man's mask; Prue found it mesmerizing. She could see herself, lit by the pale light, reflected in the mirror of the mask. She looked wobbly, disjointed. "Come," said Elgen. "I'd like you to speak to the tree. It has long desired to speak to you."

Prue began to follow the man, transfixed by his strange aura, before she remembered herself. "Do you know where Carol Grod is?"

She'd stopped in her tracks; the man kept walking. She repeated herself. "I need to know where he is."

Elgen turned. "He is close. Come."

"What, like, you have him? Here?"

"Come, Prue. Speak to the tree."

The hum had grown steadily louder in her mind. It made it hard to think straight. She could hear the weird ticking noises coming from the figures in the circle around the tree, though the sounds were quickly being eclipsed by the tree's all-encompassing low. She rubbed her temples, trying to clear her thoughts. The man continued to speak, gesturing her closer to the ring of Caliphs, the bent hulk of the Blighted Tree. "We've been waiting for you. Ever since you were brought here. When the Dowager Governess robbed your family of your brother. We saw you before anyone. We knew your power, your potential. Come closer to the tree."

"I need to find Carol. Carol Grod. We've got to remake Alexei."

"We know, we know. We only want to help you in this task. You've come at an auspicious time, Prue McKeel, Bicycle Maiden, Wildwood Regina. The tree is sending out the Word. It is communicating to its true believers in the language of the Ancients. It is the Calling, Prue. The Blighted Tree needs us." He waved his hand to the collected congregation. Prue saw them all: silent, standing in the shadow of the tree, the torchlight creating sparks against their cold, silvery face masks.

"Who are they?" she managed. The hum was now everywhere. The sound of her own voice came to her like birdsong beneath a foghorn.

"The true believers. Come closer."

Prue began walking, as if in a trance, toward the ring.

"A new tree is being born, Prue," said Elgen. "Deep in the heart of Wildwood. You've felt it. It is growing. Like an unborn child in its womb, it is pulling power from its parents. The mother and the father. It will be a difficult birth. Even now, it is sapping the energy from its surroundings. Sadly, the Mother Tree will die in labor. It is as it must be. But the Father Tree will survive. The Father Tree and the newborn will welcome in a new era. We are its midwives, Prue, all of us faithful."

The humming was so loud now, Prue could barely hear the man's words, let alone understand them. It came to her in cryptic waves. Ahead, at the tree, she now noticed a new gathering of people: Men and women stood in a line while a hooded acolyte scraped chunks of bark from the Blighted Tree's wormy trunk. The uncovered people, the men and women in the line, each in turn knelt and opened their mouths, and the acolyte dropped the bits from the trunk onto their tongues. She recognized some of the citizens she'd seen that afternoon at the foyer of the Mansion. Prue watched as each one then stood and was handed a folded robe and a silvery mask.

"We are of the same mind, Prue," Elgen continued. "We have heard the call as well. To bring the half-dead prince to life."

HUM.

"It was not just the Mother Tree who decreed this—the Father Tree as well. A champion is needed for the newborn. Alexei will be that champion."

HUM.

They were growing closer to the tree. The line toward the communion rite was longer now, curling away from the tree and through the encircling acolytes. It became clear to Prue that this was where the Elder Caliph was leading her. "Carol Grod," she said insistently.

HUM.

"We have Carol," said Elgen. "He's safe. We only need Esben. And then the Möbius Cog can be made."

HUM.

"The what?" whispered Prue. It was as if the man was speaking a foreign language. They reached the outer circle, the hooded Caliph acolytes. Prue *listened* and heard that strange ticking coming from within each of them. There was something strangely familiar, still, about these figures. Their shapes. She looked at them for some kind of sign of how she knew them, but she could only see the dark forms of their mirrored masks. Elgen called her on, noticing she'd paused by the ring of acolytes.

"Come closer," said the Elder Caliph. "The tree is calling you."

Indeed, it seemed to be; the *HUM* was now rattling in her skull like someone was holding a blender to her forehead. The other thoughts colliding in her mind simply fell away: Esben, Carol, Alexei, Curtis, her mother and father, everything. She approached the tree and placed her hand on its trunk.

A kind of electricity entered her fingertips and snaked its way along the length of her arm; it fanned out at her chest and spread through her neck and pelvis and down to her feet. She suddenly felt a kind of spirit, an energy, that made her realize just how tired she'd been before she'd touched the tree, how much the agonizing events over the last year had affected her soul. It was as if she was a dead battery, a walking dead battery, and the Blighted Tree was charging her afresh. Her eyes, alight with new vision, looked to her fingertips and saw a substance staining her fingernails a phosphorescent green.

"Yes," came a whisper at her ear. It was Elgen. "It is the Blight that gives the tree its power. The Spongiform." The strange growth, Prue saw, gathered in every nook of the tree's knobby bark. It glistened and glowed in the light of the torches. "You have come a long way, Prue McKeel," continued Elgen, "and you have tasted the beginnings of true power. Eat the Spongiform and join us. Leave your primitive life behind; become a true Caliph and help birth the One Tree."

Prue stepped away, the energy still coursing through her body, and looked to her right, where a hooded acolyte was scraping some of the foaming green stuff from the bark of the tree. Collecting it on the edge of the spoon he carried, he presented it to Prue, all glowing and wet.

"Eat," said Elgen. "Eat the Spongiform. And join us."

CHAPTER 14

A Natural-Born Saboteur;
Two out of Three

A warm bath.

It was something Elsie had not had in—literally—months. She'd almost grown accustomed to the layer of grime that had accumulated on her skin, to the ever-present sheen of grease that seemed to act like a hairnet over her curly black hair. She sat with her knees tucked against her chest while her sister used a glass mason jar to pour the warm, sudsy water over her shoulders.

Outside the room, they could hear the preparations proceeding.

A din of men shouting, things being lifted and shifted. Boxes upended and wires unspooled. Little smatterings of French peppered the men's language; jokes being shared, hearty laughs echoing in the hallway. They were the sounds of a group of actors preparing for their greatest performance, something they'd been awaiting for many, many years. And the call to places was fast approaching.

Inside the bathroom, Elsie remained quiet, feeling the warm water course over her back and shoulders.

"Okay," said Rachel. "One more time."

Elsie nodded. "Straight. Left. Left. Straight. Right. Straight."

"Uh-huh," prompted Rachel. She was looking at a map that she'd laid on the floor before her, shielded from her sister's sight by the lip of the bathtub.

"A vent opening. Hallway." She looked at her sister for confirmation.

"Yep. Then what?"

"Bathroom, just a few feet to the right. Ceiling vent. Going left from the door. Then straight. For a while. Then right. Left. Left. Right. Straight. Vent opening."

"Good, sis," said Rachel. "Careful here."

"Yeah, this is the break room, right?"

Her sister nodded.

"So we wait till it's clear. Then drop. And then . . ." She faltered here.

"And then?"

Elsie snuck a look over the tub. Rachel snatched up the map.

"No peeking, Els! This is serious. You won't have time to consult a map in the tower. You've got to commit this stuff to memory." Her face was lined with worry; Elsie could sense her sister's deep concern. "You can't get caught, Elsie. You just can't."

Taking a deep breath, Elsie continued, looking Rachel directly in the eye. "Through the break room. Down the hall. Service elevator. Wait for it to shut down." She paused here and searched her sister's face; this was to be Unthank's responsibility. One of many. The entire operation seemed to hinge on his ability to perform several challenging tasks within the sanctum of Titan Tower. Rachel hadn't

looked up; Elsie continued, "Pry the door. The car will not be there. Climb the ladder up fifteen stories. That's where the vent is, to the safe room. Break the grate and climb in. Then: Right. Straight. Left. Left. Straight. Right. Straight. And . . ."

"And?"

"There it is. Grate to the safe room. Climb in, emergency elevator is behind the bookshelf. *Extract* the captives, *rendezvous* outside at the eastern gate of the plaza." The last sentence had been Jacques's words; it had sounded cold and official. Elsie liked saying it.

"Good job, sis," said Rachel, smiling. "I think you got it."

"*Merci*," said Elsie, in the manner of the Chapeaux.

Just then, a knock came at the door; it was Michael. "You guys done in there?"

"Just about," shouted Rachel. "I think this one's got the plan down."

"Good. We need you. The rest of the Unadoptables are here." He and Cynthia had made the journey back to the warehouse in the Forgotten Place; there, they'd distributed food from the Chapeaux and briefed everyone on the action. As promised, they'd recruited several of the kids for the advance on Titan Tower.

Elsie looked at her sister, wide-eyed. It seemed as if the thing was really happening. "We're coming!" she shouted.

Outside in the main room, all was chaos. A flurry of black turtle-necks presided, a flock of black berets hovered above. The two girls waded into it uneasily; Michael sidestepped over to them, under a wooden spool of bomb fuse being carried by two saboteurs. He was followed by a trio of other children: the smallest and spryest of the young Unadoptables. They were Harry, Oz, and Ruthie. All were around nine years old and fairly short for their age. Harry was a thick kid, square-shouldered for one so young—but an indomitable force. The other kids called him Harry the Wall. Oz and Ruthie were close friends and shared an almost intuitive way of communication; it was decided that that sort of cunning would come in handy. Elsie sized up the crew and smiled. "Hey, guys," she said. "You ready for this craziness?"

They barely had a chance to respond when Nico arrived with a stack of what looked like dark tablecloths. "One for each," he said from behind the tower of cloth. He began to distribute them. "Smalls and extra smalls."

Oz unfurled the thing that had been tossed to him; it was a black turtleneck, matching slacks, and beret.

"You might be Unadoptable," said Nico, "but tonight, you're part of the Chapeaux Noirs."

"Yes, sir," said Elsie reflexively. She wasn't sure that was how they referred to one another. It just seemed right. She gamely fished the beret from her pile of clothes and perched it on her head, slightly askew. A chill of pride went down her spine.

"A natural," said Nico, winking at her.

Elsie blushed; before long, the gathered Unadoptables had donned the outfits and made their transformation into junior saboteurs.

While Elsie turned to her fellow duct-rats, as their crew was going to be known, Rachel followed Nico across the room, where an assembly line of sorts had been organized: At one table, a group of men were unpacking what looked like black, opaque iron globes, the size of large snowballs, from wooden crates and were tossing them to a second table, where a powder was being poured into the globes' cavities with a funnel. A third table, just adjacent, continued this assembly line: There, a crew of men carefully threaded wicks into the globes and sealed them with wax. Nico whistled to one of the men at the third table and proffered his hands; a finished bomb was thrown to him, and he weighed it in like a baseball.

"How's this feel?" he asked, handing the thing to Rachel.

It was heavier than it looked, and she nearly dropped it when he set it in her hands. It was cold, too, and smelled of sulfur. She squared her shoulders, set her feet apart. "It feels good," she said.

Nico seemed unimpressed. "How far do you suppose you can throw it?"

She juggled the bomb between her hands a few times, gauging the weight. "I don't know," she said. "A little ways, I guess."

"Think you could hit that?" asked Nico, pointing to a pile of discarded flour sacks in the corner of the room. It was easily twenty feet away.

Rachel took a deep breath, gave a thoughtful smirk, and tossed the bomb as best she could, underhanded, as if she were throwing a softball in gym class. It tumbled to the cement floor several feet short of its mark.

"No, no, no," chided Nico. He grabbed the bomb and walked it back to her side. He modeled the proper form by bending his arm and holding the black orb at his neck. He bent his knees, somewhat comically, before extending his arm in slow motion from his shoulder. "Like that," he said. "The power all comes from your legs." He handed the bomb back to Rachel.

She hoisted it to her shoulder and tried again; this time, the thing landed with a dull thump in the middle of the pile of sacks.

"Nice!" said Nico, clapping. "Remember: from *les jambes*." He translated: "The legs, that is."

As Rachel walked to retrieve her practice projectile, a new voice sounded behind her: "And you'll need to double that distance. From here, you're still in the blast radius." She turned to see it was Jacques.

Rachel paled a little at the notion. "I'll work on it," she said.

"Good. *Bon*. Your life depends on it." Jacques then turned to Nico. "Hopefully she won't take out any of your fellow saboteurs."

It had been a sticking point between them, having Rachel on the bombing squad. Jacques had thought it was reckless enough to send children into the tower via the ductwork; it was another thing to actually employ an unseasoned teenager as a bomb thrower.

"*Elle peut le faire*, Jacques," said Nico, steely. "*Elle a besoin d'un peu de pratique, c'est tout.*"[1]

"*Nous n'avons pas le temps pour la pratique. Nous frappons ce soir.*"[2]

Rachel walked up to the men and stood, knowing they were saying something about her. Her ninth-grade French was not enough to unscramble the men's quick speech. She glared at the two of them, until one of them spoke in English:

"Well," said Nico as he faced Jacques defiantly. "I hope your own pet project, the madman, has pulled himself together enough to not get us all killed."

"He'll do. Oh, he'll do. And I'll be glad to be nearer to him than to any bomb-throwing teenyboppers."

Teenyboppers? thought Rachel. *Does anybody say that anymore?* She cleared her throat, hoping to get their attention, to no avail. They continued to argue like she wasn't even there.

"Listen, this is *your* big project, Jacques. This is the chip on *your* shoulder."

"Well, it's not quite happening the way I'd have liked it. You had to go and make a promise to a bunch of children, that's what's got this whole thing going, you know."

Rachel had had enough. She lifted the iron bomb to her neck, bent her knees and, recalling Nico's instructions, threw it easily forty feet

1. She can do it. She just needs a little practice.
2. We don't have time for practice. We strike tonight.

across the room, letting out a very unseemly grunt in the process. The unlit bomb landed with a loud clatter some ways down the hall that led from the room, and the sound seemed to bring all activity in the chamber to a state of sudden stasis.

"We're not *children*," said Rachel, suddenly aware she had the attention of the whole group. "And I'm not a *teenybopper*." She looked over to where the bomb had fallen and, having surprised herself, exclaimed, "That's pretty far!"

Nico smiled. He looked at Jacques. "See, comrade? She'll do just fine. And now we know: When the bombs need throwing, look to *les ados*."

The room returned to its former state of commotion; Rachel retrieved the bomb and continued practicing her throw against the pile of flour sacks. Before long, several other saboteurs, apparently having been put in mind of their own lack of practice, joined her, and a good-natured competition soon sprouted.

Over in the corner, by a stack of emptied crates labeled EXPLO-SIVES, sat a hunched figure, clad in a rumpled argyle sweater-vest, shuffling through a deck of white index cards. Like an immobile object in the midst of a hectic time-lapse video, he remained still, fixated solely on the cards in his hands, while the activity in the room spun around him. Elsie watched him for a time: the almost glacial pace of his reading, the way he mouthed the words of whatever had been written on the index cards. She broke away from her group of gabbing duct-rats and walked over to the man.

"Hello, Mr. Unthank," she said.

The man seemed not to have heard her; he continued to mumble to himself, reciting the words on the cards in a low murmur. She repeated herself.

"Mr. Unthank."

He paused and looked up at her. His eyes were wide and searching. He seemed to Elsie like a confused and scared animal.

"Do you remember me?" asked Elsie. "I'm Elsie Mehlberg."

He shook his head. "N-no," he said. "I d-don't know that I do, tra la."

"My parents went to Istanbul to look for my brother, who disappeared last year. They dropped me and my sister off at your orphanage. They're somewhere in Russia now, I think. You made us Unadoptable, which is funny because we were never supposed to be adopted in the first place." It felt good, this litany, this bit of autobiography Elsie was reciting.

Joffrey just stared at her, perplexed. Occasionally he sang "Tra la, tra lee" quietly while she spoke.

"You made us go into the Impassable Wilderness, Mr. Unthank. You put weird stuff in my sister's ears and you gave me some kind of pill. And then you sent us into that place. Without food or water or anything. Do you remember? We would've starved if we hadn't found the other Unadoptables there. Do you ever think of that, Mr. Unthank?"

The man continued to babble under her words; he shuffled the index cards in his hands nervously. Elsie thought she saw tears spring up in his eyes.

"But you know what, Mr. Unthank? I think you're really a good person, somewhere down there in your belly. I think you just made a lot of bad choices in your life. You sent us into the Impassable Wilderness for your own weird, greedy reason, but we made it out. We made it out and we're the better for it, too. I know more about myself now, I know that I have a special power that I didn't know I had. And wanna know something else?" Here, she knelt down so she was looking Unthank directly in the eye. "I think it's going to help me find my brother."

She waited for a response; none came.

"So there. For all your greediness, you only made me stronger. How does that make you feel?"

More mumbling, singing. A full, bulbous tear dripped down from his eyelid and ran down the end of his nose.

Elsie started to feel very sorry for the man. "You can make things better, Mr. Unthank. You can help us. You can help us get our friends back. You can stop being crazy just for a bit and stop crying and stop singing and do your part to help us. Do you think you could do that? And then, maybe. Maybe then we'd all just get a little closer to maybe forgiving you. What do you think of that, Mr. Unthank?"

The man nodded, tears now streaming down his cheeks. He'd stopped his mumbling. He was holding the index cards firmly in his hands; they were crinkling under the pressure. Elsie heard a voice sound from behind her: It was Jacques.

"Easy, Elsie," he said. "The man's under a lot of pressure. He's got a lot to get ready for."

"Sorry," said Elsie. "I just wanted to talk to him. He just seemed so sad."

Jacques nodded gravely, turning to Unthank. "How's the practice going?"

Unthank brought one freshly scrubbed knuckle to his eyes and proceeded to wipe it free of tears. A steely look of determination had emerged from somewhere, deep inside that lumpy sweater-vested frame of his, and he wrinkled his brow in concentration. He dropped the index cards to the ground and said, "I'm ready."

*

The little dish, the dish of her mother's, the little brass bowl on top of her dresser, now contained two things: a mottled eagle feather and a smooth white pebble. Zita placed this last thing in it as she settled in for the evening, with her father turning the damper down on the woodstove just outside her room and the light of the day's dimming sun having seeped away through the veil of trees.

She climbed into her bed and waited, listening for the gas man turning on the lamps on the street outside, for her father to pad softly down the hall toward his bedroom. She watched the mirror on her dresser, waited for the mist to come. She wanted to find out more about this Verdant Empress; she suspected that the spirit was not the one that was whispered about in the schoolyard, the one whose son had been murdered. She suspected that the stories got the details wrong. This was no ghost called forth from the time of the Ancients. This spirit was someone else. And she had an idea who it was.

The moment in Wildwood, when she'd stumbled onto the Plinth, all surrounded by the bed of ivy, lingered in her mind. She'd felt something there, a kind of electricity running through the forest that seemed to connect her and the pebble to that white, fluted pedestal. It had confirmed her suspicions, that she was not simply calling some long-sleeping specter back from the dead for a kind of sideshow séance. She was implicated in something much bigger. It had been the eagle, the one that had kindly donated the first of her requested items, that had planted the seed: What *did* this thing want from the land of the living?

The night descended; Zita waited.

The moon climbed in a slow, shallow curve across the horizon; it shone into her bedroom window.

She must've dozed off, there in her bed, because the very next moment she opened her eyes and heard the clock in the hall chime midnight, and she'd toppled sidelong into her pillow. She pulled herself upright and smoothed back her hair—for what, she didn't know. For some reason, tonight she wanted to make herself presentable to the spirit. She wanted to be seen.

The clock ticked in the hall; her father snored in his bed. The mist came and clouded the glass. Zita's heart rate quickened.

GOOD, wrote the spirit.

"I know who you are," said Zita.

The glass remained unchanged.

"You're the old Governess. The one whose kid died. The one who went crazy."

The glass clouded again. Zita waited. Still: nothing.

"Is that right? Is that you?"

A breeze rippled through the room; she could feel the chill.

Zita spoke again: "It's okay. I'll still get the things for you. I just wanted to say that I know who you are. I know what happened to you. And that I guess I understand." She felt calmed, like she was speaking to an old friend. The words came quickly. "My dad told me about you. I wasn't even born yet. He said you were a great woman. He said that you went through the worst thing that anyone could ever go through, that you lost your son. He said that you maybe were a little extreme, afterward, but it was to be expected and that any parent of a child would understand. That's what he said."

Quiet; fog on the mirror.

"And while I'm not a parent of a kid, I'm just a teenager, I think I kind of get it." She paused here, drumming up the courage to say the next words. "The opposite happened to me. My mom died. About seven months ago now." She laughed a little, saying, "Funny. I haven't really talked to anyone about it. You're the first person—I mean, whatever you are. She was really sweet, my mom. She liked playing guitar and gardening. She was a really good singer, too. She was just a good person, you know? Just good. And then she got sick and she died. Just like that. Like, you think only bad people get punished and have to die in awful ways, but she was really good, my mom, and she just slipped away. So fast. Like, you'd never in a million years imagine that that sort of thing could happen to you and then it does and your whole world is just crushed, right?"

The mirror gave no response.

"I'm just saying, I know how you feel. I know why you did what you did. And maybe in some way my helping you is me just trying to help myself, you know? Does that even make any sense?"

A breeze rustled the curtains. The word *YES* scrawled across the mirror's glass.

Zita beamed. "You hear me! So is that you, the old Governess?"

YES.

"What's your name?"

The glass fogged. Then, the sound of a finger against a windowpane as *ALEXANDRA* appeared on the mirror.

"Right! Wow," said Zita. "Well, I'm glad we got that cleared up. Just so we know. Who we are. You're Alexandra, and you lost your son. I'm Zita, and I lost my mother. So we're a pretty good team, don't you think?"

She didn't wait for a response; instead, she leapt up from her bed and walked to the bowl on the dresser, her eyes glued to the foggy mirror with the scrawled words on it. "Okay," she said. "What's next?"

The words appeared, written in the fog by the spectral finger of the deceased Dowager Governess, and Zita blanched to see them, though now that she knew the identity of the spirit, it seemed to make a kind of cold, eerie sense. What's more, she felt like she'd found a new well of sympathy for the woman, deep in her heart, and she understood. Now she understood.

CHAPTER 15

The Sway of the Blighted Tree

"Eat," the Elder Caliph repeated. "And be free."

More people had arrived; the line had grown so long that it snaked away from the Blighted Tree like a long, rippling ribbon. Prue recognized more faces in the crowd: the Spokes who had carried the rickshaw when she'd first arrived, the girl who'd given her flowers when she first stepped into the Mansion. They all stood quietly and obediently, one behind the other, waiting for their time to be fed the strange substance by the hooded Caliph. The ever-present

HUM continued unabated in Prue's mind, and her vision swam as she teetered by the tree and tried valiantly to reconstitute her thoughts. The Elder Caliph, Elgen, had taken the spoon of Spongiform from the acolyte and was holding it some few inches from Prue's lips.

"Esben," murmured Prue. "I need to get to Esben."

"Esben is safe," said Elgen. "He's in good hands."

This seemed to shake Prue from her swoon. "He's hidden. You don't know where he is."

The man was growing impatient. The fungi quivered on the proffered spoon; it was a glowing brownish green. "As we speak, your friend Esben is being fetched and brought here. Soon he will be united with his old compatriot, Carol, and the reconstruction of the mechanical boy will commence. We've achieved your directive, Prue. We've done it together."

"No!" shouted Prue, deeply shaken. "That's not how it was supposed to happen!" The *HUM* grew louder; a shimmering rainbowlike aura had overtaken the margins of her vision. She wasn't sure what was happening; she was feeling the world giving way.

"It's all foretold, Prue. It was all written, long before you arrived. See: Even now, your friend the badger is here for the fungal communion."

Sure enough: There was Neil, shipped to the front of the line, preparing to receive his dose of Spongiform.

"We are the eyes and ears of this forest, Prue. No action goes unnoticed. Surely you didn't think we wouldn't follow you, wouldn't want to find out where you were keeping your ursine treasure."

Prue stared wildly at the badger; he seemed oblivious to her presence, so great was his desire to receive the substance being fed him. "This can't be happening. This isn't happening. I must be dreaming. This isn't real." The words came flowing from Prue's mouth; she couldn't shake the *HUM*, the incessant ticking from the surrounding acolytes. The ticking grew louder as she felt two figures come up behind her and hold her shoulders, hard.

The Elder Caliph persisted, "Your life, one way or another, is forfeit, Prue. Your mission is finished. Your sentence had already been written; think of this as a commutation of that sentence. In exchange for a lifelong devotion to the birthing of the One Tree. Yes: The Mansion has already turned against you. They did the moment you started speaking that hogwash about reviving the 'true heir.' Do you think for a moment that they wouldn't want to defend their positions? Do you think for a moment that your black magic interests wouldn't strike fear in their hearts? Feed on the Blight and save yourself from a fate worse than death." Elgen held the spoon to her mouth. She could feel the cold moistness of the Spongiform touching her upper lip. "Come now, Prue. Just eat it."

PLEASE, thought Prue, and she felt the grass below her feet spring to life. It wrapped around the feet of the Elder Caliph, and he choked back a shout of surprise. He merely needed to look down

251

at his ankles for the grass to release its hold, though; new tendrils sprouted below Prue's feet, and suddenly she realized that it was her feet, instead, that were now tied to the ground.

"Foolish," said Elgen. "You have no power here."

He nodded to one of the acolytes at her side, and she felt fingers curling around her neck, under her jawbone. She felt her mouth forced open. The ticking emanating from her captor was jarring in its volume. She strained to see his face; it was covered in a silver mask.

"Who are you?" she managed. His grip tightened; her mouth was opened wide now. The fungi made its way into her opened lips; she felt the cold of the spoon on her tongue.

Elgen answered for her: "They are the voice of the Wood, Prue. The sons and daughters of the forest. The midwives of the new world. And now you will join them."

Prue let her body go slack; her jaw slid open to receive the Spongiform.

She felt the hands at her jaw loosen their pressure. The bodies at either side of her seemed to relax, assured of their subject's surrender.

And that was when she acted.

The weird fungus had barely touched her tongue, an acrid, bitter flavor spreading out through her taste buds, when she spat it out with all the power she could muster. It exploded into little pieces and spackled the gold mirrored mask of the Elder Caliph before her. Simultaneously she jabbed her elbow as hard as she could into the stomach of the acolyte to her left and felt his body crumple at the waist. Pivoting to her right, she faced her second captor and, despite a prevailing instinct to not hit anybody, let alone someone wearing a mask that looked decidedly *hard*, she seized her right hand into a taut fist and slammed it into the acolyte's masked face.

The mask, seemingly made of crystal, shattered.

The face beneath was revealed.

"Brendan?" she managed, completely shocked. The red beard, the quiet eyes, the tribal tattoo on his forehead. It was all there.

Whatever energy, whatever momentum she'd collected in her adrenaline-fueled surprise attack on the Caliphs of the Synod was gone in that moment. She was floored by shock and despair. Her hand, aching from the strike, fell to her side. The *HUM* was every-where. She stared into the Bandit King's eyes in disbelief, trying to find her old friend somewhere in there. His eyes were still, almost lifeless. The ticking seemed to grow from his eye sockets, from his nostrils, and it soon became the only thing she could hear.

Until another voice spoke. "Your chance has come and gone." It was Elgen. He spoke now to a mob of acolytes who'd arrived at the scene of the scuffle. "Get her on a ship," he said, wiping the bits of Spongiform from his mask. "Let her rot on the Crag."

Prue, in despair, let her body surrender completely, and she was pushed rudely away from the congregation at the Blighted Tree. Every possible iteration of the previous year's events was flowing through her mind as the *HUM* receded and she stumbled in the captivity of the two acolytes down the sloping hill toward a line of trees. She found herself numbly mumbling to herself, saying things like, "Brendan. Here. The Synod. How *could* this?" She looked up at her captors: the masked acolytes. "Who are you?" she asked. They did not answer.

❧

The illumination of the line of torches in the meadow had faded away; a group of men holding lanterns met the group of Caliphs and their prisoner at the tree line at the far side of the meadow. The men seemed shocked to see it was Prue.

"This is the one? The one for the Crag?" asked a bearded man in a dark mackintosh.

The acolyte at her side said nothing; she was pushed forward into the arms of the group of men. They held her fast, each one looking at the others in confusion. Prue shook herself from her reverie and said to them, "This is a terrible mistake. The Synod, they're poisoning people. All the acolytes, they've been drugged!"

The men looked back and forth between Prue and the acolytes, drawn between two resisting forces. In the end, the more powerful won out.

"Bind her wrists, men," said the bearded man. "Get her down to the ship." His tone was sorrowful, surrendering.

"NO!" shouted Prue wildly. Tears were now streaming down her face. "I need to get to Esben!"

"Shhh, Maiden," said the man at her right arm. "Don't make it worse for yourself."

They marched her into the trees, down a well-worn and rutted path. A thick cord had been tied quickly around her wrists, and the tough material bit into her skin. The men smelled of sweat and pitch; Prue noticed they each wore the same little black stocking cap, the same weathered mackintosh; the thick, waxed material of the coats reached down to their knees. They seemed to be fully bearded, to a man. "Where are you taking me?" asked Prue, when she'd gathered her senses.

"I'm very sorry it's turned out like this, Maiden," said one of the men. "But it's for the good of all."

"What ship? What ship are you taking me to?"

"The *Jolly Crescent*, Maiden," said another man. "She's in dock now. Won't be long. Best to just be quiet. Don't put up a fuss."

Prue frowned and watched the road ahead of her; with her hands shackled behind her, she could feel her shoulders smarting in their sockets. She tried to relax, to focus on something other than the pain her rope manacles were causing her. She looked to the vegetation surrounding the path and began to *speak*.

WHIP, she thought.

A branch above their heads bowed a little, but soon shot back into place. That ever-present ticking noise, the one coming from the acolytes, had suddenly risen in a crescendo, and she looked behind her to see that they were being closely followed by a group of hooded, masked Caliphs. She tried again: willing her thoughts to the surrounding woods in hopes that some assistance might be given, the way that she had briefly ensnared the shape-shifting Darla Thennis when they had faced off in the refuse heap. Still, nothing. She was being blocked somehow.

She tried another angle: "You know they're cutting peoples' heads off for stuff like this. I mean, I'm the Bicycle Maiden. I'm the face of the revolution."

This got no response. The men's faces were steely and quiet.

"Aren't you afraid? I could raise an army! I could have all of you, each one, up against the wall in the bat of an eyelash." The color was rising in her face, she could feel it. She was speaking from some deeply recessed well; she was channeling all her anger into her voice.

"Times have changed," said one of the men dolefully. "It's the Synod, now, that everyone is looking to."

She jerked her head over her shoulder, looking at the several Caliphs who were following them down the rocky path. "You!" she shouted. "Who are you? Are you bandits? Are you Wildwood bandits?" She focused on them, hearing the ticking noise, trying to deduce some kind of language or syntax from the sound. The Caliphs did not respond. Their mirrored face masks glinted in the low light.

They walked for many hours, following a maze of paths that led down a steep hillside and through the thick of the trees. After a time, a light could be seen glimmering through the woods: Prue saw that it was the city lights of Portland, of the Outside. They were nearing the Periphery, the edge of the Wood. The path they were following snaked along the steep bank of a rushing creek that, some many yards down the hill, opened up into a watery inlet, surrounded by a thick weft of trees. In this inlet was anchored a very large and very old-looking sailing ship, its bevy of massive sails sitting dormant in the still air.

It looked to Prue like the ship had been swept ashore from some long-gone century, something that would be more at home battling Nelson's tall ships at Trafalgar than sitting dockside in a quaint, twenty-first-century Pacific Northwest river inlet. A moon-woman, half flaxen-haired lady and half crescent moon, was the ship's figurehead, and the shutters and eaves of the vessel's many windows were painted bright blue. The ship's central mast reached easily as high as the closest Douglas fir tree, and a veritable spider's web of ropes and rigging stretched down from its spire to the dark decks below.

Several fellow mariners came rushing up from the dock when they saw Prue and her captors approach. "What's going on?" shouted one. "Who's this?"

"Our instructions," said one of the men holding Prue, "are to bring this one to the Crag."

Soon, a crowd of seamen had gathered to greet the newcomers.

"Ain't that the Bicycle Maiden?" said one.

"Aye, 'tis," confirmed one of the men at Prue's side. "She's been indicted."

Before any of the men had a chance to speak their disbelief, they saw the hooded Caliphs appear from behind the group. It was all the proof they needed that the sentence was lawful. They cowed, visibly, under the presence of the masked men. A man with a blond, wiry beard and a black visored cap came forward. The other men seemed to step aside in deference to him, and he spoke with an uncompromising authority: "This is the one?"

One of the Caliphs nodded solemnly.

"Very well," said the man. "Let's get her onboard." He looked at Prue and said, "I'm very sorry this has to be the way, miss. I'll try to make your passage as comfortable as I can, given the circumstances. My name is Captain Shtiva. The *Jolly Crescent* is my ship. Long live the revolution." He paused and glanced at the Synod members present. "And long live the spirit of the Blighted Tree."

"Where are you taking me?" asked Prue. She still wasn't entirely clear what was happening to her. "What have I done?"

The man, Captain Shtiva, frowned. "You are an enemy of the state. I have written authority from the Interim Governor-Regent-elect to carry you to your permanent incarceration on the Crag." He held up a long and wide envelope, its seal freshly broken. "In the event of your not capitulating to the demands of the Synod."

"Enemy of the state?" gasped Prue breathlessly. "I'm the hero of the state! They're poisoning the people—they're feeding them that stuff—on the tree! It's changing them! I saw the Bandit King—the Wildwood Bandit King—behind one of those masks! I think there may be more bandits among them! Something very terrible is happening, Captain. I need to stop it. Please, let me go! I have orders from the Council Tree. I have to rebuild the prince. I have to find the makers to reanimate the half-dead prince!" The words now were flowing from her mouth in jerky rivulets. She could feel the spittle flying from her lips.

The captain watched her with a look of abject pity on his face. Her entreaties seemed to make no dent in his resoluteness; if anything, her every word seemed to erode whatever pity he had stored up. He seemed to look at her as if she were speaking a foreign language. "Get her onboard," he said finally. "There's a berth for her in the lower hold. Make sure she's locked up tight."

The men began to hustle Prue away when the captain turned and said, "But keep her safe. I don't want any harm done in the process. I will not have my hands bloodied further. Is that clear?"

The men murmured their understanding; Prue was led down the path to the bottom of the bank, where a worn dock spread out from the ground into the placid waters of the inlet. The sailors holding her tied hands sniffed at the air; one said, "No mist. How we gonna get to sea?"

"Let the captain manage that," another said. "Let's get this one belowdecks."

Lanterns, hanging from the stout wooden pilings along the dockside, lit the way as Prue was led toward the awaiting ship. She could see the winking lights of the Industrial Wastes just beyond the shade of the trees that marked the boundary between the Wood and the Outside; she assumed the Periphery, that magic ribbon that served as the protective shield around the so-called Impassable Wilderness, was somewhere in her vision, invisible.

The ship swayed as they stepped onto the deck; a crowd of like-dressed sailors stood, mopping the boards, coiling rope, shouldering wooden crates. Prue was escorted toward an opening in the floor; arriving there, she was instructed to climb down a stepladder. A smell of stale beer and moldy cheese attacked her senses as she arrived at the rough wood floor of the belowdecks. Down a crowded passageway she was led to a door made of iron bars, which opened onto a small, closetlike hold. A cot and a tin pail were the room's only furnishings. A porthole above the cot, its glass pane hatch-marked with iron bands, looked out onto the dark harbor.

Something cold was pressed to her wrists; her bonds fell away and her hands were freed. She rubbed at the sore, reddened welts the ropes had left. Her captors seemed unconcerned that she would attempt any kind of escape.

"Make yerself at home," one said. "It's a long journey."

"Where are we going?" asked Prue. To her recollection, there wasn't any kind of inland sea in the Wood; if her direction sense was not failing her, they would be plying the waters of the Willamette River.

"To th' Crag," said the other.

"What's that?" When she sensed they were not about to tell her, she tried on her best twelve-year-old-girl pleading voice: "Don't I have, like, a right to know?"

The two sailors looked at each other uncertainly before one said, "I'll tell you as much, seein' as how you're the Bicycle Maiden. I don't cotton to what they're doin' to you here, but I'm just under orders, right? You've been sentenced to the Crag. It's a rock out in the ocean. It's a hard, barren place. There ain't no escapin' it." He looked saddened by this description. "I expect you'll live out yer days there, miss."

Prue gasped. "What?"

The man shrugged. "Orders, miss."

"For the good of the revolution," said the other.

The door was closed in her face, and Prue felt her knees buckle out from under her; she caught herself on the lip of the cot and sat down heavily, her head in her hands, and began to cry. Loud, heaving sobs. They seemed to bucket up from the deepest wells of her gut.

Voices could be heard through the locked door. "Shame, what they're doing," said one sailor to another. "A shame."

"Well, we ain't going anywhere till we got a mist."

"It'll come. Calling for it tonight."

"Believe it when I see it. C'mon."

Footsteps trundled up the stepladder; the hatch slammed noisily down behind them. Prue was alone in the hold of the ship. She looked over her shoulder at the dark porthole. Standing on the thin mattress, she peered out the dirty window to watch the lantern light reflected against the water of the placid inlet.

Time passed, slowly.

Far off, the stars were beginning to be blotted out by an approaching fog. Prue turned her face away from the gray window and stared at her small prison cell. She thought about what she'd done, what had transpired to this point; she thought about the great mess she'd caused. She wondered, as people often do when faced with the very real consideration that all their plans have failed miserably, how it could be possible that she could go so wrong. Why had the tree picked her? Why had she received this communication? Certainly, there were people more qualified for the job of wrangling two missing machinists from exile to re-create a robotic boy prince in the wake of a popular revolution and an aggressive religious takeover.

The hatch on the above-decks opened, and a figure moved silently down the ladder. Prue looked over to see that it was one of the Caliphs, the silver-masked Mystics, come to hold vigil.

"Hi," said Prue.

The Caliph didn't respond. Instead he sat down on a chest directly across from the barred door of her cell. Straightening his shoulders, he set his hands calmly on his robed knees and stared straight ahead, his mask glinting in the low candlelight. The ticking noise sounded in Prue's ears, like a winding clock.

"What's your name?" tried Prue again. "Are you one of the Wildwood bandits? Jack? Eamon?"

Nothing.

"Right, vow of silence." Prue crossed her arms and stared at her feet, at the tattered canvas of her Keds.

The ship bucked in the current of the river; the boards moaned under the pressure, and Prue could hear shouting from the sailors on deck. The hatch door opened suddenly and a voice called in: "Underway!"

The Caliph on the chest did not move; he only stared straight ahead.

The hatch door closed and Prue lay back on her cot, staring at the ceiling. The ticking was there, in her mind, sounding to her from some strange source inside the Caliph.

She waited. The night poured on, like a thick syrup. Somewhere, distantly, an explosion sounded.

CHAPTER 16

The Undisputed Therapeutic
Benefits of Singing

It was not often that Desdemona Mudrak missed the Ukraine. To her, memories of that place conjured up dusty, potholed roads, disused warehouses, and brusque state employees. They brought to mind bad television, barely received by throwback TV sets in cold living rooms, and empty shelves in grocery stores. She'd grown up fairly well off, by former Soviet satellite standards, the only daughter of a self-employed florist and his wife. Her mother spent summers busily canning whatever food they produced at their modest dacha in the country and storing it in the two refrigerators that occupied their small kitchen.

But looking out over the Industrial Wastes, here in liberated, wealthy America, she found herself longing for the days of her childhood in Kiev. The smokestacks and chemical silos that she was now looking over dwarfed, by grimness standards, any similar landscape she imagined from her childhood; it seemed ironic to her that she should come here to escape the bleakness of her home country, only to arrive in a land of such emptiness as to make the industrial squalor of the world she'd left look like Disneyland. And it was all on display, every blinking light and pall of smoke, from the top floor of Titan Tower, where Desdemona was standing, etching a sad face on the windowpane with her finger.

"Whatcha doin' there, honey?" asked Brad Wigman, sitting at his desk and absently shuffling through the day's progress reports.

"Nothing," she replied. "I am to doing nothing."

"Well, why don't you *to fetch* me a cup of coffee? I've got my hands full with these reports."

Desdemona frowned; it was an unfortunate downside of being at the mercy of the Chief Titan, now that her home and business had been destroyed and her boyfriend was completely missing in action, presumed insane: She was little more than a personal assistant to Bradley Wigman, Titan of Shipping. "You have secretary for such things," said Desdemona.

"It's late, Dessie," said Wigman. "She's got a home to go to. A job she needs to rest up for. Which is more than you could say for some people in this room." He looked up, scanning the large, windowed office. "I'm only seeing the two of us in here. And *I* have a job. And a home."

Desdemona rolled her eyes and stalked away from the window. As she passed the bookcase on the north wall, she ran her hand along the fake spines that populated its shelves. She knew what the folly hid: a secret room, a panic room—the creation of a powerful and paranoid man. Which was understandable, considering the rise in industrial sabotage the Wastes had experienced over the last several months. The man couldn't be too careful. However, at present, the room was performing an altogether different function. "Shall I bring the captives some drinking or food?"

"Sure," he said. "While you're at it. I think there's some snack mix in the break room. And they'll likely need more water."

"Consider it achieved," said Desdemona. She wandered through the maze of decorative pedestals in the large space, each displaying some sort of prize or commemorative statuette honoring the Chief Titan. Opening the gigantic brass doors at the far end of the room took some doing, for a woman of Desdemona's frame, but soon she was out in the lobby, making her way toward the small alcove that served as the break room for the staff. She nodded to the two hulking stevedores who stood guard at the main elevator doors. She poured a bowlful of snack mix, grabbed a few bottles of water (emblazoned, strangely, with Mr. Wigman's chin-dominant and smiling face) and a bottle of Lemony Zip for herself. She sipped at the soda while the espresso machine gurgled its brackish liquid into a small cup.

Her arms full, she delivered the coffee to Mr. Wigman, who received it with barely a mumble. Without looking up from his papers, Brad shot the coffee back with a jerk of his head and held out the emptied cup to Desdemona. She took it with an annoyed frown and set it on the desk. Wigman seemed not to notice. Then she was off to the fake bookcase. She scanned the titles on the shelf, the very picture of an eager bibliophile, until she found the one she was looking for: Virginia Woolf's *A Room of One's Own*. She hooked her finger to the top of the spine, and pulling it back, she heard a loud click and a whirring noise. The bookcase rolled sideways, by an unseen mechanism, to reveal a small, pale-green room with two cowering individuals inside.

"Hello," said Desdemona. "I've broughten you some snack mix."

The old man barely moved; his shoulders were hunched over as he sat in his plastic chair, and his unseeing wooden eyes, which had struck Desdemona as decidedly creepy the first time she'd seen them, stared at the floor. Across from him sat the girl, Martha. She was holding a book in her hands. She nodded to Desdemona wearily as if to say, *Whatever.*

Desdemona set the bowl of snack mix and the two bottles of water on the floor. "What is it you are reading now?" she asked. She'd tried this before, to make conversation with the two prisoners, to varying degrees of success. In a sense, they'd been housemates these last few months: Desdemona had been occupying one of the temporary housing units on the lower floors. She, too, was homeless, in a manner of speaking. And so, she'd tried to remain friendly in her role as guardian to the two captives—though she suspected it was a doomed task.

Martha glared at her. She still wore the goggles on her forehead, despite her changed circumstances. Desdemona suspected it was some form of mental tic.

"What do you care?" said the girl.

"Who is it?" asked the old man, Carol, apparently having woken from some sort of trance.

"Who do you think?" said Martha.

Desdemona gamely played up her thick Slavic accent: "Yeess, hoo to think it eeez?"

"Oh," said Carol. "Hello. You've interrupted our reading."

"And I was only inquiring what the book it is you are reading, is all," said Desdemona. "And bringing you sustenance, which is a thing to thank a person for, I think."

"*The Count of Monte Cristo*, actually," said Carol.

"Ah," said Desdemona. "How fitting."

"And thanks but no thanks for the *snack mix*," said Martha.

Desdemona glared at the little upstart. Even in the orphanage, the young Asian girl had always rubbed her the wrong way. Too precocious for her own good.

"And we'll be done soon with this book," continued the little girl. "I don't suppose you got my list, did you?"

"Yes, yes," said Desdemona. "I did get the list. *War and Peace. Lord of Rings. Encyclopedia Britannica, complete.* It appears you have little positive outlook on your time in captivity."

"Should we?" asked Martha, a sneer on her face.

Desdemona glanced over her shoulder at the man at the desk. "Mr. Wigman say that man will come for you soon."

"Oh, great. Then what?"

The old man said nothing. He said nothing because he knew precisely what was next. Roger Swindon had told him when he and the girl had first been deposited in their jail cell. He was to be taken back to *that place*. Back to the Wood. And there forced to re-create the most difficult and challenging project of his entire life, the thing that had changed his life so drastically: It had both given him a new insight into the mechanics of life itself and, in turn, robbed him of his ability to see. He was to be reunited with his old partner, Esben Clampett, and together they were to take on this retreading of their old work. For what? He couldn't imagine. His mind reeled at the thought of his being a pawn yet again to a ruthless and clinically insane government power; if they had taken his eyes and his compatriot's hands so that they might never rebuild, alone, the thing they had created, what would they possibly do to them this time, after the miraculous work was done? And where would they send them? In what magic wasteland could they expect to spend the rest of their days?

They needed only to find Esben, Roger had said that. And then it was only a matter of time.

"That's for Mr. Wigman to decide," answered Desdemona. "Now, eat your snack mix." With that, she pressed a button on the side of the door and the panel slid back into place, concealing the two of them once again behind the bookcase.

"The prisoners," she said, walking back over to Wigman's desk, "are asking about when Roger will return."

This made Brad look up. "Soon," he said.

"How is it you know?"

"He told me they had a good lead on wherever this other guy is."

"If he has this good lead, why not just give him the blind man? They are now long time in that room."

Brad glared up at the woman. "Do you think I'm that thick, Dessie? I didn't get to where I am today just bending over backward for any schmuck who walks in the door. I know how to *leverage my advantage*. Unlike your old boyfriend."

Desdemona seemed to flinch at the mention of Joffrey Unthank, and Wigman softened his tone slightly, continuing, "Listen, we're all friends here. Business partners. But friends don't get the deals. He says he's got the key to unlocking whatever is going on in the Impassable Wilderness. He says he's got access. And he says that whoever can get these two guys together, they'll be like the kings of this place. Well, Dessie, I don't know about you, but when one of those guys gets caught in *my* territory, I'm not going to just turn him over with a please and a thank you. No, sir. I've got a horse in this race. And I intend to see him finishing first. No place or show for Bradley Wigman here." He cleared his throat. "As soon as I see this Esben Clampett character, then we'll talk about turning over the blind man."

"I see," said Desdemona. She was about to dig deeper, to find out what the fate of the little girl would be, when her thoughts were interrupted by a knock at the large brass doors.

Wigman looked up from his desk. He glanced at the digital clock on the wall: nine thirty p.m. It was too late for any Quartet-related business. He raised his eyebrow at Desdemona and smiled. "See?" he said. "Asketh and you shall receiveth."

Brad Wigman pushed his square-shouldered frame away from the desk and rose, striding across the carpeted floor of the top-floor office with the kind of presence of mind that only exists in high-powered executives. He reached the door in no time; throwing it open with an almost inhuman strength, he found himself face-to-face with himself.

Or rather, his own face, reflected back to him, surrounded in a dark-gray cowl.

He blinked twice, confused, before realizing that he was only seeing himself reflected in the gold mirrored mask that this strange visitor was wearing.

"What in the devil?" sputtered Wigman, shocked. "Who are you and how did you get in here?"

The figure looked confused for a second, his head cocked sideways. He breathed an understanding "Ah," before lifting a hand and removing the mask from his head. "Sorry," he said. "I forgot about the outfit. I had to get here fast."

"Jesus, Roger," said Wigman. "You really gave me a scare."

Roger Swindon, clad in a gray robe and gray cowl, pulled a handkerchief from some unseen pocket in the robe and mopped his face of perspiration before setting a little silver pince-nez on the bridge of his nose. "There we are," he said. He breathed a sigh, clearly relieved to be free of the mask. "Can I come in?"

"We were just talking about you, Roger, my boy," said Wigman,

273

gamely waving the way forward. "We were beginning to wonder when you'd show up."

"Good news, good news, my friend," said Roger as he walked briskly across the office floor toward the bookcase. "I have our second maker. The circle is complete. The construction can begin."

Wigman trotted to keep up with the man. "Well, that's fantastic news. Really great, Roger. Now, we'll just need to . . ."

But Roger was not listening; instead he was searching the bookshelves for the latch to operate the panel. Wigman, catching up, slid between him and the bookcase. "Hold up, there, Roger, m'friend."

Roger paused and glared at Wigman. "Yes?"

"Where is this guy, this Esben?" He looked around the room. "I don't see that you brought him with you."

"No, I didn't *bring him with me*," responded Roger, sounding annoyed. "What a ridiculous idea. He's safe in the Wood, the Impassable Wilderness, where he will soon be reunited with his old partner and our work will commence. Now: Which is the book that opens the door?"

Wigman laughed. "Which book. That's rich. As far as I'm concerned, nothing's changed here. As far as I'm concerned, you still don't have your guy. I'm not turning over *anyone* until I'm assured of my position here, Roger. And while we're at it, what's with the getup?" He flicked his finger under a fold in Roger's robe.

"Nothing," said Roger. "None of your concern." He seemed

thrown by Wigman's obstructionism. "Listen, the deal remains the same. You can have your access—exclusive ties to the Wood. You will have control over a percentage of—"

"Blah, blah, blah," said Wigman, sock-puppeting his hand. "That's just talk. Anything that goes down, any kind of cog that's going to be made, has to happen right here, in plain sight. Do you hear me? That was the deal."

Roger massaged his forehead, his exasperation shining through. "Just . . . trust me on this, Mr. Wigman. Between business partners."

"Trust you? Trust you? Do you think I got to where I am today by just willy-nilly trusting anyone who had the great fortune to call me, Bradley Wigman, a *business partner*? No! I didn't get Industrialist of the Year *three years in a row* from *Tax Bracket* magazine because I am a trusting soul. I didn't become the godfather to not three, but *four* children of Portland's esteemed mayors because I believe in human goodness. I got to where I am because I am ruthless, Roger. And I don't think I'll be stopping now, thank you very much."

Roger had no response. He backed away from the bookcase and sized up his opponent. Wigman lifted his dimpled chin defiantly. Desdemona, by the desk, watched the standoff with bated breath. Neither man spoke nor moved a muscle. The awkwardness was terrible, all-consuming, and Desdemona shifted uncomfortably in her high heels, trying to think of something to say that might dispel the tension. Thankfully, in the end, she didn't have to think of anything, because something presented itself that did the job fairly organically, snapping both of the men out of their current states of agitation.

It was the buzzer on the intercom.

Wigman looked at Desdemona. "Get that?"

Desdemona pushed the button on Brad's desk, and a voice chirped through the speaker. "Mr. Wigman, sir?"

"Yes?" called Wigman; his eyes remained fixed on Roger.

"Someone to see you, sir. At the front gate."

One of Wigman's eyebrows broke away and intrepidly scaled his forehead. "Who?" he barked, annoyed.

A pause. "It's the Machine Parts Titan, sir." Another pause. "Sir, it's Joffrey Unthank."

Desdemona felt her face flush; Brad glowered. He glanced over at the intercom. He nodded to Desdemona, who depressed the talk button while he spoke. "Tell him it's late. Tell him to come back tomorrow."

There was a pause; Desdemona let go of the button. She looked at Brad imploringly. "He might be hurt, Bradley. He's been missing for these months!"

"Joffrey Unthank means nothing to me now, Dessie," said Wigman. "He should mean less to you. He ran that factory into the ground; he allowed a rebellion to happen on his watch."

"Please," implored Desdemona.

"All he wants is to horn back in on this deal. And if you think for a moment I'm going to send the welcome wagon, you don't know Bradley Wigman," said Wigman, referring to himself in the third person, which was something he did occasionally.

The intercom buzzed again; Desdemona answered. "Yes?"

Bzzz. "He says it really can't wait."

Desdemona, dredging from the depths every last reserve of actorly charisma, fixed Wigman with a look that both scorned and pleaded. "Please," she whispered.

Brad swore under his breath and shouted, "Let him in, but don't send him up. Keep him in the lobby. I'll meet him there." He wagged a finger at Roger and said, "You stay put. Dessie, keep an eye on this one. I don't trust him as far as I can throw him. Though considering what I'm benching these days, I could probably throw him pretty far. So that's a bad analogy. What I mean to say is: Don't let him out of your sight."

"Yes, Mr. Wigman," said Desdemona. "Thank you, Mr. Wigman."

The Chief Titan spun around on the heels of his tasseled loafers and strode out of the room, with purpose.

Desdemona turned back to look at Roger, who had begun absently browsing the titles on the bookshelf.

"Don't even think about it," said Desdemona.

🌿

Smile.

This was the word that Joffrey Unthank created in his mind as a beacon. It was the thing that harnessed him to the rocky shores of his own sanity, his own loose grip on the reality that had been swirling around him, somewhat amorphously, for the past several months.

Smile.

Simple, really, when you thought about it. Which he did a lot.

He'd braved a cold winter, wandering the Industrial Wastes in little more than an argyle sweater-vest and a tattered overcoat. He'd slept in culverts and had his toes nibbled clean by rats; he'd escaped wandering bands of feral dogs and had even befriended one, named Jasper, and the two of them had had a few spectacular adventures before Jasper vanished one morning over breakfast and it dawned on Unthank that the dog had, in fact, been a hallucination the whole time.

Even in the face of this unspeakable (and somewhat jarring) tragedy, Unthank remembered to *Smile.*

And *Sing.*

But singing was not supposed to happen now; that's what Jack had said. Except his name wasn't Jack anymore, was it? It was Jacques now. His old fellow Titan, his fellow fallen Titan. He'd liked Jack very much, back when he was Jack; they'd both been born to important families in their respective Divisions. They'd both taken a kind of preternatural shine to their respective responsibilities, and where other children of Titans squirmed uncomfortably in the shackles of their parents' expectations, Joffrey and Jack had worn them like shining crowns. And when Jack fell, when he was shunned and his Division destroyed, Joffrey felt awfully sorry for his old friend. Not that he could afford to say anything to that effect—Wigman would've ostracized any sympathizer. But Joffrey always loved Jack. Always trusted him.

And so he trusted him when he told Joffrey not to *Sing*.

But he could still *Smile*.

Which was what he was doing now, while the linebacker-like stevedore pressed his stubby finger into the telecom at the front gate of the looming Titan Tower and announced that Joffrey Unthank, former Machine Parts Titan, had returned.

Smile.

A second stevedore stood on the other side of the gate, watching Joffrey closely. He felt studied, there, in the brilliant shine of the klieg lights, a specimen under a microscope. He suddenly felt the urge to sing, something he'd often done in his few months in the wilderness, in his mental wilderness, to comfort himself. But he knew—Jacques had told him—that it was very important that he not sing. That singing, somehow, would give away his disguise. And what was he disguised as? Himself. Shouldn't his disguise be improved if he were to sing, just to hum a few times? Wasn't that being himself more? Wasn't *not* singing betraying his true self?

The stevedore at the intercom walked over to him and said, "He says he's busy. He says come back tomorrow."

Sing.

Don't sing, he countered. That's what Jacques said. The role he was playing was not himself, but a version of himself. A long-gone version of himself. The himself who had perished in the factory fire, when the orphans broke the windows and destroyed the machines. The children. Those children, who deserved his thanks and forgiveness. They allowed the chrysalis to open, to let the real Joffrey Unthank uncoil and fly.

"It's very important," said Unthank. *Tra la.* "Could you please tell him that I need to see him now? It really can't wait." *Tra lee.*

Again, the stevedore returned to the intercom; the other stevedore continued his studied stare. Unthank flared his eyes at him and the guard blinked, surprised, and looked away.

"Okay," came the answer. "He'll meet you in the lobby."

Something smarted, deep down. Some crucial piece of his innards made a quick flex and sent a spark up through his esophagus to his cranium. "N-no," he said. *Don't sing. Smile.* He answered his own demand and smiled widely, saying, "No need to trouble the man. I'll just go up to him."

"He said he'll come down to you," said the stevedore, cocking his eyebrow.

"But it doesn't work that way," Joffrey said, before remembering: *Don't say that out loud.* It was too late.

"*What* doesn't work *what* way?"

The stevedore on the other side of the gate had resumed his stare; he seemed to be listening in, intently, to the conversation.

Smile. "Never you mind," said Unthank. "I'll just meet him in the, as you say, lobby."

The response seemed to disarm the moment. The stevedore looked sideways at Unthank before letting him pass through the gate, saying, "They all said you went crazy."

Sing.

Don't sing. "Well, that's how rumors start, you know," said Unthank. "Don't believe everything you hear." And then, quite inadvertently, he let slip: "Tra la!"

"What?" The stevedore stopped short.

"Nothing. Nothing. Just. Humming a tune, you know. Earworm. Can't get a song out of my head. Don't you hate it when that happens?"

The stevedore stared at Unthank for a moment before giving his grumbling reply, "Whatever. Just wait in the lobby there. Wigman'll be down in a moment."

Clear. First hurdle. First obstacle. *Walk normally.* Unthank had developed a kind of shuffling, hunchbacked gait in his time wandering the Industrial Wastes, owing to the great pile of blankets and discarded coats he'd had to bear on his shoulders to ward off the winter cold. It had become habitual. But he knew: Now it was of utmost importance that he walk upright, back straight. Chin high. It was all he could do to keep himself from toppling his shoulders into the Quasimodo-like stance; he knew it would betray him, it would betray the fact that he was merely pretending to be his former self.

He walked into the glistening, pristine white lobby of Titan Tower and nodded to the night secretary at the front desk. The secretary, a clean-shaven young man with glasses, looked shocked to see Unthank appear through the sliding glass doors. "H-hello, Mr. Unthank," he said. "Haven't seen you in a while."

Unthank froze, unsure of what to say; he hadn't rehearsed this bit in his run-throughs. Conversation with the lobby's secretary had not been on the cue cards. "Nor should you have," he said finally. "I've been off."

"Off?"

"Off. You know."

The secretary smiled, clearly wanting to give Unthank the benefit of the doubt. "I guess I don't know. But I'm just a night secretary."

"No one's just a night secretary," said Unthank. *Don't sing.* "Do you sing, by chance?"

"Sing, sir? I mean, I do occasionally when—"

"You'll find it does you a world of good. I'd like to sing right now. Do you mind if I do?"

The secretary's face had gone pale; he looked over Unthank's shoulder at the two stevedores just beyond the doors. "G-go for it," he said.

"Thank you. I will." Unthank cleared his throat and was about to warble some calming note when he remembered himself. "But first: I'm fairly parched. Awfully parched, actually."

"Can I . . . get you some water?" asked the secretary uncertainly.

"Water! Yes, that's just what I need. A nice bottle of water."

"Have a seat, Mr. Unthank, I'll be right back with it." The night secretary seemed happy to have some excuse to leave the room; he jogged off with the briskness of a man who'd arrived at the wrong party and had only found out too late it was a reunion of old Star Trek fan club members.

Unthank glanced at the elevator that stood directly to the right of the desk; the digital panel above the doors gave the location of the car as the thirtieth floor. Suddenly, it began to change: 29. 28. Wigman was descending.

Quickly, Joffrey sashayed around the corner of the desk and took in the massive apparatus that was the lobby's security system. Images swam in his mind: a deck of white cue cards, riddled with notes, splayed out before him. He saw Jacques, calmly coaching, in his mind's eye. He began tapping on the computer's keyboard.

26. 25. 24.

ADMINISTRATIVE ACCESS ONLY, read the monitor. PLEASE AUTHEN-
TICATE.

To the right of the screen was a touch pad with the outline of a hand. Joffrey placed his palm against it and waited, praying inwardly that his security access had not been deleted or suspended during his months-long sabbatical in the hinterlands. He glanced at the digital readout above the elevator.

23. 22. 21.

"Come on," he swore. "Come on, tra la, tra lee."

ACCESSING . . . , dithered the computer screen. ACCESSING . . . PLEASE WAIT . . .

20. 19. The elevator stopped there, apparently having taken on a passenger on the nineteenth floor. Joffrey envisioned Wigman nodding politely to the new rider, then staring ahead at the array of numbers on the keypad.

ACCESS GRANTED. HELLO JOFFREY UNTHANK. Joffrey let out a breath of relief. He began madly tapping out commands, his two index fingers quietly punching at the keyboard. Suddenly, he heard the sound of footsteps in the hall. The secretary was returning.

Sucking in his breath, he scooted around the front of the desk, getting only as far as the counter before the young secretary reappeared, carrying a bottle of water. A little plastic flower on the surface of the counter caught Joffrey's attention, and he pretended to be intently studying it.

"Funny," he said as the secretary came closer. "This is a very funny little flower. Ha! It dances a little when there's light, huh? What a little contraption. What an amazing little contraption." He gave the secretary a feigned look of surprise and said, "Oh, hi! I've been standing here, looking at this little gizmo, the whole time you were gone. Literally. Just right here. Looking at this little flower."

The secretary appeared nonplussed. "Here's your water, Mr. Unthank."

"Oh, thanks very . . . ," began Joffrey as he took the water from the secretary. "Oh. I'm sorry. I need tepid water. I should've said as much." He handed the bottle back. "Overly cold water is bad for your digestion. Did you know that?"

"No, I did not," said the secretary. "Tepid water?"

"If you don't mind," said Unthank. He made every effort to retain close eye contact with the secretary; he couldn't afford the man looking down at the computer screen behind the desk, which was now advertising the following words in fairly large block letters: YOU ARE ABOUT TO SET ALL SECURITY SYSTEMS TO BYPASS. ARE YOU SURE YOU WANT TO DO THIS? Y/N.

"Not at all," said the secretary. He wheeled about and walked down the hall and out of sight. Joffrey rolled around the side of the desk nimbly and jabbed his finger down on the Y key of the keyboard.

RETINAL SCAN REQUIRED.

He glanced at the elevator. The readout above the doors was proclaiming, in Joffrey's inner ear, that the elevator carrying Wigman was now on the EIGHTH FLOOR.

"C'mon, c'mon," hissed Unthank as he positioned his face in front of the monitor's webcam. "Take your pretty picture."

ACCESSING . . . ACCESSING . . . PLEASE WAIT.

7. 6. 5.

Little droplets of sweat appeared on Unthank's brow; he could feel his face growing pink and warm. His heart began beating wildly in his chest. "Tra la, tra lee," he murmured helplessly.

ACCESS GRANTED. SECURITY SYSTEM BYPASSED. THANK YOU, JOF-FREY UNTHANK.

"No, thank you, tra la, tra loo!" he nearly shouted as he heard the elevator ding. He shot upright and spun around, staring helplessly at the elevator doors as they slowly hissed open. Like a video paused on a particularly unflattering frame, Unthank's body was frozen, contorted into a bizarre and unbecoming shape, his mouth stretched sideways and his hands cocked in surprise like a campy vampire in pre-attack mode.

He had come face-to-face with Brad Wigman; or rather, face-to-bald-spot, as Brad Wigman was bending over, wiping some offending speck from the front of his chinos, presenting his blond pate and revealing to Joffrey that the Chief Titan was, in fact, losing a little hair on top.

Unthank thought fast; before Bradley had lifted himself upright, Joffrey dashed to the side of the elevator doors, safely out of sight. He then watched as Wigman stepped out of the open elevator and into the lobby. Joffrey silently slipped into the car as the doors began to *shush* closed, taking Wigman's place. He watched as the closing doors slowly concealed the Chief Titan's broad shoulders. Still holding his breath, Unthank punched the number twenty-two on the elevator's keypad and glanced up at the readout above the door; the numbers began climbing.

Joffrey smiled. He allowed himself a long, loud melody, sung from the depths of his belly.

And then: the first explosion.

C H A P T E R   1 7

Where Everybody Was

When the explosion happened:

Joffrey was in the elevator, singing loudly to himself. He was thrown to the back of the car by the force of the detonation; the lights went out. A red bulb flashed on, bathing the elevator in a stark light as the elevator's climb became stuttered and uncertain, powered by some unseen generator.

Desdemona Mudrak was standing by the desk on the top floor of the tower, picking at her cuticles and watching Roger as he casually read the titles of the book spines on the shelves and tried to intuit which one was the hidden lever to open the case. The explosion made a ripple-like tremor, decreasing in strength as it made its way up the massive structure of Titan Tower, until it reached the top floor and merely rattled the trophies in their cases and caused Desdemona and Roger to look at each other in a confused silence.

Martha and Carol were in the safe room behind the bookcase, absently munching on pretzels and preparing to dig into the final chapter of Dumas's jailbreaking masterpiece. The sound of the explosion caused Martha to drop the book.

Wigman had just stepped into the ground-floor lobby of the tower, having just removed an obstinate strand of lint from his otherwise pristine and pleated khakis. He was surprised to find the lobby empty; even the night secretary was missing from his station behind the desk. Wigman was about to say something when the secretary appeared, holding a plastic bottle of water. They both looked very surprised to see each other and equally surprised to see no one else. The explosion's epicenter was some yards off, just beyond the gate of the guarding wall, but its power was enough to completely shatter the tall plate-glass windows that surrounded the ground floor and throw the furniture, which had been purchased cheap at a liquidator's warehouse, into the air like beanbag chairs freed of gravity.

Rachel Mehlberg was huddled behind the cover of a stack of pallets with a cohort of fellow saboteurs, holding an unlit bomb in her hand. The explosion sounded, echoing off the cement walls and chemical

silos that surrounded the tower, and splashing the dark nighttime
scene with bright yellow light and a very sudden and intense heat.
She could feel the shock wave rumble her lungs and she nearly fell
backward, balanced as she was on the balls of her feet in a crouched
position. Someone caught her; it was Nico. He was smiling. "Now,"
he said. He lit a match and held it to the fuse of Rachel's bomb. She
let out a loud, prehistoric "*WHOOP*" and threw it as far as she could.

Elsie Mehlberg was crouched in a square, anodized aluminum
duct, barely three feet across, at the front of her fellow Unadoptables-
turned-saboteurs: the duct-rats. They'd been waiting for the little
blinking red light above the latticed gate that blocked their way to

turn green, at which point, they were told, they could safely open it without incurring a shock that would turn them, instantly, to small fuzzy piles of ash. This was a fate that none of them were interested in experiencing. When the green light came on, it was Elsie's job, being the first in line, to reach out gingerly and undo the latch. It opened with a yawning creak, happily absent of any kind of electric flash, and she began shuffling on her hands and feet down the squat corridor toward the white light in the distance. When the explosion came, it shuddered the building and a very loud noise echoed up the metal vent, causing all the children to duck their heads. The light in the distance blinked out, only to be replaced by a strange red one. Elsie continued forward.

Michael and Cynthia had just returned to the Forgotten Place, to their warehouse home. They'd come back to resume leadership over their fellow Unadoptables as the eldest of the clan; they'd arrived with fresh blankets and fresh food and a promise that their two missing members would soon be rescued. Just as they'd announced this, the high, cracked windows of the warehouse were suddenly illuminated with a glowing light and the children *ooooooh*ed their appreciation, knowing that the great operation had begun.

Prue McKeel was on a ship, a prisoner in a belowdecks hold, staring out a barred porthole. The explosion sounded like a distant thud; she saw a flash light up the night, outlining in white the monolithic shape of a tall tower. More explosions followed; many of them, in fact, but a mist had settled over the river basin and she could no longer see the outline of the tower, and the ship's wooden hull groaned as it began to move its way out of the inlet and onto the surface of the river, safely concealed from prying eyes by the presence of the all-consuming mist.

The Earth was revolving, orbiting a distant sun, one of a series of planetary chunks of rock and magma spinning in the vastness of space.

CHAPTER 18

The Assault of Titan Tower

Several more explosions followed the first, but they seemed fairly ordinary at this point, with all the windows of the ground floor stove in and the entire honor guard of stevedores rushing from various outposts to stem the attack that had been launched. It was very dark, being sometime just after ten o'clock, and a dense fog had descended over the river valley and was rushing across the Industrial Wastes like someone laying out a heavy winter duvet.

Elsie Mehlberg tried to subdue her very present fear as best as she could, her knees now feeling rubbed raw from the extraordinary stretch of ductwork they'd crawled so far.

"*Pssst,*" hissed a voice behind her; it was Ruthie. "How much farther?"

Left. Right. Left. Straight. Elsie was trying to remember the schema of the ductwork. "Not far, I think," she said.

They'd arrived at a four-way intersection.

"We go left," said Elsie. Her memory had served her well: It was only a few moments before they arrived at the vent covering. She peered through the mesh and saw that the vent let onto a stark white hallway.

A gust of hot air blew over them; the slightest smell of smoke was in the air. "Harry," whispered Elsie. "You ready for this?"

"As I'll ever be," came the voice, holding up the rear of the foursome.

Ruthie, Oz, and Elsie pressed themselves sideways against the wall of the duct so Harry could squeeze, feet first, to the front. There, he placed his shoes against the metal vent covering and waited.

"That security system's disarmed, right?" he asked.

Elsie, at his ear, nodded. "It should be," she said. But she knew: Their lives were now entirely in the hands of Joffrey Unthank and his ability to keep his madness at bay. She imagined the worst-case scenario: They kick open the covering, the security system engages, they get nabbed after a feeble chase and are thrown into the safe room with Carol and Martha, the very people they'd intended to save. Or worse: They suffer the same fate that so many captured members of the Chapeaux Noirs had faced—disappeared. Drowned. Fed to the dogs. It was enough to send Elsie's stomach spasming in fear.

Harry looked back at Elsie. "Should I just do it?"

"Wait for the explosion."

Just after she'd said it, it came: an explosion; a soft thud sending another shock wave through the building. Harry coiled his legs back and gave the covering a tremendous kick; it went clattering into the hallway beyond. He quickly peeked out of the opening, jerking his head right and then left. "Clear," he said.

"Go!" whispered Elsie, and Harry, grabbing the outside lip of the opening, slid himself out into the hall. The other three were quick to follow.

"Which way?" asked Ruthie once they'd all assembled in the hallway.

Elsie ran the schema in her mind. "Left," she said.

"I'll scout ahead," said Oz. The boy disappeared around a corner, briefly, before scrambling back. "Stevedores!" he reported in the loudest whisper he could manage.

Sure enough, a gang of the overall-wearing giants came stomping into view. They crossed the children's vision, running along an intersecting hallway. The duct-rats all froze in place; they'd had too little notice to do any kind of evasive action. Thankfully, whatever it was that the goons were off to do seemed more important than anything down this side hallway, and the four of them survived unnoticed. Elsie looked around at her friends with wide eyes. "Let's be careful," she said. "This place is jumping with those guys."

Oz scouted again and gave the all clear, which they'd agreed would be a kind of clicking noise the boy was able to make with his tongue. It sounded like the rattle of a radiator. They rounded the corner and made their way to a second vent cover, which presented itself, as the blueprint promised it would, at ground level just a few feet past the intersection. Ruthie, charged with the task, pulled out the screwdriver and began removing the screws from the four corners of the vent. Oz and Elsie edged outward to either side, their eyes trained on the empty hallway.

The vent grille clattered to the ground and the four duct-rats, one after another, slid into the tunnel with Elsie in the lead. She paused a moment, collecting her thoughts. "Straight on," she said. "It branches in a little ways."

They scuttled down the short passage, listening to the reverberant sounds of explosions somewhere far below them. Elsie thought they sounded like they were getting closer. She'd been disturbed by an exchange between Jacques and Nico, just before they were leaving for the action: Jacques had suddenly, emboldened by promised success, been very adamant that they achieve the thing they'd long angled for: the complete destruction of Titan Tower. He'd said that they weren't likely to get this close again. That the time to strike was now, to deal the final blow. Nico'd warned against it, saying it was too rash. Their objective, as they'd promised the Unadoptables, was to simply free the Chief Titan's hostages, full stop. And that's how they'd left it, but once the explosions started happening—louder and closer than Elsie imagined they would be—she couldn't help wondering if that wasn't the sound of Jacques getting his way.

But there was no time to fret: They arrived at a T-intersect; following the blueprint of Elsie's recollections, the four duct-rats crawled leftward and soon arrived at a vertical duct. One after another, they began their upward climb, spidering themselves against the walls of the duct and inching, ever so carefully, toward a glimmering light some five floors above them.

ʑ

The elevator climbed; Unthank watched the numbers change in the readout above the door. The chaotic noises of the ground floor: the breaking glass, the howling voices, the sound of a multitude of footsteps running desperately to the scene of the explosion—they all ebbed away until Unthank was alone with his thoughts in the silent space of the elevator car.

"Tra la, tra lee," he sang to himself. He felt at the small black package in the left-hand pocket of his coat. The thing was still there. He sang again: "Tra loo, tra lee." The elevator dinged its arrival at the twenty-second floor. He waited cautiously as the doors slid open, revealing an empty hallway.

He stepped out uncertainly, unnerved by the quiet on the floor. He looked at his watch and confirmed that despite the inconsistencies in the plan, he was still on schedule. A tentative beep could be heard somewhere in the distance, and he began walking toward it, humming all the while.

❧

The duct-rats had arrived at another vent cover; the dusty light from the hallway cast a hatch-marked etching on the floor of the duct. They waited for another explosion; it came, and Harry kicked the cover out into the hall, sending a spray of chalky drywall dust onto the floor. The way was clear; they extricated themselves from the low conduit and stretched in the open air of the hallway. Despite their small size, each of them was feeling the pinch of having to crouch so low for so long; what's more, the five-story free climb through the vertical duct had taken all the energy they could muster. They were breathing deeply, gulping in air.

"To the bathroom," instructed Elsie, and they all filed toward the door, which, as she'd known, was only a few feet to their right.

The bathroom was sparklingly clean; truly, the work of an organization that prided itself on spotless, bacteria-free cleanliness. To the children, having spent the last several years of their lives either in an overcrowded orphanage, in a woodland cottage with no working plumbing, or in an abandoned warehouse with even fewer amenities, the sight of the immaculately clean restroom facility was enough to bring tears to their eyes. Or at least Harry's.

"I've never seen anything so beautiful," he mused aloud.

"C'mon," hissed Elsie, who, of the children, had had the most recent exposure to the everyday cleanliness of twenty-first-century life. She was committed to her task, which involved the careful cataloging of the byways of a ductwork that spanned hundreds of yards and stories. One kid's potty break could be enough to throw that off. "The vent's in the ceiling. Over here."

"Can I just go to the bathroom once?" pleaded Harry, in thrall to the beautiful, snow-white porcelain that presented itself throughout the restroom.

"No," whispered Elsie. "Let's go!"

"What if it's just a number one?"

Elsie grabbed Harry by the arm and dragged him toward the end of the room, where a black grate interrupted the cool white of the tiled ceiling. It hung directly above one of the bathroom's toilet stalls, and Elsie had seen enough movies to know that one must look both under the door and above it to see if anyone is hiding within. The stall was clear; Elsie and Ruthie scaled the opposing stall walls and sat there, balanced on the metal dividers. Oz stood on the back of the toilet and braced Ruthie's slippered feet while she undid the screws holding the cover in place.

The screws dropped, one after another, into the toilet. Ruthie slid the grate aside, into the interior of the duct, and they all climbed into the hole in the ceiling. All of them but Harry.

He'd been so taken by the bathroom that he lingered a moment longer, apparently ogling the facilities, before the hissed whispers from his fellow duct-rats shook him back to attention. Sitting on the edge of the top of the stall, he kicked one foot down and flushed the toilet, apparently just to see it work. The sound masked the noise of the bathroom door suddenly swinging open, though Harry saw the stevedore, moments after, as he came around the corner and made his way toward the stalls.

Elsie, her head sticking out of the hole in the ceiling, saw the intruder too; it all seemed to be happening in slow motion.

A voice shouted to the stevedore from the hallway beyond. "Come on, Tony! We got to get down to the lobby. This ain't a drill."

"Hold up," said the stevedore as he walked along the corridor of closed bathroom stalls. "Nature calls."

Elsie jerked her head backward into the duct; peeking over the edge, she stared wide-eyed at Harry, who was poised, spread-eagled, across the top of the toilet stall. The toilet stall that the stevedore had hurriedly selected.

Elsie held her breath. She could hear Oz and Ruthie suck in theirs as well. She only imagined Harry was doing the same.

The stall door swung open. The stevedore gave a cursory look at the empty toilet bowl before dropping his overalls and turning around, sitting heavily on the white toilet seat. He cupped his forehead in his hands and stared at the space between his knees as Harry, pale and terrified, stood only a handful of feet above his head, his legs painfully tenting the distance between the metal walls of the stall.

And they waited. Elsie couldn't stand the strain, and she slid down the corridor, covering her face with her hands, as if willing the world away. A minute passed. One of the man's fellow stevedores hollered out an impatient word before the toilet flushed noisily and the stall door slammed open and closed and the stevedore, freshly relieved, walked loudly out of the bathroom.

Only then did Elsie creep her head back over the lip of the vent opening.

Harry was still straddling the stall. He looked up at the shocked faces of the three Unadoptables, who were peeking down at him through the hole in the ceiling.

"That," he said, "was disgusting."

Before another stevedore had a chance to wander into the bathroom and disrupt their plan, Elsie and Oz had thrust their hands down through the vent opening and yanked Harry, with all their strength, into safety.

❧

Joffrey Unthank's goal was in sight. There, at the end of the hallway, was a door marked AUTHORIZED PERSONNEL ONLY. Beyond it was the very small and dark room that housed the operational protocols for the Tower's two auxiliary elevators. Only one of those elevators was known to most of the staff of the Tower: the service elevator, a nondescript apparatus that was used mainly by janitorial and, if needed, in emergency situations. However, unbeknownst to everyone apart from the few who had high-level security clearance, the console inside the room could also override the security lock for a more clandestine elevator: the small caged contraption that served as an escape route from Wigman's safe room. Joffrey rubbed his hands eagerly; *he* had high-level security clearance. It was a benefit of being a Titan of Industry. And now: His penultimate goal was at hand.

However, no sooner had he finished rubbing his palms when a pair of lumbering stevedores came crashing toward him, barreling down the hallway and blocking Unthank's view of the door. He immediately recognized both of them, which was surprising considering the strange uniformity among the stevedore ranks: They all looked as if they'd been engineered by a remarkably unimaginative geneticist. But Joffrey knew them: They were Wigman's two right-hand men, and they were steaming toward Joffrey and looking very angry.

They saw him, and genetically inseparable looks of surprise fell across their faces.

"Machine Parts?" said one, surprised.

"Jimmy!" said Unthank, smiling excitedly. "Bammer! Been a while, hasn't it?"

"What are you doing here?" growled Bammer. He was holding a very large, red pipe wrench in his right hand.

"I thought you went crazy," said Jimmy.

Unthank shrugged his shoulders as if to say, *It happens.*

"Do you know there's an attack on the tower happening *right now?*" added Jimmy.

"An attack? Had no idea, tra la." It just slipped out, the singing. He bit his lip, hard.

The two stevedores, so confused by the random meeting, seemed not to pay the little tic any mind. "Chapeaux Noirs," said Bammer. "Gettin' brazen. Whole lobby's blown out."

"Oh wow, really?" said Unthank.

"Yeah. It's real. The Chief's down there. We got to get him to safety."

"What horrible people," said Unthank. "Those saboteurs."

"We'll show them, though," said Jimmy, who was also holding a very large pipe wrench. Joffrey couldn't imagine the kind of plumbing repair that would require such a large tool. The stevedore whacked it against the palm of his opposing hand a few times.

"You sure will," said Joffrey. "No doubt about it."

"You shouldn't be in here," said Jimmy. "Ain't safe."

"Yes, yes," said Joffrey. "I'm just making my way out. I know the drill."

Just then, another explosion sounded from below. The hallway was rocked slightly by the detonation. Joffrey braced himself against the wall.

"We gotta get down there," said Jimmy. "All hands on deck."

"Watch yourself, Machine Parts," said Bammer as the two stevedores shoved past him. It was an annoying entitlement the two stevedores enjoyed: being able to refer to the various Titans by their Division, something only Wigman typically did.

"Will do, guys," said Joffrey. "And good luck down there." He waited until they were out of sight before continuing his walk toward the door. He breathed deeply, desperately tamping down the violent urge he had to sprint for the door, screaming epithets. He still had appearances to keep up; his narrow escape from Bammer and Jimmy was testament to that.

He reached the door in a few short steps. Access required handprint identification, which he provided, along with another retinal scan. "Good evening, Joffrey Unthank," said a robotic voice from the panel by the door once the procedure had been completed. A click sounded by the handle; Unthank pushed the door in and entered the room.

✌

The break room had exhibited all the signs of a speedy departure; benches were upturned and magazines thrown carelessly to the ground. Several of the stevedores' metal locker doors were wide open, and denim overalls poured out like blue tongues. A few maroon beanies littered the floor. Cold cups of coffee. Half-eaten bagels. The duct-rats had managed their scurry through the room without incident, and they were now running down the hall toward the service elevator that would, if all things were going according to plan, be powered down.

Harry led the pack this time; arriving at the shut doors (a sign above them read SERVICE ELEVATOR! AUTHORIZED PERSONNEL ONLY!)

he sized up his challenge with a steely eye. He was ten years old—he'd have been twelve if it weren't for his two years in the time-stasis of the Periphery—and it was as if someone had held their thumb on his head as he'd grown. All of his development seemed to have occurred in his thighs and biceps, while his height stayed remarkably stunted. Even Elsie, who was shorter than most of the nine-year-olds in their crowd, met him eye to eye when they spoke. He squared up his stumpy legs and fished his thick fingers into the gap between the elevator doors and *pulled*.

Nothing.

Again: He *pulled*. He grunted as he did so, and little veins popped up in his neck.

Elsie gave a look behind them. "Hurry!" she whispered.

"I'm trying," said Harry, annoyed, before he gritted his teeth and tried again; the doors gave a little this time, and a thin red glow appeared between them: the light from the interior of the elevator shaft.

"You're almost there!" said Ruthie. She and Oz thrust their fingers into the fissure to try and help.

Harry grunted again, and soon the doors had been pried some eighteen inches apart and the boy was able to slide between them and brace them open with his feet. "Okay!" he whispered breathlessly. "Get in!"

Oz went first, climbing through the lattice of Harry's splayed shins and elbows, and gasped loudly. "Long way down, guys," he said.

He then inched his way out of sight and presumably began climbing. Elsie and Ruthie followed suit.

Just beyond the doors was a red-lit shaft that seemed impossibly tall; the floors below were distinguished by metal doors that appeared periodically along the wall of the cement corridor. The car was nowhere in sight. They could only hope that Mr. Unthank had managed to shut the thing down; it was understood that if the car were operational and it were to run over them as they climbed, well, the less said about it the better. Above them, the shaft stretched into the unseen distance, a constellation of little red lights extending into a pinkish blur. The metal rungs of a ladder were set into a shallow channel in the shaft wall, and the four children began climbing them, mindful not to look down.

"Come on," said Elsie. "We got a long ways to go."

🌿

Adopting the bearing of a service technician finishing his rounds, Unthank backed out of the room and gently closed the door behind him, ensuring that the door was locked as he did so. He couldn't help, at this moment, but feel a little impressed with himself. Not only had he steeled himself against the constant barrage fed by his enfeebled mind, bursts of manic suggestions and reality-tilting images, but he'd managed it all rather flexibly, adapting his actions to all the curveballs that fate had thrown at him. What's more, he'd done an incredibly good turn for the children. Now they would be well on their way to freeing their friends from the grip of the Chief Titan and thereby scuttling any chance of Bradley Wigman achieving what would have *rightfully been Unthank's*, what he had worked at for *so long*. . . .

He stopped. That was the old himself.

He was working to free the children. To allow them their justice. *Smile.*

He was, he had to admit, fairly good at this sort of thing. Perhaps there was a place for him among the ranks of the Chapeaux Noirs. He had to admit: Being a saboteur was rather satisfying.

But no: He had one last task. One last goal. One last wish to complete. He patted the thing in his pocket, took a deep breath, and began walking toward the end of the hall.

That was when Bammer and Jimmy showed up again.

You're not supposed to do that, Unthank fought the urge to say aloud when he saw them. He chided himself. *Remember. Flexibility. Smile. Don't sing.*

"Hi, gents," he said amiably. "Back so soon?"

"Elevator's down. Service elevator isn't taking our credentials."

"Oh," said Unthank. "That's strange."

Bammer cocked his eyebrow. "I thought you were making your way out."

"You were goin' the wrong way to get out," added Jimmy.

"Was I?" said Unthank. "I was, wasn't I? Oh well, I guess you both should lead the way."

The two stevedores paused and shared a look. "I said: Service elevator ain't takin' credentials. Think it's been shut off. We need it on."

"You got security clearance for that, don't you?" asked Jimmy.

"I do, in fact," said Unthank. *Flexibility*. He thought of the children. They would be climbing by now.

"Well?" prompted Bammer.

"I suppose we ought to, well, turn it on," said Unthank.

"Yeah," said Jimmy. "Like, now."

"Right," said Unthank. "Now."

The three of them stood there in the hallway for a minute; another explosion rocked the building.

"NOW!" shouted Bammer.

The two stevedores grabbed him by the shoulder and spun him around to face the door he'd so recently closed and locked. He focused his power into his legs to stop them from buckling, before realizing that he needed an equal amount of brainpower to consider all the implications of turning the service elevator back on. He and the stevedores were on the twenty-second floor; he knew that the duct-rats would be climbing into the shaft at the fifteenth. Surely, unless the children had already climbed above the elevator car, they would be meat loaf in the workings once the apparatus had passed them by. A shiver went up his spine.

"C'mon," said Bammer. Unthank then realized they'd already

arrived at the door, and he defeatedly presented the required body parts to the palm and retinal scanners.

"Welcome back, Mr. Unthank," said the robotic chirp.

Jimmy cast a sidelong glance at Joffrey.

"Did you—" he began.

Unthank interrupted him. "C'mon, gents," he said with a forced urgency. "The Chief Titan might be hurt."

This, apparently, was enough to distract them from their sudden suspicions. They entered the room, gently shoving Unthank forward. A myriad of television screens presented themselves, flickering

in the dark of the room. The monitors displayed the footage from the tower's manifold security cameras and they played in stark, cinema verité black and white the violent scene that was playing out all around the tower's ground floor. Several of the screens only showed static; three of them showed the dust-and-debris-covered lobby. Another explosion sounded; its source was shown in grim depiction by one of the television screens: a tremendous white cloud overcame a section of the south wall; a phalanx of stevedores came rushing into the frame.

"Quick!" shouted Bammer. Or was it Jimmy? Unthank couldn't tell; his eyes were fixed on the monitors.

One of the screens showed the interior of the service elevator shaft. Four small children were there, gingerly scaling a narrow ladder, bathed in a dim light. One reached a hand out to the other, helping their compatriot over a difficult spot. Unthank looked down and, typing in the pass code he'd been given when he'd been named a Titan of Industry, restarted the power to the elevator.

CHAPTER 19

Martyrs for the Cause

Elsie had climbed nearly five stories (the numbers were painted in bright yellow by every door they passed) when she heard the elevator power up. It sent a jolt of adrenaline through her body. The car itself had come into view once they'd climbed a few dozen yards, lost in the hazy distance above them. A single white bulb dangled from its underside. But now: She'd heard a kind of buzzing hum echo through the shaft, and she looked down at Harry, who was some feet below her.

"Did you hear that?" she asked.

"Yeah," he said.

Hoping it was a fluke, Elsie kept climbing. It wasn't long, however, until her worst fears were confirmed: The elevator car began to move.

Harry swore. Elsie looked up at Oz and Ruthie, who were close together, some thirty feet up. They both looked down at Elsie and Harry, a look of identically abject horror in their eyes.

"Guys!" they shouted. "It's coming down!"

Elsie desperately began looking around her for some crevice to crawl into; none presented itself. Some ways up the shaft, she saw a small notch in the concrete, potentially big enough to house her small body. She began climbing toward it.

Just then, the elevator stopped at one of the doors, a few floors above them. Elsie barely had time to breathe a sigh of relief when it started up again, having presumably taken on passengers, and was now once more barreling toward them.

"Guys!" she shouted, disregarding the need for quiet. "Get to someplace safe!"

The elevator was picking up speed. A loud hum echoed through the long chamber. Elsie could hear the clacking of the cables as they struck against one another, dangling in the center of the shaft. She stepped away from the ladder and pressed herself into the small crevice she'd found, trying to flatten her back as well as she could. She willed her every inch of flesh to worm its way into the corners.

Looking down, she saw that Harry was busily scrambling for a similar safe point, though it seemed to be some feet below him. Oz and Ruthie hadn't had as much luck; the elevator was approaching them at a remarkably fast speed, and they were many yards away from one of these pockets in the shaft wall. Oz, dangling from the ladder, was trying to pry open one of the doors in the wall to no avail.

"Guys!" shouted Elsie.

Ruthie, unbelievably, was climbing madly toward the oncoming car, desperately attempting to reach the divot in the wall closest to her, which happened to be about ten feet above her. She arrived at it just as the speeding car passed her and she screamed as she thrust her small body into the cavity; the noise was swallowed by the groaning cry of the elevator as it plummeted downward, and Ruthie was gone from Elsie's sight.

Oz, acting quickly, leapt from his place at the ladder and caught the looping cable that hung from the bottom of the car. He swung dramatically there, his legs kicking at the empty air below him. He joined the downward plummet of the car, rocked impotently by the swing of the cable. Elsie pressed herself farther into her crevice, preparing herself for the car's arrival. It was now approaching her with the speed of a locomotive.

Elsewhere in the building, Joffrey Unthank watched the two stevedores as they marched out of sight down the hall. He knew he was trapped. Shutting down the elevator now would merely bring the two stevedores steaming back to him, demanding action and, more complexly, answers as to why the Machine Parts Titan was repeatedly turning on and off the service elevator. He could only watch. And wait.

He looked up at the security-camera feed of the elevator shaft; he saw the children climbing. When the stevedores called the elevator, he saw the children panic in reaction to the movement of the car.

Move, he hissed to the grainy black-and-white image of the Unadoptables.

The car was heading down.

He realized that the children would not be able to get out of the way.

His fingers dove for the keys; he began madly jamming in his pass code. His fingers were shaking.

Tra la tra lee.

It was a hopelessly long string of numbers (*why did they have to make it so complicated?*); the keypad below his fingers seemed to shimmy and dissolve as he punched at the keypad.

ERROR, WRONG PASS CODE, read the screen.

He swore; he cracked his knuckles and tried again.

✦

A shout sounded below Elsie. She looked down in time to see Harry fall away from his perch on the side of the wall; he'd been spooked by Ruthie's scream and had looked up, momentarily losing his balance. He managed to catch his arm on a rung of the ladder, and Elsie could hear a *thump* resound through the chamber, and Harry let out a pained yelp. The boy swung there by the crook of his elbow, fully in the path of the charging elevator car.

"HARRY!" shouted Oz, dangling from the bottom of the car. He reached out his hand, valiantly. "JUMP!"

But Harry was stuck; he couldn't manage to get his arm unlooped from the ladder rung. Elsie closed her eyes as the elevator rushed by her; she could feel the wind it carried with it, the acrid reek of grease and synthetic adhesives. She knew the car would arrive at Harry within seconds and would either crush him with its weight or knock him from his perch to fall some twenty-odd stories to the bottom of the shaft.

🌿

ERROR, WRONG PASS CODE, the screen advertised brightly, once again. And then: TWO MORE ATTEMPTS ALLOWED.

Unthank slapped his cheek firmly, trying to banish the needling urgency that was making his fingers fail so spectacularly. He closed his eyes; he breathed deeply.

Smile.

He tried again.

ERROR, WRONG PASS CODE.

Unthank grunted, once, very loudly. Did it have to be so hard?

ONE MORE ATTEMPT ALLOWED. IF ENTERED IN ERROR AGAIN, CLEARANCE WILL BE SUSPENDED. CHECK EMAIL TO RESET PASS CODE. THANK YOU!

Unthank waved his hands impatiently at the little screen above the keypad. "Okay, okay, I get it!" he hollered. He channeled his thoughts; he calmed his quivering digits. He thought of the kids, of the orphans. He thought of what he owed them.

He tried again.

❧

The elevator stopped. It hadn't just come to a smooth halt, like it would if it were to arrive at a floor, but jerked and froze. It had just cleared Elsie's feet; she felt a tingling sensation over her entire body, as if she were a freshly torn strip of Velcro. Looking down, she could only assume the worst: that somehow Harry's body had stopped the downward momentum of the elevator. She called out weakly, "Harry?"

Ruthie, having just extricated herself from her hiding place, called down to Elsie. "Are they okay?" she shouted desperately.

Elsie shook her head, mouthing: "I don't know."

A minute passed. No sound came in response. Elsie felt a sob welling in her chest.

Suddenly, from a shallow chink in the wall, she saw two dirty hands reach up and grab the top of the elevator car. Shortly, a face presented itself: It was Harry. Squeezing his thick frame between the car and the wall of the shaft, he managed to get himself onto the top of the elevator. His face was streaked with grease, and little red scratches crisscrossed his forehead. He had a wild-eyed look on his face. He turned around and thrust a hand back down the little crevice he'd climbed through and brought it back out with another hand firmly in its grip. It was Oz, who arrived at the top of the car similarly covered in soot and lacerations.

"It stopped . . . ," mumbled Harry once Oz had been pulled from the crack between the wall and the car. "Just . . ." He held his greasy fingers up, his thumb and forefinger only inches apart.

Elsie wanted to hug him. She wanted to throw her arms around him and just fiercely *hug* the boy, this greasy boy. But before she could act on the very friendly and comradely instinct, they all heard the sound of whoever it was inside the elevator car they were standing on, trying to get out.

It sounded like a herd of rhinos contained in a small metal box.

Suddenly, a small door at their feet flew open, slamming back with a loud *clang*.

Elsie looked into the elevator, expecting to see rhinoceri. Instead, she saw two frothing-mad stevedores.

"Let's GO!" shouted Elsie, and the four of them—Elsie, Harry, Oz, and Ruthie—leapt back onto the ladder and began climbing as if their lives depended on it, which, in point of fact, they did.

They managed to buy themselves some time; the stevedores had a hard go of it, extracting their broad frames from the small opening in the top of the elevator. When they finally managed it, two genies being sucked from the opening of a bottle, they ground their teeth angrily—so angrily that Elsie could actually hear the grating noise from her position on the ladder, twenty feet above them.

"ORPHANS!" shouted one of them, waving his overlarge pipe wrench above his head. "The attack is a DECOY!"

"UNNNTHAAANK!" shouted the other, rather dramatically.

The ladder gave a little quake as the two stevedores, one after the other, clambered onto the nearest rungs and gave chase to the duct-rats.

What the stevedores had over the children in terms of strength and arm span, the Unadoptables well made up for by sheer agility, speed, and a seemingly perpetual supply of adrenaline. They flew up the rungs of the ladder as if it were a web and they were its spider-creators, dashing for a fly caught in the center. Elsie took up the rear, keeping an eye on the progress of their pursuers; they were not far behind.

"Move, guys, move!" she shouted to the three climbers ahead of her.

"We command you to stop!" shouted one of the stevedores. He pulled his pipe wrench from a loop at his leg and swung it in Elsie's direction. "I'm going to kneecap the lot of you!"

This gave Elsie a needed extra jolt of energy and she doubled her efforts, climbing the ladder rung over rung.

The elevator shaft wheeled below them; the distance, and thereby the potential free fall, to the stopped elevator car grew and grew. The stevedores continued to howl; the duct-rats climbed as fast as their little bodies could manage.

Elsie craned her head upward; she could see the clambering feet of Ruthie, leading the pack some thirty feet above her. "Keep an eye out, Ruthie!" she shouted. "The vent!"

Per the tower's blueprint, Elsie knew there was a ventilation duct that let out into the service elevator shaft; it led, after some meandering, into the panic room itself.

"I think I see it!" Ruthie shouted back. She pointed upward and began climbing again. Elsie looked down at the approaching stevedores; they were gaining, fast. She slapped the shoe sole of Harry, who was just above her.

"Faster, Harry!" she shouted.

Ruthie hollered her arrival at the vent; it was just a few feet off the rungs of the ladder. The girl pulled her screwdriver from her pocket and began carefully removing the screws from the cover's four corners. Soon, the traffic on the ladder slowed as each kid's progress was halted by the one before them.

Elsie stopped some yards below Ruthie's frantic activity, just below Harry, and locked her elbow around a rung of the ladder. "Don't come any closer!" she shouted to the approaching stevedores. "I'll kick you in the face!" She swung her leg around threateningly.

The stevedore in the lead gave a leering smile. "Won't do you no good, kid," he said. "You ain't gonna last on this ladder. Gonna pick you like a ripe apple and give you a toss. Gonna make applesauce with ya." He kept climbing, rung over rung.

Trying to ignore the stomach-turning image the stevedore's threat had evoked, Elsie looked up, watching Ruthie's progress, willing her fingers to work faster. The girl handled the screwdriver carefully, unthreading the screws and letting them fall into the open shaft below. "Two more to go!" she shouted.

Elsie felt something at her ankle; it was the meaty hand of one of the stevedores, grabbing her shoe. She screamed and kicked; the man swore loudly as her toe connected with the bridge of his nose.

"Move, Harry! UP!" she shouted.

The boy bolted a few feet up the ladder until he was practically on top of Oz. Elsie scrambled the short distance the boy had bought her, but still their pursuers came on.

"You'll pay for that, missy," said the freshly kicked stevedore, a palm held to his face. He lifted his hand away and looked at the results: His sausagelike fingers were stained with blood. "Oh, you'll pay. You're gonna fly." He swatted his hand upward again, just brushing the bottom of Elsie's feet.

"Only one more to go!" shouted Ruthie; a little screw went whizzing by Elsie's face.

"Get going!" Elsie yelled at Harry.

"I can't! Oz's right here!" It was true; the boys were practically embracing on the ladder.

CLANG. The vent cover came loose and cartwheeled down the elevator shaft, banging its way down to the car far below. Ruthie swung away from the ladder and climbed into the shaft, followed close behind by Oz, having unbraided himself from Harry's embrace.

Suddenly, Elsie felt a rough pain at her ankle; she looked down to see that the stevedore had her foot in his grip.

"Got you," he said, calmly, quietly.

Elsie screamed and jerked her body around, trying to lose the man's grip, but it held tight. Harry had already started to scramble into the duct when he heard Elsie's shout. Reversing his steps, he climbed out and, firmly catching a ladder rung in the crook of one elbow, reached his hand down to her.

"Grab hold!" he yelled.

Elsie shot her hand up and laced it tightly with Harry's. Suddenly, she was being torn in two directions, her spine stretching like a piece of taffy as the two opposing forces fought against each other.

Something had to give.

Finally, something did.

It was Elsie's shoe. It glided off the heel of her foot like the burned outer skin of a marshmallow too long over the campfire, and remained in the grasp of the suddenly bewildered stevedore. Elsie shot upward, buoyed by the pull of Harry's strong arm. They clambered, arm over arm, the remaining distance on the ladder, and within moments the two of them were crawling into the safety of the ventilation duct.

They could hear the wild and enraged cries of the stevedores, just at the entrance to the vent. They even heard a few pained grunts as the stevedores evidently tried to fit their massive frames into the small profile of the duct opening—to no avail. The duct-rats turned a corner in the tiny corridor, and the stevedores' cries soon echoed into nonsense and were assimilated into the ambient noises of the building itself.

※

Unthank stared at the television monitor breathlessly, watching the scene play out in vivid black and white. He had his hands to his lips, his mouth slightly open. When he saw the children escape through the duct, he couldn't help letting out a little victorious yelp.

"Yes!" he shouted, shaking his fist at the screen. "YES!" He then broke out into a song, a song he'd been storing up for a while now, and he belted it loudly in the privacy of the small room. His feet cut a kind of shuffling tap dance on the laminate floor.

And then it dawned on him what must come next. His hand dropped to his side and he backed out of the room, letting the flickering monitors televising the very real revolution that was happening within its many-eyed purview fall away. He closed the door. He locked it. He patted the little box in his pocket and turned around, heading for the stairway and from there to climb the remaining floors to the top of the tower. To Wigman's office. While he climbed, he remembered.

"You do the honors?" Jacques had said to him, there in the half-light of the saboteurs' hideout, safe away from the onlookers. The room was alive, so many people, so many children, planning this elaborate caper.

"Yes," he'd said. "I do the honors."

"One charge, top floor. Wait till the kids are out."

"One charge, top floor." He'd stopped there. "What if the kids aren't out, tra la tra lee?"

Jacques had shaken his head, hadn't he? "No singing," that's what he'd said. Another reminder. Had he answered the question, though? Unthank had asked him again:

"What if they aren't out?"

"The kids will be out," Jack—Jacques—had said.

"And if they're not?" Unthank had pressed. He'd remembered.

Jacques stared at his old compatriot, hard. He perhaps hadn't expected blowback from a reportedly crazy person. "Then we've got a few more martyrs for the cause." That's what he'd said. "All in the service of bringing down the greatest industrial power this country has known. We're dealing the killing blow here, Joffrey. No time for cowards and quitters."

"No time," repeated Unthank. "Yes. No time."

And so here he was, panting wildly as he walked the eight stories to the thirtieth floor, the thing in his pocket weighing more and more with every flight he climbed.

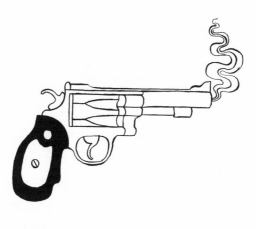

CHAPTER 20

The Kiss; Across the Threshold

Martha Song was dreaming. Or at least she thought she was. She was standing in front of a large crowd of people, receiving an award. Someone was standing near her; she turned to see who it was and immediately recognized the man as the mayor of Portland himself. She'd never actually known who the mayor was—Unthank had kept the orphanage under a pretty serious information lockdown—but it was as if her unconscious self was implying that the man in front of her—tidy three-piece suit, horn-rimmed glasses, neatly pomaded hair—was, in fact, the mayor. She must've remained suspicious, as, out of the ether, a sash suddenly appeared over the man's shoulder, reading MAYOR OF PORTLAND. The bespectacled man pointed to the sash, smiling.

"Oh," said Martha. "Hi."

"It is my utmost pleasure to present to you, Martha Song, the key to the City of Portland," the mayor said, speaking into a funny spaceship-like microphone. The jubilant crowd that stretched out into the horizon cheered loudly. The mayor continued, "For your hardships, for your sacrifices. Just so you know they have not gone unnoticed."

"Well, thanks," said Martha, bowing her head so that something could be placed over it. It felt strange, the award, and Martha put her hand up to her face, feeling the wispy tendrils of a long, gray beard.

She looked up and saw that she was suddenly in the middle of a very dark chamber, made of smooth stone. A small glint of light came in from a barred window, high above. Her hands were dirty; she saw that she'd been using them to dig a tunnel. The opening to this tunnel presented itself, clawed out of the corner of the stone wall. She spat into her palm and crouched low, preparing to continue her labors.

That was when she was shaken awake. An alarm was sounding. Soft, thudding explosions could be heard somewhere, far off, like pillows dropping from a great height. She opened her eyes.

"Elsie?" she managed. Another thing presented itself to her: The back of her head was slightly damp and pounded with a very rare kind of dull pain. The blur of her eyes gave way, and the girlish contours of the nine-year-old's face came into focus. "How did you—"

"We don't have time!" shouted Elsie. She was out of breath; it seemed that she'd just undergone some great travail to be there, looming over Martha like an orbiting planet. "What happened to Carol?"

It all came wheeling back to her: They'd just been sitting there, in the room. The room that was not the dusky basement of some craggy castle, but in fact the weird room that led off from Brad Wigman's office. They'd been there, Martha and Carol, when the first explosion rocked the building, sending a tremulous shake up to this, the top floor, like a shiver up a spine. They'd been in the middle of reading, hadn't they? She'd dropped the book and locked eyes with Carol, even though Carol couldn't see. That was when the door to the room had drawn back and that man Roger had appeared, strangely dressed in some kind of ceremonial robe.

"He closed the door behind him," Martha continued to explain, lifting herself onto her elbows, "murmuring something about a book, about how easy it had been. Then he grabbed Carol, really hard, by the arm. I jumped up to stop him and he hit me over the head with something. A bottle, maybe? I don't know. It hurt. I fell. Everything kind of went dark. And that's when you showed up."

More of her fellow Unadoptables were now appearing, as if materializing from the walls. She rubbed her eyes and tried to refocus. "Oz? Harry? Ruthie? What are you all doing here?" She couldn't help but feel a warm glow of relief spread through her chest.

The three other children, all piled into the small room, had the same look of desperation on their faces as they studied the room's every corner with the flightiness of spooked jackrabbits.

Another thing was happening, something that Martha realized had somehow figured into her dreamlike unconsciousness: Someone was pounding on the wall. Martha sat up; the other children froze. A voice came through, a voice dipped in a dialect that sounded like something one might hear pealing away as one rode a belled troika across the Russian steppe.

"I demand the door is opened!"

The children all recognized the voice: It was the voice of their old orphanage matron, Desdemona Mudrak.

"No!" shouted Elsie, taking initiative. "Not until you tell us what happened to Carol!"

Silence reigned on the other side of the wall; Desdemona was evidently rejiggering her circuits to these strange new phenomena. Apparently Carol was not in the room, but instead had been replaced by one of the other orphans—an orphan who had not, to her best recollection, been in the room before.

"Who is speaking?" she called.

"It's Elsie Mehlberg, Miss Mudrak," cried Elsie. "And we're here to save our friends."

"Carol is not in the room? Not Mr. Swindon, neither?"

Elsie glanced around the room, as if to confirm. The room was barely ten feet square; its interior decoration was limited to a wall of shelves faced by two chairs, one of which was toppled over. The other now carried the weight of Martha Song, who had her head in her hands. "Nope," said Elsie.

Desdemona seemed to chew on this information for a second before saying, "Open door. I help you."

Elsie looked around. "There's no door."

"There is," came the response. "Keypad is below shelf."

Sure enough, a small ten-key calculator-like pad presented itself below the first shelf on the far wall.

"Punch in five-eight-three pound key nine," instructed Desdemona.

Elsie did so, and the door slid open. There, standing silhouetted by the lighting in the gigantic room beyond her, stood Desdemona Mudrak. She eyed the five children in the small room and frowned. "That ТУПИЦЯ, " she said, directed at the man who was not present, the man who had scuttled off with Carol. Elsie guessed it had been a bad word. "What happened?"

"You tell me," said Martha. "We were in here one moment, next moment your guy comes in wearing a dress and hits me over the head. Grabbed Carol and"—she made an explosion noise with her lips—"vanished."

"Elevator," said Desdemona. "They take secret elevator."

"Right!" shouted Elsie, remembering herself. "They didn't just vanish."

"There was an elevator in here?" asked Martha, suddenly very deflated.

"Secret elevator," qualified Desdemona. "Required access pass. Roger must know pass."

"He didn't need to know the pass. The security is turned off," said Elsie. "Mr. Unthank did that. That's our escape route."

Desdemona, on hearing her former boyfriend's name, seemed to lapse into a silent stupor. As if moving by a control that was not her own, she walked into the room and proceeded to peel back a panel on the other side of the small space. It rolled sideways fluidly, following unseen tracks, revealing the twin metal doors of a rather small elevator. An illuminated button, the size of a silver dollar, was inset in the panel to the left of the doors and it flashed a few times; an upward-pointing red arrow, lit, suggested that the elevator had just deposited its load and was in the process of returning to the top floor.

Martha forgot the ebbing pain in the back of her head where the man's bottle had connected with her skull and leapt up, along with the other Unadoptables in the room, and dove for the elevator. Elsie managed the leap first; she was stabbing her finger repeatedly against the call button.

They would've been joined by Desdemona, had she not heard her name called to her, loudly, from inside Wigman's office. She turned around to see Joffrey Unthank standing in the cavity between the massive brass doors at the front of the room.

"Joffrey," she said.

"Dessie," said Unthank.

Elsie glanced over her shoulder, witnessing the scene briefly before hearing the elevator arrive and the doors whisper open. She ushered the four other Unadoptables into the waiting car. The doors closed in front of her as she climbed in, leaving Desdemona and Joffrey to their private reunion.

"What is happened to you?" asked Desdemona, walking slowly toward Joffrey.

"I had to take some time, Dessie," said Joffrey. "I had to clear my mind. Tra la tra lee."

They arrived at the center of the room together, and Desdemona reached out her hands. "Oh, Joffrey, I'm so sorry for what it is I've done," she said softly. "I did not mean to hurt."

"I know, darling," said Joffrey. "I know. In a way, you taught me. I emptied out, baby. I lost it all. But I found *me*." He seemed to then shake himself from his surprise in seeing his girlfriend. He seemed to apprise himself of something much more serious. "But you shouldn't be here now. You weren't supposed to be. It's not safe."

A quick succession of explosions happened just then; a trio of soft, blossoming glows erupted outside the tall windows of the office, one after another, like fireflies. They backlit the two of them, Desdemona and Joffrey, as they gripped each other's hands tightly, the line of their arms an obtuse angle.

"What's happening?" asked Desdemona, searching Joffrey's eyes.

"The Chapeaux Noirs, they're attacking. This is it, Dessie. This is the big one."

"The Chapeaux Noirs? But how do you know?"

"I'm with them now," said Unthank, tears welling in his eyes. "Like I said. I found *me*. I'm changed. I've found my true self. And I want you to come with. I forgive you, Dessie. It was you who led me out of my darkness, tra la, my internal darkness. The fog of my mind. You set me on the right course, tra lee. You were my beacon, my guiding light."

"Oh, Joffrey," smiled Desdemona as another explosion *pummed* and lit up the windows. Suddenly, there, in that moment, she felt something soft and warm encompassing her, a sparkle of déjà vu that seemed to descend on the two of them like a summer shower. She realized what it was: She was suddenly and acutely recalling her first onscreen kiss. The one she'd shared with Sergei Goncharenko on the set of *A Night in Havana*, there in a dusty back lot in Kiev, when they'd had only one shot left and the crew was getting tired and the budget had been strained and they had to nail this one final shot, a bare minute of film, and they'd fired the pyrotechnics and the rain was pouring down from hoses suspended above them and Sergei had said his one line ("Let's make this one count, then.") and Desdemona had felt such an upswell of emotion that she'd completely trans-ported herself to that place, to that café in Havana, amid the chaos of a popular uprising, and had kissed Sergei so deep and long that when he'd gasped and fallen back, per the screenplay, and feigned the first spasms of his character's death, she'd *gone there*, hadn't she, *she'd believed it*. And now: Desdemona, as if reenacting the screen directions of that seminal film, leaned in to kiss Joffrey and their lips met.

A very loud bang sounded. It seemed to shake the white paper chandeliers that hung over the wide room. Then a look of intense surprise awoke in Joffrey's eyes as he pulled away from the kiss and his eyebrows jutted upward and his face slackened and his mouth fell open. Then, a little trickle of blood, the bloom of a rose, appeared on his argyle sweater-vest and as it was absorbed by the fabric, it flowered out like an opening poppy, red and full, across the breadth of his chest.

Desdemona looked over his shoulder, shocked, and saw the figure of Bradley Wigman standing in the gap between the brass doors, holding a pistol, straight out away from him. A thin tongue of smoke licked away from the barrel. A cough escaped Joffrey's lips and he tumbled, a rag doll, into Desdemona's arms.

"My beacon," repeated Joffrey weakly. "My guiding light."

"Bradley!" Desdemona shouted in disbelief. "What have you done?"

Wigman drew closer, the gun still outstretched. As he came into the light, she got a better look at him—he looked as if he'd just escaped some horrible car accident. He was covered in a fine black spray, head to toe, like a coal miner in some old photo, and his bespoke shirtsleeves were torn into little shreds along his dirtied arms. His hair, typically so immaculate in its pomaded wave, literally could not

have been more mussed up—if you had tried to muss it any more you
would have only succeeded in making it more groomed.

"He's the enemy," said Wigman, a kind of traumatized gravel to
his voice. "He's a turncoat. A rat."

"You shot him," she replied, barely able to speak.

"Damn right I did," said Bradley, approaching them. "For the
good of the Wastes. For the good of the Quartet."

Joffrey coughed and his knees buckled and Desdemona fell to
the floor under his weight, kneeling and cradling him in her arms.
"Oh, Joffrey," she cried. "Dear Joffrey." His head jerked a little in
her palms, and he turned to look up at her face. He became still. He
smiled warmly, lovingly at Desdemona. His hand moved impercepti-
bly toward his left coat pocket.

When Titan Tower exploded, erupting in a shower of glass and concrete and bathing the entire Industrial Wastes in unearthly light, the five Unadoptables had only just made it out of the emergency elevator and were running across the grounds of the tower, racing after a pair of figures they'd spotted who were, in turn, struggling away down a gravel road toward a distant line of trees.

All of them, the five Unadoptables, the two figures struggling away (revealed in the light of the detonation to be Roger and Carol), the little groups of warring stevedores and Chapeaux Noirs on the outskirts of the containing walls—all of them stopped to watch the magnificent immolation of Titan Tower. It was as if day had arrived in the middle of the darkest night. The world was flooded with illumination. The stevedores, some frozen in position with their red pipe wrenches held high above their heads, blinked and stared at the sight. The Chapeaux Noirs saboteurs, in midthrow, tossed their lit bombs to a safe distance and watched the glass cascading from the top floors like a shower of crystalline rain, ignoring the detonation when their own bombs had landed, some feet away, and exploded impotently.

The stevedores all but shriveled at the sight; the heart of their entire operation, the center of the hive mind, was crashing down before them in a cataract of silver light and heat. They dropped their wrenches, each one, and fell to their knees. The Chapeaux Noirs gaped and stumbled; some pulled their black berets from their heads and held them, crushed, to their chests, so great was their reverence for this single gorgeous explosion. The tremendous light made long shadows across the blasted ground of the Industrial Wastes from all the combatants; the light touched the farthest reaches of the Wastes, the boom and rattle soon after. In Portland, even, among the quiet, dormant houses filled with Outsiders at their evening leisure, the light could be seen, a beacon of flame in some far-off field. Somewhere in the north part of the city, a child ran to his window and called out to his parents to see the strange light; he was loudly shushed and sent back to his bed so his parents could finish watching their television show.

Rachel Mehlberg, standing by a group of similarly shocked and frozen saboteurs, spied the group of five Unadoptables, shadows cast by the burning building, racing across the tower's grounds toward some unknown goal; she'd been waiting for them at the East Gate of Wigman Plaza, having long deployed her allotted four bombs, worried sick about the welfare of her sister and cursing herself for ever letting Elsie out of her sight. The sound of the battle had been deafening; a high-pitched whistle was singing in her ear. She'd just checked her watch, the chain watch that Nico had given her, and was chagrined to see that ten o'clock, the time of the rendezvous, had long passed. That was when she saw them running, charging across the budget-bin landscaping that served as greenery in the tower's interior square, now covered in a squall of glass and ash.

"There they are!" shouted Rachel. She'd counted five children;

she made the quick guess: "They've got Martha!"

Nico was standing with her. "Let's go," he yelled over the sound of the tower's residual collapse. The two of them arced out, away from the falling debris, in line to bisect the Unadoptables' course.

"Elsie!" screamed Rachel, as she charged after them. The noise of the settling wreckage of the tower blotted out all sound. A cloud of smoke and dust was barreling out from the base of the demolished building, obscuring everything in a deep, dark haze.

Just as this fog consumed them, Rachel and Nico managed to fall in line behind the running Unadoptables. "Elsie!" Rachel tried again.

Her sister quickly looked over her shoulder, seeing Rachel in pursuit. "He's got Carol!" she shouted between heaving breaths.

"Who?"

"Just . . . follow them!" shouted Elsie, exasperated.

Rachel looked ahead; they were now funneling into one of the narrow corridors that etched the face of the Industrial Wastes. The buildings in the smoke and fog were just shapes in the dark. Ahead of them, the way was lit by the occasional yellow streetlamp, glowing dimly in the haze; about fifty yards away, she could see two figures emerge into the light and disappear again.

The air around them was hot and close. Enveloped by the cloud of dust, they each pulled their black turtlenecks to their mouths to filter the grime and charged ahead. No sooner would the two figures, stumbling through the fog, disappear from sight, than they would appear again as the swirl of cloud parted and eddied away.

"STOP!" yelled Rachel, pulling her mouth away from the fabric of her shirt long enough to shout that one, sharp directive. She was immediately thrown into a fit of coughing, and she stumbled as she ran. Elsie saw her sister falter and fell back to help.

The dust cloud grew all-consuming. The horizon was blotted out. Only the closest streetlamps could be seen on the road. The looming chemical silos along the gravel roadside became deeply shrouded in the gray dust, transforming into still, white ghosts in the dark. The pursuers continued forward, arriving after a short time at a chain-link fence.

"Look!" shouted Nico, pointing to a ripple in the fence where the bottom had been lifted from the ground. A piece of rough gray fabric was caught in the wire mesh; Nico grabbed the wire and pulled, holding it open as the six children scrambled through. On the other side of the fence was a wide, fallow stretch of scrub brush and scotch broom. Just at that moment, a gust of wind picked up and peeled away the curtain of clouds like a hand on a fogged windscreen, revealing the way ahead: a looming line of trees, a dense weave of bracken and greenery, a whining creak from ancient boughs.

Ahead, not far off, a robed figure could be seen, ankle deep in fern fronds, dragging his reluctant companion past the threshold of trees and into the Impassable Wilderness.

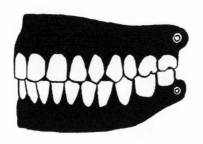

CHAPTER 21

A Revival Is Born

It was like a wave of gray had crashed over the village, lapping up every citizen in its tide. That was the only way to describe it. Where one day there had been only a few of them, the next it was one out of every five; and suddenly they were everywhere you looked: hooded robes and swinging censers, silvery masks and silent stares. The South Wood Guard, an honored institution since the first brick of the Mansion had been pulled from the kiln, was immediately dissolved, its ranks subsumed into the Synod's new security force, the Watch, whose members walked through the village distributing pamphlets describing the laws of the new regime.

It seemed as if it happened overnight, this sudden takeover, and yet its seeds had been planted months before.

No one quite knew what happened to the leaders of the post-revolution regime, whether they had been absorbed into this new vision of leadership or had simply been disappeared like the Svikists of old, but it was a hardy Spoke indeed who would pine for the revolution's endless social and political protocols that had been stripped away—the sashes and the sprocket brooches, the forced honorifics, and the always-looming fear of the guillotine—with the rise of the Synod. The revolutionary leaders, those who had survived the months of purges within their own ranks, had made such a hash of governance that when the wave of gray robes crested and fell upon the people of South Wood, they were, from most quarters, welcomed as long-awaited saviors, and their edicts, though strict, were adopted almost immediately.

"One has to give up some liberty," a village elder was heard to say, "in the service of the greater good. At least initially."

A strict curfew was imposed; no one outside the Synod's inner ranks and those employed by the Watch were to be on the streets, outside their homes, after ten p.m. The uniform of the Spokes—the bicycle pants, the caps, and the sashes, not to mention the ever-present brooches—was absolutely verboten. Anyone found wearing such a costume would be detained by the Watch and put on trial in front of the Blighted Tree for the crime of inciting unrest. Any literature or paraphernalia connected to the former revolutionary movement—deemed a fascist junta by the Synod—was to be collected and destroyed. No questions asked, the wording of the pamphlets emphasized. The good folk of South Wood were to be received with open arms by the Synod and forgiven their past missteps, according to the teachings of the Blighted Tree—provided no unfortunate backsliding was exhibited. And despite their prior allegiances, all were expected to show their devotion to the Blighted Tree by congregating in the Glade every Wednesday morning at nine and again at noon for those who couldn't make the earlier service.

Those so moved would be welcome to petition the Elder Caliph (or, in case of his absence, his second in command) for a role within the clergy—perhaps even an acolyte-ship, provided they received the tree's communion and were prepared to take the vow of silence required of the inner circle of Caliphs. Those who had felt lost within the revolutionary fervor of the prior regime, those who had felt threatened by the all-as-one mentality the prior regime sold, those who had longed for more security and control, gladly gave themselves to the edicts of the Synod, and peace, of a sort, reigned over South Wood for the first time in quite a while.

And so, Zita could not blame her father for his newfound religiosity. There'd been a pretty sizable void in his life since the passing of her mother, and, once the Synod's influence had found its way into their home, a new life sprang into his eyes. He'd been given a position in the civilian ranks of the Synod, a job that entailed organizing events within the community and occasionally assisting in the services that were held at the Blighted Tree. It gave him a renewed perspective, and a fresh intention.

That morning, he'd been pulled in by a group of other low-level Caliphs who'd been tasked to whitewash the many pro-revolution murals that had been painted on the village walls over the last several months, and he'd arrived home, sometime after nightfall, achingly tired. He'd been surprised to see his daughter, quite awake, sitting in the living room, reading a book.

"Hey, Dad," said Zita, seeing him come in. She recognized him, despite the mirrored green mask and the floor-length gray robe he'd been asked to wear when he was doing the work of the Synod.

He hung his robe on the rack by the door and slumped in the chair opposite Zita; he pulled the mask from his face, dropping the loop of his cowl to the back of his chair. "Hiya," he said. He looked exhausted. "What are you doing up?"

"Can't sleep," she said. "Plus, we just got all new textbooks at school. Everything's changed to meet the Synod's new rules."

Her father frowned. "Ah," he said. "Well, it's really for the best. We have a lot of lost time to make up for."

"Yeah," said Zita. "Oh—did you hear? Kendra's eating the Spongiform tomorrow."

"Really? She's so young!" Zita could hear a little disappointment in her father's tired voice; she knew that it was his goal to receive this communion. He only needed to prove himself within the organization.

"Well, her dad's been involved in the Synod for a while now," said Zita. "She got a little help on the way."

"Good for Kendra," said her father, heaving a sigh. "Well, I'm bushed, dear. Gonna head in for the night."

"Okay, Dad. Sleep well."

"Don't be up too late."

"I'll try."

"Good night."

"Good night." She waited until he had closed his door behind him, listened for the shuffling of his bare feet. Before long, the seesaw of his snoring was emanating through his bedroom door, and Zita snuck a glance over her book at the cascade of gray sackcloth he'd hung on the coatrack. A shiny green mask, its chin exposed beneath the cloth, glinted in the candlelight.

She had to fold and pin the hem of the robe up a few inches above her ankles to keep it from dragging along the ground as she walked; the mask's eerily cold inner surface clung to her skin and seemed to amplify her labored, excited breathing. The night lay on thick, thick with fog, and she hurried through the glow of the gaslights. The clock tower, sitting vigil over the empty town square, chimed the hour as she passed through the shadow it cast by the gas lamp's light.

In the pocket of her robe sat two objects: a small white pebble and an eagle's feather.

For ceremonial effect, she'd worn her unwashed white dress beneath the robe—the same dress she'd worn for her coronation as May Queen. She'd even set what little remained of the desiccated wreath of flowers, her crown, over her head, hidden beneath the shroud of the gray hood. She thought it was fitting, wearing this costume. She thought the final conjuration would feel more like a completed circle this way.

The cobbled street she was following, an artery off the square, was suddenly filled with a company of Watch members. Their masks were black, befitting their rank, and they carried black truncheons, which they swung idly by their sides as they walked. Zita counted seven of them. She stood to one side of the road and bowed as they passed; they seemed to size her up, this green-masked Caliph, but apparently thought little of her appearance on the street after curfew. It was allowed, after all. The edicts stated that anyone who'd earned his or her robes could be out on official business past curfew. She was thankful they hadn't stopped her to ask what that business was; she'd had a hazy excuse but wasn't sure if it'd pass muster.

No matter; the gang disappeared around the corner behind her, on their way to prowl the square for other curfew breakers. One thing was certain: The village had become much safer since the Synod took over—there was no denying that. Before, in the weeks leading up to the takeover, people tended to impose their own curfews on themselves and their families. It simply wasn't safe to stroll the streets after dark.

But here, in her cocoon of gray cloth and green mask, Zita felt empowered. What's more, she knew that her arduous work, her job as gofer to a disembodied spirit, was coming to a close. Now she would see the fruits of her labors. She would see the woman reborn. She would give that woman a child to love.

The lights of the village grew distant; she found herself on a quiet, dark road that led out into the surrounding forest. It wormed its way around the landscape, having been laid in deference to the older trees in the wood so that they would not be disturbed. Even so, with the passing of centuries, the old oaks and walnuts had expanded their territory and buckled the cobbles such that there were ripples like mountain ranges erupting here and there and Zita had to watch her steps carefully.

Finally, she arrived at the spot. She'd known the way fairly well; it was a place she and her father frequented, making the trek every Sunday afternoon. A metal gate stood guard over the entrance; it hung permanently open, having been shoved aside by a ripple in the cobblestones. A wrought-iron arch bridged the distance between the two sides of the gate. Zita pulled a flashlight from her robe and flashed it

over the words that had been ornately spelled out there: SOUTH WOOD CEMETERY.

Zita lifted the mask from her face, letting it rest on the crown of her head. She didn't expect she'd see any Caliphs here, at the cemetery, where few people would think to go after eleven. But she kept the mask poised, just in case, so she could bat it down over her face at a moment's notice. She gave the gate a push; it creaked a little, and she squeezed herself through the opening.

She made her way by the rows of headstones, along the avenues of memorial plaques, all littered with drying flowers, toward a shape she could just make out through the thickening mist: a gabled roof, on a little rise in the earth, with a fluted portico. She'd seen it often—it was impossible to miss. Every Sunday, when she and her father made their way drearily to this cemetery, their arms filled with fresh-cut flowers, she would look at that strange, noble mausoleum and wonder: what an incredible testament, what a gift, to be housed in such a glorious tomb. She wondered at the person resting within—her father had explained to her that it housed the remains of Alexei Svik, the son of the old Governess. Her mind boggled at the importance of the child, the heir to the Mansion. How his greatness required such an elaborate monument be made over his deceased form.

But then she changed her mind; with every visit to her mother's gravesite, some yards below where the prince's mausoleum stood, she grew disgusted with the building. No one ever visited it, not that she could tell, and no flowers were scattered across its granite veranda. What an ostentatious display of reverence, she thought, for just another person dead. What made his death more important than any other's, that he required such a monument? Her heart was broken, her father's life was a shambles, and every Sunday they came to remove the old flowers and replace them with the new ones at the simple grave of her mother, a woman who had meant more to them than any deceased royal or gentleman-in-waiting, while the prince's cold tomb remained unvisited, unloved. She wanted to tear it down, piece by piece, and use the salvaged remnants to build a shrine to her grief for the loss of her mother, one that she and her father could visit every day and cry over. Something big that towered over everything around it; something so big that it blocked the sun.

So she did not feel an iota of remorse about what was asked of her—to violate the tomb and desecrate its lifeless occupant. To push back the lid of the sarcophagus and remove the body's teeth.

Strangely, she found she was numb to the macabre nature of the act; she was now too determined to be thrown by anything. The Verdant Empress had asked this much of her. She would show the spirit that she was not cowed.

Zita did not stop at her mother's grave. Not tonight. Her eyes remained locked on the prince's tomb and she walked steadily toward it, weaving between the tidy, moss-grown plots along the way.

The door to the tomb was made of iron and hung on ancient metal hinges. Zita gave a quick look around her before she pried the door open and slipped into the mausoleum. Inside, all was dark. She shone her flashlight around the small entry chamber and watched as the light fell on various items that had been laid there: a child's doll, a toy castle, a riding crop. Evidently the things the family of the deceased boy had thought should be interred with his body. The room let onto another, larger room, and in the center of this chamber she saw the sarcophagus.

It wasn't too long or wide; it was the size you would expect to hold the body of a teenaged boy. It was made of polished stone, and some coffin maker had gone to the extra trouble to carve a frieze around the beveled edge of the lid: a woodland scene with a group of elk being chased by a boy on a horse through a grove of flowering trees. Zita ran her fingers along the decoration as she looked for the seam between it and the container itself. Finding a spot, she gritted her teeth and pushed; the lid groaned and slid slightly to one side.

It had taken, really, all the strength she could conjure to push it a scant few inches. She peeked into the crack she'd made between the lid and the coffin; the light from her flashlight caught the fringe edge of an epaulet. She pushed again, setting the flashlight down on the ground next to her. Again, it moved a few inches before she had to stop and take a deep breath. She glanced heavenward, wish-thinking to the spirits of the air that maybe the Verdant Empress could just come now and help her. But no: She had a rite to complete.

She knitted her brow, braced herself against the cold stone of the floor, curled her finger around the edge of the coffin lid and again, with all her strength, pushed. The lid gave and an opening spread out; the body was revealed. The far edge of the coffin lid suddenly tipped, and the weight of the lid came toppling down on the other side of the container, cracking into pieces with a loud crash. Zita screamed and leapt back—she hadn't intended that.

Her hand to her face, she walked slowly toward the open coffin and looked inside.

There, lying peacefully, was a boy.

A boy her age, she judged. Untouched by the weathers of time. His skin was perfectly pale and placid. His eyes were closed and his face was set in a look of almost resigned quiet. He was beautiful, this boy. Suddenly, Zita felt a shock of remorse for her loathing of the mausoleum, of the monument to the boy. It wasn't as if he'd had a say in how he was memorialized; he had no more choice in his death than in his birth. The garish display of his mausoleum had been the work of a state intent on creating a symbol of this boy and of the enduring legacy of his family name, no more.

He wore a tidy and pressed uniform, with gold-fringed epaulets at the shoulders, and tarnished brass buttons ran in a clean line down his chest. Looking closer, Zita noted that there were little rivets along the side of his chin and a hinge—yes, it was a hinge!— had been soldered at his jaw. She shone the flashlight closer and saw that his face was not, in fact, made of flesh but instead a kind of pearly-white metallic material. She reached into the coffin and, experimenting, tapped a finger against the boy's cheek; the sound came back hollow, tinny.

"Huh," said Zita aloud.

This much she'd known, that the Governess had re-created the boy as a mechanical facsimile of her deceased child. What she hadn't realized or reckoned was the incredible care that had gone into the making of this automaton. It was uncanny, really, the resemblance it bore to the organic thing it was modeling. The craftsmanship involved was dizzying.

Recalling herself to her task, she balanced the flashlight on the edge of the coffin and set about managing her first-ever postmortem dental extraction.

Using both hands, she pulled the jaw of the boy open and found that the lips separated with the ease of a well-oiled pair of garden clippers. Holding the jaw carefully prized apart with two fingers, she grabbed the flashlight with her other hand and shone it into the cavity of the boy's mouth. There, set into the metal, were a set of handsome—and very human—teeth.

Somehow, the synthetic nature of the rest of the boy's head and face tempered the wave of nausea that had begun creeping up through Zita's chest as she began the careful extraction. She'd laid the flashlight by the boy's ear in order to get the scant light right, and, with two fingers keeping the metallic jaws pried apart, she gripped the top row of teeth and pulled. To her surprise, the entire row released from the jaw with very little resistance—a kind rubbery pop sounded as she did so—and she held the thing in her hands up to the flashlight's beam: Some sort of pinkish material held the teeth in formation; little copper rivets seemed to hold them to the mold. Sticking the thing in her pocket, she pulled the bottom row of teeth out in a similar fashion. The jaw, apparently set on springs, clicked back into place.

Something stirred somewhere, something almost imperceptible.

A slight change in temperature, a shift in the timbre of the ambient noise in the mausoleum. Zita glanced around the room, at the cold, fluted pillars that supported the four corners of the slanted roof. She backed away from the opened sarcophagus and edged toward the entrance. A sudden breeze erupted out of nowhere, strong enough to make the heavy iron door at the entrance moan slightly on its hinges.

She shoved the second set of teeth into the pocket of her robe. They were now joined with the eagle feather and the white pebble. She turned and began to run for the entrance of the tomb, suddenly overcome with anxiety. The green mask fell over her face, startling her. She dashed out of the door and into the cemetery.

A wind had picked up, and it shook the ancient trees of the grave-yard; the beam of the flashlight danced before her as Zita ran down the little paved walkways between the graves. She squeezed back through the wrought-iron gate and onto the road. A gang of robed guards, the Watch, appeared from around the bend in the road. Taking a deep breath, she calmed herself and slowed her walk. She noticed they seemed to be agitated; they were all looking up at the waving branches of the trees. They seemed alarmed by the sudden and strange shift in the weather.

They saw her and hollered something; it was lost in the wind, which was now blowing powerfully enough to bend the thickest boughs on the oldest tree. Something cracked; a limb fell noisily to the cobbled street below. It fell into the midst of the gathered figures, scattering them, and Zita ran in the other direction.

The wind barked and the trees shook all around her; it was as if the forest itself was trying to stop her from finishing her rite. Leaving the road and breaking through a thicket of briars, she felt the thorns tear at her robe as if they were fingers holding her back. The branches lashed at her face; the green mask protected her, but she felt battered nonetheless.

Finally, she arrived at her destination. The glow of the flashlight lit up the mossy green walls of the old stone house; the village clock, somewhere, chimed midnight. The wind howled through the empty cavities of the house's windows and whipped down through its open roof.

She stumbled through the broken door and fell to her knees in the thick carpet of ivy that was the house's floor. The wind was practically roaring now and a heavy rain had started, thrashing sideways across Zita's face once she'd thrown her mask to the ground. She dropped her father's Synodal robe from her body, revealing the white dress beneath, and adjusted the flower crown on her head. Her brown hair was soaked through almost instantaneously. The water was pouring down her face as she thrust her hands into the robe's pocket and retrieved the three things she'd stowed there: an eagle's feather. A pearly stone. A boy's full set of teeth.

From the other pocket, she pulled the little bowl, the bowl that had been her mother's, the one she'd kept on her dresser. She set it carefully down in the bed of ivy (which was now writhing in the wind) and, one after another, she placed the three items in the bowl.

First, the feather.

YES, came a voice—or was it the wind?

Then the stone.

YESSS, repeated the voice. Couldn't be the wind.

And finally, the teeth.

NOW, said the voice.

Zita looked up at the sky, laden with clouds and shaking tree branches, and calmly intoned the following incantation:

> *"I CALL YOU,*
> *VERDANT EMPRESS."*

The sky ceased its bucketing rain. The clouds froze in place. The trees quivered and gasped.

The ivy came alive under Zita's knees. It was as if the ivy was a body of water and someone, from a very great height, had dropped a rock into it. The point of contact was the bowl of offerings, and the wave rippled out in concentric circles from the center. Now the circle came again, this time as if the thing that had been dropped was the size of a basketball, and Zita, to her shock, was carried along in the crest; she fell backward on her elbows. Then it happened again, again larger, and Zita was thrown to one side of the house, where she braced herself for another wave.

Quiet. Silent stillness.

Then: an eruption from the center of the ivy bed, from the spot where the bowl had been laid. A single column of ivy blew from the earth and rocketed upward, a writhing, pitching obelisk of the plant; the green vines twisted and braided themselves, controlled by an unseen power, and began to take shape into something other. Suddenly, from the cocoonlike tangle of ivy, Zita saw an arm outstretch.

She was watching a human, slowly being created out of ivy.

Zita watched as the ivy, suspended in midair above the floor of the stone house, formed twin limbs—human limbs—that licked out into long, thin fingers; fingers that unfurled and straightened as life channeled through them. The ivy, at the center point, curled in on itself, making the trunk, and two breasts extruded from the leaves, and Zita realized she was watching the creation of a woman and, in her wildness of thought, suddenly knew it to be the Verdant Empress herself.

The vines atop the columns busily coiled in on themselves, and soon a head and a face became clear, and a clutch of the plant grew down from the crown of the head to form two braids of hair. A wide brow, an elegant cheekbone—all framing two closed eyes that hung over a nose and a pair of sweet green lips. Zita watched it all take place, absolutely transfixed by the miracle that was happening, that she had called into being. What power! What incredible magic!

And then the eyes opened.

They flared like fire, a fire that overtook the figure's placid expression and twisted it into a look of absolute spite.

Seeing this, Zita screamed, and the figure looked down at her piti-lessly.

The ivy-woman's mouth yawned open, and a terrifying and heart-rending moan issued from its lips, and Zita realized that what she had done was a very bad idea. A very bad idea, indeed.

*

The three sets of ripples that had started from that center point on the floor of the old stone house on Macleay Road continued, as all waves must, on past the walls of the house and pulsed out into the neighboring woods. With each spasm of energy that was created, the wave in the ivy poured out, concentrically, and the wave grew as it moved, pushed forward by its own momentum. It rolled through the vegetation that surrounded the cemetery and out into the villages of South Wood; it contorted the roads and shattered the windows of the sleeping houses. It woke children and adults alike from their sleep; sent fathers and mothers running for their windows to see what the disturbance had been. It swept outward, farther still, and rent the hard stone of the North Wall and quaked the massive cedars of the Avian Principality, sending birds scurrying to flight while their nests, brittle in the wave, broke to pieces and scattered into the wind. The wave roared through Wildwood, awaking every tendril of ivy as it went, pulling every vine into its movement and through the Ancients' Grove. It broke under the feet of a mob of young children who had just crossed into the woods, only momentarily slowing them in their pursuit of the two men who were making their way, farther and farther, into this strange and unknowable wilderness. It rode across these deep, uninhabited forests and wrecked the cobbles of the Long Road and crested, unstoppable, over the passes and the peaks of the Cathedral Mountains; it rolled into North Wood and pulverized the freshly plowed furrows of the farmers' lands and shook the roots of the Council Tree, sending a flurry of dead and dying leaves into the cold, gray air.

It went out, farther still. It became a loping wave on the churning Columbia River and sent bucking breakers to smash into the hull of a four-masted ocean-bound ship. The vessel rocked violently and sent a flurry of seamen scrambling about the decks, trying to right the ship. Down in the belowdecks, a black-haired girl, held captive in a locked cell, awoke from a fitful sleep and gasped.

She stood up quickly, feeling something—not just the feel of the ship quaking in the sudden wave—but something else entirely, as if the physical force of the wave had been accompanied by a cry for help from every leaf and branch and stem and petal of the forest.

She stared out of her barred porthole, her eyes agape.

"She's come back," said the girl.

PART THREE

CHAPTER 22

An Owl's Tale

In the woods, there lived an owl.

He was a quiet owl, one who liked to keep to himself. He considered himself lucky to be living in a fairly untrammeled patch of the forest, and he rarely had much fuss with his neighbors. He slept through the days, typically, in a cozy nest he'd built in the hollow of a very old tree, which had snapped in half during a storm some twelve years prior. The hollow made a very nice home for an owl who was getting on in years.

He had relatives who were living in other, more populated areas of the Wood, and they were forever bothering him to come and join them; that somehow, in his advanced age, he could benefit from the help of others. To him, this suggestion implied that he was unable to look out for himself, and he took umbrage at this. Deep, deep umbrage. It only made him more content in his daily and nightly habits, his everyday activities, here in this farthest frontier of the woods in his quiet and cozy hollow-of-a-tree.

Every day, he slept away the sunlit hours and woke himself at dusk. Every night, he busily tidied his hollow-of-a-tree and then set out for his breakfast, which happened at night, as it does for most owls. However, rather than expending an awful lot of energy, flying around and searching the forest floor for food, this owl simply climbed out of his nest and made his way, slowly, some three feet down the edge of one of the tree's surviving limbs and sat there for the remaining hours of the evening, watching the ground. Occasionally a small rodent would run across his field of vision and he would unfurl his large, weatherworn wings and soar down and grab it for lunch or dinner, depending on what time of night it was. But mostly he just sat there, staring at the ground.

When the first glints of sunrise awoke the early morning birds and the waxy leaves of the salal vines glowed in the light, the owl would yawn and make his way the few feet to his nest in the hollow-of-a-tree and happily brew himself some hot chocolate and cozy up with a book in a small chair by the fireplace and doze off.

Life went on like this for the old owl, fairly uninterrupted, until one day, while he was holding his vigil on the tree limb, casually scanning the darkened underbrush for rodents, as he did every night, a slight tremor alerted him to someone or something that had joined him on the branch.

He looked over to see that it was a squirrel.

"Go away," said the owl.

"What're you looking at?" asked the squirrel.

"Nothing," said the owl, not wanting to engage the newcomer in conversation. He enjoyed his privacy, his solitude. He wished the squirrel would respect that.

The squirrel cocked his head. "Nothing? Like, nothing?"

"Nothing," said the owl. "Now leave me alone."

The squirrel remained, transfixed, as the owl was, on the ground below.

"You're still here," said the owl, after a time. Which the squirrel was.

"How do you do it?" asked the squirrel.

"Do what?"

"Just sit here, staring at the ground. Don't you get bored?"

"For your information, I am hunting," said the owl. "I am hunting for small, furry creatures that I might eat. Technically, you fit that description."

"Is that a threat?"

"I'd just prefer to be left alone, is all," said the owl with a deep sigh.

"I get it," said the squirrel.

They sat in silence for a moment, while the owl continued to search the ground. He didn't like confrontation or conflict, this owl, and so he chose to simply pretend that the squirrel wasn't there. He would make good on his threat and eat the squirrel, except that the owl didn't particularly like the taste of squirrels—and, what's more, they were a little too big for him. Maybe in his younger days, but now, he found he preferred the ease of hunting mice and voles and the like.

"Question," said the squirrel.

"What?" asked the owl, annoyed. Perhaps if he engaged the squirrel briefly, he could satisfy the animal's curiosity and he would then leave the owl in peace.

"Don't you think there's, you know, more to life? I mean, more than just sitting here on this limb and waiting for some food to come walking along."

"What do you mean?" asked the owl, now having a hard time pretending the squirrel wasn't there.

"You know, seems an awful waste of one's time on this stretch of earth, just satisfying the urgings of the old tummy without a thought given to the bigger questions of the day."

The owl thought about this for a second, before replying, "Seems okay to me."

And then: "Seems like a very good life, actually."

The squirrel shook his head. "But there's, like, a whole *world* out there! Filled with mystery and awe and sorrow and happiness. And all you're doing, night in and night out, is sitting on this old branch and watching for a mouse to come along." The squirrel held out his paws, palms up, and shook them. "Don't you just, you know, *long* for more?"

"Guess I hadn't thought about it that much," was the owl's reply. "Now if you wouldn't mind, I don't want to—"

"Hold up," said the squirrel. "Can I show you something?"

"No," said the owl.

"Oh, c'mon," the squirrel chided. "It'll just take a sec."

The owl glanced ruefully at his branch-mate and gave no answer, which the squirrel took to be an emphatic *yes*. He held up a single digit of his paw before leaping from the branch and disappearing into the canopy of trees.

Hmm, thought the owl. *That was easy.* He returned his attention to the ground below, a dark blanket of ferns and vines, hoping for the promise of a lunchtime meal. He sat there for a time and only occasionally did his thoughts go to the squirrel and his strange question about the nature of the owl's simple and, he had to admit, fairly contented, way of life. Why *should* he long for more? Wasn't everything he needed right here? Wasn't there a kind of solace in the repetitions of his life, how every evening and every day were, more or less, exactly the same, barring whatever minute interruptions he might have to suffer on very rare occasions—like, say, a squirrel distracting him from his nightly surveillance? Oddly enough, the more he pondered these questions, the more he began to see holes in his timeless logic. Maybe the squirrel was onto something. . . .

Before he had a chance to delve deeper in his own meditations, the branch shook and the squirrel reappeared at the owl's side. "Hi," said the squirrel.

"Hi," said the owl.

The squirrel was carrying something. He held it up and showed it to the owl; it was a large postcard, human-sized, and on it was a photograph of a very strange and elaborate structure. The structure seemed to be made of sticks, or sticklike objects, and it stood on four stick-made legs. The sticks made a kind of lattice as the four legs met each other at the midsection, and from there a pinnacle-like tower sprouted upward, skyward, to reach a fixed point at the very top, which seemed to end in a spired arrowhead-like design. What's more, there seemed to be a viewing deck at the top of the structure; small figures, ant-size relative to the structure they were standing on, milled about on the observation deck.

"What is it?" asked the owl.

"That's the thing," said the squirrel. "I don't know. But look at it. Look at that thing. I have no idea how big it is, or how many squirrels it took to build it, or even *where* it is. This picture just literally fell out of the sky one day while I was busily collecting sunflower seeds. Like you, I spent my days as if I were *adhered* to a track, like I was trying, busily, to simply *re-create* the exact events of the day before: forever collecting seeds and nuts, forever skittishly running up and down tree trunks, forever making this kind of weird squeaking noise with my front teeth." Just then, he made the noise. It surprised the owl, whose attention was firmly engaged with the picture the squirrel was holding. "See?"

"Mm-hmm," said the owl.

"But *boom*. This picture floats down from the sky and I look at it and suddenly—wow—my worldview, like, *instantaneously* doubles. Or triples! And suddenly my rote daily exercise of sustenance and survival seems awfully puny in the face of such, like, flourishes of creative spirit. You know? Simultaneously, I experienced this very true understanding—this *epiphany*—of the oh-so-trivial nature of life, and yet, despite the trivialities, a life that is so full, so *chock-full*, of an almost infinite promise. You see?"

The owl was dizzied by the squirrel's monologue. "I guess so," was all he could say.

"It's okay," said the squirrel. "I was where you were, once. I was in the dark. My eyes were closed to the possibilities." He flipped the postcard in his fingers, away from the owl, and gave it a long glance. He then handed it to the owl.

"Here," he said. "I want you to have it."

The owl gulped. "Don't you want it?"

"It did me some good. Time for me to pay it forward."

"Okay," said the owl, taking the postcard in his talon. And then: "What are you going to do now?"

"I'm off to have some adventures," responded the squirrel. "I'm off to see the world."

And with that, the squirrel gave the owl a puckish wink and a little salute. He then tiptoed off the end of the branch and nimbly dove into the surrounding dark.

The owl sat for a time on the branch, alternately looking at that same patch of forest floor he had for years upon years, and looking at the postcard picture the squirrel had given him. The thing—the tower—on the postcard was truly a work of dizzying beauty. The night passed like this, with the owl in deep contemplation. Finally, a hint of sun broke through the low branches of the Douglas fir saplings, and the forest awoke to the morning. The owl walked back into his nest in the hollow-of-a-tree, and he proceeded to do his morning ritual: He made himself a cup of cocoa and he climbed into his cozy chair with his book—but not before he had taken the postcard and attached it to a little twig that had ingrown just above the fireplace. And there he continued to look at the strange structure until he drifted off to sleep.

When he awoke, he knew what he had to do.

That night, rather than standing on the branch, as he had for so

many nights prior, he instead began flying around the neighboring trees, retrieving branches and twigs in his talons. Once he'd amassed a nice pile at the base of his broken tree, he began to select the straightest and the strongest of these branches.

He then began to build.

Using the picture as a rough template, the owl, in the dark of night, began assembling the tower's four legs. They each collapsed a few times, that first night, before he was finally able to get one to stand firmly. From that, he guessed that the little maple branches he'd salvaged were best for the job, and once he'd built a strong enough foundation, he fortified the legs by weaving dogwood twigs through the branches, which also managed to fabricate the latticed look of the tower he was modeling. Before he knew it, the sun was rising and the songbirds were chirping, and he settled back in his hollow-of-a-tree for the night, staring at the tower on the postcard until he drifted off to sleep.

And so his life continued, for some time, night in and night out, as he collected scavenged forest debris and used it as building blocks for a scale model of the incredible edifice on the postcard he carried with him wherever he went, a structure that the owl believed to be a testament to the dynamic thinking and ambition of organic life. The squirrel had mentioned that he believed it was his fellow species that had built the original; the owl now suspected that his own, *Strix varia*, had been responsible for this particular feat. He was intent on re-creating it.

It happened, after many months had passed, that the owl finally came close to finishing his laborious endeavor. The neighboring forest floor had been largely picked over in his pursuit, and he found he often had to go farther afield to source the right building materials; some miles off, he'd found a green pinecone, perfectly conical in shape, that would serve perfectly as the final piece, the pinnacle of the tower's top. That night he intended to set it.

And set it he did, in a moment that seized his little owl heart and gave him such an electricity that he could barely keep his talons from quivering as he laid the pinecone at the apex of the latticed tower. Seeing it affixed, the owl flew back to his perch on the branch on the broken tree and looked down on his creation with pride.

Just then, the owl heard a noise. It was a kind of rumbling noise, coming from somewhere distant, and it seemed to unsettle the forest in its growlings. The greenery rustled and the birds whistled in alarm; within seconds, it rolled into the small clearing below the owl's hollow-of-a-tree: a kind of bulbous wave, echoing out from some far-off point, in the vegetation itself. He saw it coming several yards away, creating a weird roll to the landscape, but could barely dive down to his creation before the wave had come upon him.

It bucked the wooden tower and caused it to sway, dangerously, in the wake. The pinecone, so recently affixed, began to topple from its perch and the owl swooped down, in a panic, to catch it. But no sooner had he saved the cone from falling than the rest of the structure began to tremble and snap. Seized with terror that his beloved creation was about to come tumbling down, the owl desperately flew about the tower, bracing all the struts and supports that were threatening to break apart. Seconds passed like hours. Time seemed to still to a stop. Finally, the owl, his one talon braced on one of the legs of the tower, his other talon somehow extended to the midsection, felt the structure settle back into place, and he breathed a long and very exasperated sigh.

Two men, one fairly dragging the other along, suddenly entered the clearing and, their eyes trained behind them, ran headlong into the owl's creation and knocked it, every maple branch and every twig of dogwood, to the ground in a splintering crash.

The owl fell backward, devastated.

The two men seemed to not even have reckoned what damage they'd done, as they were gone from the clearing within the bat of a wing.

The forest floor lay littered with little scavenged sticks; a single pinecone rolled to a stop at the base of the owl's broken tree. And then, some moments after, adding insult to injury, a group of kids came charging through the clearing and sent the piled remains of the tower cracking and spinning into the surrounding bracken.

The owl put his wing to his brow and sighed.

🌿

*She thrust her hands into the robe's pocket and retrieved the three things
she'd stowed there: an eagle's feather. A pearly stone. A boy's full set of teeth.*

When the fog and smoke had cleared and the trees seemingly materialized on the horizon before them, as if conjured, Elsie immediately knew where the man was taking Carol. Inwardly, she knew that her path, and her sister's, would eventually lead back into the Impassable Wilderness. She just hadn't anticipated it quite happening like this. Once they'd come to the end of the barren, scrubby skirt of land that served as a sort of buffer between these two I.W.s, they knew what to do.

"Nico," shouted Rachel. "Grab hands!"

"What?" called the saboteur, his breath labored from the pursuit.

"Just do it!" called Elsie from the front of the pack.

The group locked hands, with Nico in the center and Rachel taking up the rear. They recalled how they'd left the Periphery, so many months ago; they could only hope that the enchantment remained.

They heard a shout from behind them; jerking her head around, Elsie saw that the sound had erupted from an enraged mob of stevedores, some two dozen in number, that were steaming toward them at full speed. The burning remnants of Titan Tower smoldered behind them.

"Quick!" yelled Elsie. Mindful to keep a tight grip on the hand of the soul behind her—who happened to be Oz—Elsie led the troupe beyond the veil of trees and into the forest. The rumble and yell of the stevedores grew louder; they were getting closer.

Rachel, being the last in the line, glanced back at their pursuers just as they crossed over; the hulking shapes of the stevedores seemed to blur and shimmy in the dim light until they disappeared completely. Perhaps she saw a single maroon beanie fall to the ground behind her, or perhaps it was just a trick of the light.

The woods surrounded them. The trees seemed, in a way, to swallow them whole.

A rustle from ahead, a strangled shout, alerted them to Roger and Carol's trail; they pressed on, stepping through the knee-deep vegetation. Once they were certain they'd crossed far enough, they unlocked hands. Nico retrieved a flashlight from his knapsack and stepped up to the front of the pack. He and Elsie, together, led the team forward, ever watchful of the ground at their feet and of the path of disturbed undergrowth that the two men ahead of them left in their wake.

"Carol!" shouted Elsie when they'd taken a wrong turn.

A holler came from their right; it was immediately choked off.

"This way!" shouted Nico.

The forest crowded around them, hampering their every step. The dark spaces in between the trees loomed menacingly, and Elsie thought she heard strange rattlings in the underbrush. She kept her eye trained on the bouncing ray of Nico's flashlight as if it were a rope and she was dangling from a cliff. She feared that were she to leave the safety of the light's bare glow, she would be lost forever in a wood that felt more inhospitable and more threatening with every step they took.

A light danced off the branches ahead of them, giving away Roger and Carol's location; they were making their way up a steep slope some ten yards distant. The children and Nico had no sooner seen the two men, however, than the light disappeared and the two were gone again, deep into the bushes. They followed the path, scrambling up the hill and through a dense clutch of ivy vines. They tore through a small clearing, their feet trundling over what looked to be a massive stockpile of sticks and branches scattered about the forest floor; Elsie looked down at this in horror, briefly, wondering at the sort of obsessed animal that would make such a bizarre collection as this. They'd already gone farther, she guessed, than she'd ever ventured before into the Impassable Wilderness.

They'd grown close enough now that they could hear the two men as they crashed their way through the trees; Nico stopped the rest of the Unadoptables with a wave of his hand as if to say, *Listen.*

They stopped. Silence. It was evident that the two men, Carol and Roger, had paused in their escape.

"Mr. Swindon!" shouted Elsie. This was the name Desdemona had used describing the man; she guessed it was the same gentleman who had initially demanded Carol be delivered to him, back when they'd had the standoff with the stevedores during the orphanage rebellion. It was a hunch, anyway.

"How did you . . . ," came the shout in response. "Who are you?"

It was the voice of a fatigued and very confused man.

"We want Carol back, that's all!"

"Well, you can't have him!" was the response. Then: the two men's noisy retreat started up again.

The six Unadoptables and Nico continued their pursuit.

The forest here felt older, more ancient. The tree trunks they rounded were the heft of midsize automobiles, and the fern glades they stumbled through looked straight out of some computer-generated cut-scene from a dinosaur documentary. Elsie felt her attention being drawn in a million different directions. Her eyes were fixated on the way ahead, the bouncing glow of Nico's flashlight and the sound of the two men's shambolic running in the distance; her heart and her mind were constantly being drawn to the crowding forest, to the sounds that sparked in the night, strange and alive.

Nico screamed, once, suddenly.

"What is it?" shouted Rachel from behind.

"There's creatures! In the woods!" he shouted frantically as they ran.

Elsie took her eyes off the way ahead and scanned the nearby bushes; she saw it too: A head appeared, a bulky torso. "Run!" she shouted. "Faster!" Spikes of fear shot through her limbs, and she charged forward.

Their pace quickened; still, they saw the figures in the trees, as if silently watching them, following them.

Just then, they heard a shout sound from the trees ahead: It was

Carol and Roger, their voices united in a single, surprised exclamation. A great crash followed the sound quickly, and the trees ahead were seen to shake wildly.

Nico aimed the flashlight dead ahead, and they followed the two older men's path through a thick stand of salmonberry stalks to arrive at a small and very empty clearing. The surrounding bushes seemed undisturbed; it seemed as if the two men had simply entered the clearing and disappeared completely. Nico shone his flashlight wildly in every direction, trying to puzzle out where the two men had vanished; the beam fell on a figure, his face darkened, between two tree trunks.

Ruthie and Oz yelled, simultaneously. Nico wheeled the flashlight to the other side of the clearing to reveal another looming, darkened figure, watching them silently from behind an ivy-covered stump.

"Who are you?" shouted Rachel. "What do you want?"

Elsie stepped forward, having seen another figure in the near dark. There was something vaguely strange about him, she decided. Before she was able to get a clear view, a small *click* sounded below her feet. She looked down, just in time to see the world erupt from beneath her toes and carry her skyward.

It had happened too quickly, really, for anyone to reckon exactly what had transpired. By their minds, the six Unadoptables and Nico, they had simply been standing in the middle of the clearing, seemingly surrounded by mysterious, silent watchers, when, the very next moment, they were dangling an easy thirty feet above the forest floor. All they'd heard was a wheezy creak, a snap of a branch, and they'd been conveyed thus, heavenward, dangling in the ether. A quick catalog of their situation revealed that they were in some sort of net, woven from very organic-looking material, a net that had bagged the six of them as if they were the evening's groceries. What's more: A survey of the surroundings alerted them to the presence of both Mr. Swindon and Carol, who were swinging in a similar webbed container, not ten feet away from them. Jumbled together like action figures in a pillowcase, the captured seven had been forcibly entwined, and Elsie felt Harry's elbow locked around her fibula; the surprised face of her sister was dangling directly above her, and the girl's long black hair was draping into Elsie's mouth. They all groaned, as one, as they tried desperately to unlock themselves from one another, still in shock from their sudden change of circumstance. Elsie, her face pressed to the mesh of the net, looked down on the mysterious figures that had surrounded them, waiting for them to approach and claim their quarry.

A groaning could be heard from the opposite net. Martha cried out, "Carol! Are you okay?"

"I'm okay, dear heart," came Carol's voice. "Just a little bruised up is all."

"Quiet, old man," shouted Mr. Swindon.

"Why?" Carol was heard to say. "What are you going to do? Gnaw my arm off?"

From the looks of it, the net that had captured Carol and Roger Swindon had cinched very tightly, owing to the lesser cargo, and the two men were immobilized in an unwilling bear hug.

"What happened?" Elsie shouted.

"Was this your doing?" Nico yelled at the opposing net.

"Quiet!" shouted Roger, considerably perturbed. His plan had clearly gone very south, very quickly. He began to mumble to himself loudly; Elsie made out the words "Wigman" and "Bicycle Maiden" and "Wildwood," interspersed with the sort of swear words one usually hears emanating from grumpy biker gangs.

"As soon as we get down from here," threatened Nico, "we're going to give you the what-for, so help me God."

"We won't be getting down," said Roger. "Or at least we won't be getting down alive. We're in Wildwood now, kiddies. There's no telling what baleful souls have captured us." He laughed an ironic sort of laugh, one that sounded as if it had been steeped in sulfuric acid. "I'd chalk this up to brigands, but the Wildwood bandits are no more. Must be some other desperate, starved creatures. No doubt we'll all be making some tribe of cannibals a decent meal come morning."

Elsie shivered at this suggestion. She looked down at the figures surrounding them; she found it strange that they had not advanced or said anything. "Hello?" she called out. "Who are you?"

No answer came. Roger, with some difficulty, moved his head so he could see the ground below. He made a surprised exclamation, having just now seen the silent figures watching them writhe in their nets. "It can't be!" he shouted. "I wiped you out! I saw to it myself!"

The figures in the darkened patches between the trees gave no response.

"Show yourselves!" shouted Nico, exasperated.

Finally, after some time had passed, the sound of crunching footsteps in the dark alerted them to someone—or something—drawing closer. They all ceased their mutterings and shiftings and trained their eyes into the muddled distance, trying to make out who their captors were. Elsie grasped the vines of the net and stared out, watching carefully, breathlessly, as a humanoid shape emerged from between two wide tree trunks, bathed in the dark. She blinked her eyes rapidly, willing them to grow accustomed to this blackness, lit only by a sliver of a moon (Nico's flashlight having fallen during the capture; its batteries had spilled out into the blanket of vines on the ground), which cast the forest floor in a dim white sheen. A stand of ferns parted; the form walked through it slowly, a stalking creep, and Elsie's heart rate began to quicken, her racing imagination set loose to envision whatever horrific creature it chose, bent on whatever terrible, wicked desire her mind could conjure. And suddenly, just as she'd dreamed up the worst possible fate for her and her friends—something that involved a large cast-iron pot, a fish paring knife, and, oddly enough, a kind of reptilian creature with a lightbulb for a head—the glow of the slim moon glinted against a pair of wire-rimmed eyeglasses perched on the figure's nose, and Elsie let out a gasp.

"Curtis!" she shouted.

CHAPTER 2 3

The Lonely Crag

P rue must've fallen back asleep; she dreamed of Alexandra, the Dowager Governess. The woman stood over her, a motherly smile on her face. Alexandra reached out her hands to Prue, lovingly, and Prue was shocked to see them transform, slowly, into long vines of ivy. The horrible vision was soundtracked by the ever-present ticking noise she'd heard coming from the silent Caliph in the hold. In her dream, the ticking suddenly transformed itself into a language, clear words that were both English and not English. She woke with a start and saw that a plate of food had been slipped beneath the bars of her door. A dim light was shining through the gray of her porthole; dawn was breaking.

Prue sat up and saw that the Caliph had remained unmoving from his position, a strange statue holding guard, throughout the night. Prue grabbed the plate of food—rice and beans, it appeared—and began shoveling the savory stuff into her mouth. She was famished, she suddenly realized. Adventuring really had a habit of throwing off one's eating schedule.

The ticking noise continued unabated after she'd finished, and she set the plate down, remembering her brief dream. Rather than speak to the Caliph, she instead chose to quietly address the ticking noise itself.

She found that it was responsive.

She breathed a gasp of surprise as she began to almost converse with the noise; it suddenly dawned on her that the sound was some sort of vegetation *inside* the Caliph himself. Something caught her attention; she looked up and saw that the Caliph's shoulders had *twitched*, just slightly.

She tried again, addressing the tick: *WHO ARE YOU?*

The noises she received in response were unintelligible. The Caliph twitched again, his shoulders jerking slightly on his frame.

The tone of the noise suggested it was some kind of organic living thing, but decidedly not human. It had all the cadences she was accustomed to hearing from the plant world, just in a different dialect—if such a thing could be said. And then she realized:

She was speaking to the Spongiform.

WHERE ARE YOU?

Ticking. Ticking. The Caliph shook his head slightly.

She took that as a sign. *IN THE SKULL?*

YESSSSSSSS, the ticking codified into a word.

She recalled learning in life science about the strange and delicate relationship between parasites—particularly fungi—and their hosts. There were bacterial parasites that could change the makeup of someone's thinking—certain parasites that transformed action and behavior, drawing the host toward more environments where the parasite might be better distributed and ingested by other organisms. The whole class had chittered with disgust and disbelief; now Prue found herself face-to-face with such an example.

COME, she thought. *COME FORWARD.*

She channeled her language, commanding the noise forward. She used the same tone she did when she found herself able to make grass weave around her toes, to make branches bow in still air. *COME.*

The Caliph, still silent, shook in his chair, as if an earthquake had erupted just below his feet. And then: a noise, a human noise: a cough, a sputter.

The ship tilted in the wind, the crewmen shouted from above, and the Caliph on the chest went spilling to the floor, his hands grabbing for his face mask.

Prue leapt up from her cot and pressed her face between the bars of her cell door: *FORWAAARD!*

The Caliph on the floor made loud retching noises, and his hands flew to his face and whipped off his headgear, the mask and the cowl, as if he were suffocating and his strange outfit was the cause of all his discomfort. The silver mask went skittering across the floor of the belowdecks and Prue was surprised to see, revealed beneath the mirrored thing, none other than Seamus, the Wildwood bandit. His beard was matted with sweat, and his skin looked as if it had been deprived of sunlight for a long time. His eyes were wild and blood-shot as his dirty fingers scraped at his face, like he was trying to peel his own skin away.

"Seamus!" shouted Prue, reaching her hand between the bars. "Seamus, it's Prue!"

But the man couldn't hear her. He was too busy writhing on the floor, jamming his fingers into his mouth and nostrils. His chest spasmed in great gasps as he dry-heaved repeatedly, his knees jammed firmly into his chest. Finally, something seemed to give as there was a kind of liquid chok-ing noise from his throat and something very brownish green and viscous, the size of a walnut, was ejected from his right nostril. Wide-eyed, he grabbed it and began to pull; little tendrils ran away from the greasy little object, a tangled mesh that connected it to the inside of his nose. Carefully pulling at the stringy lattice, retching all the while, Seamus managed to extract a veritable spider's web of mucus-covered tendrils that, when collapsed into a ball, resembled a leftover pile of mutant brown spaghetti. It lay there in a quivering lump, ticking away in Prue's brain.

"Seamus," she hissed. "Throw it out the window." It seemed imperative that he do this; it was sucking at the air, it was ticking loudly in her mind.

Pulling himself together, as one does when painfully sick yet desperate for a drink of water or access to the television's remote control, Seamus grabbed the slimy stuff in his hand and crawled to the nearest porthole. Heaving himself up onto an obliging crate, he opened the window and tossed the contents of his fist out into the fog-covered river basin.

The ticking stopped. The creaking of the ship, the whining of the rigging, was all Prue could hear.

"Where . . . ," gasped the man in the robe. "Where am I?"

"You're on a ship. Bound for the Crag."

He looked up at the speaker; his sudden recognition of his old friend Prue seemed to fall on him like a barrel of rocks. "Prue!" he shouted. "Prue McKeel! What are you doin' all locked up?"

"Well, to be honest, you sort of had a hand in putting me here."

"I did?" He was busily wiping a layer of snot and grime from his face. He held a strand of it at arm's length. "What was that stuff?"

"Spongiform. The blight on the Blighted Tree. Someone fed it to you."

"Who?"

"I don't know. Someone from the Synod."

Seamus seemed to search his memory; he stared at his feet for a moment before saying, "The Synod. The Blighted Tree. I'm remembering. I was in South Wood, wasn't I? I was there." The memories now seemed to be flooding back, a deluge of lost time. "I was the emissary. The bandits' emissary. Left in South Wood after the Battle for the Plinth. The Synod; they reached out to me. Took me in. I didn't know what was happening, Prue, swear I didn't."

"It's okay, Seamus. It's not your fault."

"But what did I do? Where are the others? Where's Brendan? What's become of the other bandits?"

Prue curled her fingers around the bars of the door and said, "I think they've done the same thing. I think they've eaten that stuff. And become part of the Synod."

"But how?" The realization slowly overcame him. "You don't think . . . did I? Did I convince them?"

"Do you remember anything?"

"No, the memories go foggy at a point." He squinted in

concentration. "I remember meeting with the Synod. Those masked fellows. Something about reparations for the battle. Then everything goes hazy. Though maybe . . . Oh gods." His chest sank in and his head fell. "I do remember now. A trip to Wildwood. Sent by the Synod. A package of food. Supplies. Provided by the Synod." He looked up blankly at Prue, his eyes shot through with tears.

"I did it, didn't I?" he managed. "I fed it to them."

Prue could only stare, her hands gripping the bars. The idea seemed ludicrous; and yet she'd seen the effect of the Spongiform. The parasite, growing inside the cavity of the host's skull, seemed to reduce the host to a catatonic stupor, highly suggestible to the Blighted Tree's authority.

"It's not your fault, Seamus," she said. "You were duped. You were poisoned."

"And now what? How did I—how did you—end up on this ship?"

"Long story. I'm being sent off to the Crag, which is like a rock in the ocean. I'm sentenced to be marooned there. Forever."

"But why?"

"I guess I'm the enemy now. In the Synod's eyes, anyway. Oh, Seamus, so much has happened since I last saw you. I was there, at the bandit camp, right after everyone had left. Me and Curtis. We thought that you'd all been wiped out by these Kitsunes—shapeshifting monsters—but it turns out everyone had abandoned the camp only the night before. That must've been when you'd gone there, fed them the stuff. . . ." She was piecing everything together in her mind as she spoke; she didn't see Seamus smart at the mention of poisoning his fellow bandits. "I came back to Wildwood to have Alexei, the heir to the Mansion, rebuilt. It's what the Council Tree told me to do. And now . . . And now . . ." She paused here, trying to wrangle her colliding thoughts. She remembered her revelation from the night before, when the wave had buffeted the ship and she'd felt the strange *presence*. "I—I can't be sure," she said, "But I think Alexandra has returned."

The bandit gave her a wide-eyed look, seemingly cataloging, internally, everything she'd told him. "First and foremost, we'll escape here," he said, standing up. "We'll get our revenge. We'll free my brothers and sisters." He paused. "Curtis is saved? Did I not poison him as well?"

"No, he was with me. I don't know where he is now. We split up months ago; he went to find out what happened to you, to the bandits." Prue pulled on the bars, testing their strength. "As for getting me out of here, I'm not sure how. There's a whole crew of sailors up there. We're miles from the Wood."

Seamus stood up, a little rickety on his feet, and walked to the porthole. He peered out and confirmed Prue's worst fears: "Water everywhere. We're in the open ocean, Prue."

"How does that even happen? Aren't they beyond the boundary—the Periphery?"

"It's been going on for centuries. Even I know about the Crag. It's the ruins of an old castle, built on the top of a rock in the water. The Ancients built it, it's said. It was a great achievement, the Crag. And then, like most of the Ancients' creations, it fell into ruin. In the second age, folks started using it as a punishment for the worst offenders—the criminals who deserved the worst death imaginable: slow and tedious."

"Why haven't the Outsiders seen them? Like, all of Portland? Seems like a ship like this would be pretty conspicuous."

"Like all ship trade, they travel under the veil of fog."

"Bizarre," Prue whispered.

"But we need to free you, Prue," said Seamus, walking to the barred door and giving it a rattle. "First thing. Do I have a key?" He'd asked it almost rhetorically; he was fishing through the folds of his robe. His hands came up empty. "Nope. Guess they wouldn't entrust that kind of responsibility to the religious nut on the ship."

"Plus, there are about a dozen men up there, as far as I can tell," put in Prue.

"Yep. This is a sticky situation. No doubt."

There was a scraping noise above their heads; the hatch was being opened.

"Quick!" hissed Prue. "Back into your outfit!"

Seamus was already on the job. Speedily picking up the cowl and mask, he was once again the silent watchman, sitting on the chest.

Light flowed in from the open hatch. A sailor climbed down the ladder. Arriving at the floor, he put his hands on his hips and looked at Seamus. "You ain't moved this whole time?"

"He's kind of weirding me out," said Prue through the bars. It had just sprung to mind; she hoped it wasn't overplaying things.

"Don't blame you," said the sailor. He snapped his fingers a few times in front of Seamus's masked face; the bandit remained unmoving. Prue could see his chest rising and falling under his robe a little more rapidly than it had when he was a soundless Caliph, but otherwise he seemed to pull off the mimic fairly well. The sailor, a thin man with a spotty mustache, walked over to Prue's cell door and said, "Gettin' close, Maiden. We'll be mooring at the Crag soon. I've been instructed to take you to the foredecks."

But before the seaman had a chance to remove the key from his pants pocket, a meaty *thunk* sounded and his eyes rolled back in his head. Like a scarecrow loosed of his wooden frame, the sailor crumpled to the ground in a pile of wool clothing and poorly washed skin. Behind him was Seamus, his hands still held in the after-position of the Bandit Backblow, something that even the most junior bandit learns within weeks of receiving the oath. Done correctly, it can put its victim into a deep and fairly pleasant sleep.

"Wow," said Prue.

Seamus whipped off his mask and breathed a silent curse at the thing, before fishing the key from the sleeping sailor's pocket. In a moment, he had Prue freed from her cell and they were both standing amid the crates, bales, and snoring sailor of the belowdecks hold.

"Now what?" asked Seamus, seemingly at a loss.

"Good question," said Prue.

Just then, the whole ship jerked and shuddered. Prue ran to a porthole and, climbing atop a box, looked outside. There, in the midst of a wide, gray ocean, she saw the Crag.

The sky hung low, like a dropped ceiling oppressing a drab schoolroom, and the clouds splayed out in all directions, an unchanging ripple of gray light. The rough waters of the Pacific Ocean, equally gray, crashed wildly against the object in their midst: A giant, moss-covered rock, some dozens of stories high, was the rough pedestal for the stone structure that had, impossibly, been built on top of it. The structure resembled a castle, or a fortress, though its skyward-reaching battlements were toppled and its ramparts were in ruin, as if the thing had reached too high or defied the elements for too long; a long stone staircase wound around the side of the rock, a testament to the fact that this place had once been accessible, that it had once been a place people wished to reach. The ship pitched in the waves that drew it closer to the rock's only visible landing spot: a wave-racked wooden jetty.

Prue turned back to report the sight to Seamus when she saw the bandit had drawn a cutlass from the sailor's belt and was brandishing it, his eyes wild.

"Only one way out," he said dramatically.

"Do I get one?"

Seamus frowned. A table leg, propped against the hull of the ship, would suffice. Prue gripped it and nodded. "Let's do this," she said.

What "this" was could be easily summed up in a short, and fairly sad, paragraph. The two of them, without much of a pregame conference, noisily climbed up the ladder, threw aside the hatch, and proudly presented themselves to the sailors, who, for their part, seemed a little surprised to see their prisoner freed and the man who they assumed to be a member of the silent Synod now sporting a raffish beard and a scimitar and howling things like: "Have at ye, scoundrels" and "This is a mutiny." However, there were only two of them, scimitar and table leg notwithstanding, against a healthy dozen stolid seamen, and Prue and Seamus were quickly disarmed and bound against the main mast, causing only a slight ruffle in the sailors' continued work getting the ship safely navigated into the jetty of the Crag.

"Wow," said Seamus when it was all done and his back was pressed tightly against the solid wood of the mast. "They're good."

"That could've used a little more planning," said Prue. At least she was enjoying some fresh sea air; it was one improvement that her current state of bondage had over her prior.

"Next time."

"Don't expect there'll be a next time," said Captain Shtiva, who had overheard their conversation. "You'll be spending your days on the Crag. Rescue is unlikely."

The broken fortress bobbed on the horizon; the sailors worked at their various tasks, wrangling the loping ship into the jetty. The air was full of seagull cries and ocean mist; the canvas sails whipped and cracked above Prue's and Seamus's heads. The sailors shouted commands and calls to one another. Before long, the ship had sidled angrily against the dock and the lines were figure-eighted around the dock's rusty cleats. A plank was thrown over the gunwale, and Prue and Seamus were freed from their place at the mast. A sailor cohort escorted them at pistol-point over the plank and onto the dock. Captain Shtiva led the group.

Prue stayed silent. Her eyes remained fixed on the ruined battlements atop the rock. She and Seamus were led up the twisting stone staircase, made of a kind of yellowing sandstone, around the base of the rock. It followed the contours of its foundation, dipping and falling with the rock's inconsistencies, until finally ending at a crumbled stone arch. Beyond the arch was a scene that nearly caused Prue's knees to give out.

A weathered veranda, its flagstones littered with the remains of former convicts, stretched out before them, surrounded by walls in various states of ruin. Pieces of bone covered the ground like confetti on a parade ground.

"You can't do this," said Prue, in shock. "This is wrong."

Captain Shtiva seemed to be mindful of the grim scene. "I'm sorry,

Maiden," he said. "These are my orders."

"I spit on your orders," said Seamus, which he did, his spittle flying over the piled remnants of some poor individual's bottom half.

"You don't have to follow them," pleaded Prue. "You can follow your gut. You know this is wrong. You know this is not 'for the revolution.'"

The captain remained silent. "Untie them," he said.

They were led to the center of the veranda; the wind buffeted through the broken walls, chilling everyone present. The sailors held their pistols straight, their flintlocks cocked, and began to back away from the two convicted prisoners.

"Look what they did to Seamus," shouted Prue. "They changed him. They fed him that stuff. Don't think they won't do the same to you."

"Fools!" said Seamus. And again, softer: "Fools."

The sailors said nothing; they were soon out of sight and away down the long staircase toward the *Jolly Crescent*, which was bucking in its moorings down at the jetty. Prue and Seamus remained standing in the center of the veranda, at the top of the Crag, ankle deep in a wide carpet of discarded bones.

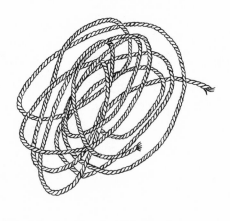

CHAPTER 24

The Last of the Wildwood Bandits

Elsie had never known what it was like to be speechless before; she'd read about it in novels and heard people refer to themselves as such (though it seemed to her there was something problematic in someone *saying* they were speechless) but had never known what the feeling was truly like until that moment, in the deepest woods, caught in a handwoven trap net, and seeing her long-lost brother for the first time in many, many months.

She'd shouted his name, first, but then all speech was robbed from her and she sat there in the captivity of the net, staring at the lanky boy as he walked into the clearing, holding a lit torch. Always a little skinny, he seemed to have only grown more so; his face looked unbelievably older. There also seemed to be some sort of rodent sitting casually on his shoulder.

Her brother appeared to be similarly shocked, as he lifted the torch hesitantly and peered up into the netting, saying, "Els?"

And that was when Elsie became really, truly speechless. In that she could not manage a single noise in response to her brother's call. Thankfully, her sister, just up and to her left, her hair dangling in Elsie's face, was not so affected.

"Curtis!" she shouted, not adding much to the dialogue.

"Rachel?"

Suddenly, Elsie got her speech back. "Curtis!" she yelled.

"Elsie!" shouted Curtis, as if just now understanding what this conversation was about.

"You guys know each other?" asked Nico, breaking up the monotony of the exchange nicely.

"He's our brother!" said Rachel loudly, with a good deal of uncharacteristic enthusiasm.

"Mreally?" This was Harry; his face, Elsie realized, was planted firmly in her rear end. She could tell because she more felt the word pronounced than heard it.

Just then, to the great surprise of everyone present (except perhaps Carol and Roger, who were swinging in their own net just ten feet away from the Unadoptables, and were accustomed to the strange ways of the Wood), the rodent on Curtis's shoulder opened his little mouth and spoke. Words. In English.

"These are your sisters?" said the rat.

Before anyone had a chance to answer the question, Nico, apparently deciding that a talking rat was more shocking than the incredible coincidence he was witnessing—that these three siblings should be united after so many months of wondering and searching in the strangest possible circumstances—said, "Did that rat just say something?"

"Yes," said the rat, sounding affronted. "I did. Do you have a problem with that?"

"None whatsoever," said Nico. He then looked down at Ruthie, whose forehead was jammed beneath his chin. "The rat talks," he said.

"I think he does," said Ruthie, similarly bowled over.

Curtis, meanwhile, was sputtering. He was sputtering like a broken faucet. "You—" he started. "How—What did you—Where's—" Finally all his momentum ended in the question: "Where's Mom and Dad?"

"Russia!" shouted Elsie. "They're looking for you, stupid!" Elsie found that during her speechlessness, she had overcome her shock and was now feeling a little angry. She heard her sister join in, heaving a string of vitriolic curse words at their brother like she was breathing fire.

"Wow," said the rat. "Charming siblings."

Curtis began to defend himself, shouting back his meager defenses to the two girls, who were now yelling at him in loud unison. "But I . . . ," he sputtered between the girls' invectives. "You know, I could . . . It's just all really complicated!"

Finally, Nico raised his loud, grown-up voice above the yelling children and said, "STOP!"

They did.

The saboteur, whose right leg had been unfortunately caught in the webbing of the net when it was tripped and was now currently positioned slightly upside down with his knee linked around one of the ropes, like a practiced trapeze artist mid-performance, said, simply, "Can you get us down, please?"

"Can we get some reassurance that those two girls won't attack us?" asked the rat.

"Shhh, Septimus," said Curtis as he turned from the two dangling nets. "Those are my sisters." He climbed into the nearby brush and began working at some unseen mechanism; soon, Elsie felt the net loosen and shake and they were lowered slowly to the ground. Before he'd gone to do the same to the other trap, Rachel shouted out to her brother as she tried to untangle herself from the grounded webbing and the other bodies:

"Don't let them go yet, Curtis!" she yelled, pointing desperately at the other net.

Curtis popped his head out from behind a bush. "What?"

"One of them is very bad," was the best she could do on a moment's notice.

By the time Curtis had paused in his undoing of the ropes that held the second trap in place, Nico, Martha, Rachel, and Harry had leapt to the open space below the dangling net and readied themselves. Elsie stood up and stared at her older brother, still in disbelief at his sudden appearance, here in the Impassable Wilderness.

"Okay," said Nico. "Lower 'em down."

Curtis did so, apparently undoing some hefty knot on the forest floor, and the net began descending with an aching creak. Roger's and Carol's arms and legs, pretzeled ridiculously in the ropes, stuck out from the bulbous trap like tendrils on a sea anemone. When they'd touched the ground, Nico and Harry dove into the scrum, nabbing Roger by his arms, and held him back while Martha grabbed Carol and lifted him to safety.

"Thank you, dear," said Carol.

Curtis tied off the anchor rope and began to walk back into the clearing when he was set upon by Elsie, who jumped on him, her arms thrown around his neck in a strangling hug. "Curtis!" she yelled. "I knew it. I knew it! I just knew we'd find you. I missed you so much. So much. But I was also so, so angry at you."

Curtis returned the hug, wrapping his arms around his little sister. "You too, Els. I'm so sorry. So much has happened. There's so much to tell. I don't even know where to start."

They were drawn away from their conversation by the impassioned objections coming from Roger Swindon, who was held fast by Martha and Nico. "Rope!" called the saboteur.

"Right, one sec," replied Curtis, and he dove into the trees, retrieving a short length of what looked to be hand-spun rope. He rushed over to the squirming man and, within a few scant seconds, had deftly manacled his hands.

"Nice," said Nico, impressed by the boy's ability.

Rachel and Elsie watched their brother, agog. He seemed to be suddenly embarrassed. "It's one of the first things you learn," he said, by way of explanation.

"What do you mean, first things you learn?" asked Rachel.

"In Bandit Training," said her brother. A brother who, Rachel recalled, had been given a note from their mother so that he could sit out his gym class's mandatory presidential fitness test.

"Bandit Training?" repeated Rachel. "What *are* you talking about?"

"That's what I am, guys. That's what I've been doing in here. I'm a bandit. A Wildwood bandit."

"Cool!" shouted Elsie, letting the weird explanation wash over her. She'd never imagined she'd have a bandit for a brother. Not that that was something she'd ever expected; it was just a pleasant surprise.

"Wildwood bandit?" questioned Rachel skeptically, ever the big sister. "What's that? Does that even exist?"

Curtis was strangely shamed by his sister's comment, and he seemed to inwardly collapse until Carol said, "Oh, it does. They do. I did not expect to run into a band of the Wildwood bandits, but it's a good thing we did. What's more, one that seems to be an ally. Where are the rest of your brethren, good bandit?"

"They're watching from the woods," said Nico, peering into the greenery. "Why don't they come out, your fellow bandits?"

While Curtis seemed to be heartened by the old man's defense, his voice lost some of its previous color when he said, "Because those are just dummies. Mannequins. I made them. The Wildwood bandits are . . . gone."

"Oh," said Carol, frowning. "That is very strange."

Martha stood at Carol's side. "Are you all right?" she asked.

"Just fine, dear," the blind man said, blinking his two wooden eyes. "We're free, at least."

"Yep," said Martha, squeezing the old man by the waist. "I knew we would be." She turned to the assembled crowd and spoke, smiling widely. "Thanks, guys," she said.

The children, reunited with Carol and their fellow Unadoptable, swarmed one another, high-fiving and trading quick remembrances

of their hair-raising ordeal in Titan Tower. Carol beamed down, unseeing, on the children, the proud godfather to an impressive brood.

Once they'd regained themselves, Rachel and Elsie quickly besieged their brother, and the long telling of his incredible story was unspooled to his disbelieving siblings. Elsie stood with her hand at her mouth the entire time, her eyes filled with tears, marveling at the extraordinary adventures her brother had experienced since they'd last seen each other, walking to school that early fall morning like they had untold mornings before. When he got to the point about the City of Moles and Prue's quest to reunite the strange machinists to bring back the mechanical boy prince, Elsie let out a little shout. "What was his name, the other machinist you were looking for?"

"Cary, I think? Something like that," said Curtis. "I don't know. It's been so long and I've been so intent on my own survival here, that I'd kind of forgotten about him."

"But he was blind?"

"That's what the bear said, anyway. Had his eyes taken out by the Governess."

An awed silence fell over the two sisters as they swiveled aside and looked at Carol Grod; the old man had been listening in and began walking toward the young bandit.

"Indeed, she did," he said. "But I made these old wooden ones, didn't I? Suit me just fine."

"No. Way," said the rat at Curtis's shoulder.

"That's it. Carol Grod," said Curtis, staring at the old man. "You're the other machinist. The one who made Alexei."

Both Elsie and Rachel let out an amazed gasp.

"That'd be me," said the old man matter-of-factly, before correcting him: "But I couldn't have done it alone."

"No, you couldn't have," said Curtis, dazed. "You needed another. Esben Clampett, the bear."

"That's right. Don't know where he ended up. For my part, they sent me to the Periphery. Exiled me there."

"That's where we met him, Curtis," said Elsie. "We were there,

The ship pitched in the waves that drew it closer to the rock's only visible landing spot: a wave-racked wooden jetty.

stuck in the Periphery." She then turned to Carol and said in a stunned voice, "That was why you were exiled, huh? Why didn't you tell us?"

"Didn't come up, really," the old man said coyly, before adding, "It was a touchy subject, dear. I don't particularly like talkin about it. What she did left more than just physical scars. I was tryin to forget, there in that place."

"How did you get out?" asked her brother, awash in all this bizarre new information. "And how did you get in—here—now?"

"Same way you did," put in Rachel.

"Woods Magic," said Carol, hobbling over to them with Martha's help.

"We must have it," said Curtis. "I was never sure. I mean, I seemed to pass through the boundary fine, but I just couldn't ever figure why. We must have it, in the blood." He turned to Carol, his intention renewed. "We have to get you to Prue. She's got Esben."

The old man's eyes opened wide, and the wooden orbs goggled in his skull. "He's alive?"

"He was exiled, too. Sent to the Underwood. We found him, Prue and I. Another sort of crazy coincidence." He looked around him, as if taking in the thatchwork of trees surrounding them. "Though I think Prue would say otherwise. She'd say it's the workings of the tree. In any case, Esben is with Prue now."

"No, he isn't," came a voice from the dark. The gathered crowd looked over at Roger Swindon, sitting cross-legged on the leafy ground, his arms pinioned behind his back.

"What did you say?" asked Curtis, waving the torchlight in his direction. A few sparks erupted from the flame.

"She doesn't have the bear. We have the bear."

"Who's we?" asked Curtis, dumbfounded.

"The Synod. The Caliphs of South Wood."

"What happened to Prue?" pressed Curtis.

"She's gone."

Nico gave the captive a swift kick to the ribs. Roger toppled sideways with an anguished shout. "Stop being difficult," said Nico. "You're our prisoner now."

"Hey," said Elsie. "Go easy."

"Sorry," said the saboteur.

"What do you mean, she's gone?" asked Curtis.

"Gone, gone. Forever gone. Marooned on the Crag. She won't last out the week. I'd say your best bet is to simply let myself and Carol go. You are all, in one way or another, Outsiders who are simply out of your depth. This is much bigger than you." The man shifted in his bindings awkwardly as he spoke. "As we speak, the Synod is expanding their control over the Wood. You will all eventually be assimilated, should you choose to stay, or simply be pushed out of the way."

"Assimilated?" breathed Nico.

"Yes," said the man as he, with some difficulty, righted himself back into a seated position. "Like your fellow bandits. They're part of the Synod now."

"What?" shouted Curtis, suddenly walking toward the man as if he were intent on setting him on fire with the torch. The man flinched to see the boy approach. "You know where the bandits are?"

"Oh yes," said Roger, clearly amused that his words had stung. "They're with us now."

Curtis stumbled a little; his face slackened with shock.

"What's the Synod, anyway?" asked Rachel, staring curiously at her brother.

"The Holy Mystics of the Blighted Tree," said Roger. "Or some such rubbish. Doesn't matter. Now that the Synod has imposed its rule, there's little to stop us. The Spongiform is all-powerful."

"I don't really have a clear idea what you're talking about, but I don't particularly like it," said Nico, staring down at the man. He looked back to Curtis. "Can I kick him again?"

"Wait," said Curtis, shaking himself from his reverie, holding up his palm. He knelt down beside Roger and grabbed him by the scruff of his robe. "Tell me," he said. "What happened to the bandits? What did you do to them?"

"Oh, it was all fairly innocent," said Roger. "We'd known you were looking for the makers. We discovered where you were hiding. We *assimilated* your friend first. I believe his name was Seamus? The emissary, left behind after the revolution. To 'represent' the Wildwood bandits. Needless to say, he didn't do a very good job. We fed him the Spongiform and then commanded him to do the same to your fellow bandits. It's quite miraculous how that little fungus works, actually. It spread so easily—"

He was interrupted when, on Curtis's signal, black-bereted Nico gave him another kick in the ribs. He let out a groan and toppled over again. Curtis dragged him and held his face within inches of his own. The talking rat perched on his shoulder stuck out his snout so that he, too, was staring down the captive.

"I don't know who you are or what your master plan is here," said

Curtis. "But you're going to take me to the bandits, and you're going to make this right."

"What he said," said the rat.

ᘐ

The spectral figures in the trees, the ones the Unadoptables and Nico had seen surrounding them when they'd still been in pursuit of Roger and Carol, had been a particular challenge. Curtis had apparently started with one—he'd named him Jack after one of his departed fellow bandits—and slowly expanded once he'd gathered enough resources. It was hard, he said, finding the right shape tree branches and trunks. Moss could be used to mimic the scraggly beards that were a hallmark of the bandit style; the right angle of maple branches made apt arms, resolutely crossed at the chest. He'd decided, in the bandit band's absence, that at least a show must be made. Like the extinction of some vital organism, Curtis believed that were the Wildwood bandits to disappear altogether, it would upset the delicate balance of Wildwood's ecosystem.

This was the story he told as the group made their way, in the dark of night, toward South Wood. Their goal seemed simple, if somewhat challenging: to free the bandits, rescue Esben Clampett, and hopefully, save Prue from her harrowing sentence on the Crag. They were an interesting group: The boy with the brocaded uniform and the talking rat led the way with his two sisters, dressed in identical black turtlenecks, at his side. Directly behind him was the blind man, Carol

Grod, who was being guided along the road by goggled Martha Song. Their captive walked slowly in the midst of the group, his head solemnly downcast, while Nico and the other three Unadoptables kept a wary eye on him, lest he should escape into the surrounding woods.

The traps were another matter altogether, Curtis explained to the group, and he hadn't taken on the challenge until he'd found that he was becoming more and more handy repurposing the salvaged flora of the woods. He'd expected to catch food or intruders; he had not, in a million years, thought he'd nab his sisters.

"But why?" It had been Elsie's nagging question, all along. "Why'd you go through with all of it?"

"I made an oath, Els," replied her brother. "The Bandit Oath. I swore to uphold the band. I figured this was the way to do it."

The story went like this: He'd returned to the Wood, crossing through metropolitan Portland in the dead of night. He'd left Prue to her own devices, having decided, once and for all, that his loyalty remained with the Wildwood bandits. He'd witnessed the scene at the bandit camp, that day when Darla and her fellow Kitsunes had attacked the two children and sent them spilling into the depths of the Long Gap, and was longing to get back to investigate the bandits' disappearance.

"You walked through Portland?" interjected Rachel. "You were there?"

"Yeah," said her brother, a little sheepishly. "I walked by the house. Everyone was gone. Figured you guys were on, like, vacation or something."

"You walked by the house," repeated Rachel plainly.

"Yeah." The boy seemed to suspect what was coming.

"Well, we weren't on vacation. Actually we were in an awful orphanage-slash-factory and Mom and Dad were in Turkey and Russia and wherever else, looking for you," said Rachel.

"C'mon, Rach," chided Elsie. "We've been through all that."

Rachel mumbled something grumpily in response while Curtis, thankful for his younger sister's defense, continued.

He'd then retraced his steps, back when he'd first followed Prue into the place he'd always known as the Impassable Wilderness and his life had changed so precipitously. He crossed the Railroad Bridge, thankfully avoiding any sort of run-in with another southbound locomotive, and crossed over the thick mantle of trees. He found himself, very quickly, back in Wildwood.

"It's where we are now," he explained, gesturing to the darkened trees around them, lit by the bare throw of the torch's light. "It's the frontier, the wild part of the Wood. Everything that goes on here, it's still kind of a mystery. Even the oldest bandits would tell stories about ghosts and sprites living in the trees."

The mention of his fellow bandits, his lost comrades, always came with a softening of his voice. The loneliness of the search became all-consuming for the two searchers: Curtis and the rat Septimus.

The rat would spend his days climbing through the high boughs of the trees, scanning from this aerial perch for any sign of the bandits, while Curtis trudged through the bracken of the forest floor. They'd assumed that whoever had survived the attack on the camp would strike out and build another hideout. Bandits were known for their secrecy and their ability to completely conceal any trace of their habitation, so it was no wonder Curtis and Septimus had had a hard time tracking the survivors down.

Days passed. Weeks passed. Still no sign. They subsisted on what meager provisions they could scavenge from the forest, taking shelter in whatever crude lean-to their exhausted limbs allowed them to construct. They spoke little; they woke early and fanned out, combing the nearby woods with an obsessive scrutiny, not moving on until they were certain that no bandit tread had left its footprint.

But as the days piled on, it became clear that the Wildwood bandits were, in fact, gone. Extinct. It was over a low campfire, one clear evening, that Curtis and Septimus decided to rebuild the band anew. It seemed to Curtis that in the event of a total decimation of the Wildwood bandits, the oath required the survivors to carry on. "To live and die by the bandit band" was the final line of the oath, and Curtis intended to stay true to that, to the letter. There was no indication about whether the band should be dissolved in the case of their numbers being whittled down to two. They were now the Wildwood bandits, he and Septimus, from first to last. They alone would uphold the code and creed.

Brendan being absent, assumed dead, Curtis performed the rite of fealty for Septimus, who'd up to this point not taken the oath. He figured Brendan would approve. The rat was a little leery of the bloodletting part, but beyond that, he seemed to take on his new position with a stoic resolve.

And then? Curtis had to put the memory of his bandit brothers and sisters behind him. There was something in that, something that made the whole situation easier to swallow. No longer was there that question mark etched in his mind, following him around like some thought-balloon from a comic book. He put the Wildwood bandits, the old Wildwood bandits, away. He steeled himself in his new role as one of two sole survivors of a long-lost tribe.

They built a new hideout, high in the trees. They built wooden walkways connecting the platforms they'd built in the highest limbs of the oldest cedars. And, in a moment of genius, Septimus suggested they build mannequin bandits to guard the pale of their hideout; so that anyone or anything venturing into these woods would see the shapes and retreat, knowing that the territory belonged to the bandits. The Wildwood bandits, as strong as ever.

They even mounted a few Long Road holdups, which was difficult considering their number and the fact that they did not have horses. Several coaches went flying by, undaunted by their presence in the road, before they managed to stop one. Their first robbery was a South Wood merchant, returning from a successful market day in

North Wood. It was getting on in the evening and the coachman was thankfully daunted by the weird, spectral figures that stood resolutely alongside the road. When Curtis and Septimus had appeared from the depths of the forest, the driver assumed that he'd been jumped by an usually large raiding party.

"Take what you need," he'd said, his voice quavering. "Just let me live!"

In truth, though, the chest of gold doubloons they'd liberated from the merchant's possession did little by way of easing Curtis's melancholy. He found that the only reason he'd even staged the holdup was to keep up appearances. He hated the idea of word getting around that the Wildwood bandits were no longer a threat when passing through this most inhospitable part of the Wood.

And that's how he'd been, that evening when the fog was heavy on the river basin and the stars were blotted out and his two sisters had come running into his territory, just a few scant miles from his tree-bound camp, and tripped his two biggest traps. He'd just returned from another vigil on the Long Road, scouting out for traveling coaches, surprised that none had come in several days, when he'd felt the strange earthquake-like rumble and the undulating wave that had upset the forest floor as it passed.

"I felt that too!" said Elsie, when he'd mentioned it.

"I couldn't figure it out," said her brother. "I assumed that there was some attack being staged somewhere. I imagined that maybe the coyotes had regrouped and had set out to go after us. That's why I went out to check the perimeter of the hideout, and I saw you guys had been caught in my nets."

It turned out that they'd all felt the quake, but were so consumed with their chase through the mysterious forest that they hadn't really processed the feeling.

The rat, Septimus, leapt from Curtis's shoulder and scurried over to the hem of Roger's robe; before the man had a chance to flinch, the rat had climbed up his leg, rounded his hips, and was whispering into his ear. "I don't suppose you have any knowledge of such a thing. Are your minions on the attack?"

"Can you call your rat?" the man asked Curtis. "He's crawling on me."

"Hey, he's not my person any more than I'm his rat," said Septimus drily.

"I don't like rodents," said Roger Swindon.

"Well, I don't much like despotic theocrats," said Septimus.

The man took a deep breath before saying, "This is a lost cause. It won't be long before we are overtaken by the Watch. Even now, as we speak, the North Wall is being deconstructed and the Avian Principality is being dissolved into a united One Nation, under a One Tree. You'll all be held as betrayers of the one true religion and will likely be joining your friend the Bicycle Maiden in her lonely existence on the Crag. If you're lucky. As the Elder Caliph, I can say that how quickly you capitulate will determine what sort of sentence you will receive."

"Well," said Septimus, unperturbed, "I'd say you're a pretty valuable hostage, then."

The man said nothing. The rest of the group seemed thankful for his silence. Nico turned his attention to the rat at the man's shoulder.

"How long have you been able to do that?" he asked.

"Do what?" asked Septimus.

"You know, talk."

"How long have you been able to?" shot back the rat.

"Point taken." The saboteur paused, thinking. "Do all animals in here do that?" he asked finally.

"Do try to keep up," chided Septimus, traveling back to Curtis's shoulder at the front of the pack. "You're in Wildwood now."

*

"Welcome," said Curtis, putting his hand proudly on the base of the ladder, "to Bandit Hideout Deerskull Dragonfighter."

"I helped come up with the name," said Septimus.

"Cool," whispered Harry breathlessly.

They'd traveled many miles in their journey, and morning had come to the wild forest; the air was cool and bright and lit up with birdsong.

"A few things you should know before we head up," continued Curtis. "It's not super entirely safe yet. Like, the banisters are mostly temporary, so don't go putting all your weight on them." Curtis looked at each member of his small audience, as if to underscore the importance of his words. They all looked attentive, though incredibly tired. "You guys are beat, aren't you," he said.

Elsie nodded emphatically. The rest murmured their yeses. It'd been a long night; they'd all agreed that they should stay a day or two before they made their way to South Wood, there to confront this strange religious sect that had enslaved Curtis's bandit brethren. Elsie was still floored by all that had happened the night before. She'd been part of a miraculous rescue mission, a daring chase through this mysterious world and, in the end, been a part of a dramatic reunion with her brother. It was about as much as her nine-year-old mind could take.

"Up we go," came her brother's voice, and she saw that she was next in line at the ladder, the rest of the group having already climbed. Her arms felt rubbery and spent, but she found the energy to heave her little body up into the boughs of the great tree where Curtis had built his own wooden world.

And what a world it was.

It became startlingly clear that he and Septimus had utilized every idle minute of their days in the construction of this new hideout. The ladder led up through a small opening onto a platform that encircled the trunk of an ancient cedar tree. From there, a staircase had been built that spiraled up and around the trunk, the steps made of planed beams that seemingly sprouted from the tree's surface. The group fell into a single file, at Curtis's instruction, as they made their way up the stairs. The climb was enormous; soon, the canopy of the tree and its surrounding neighbors had completely concealed their whereabouts from the ground.

"Wow, Curtis," Elsie said, watching the world disappear below her. "You built this?"

"Me and Septimus, yeah," said her brother. "I'd learned a lot of this from Bandit Training. Pretty basic hideout construction, actually."

"And Mom and Dad were all worried that you were missing school," said Rachel, from a few steps above them.

Finally, the seemingly endless string of steps climbed through an opening to arrive at another wooden platform, this one much larger, made of rough logs that fanned out from the tree's trunk. The floorboards seemed to be tied together with more handwoven rope and were supported by rough-hewn joists from below. Elsie gasped to see that several rope bridges led out from this platform, connecting the tree to its neighbors. There, she could see more structures had been built: Small huts with neatly shingled roofs and wooden walkways dotted the tops of the surrounding firs and cedars. It was a neat little village, camped some several hundred feet above the forest floor.

"This is incredible," said Nico, inspecting the handiwork.

"I had a bit of a one-up on the other guys in training," said Curtis modestly. "They hadn't heard of an Ewok village. I just followed that model, really."

A holding pen, crudely constructed of crosshatched pine boughs, had been built in a close-by fir tree, accessible by a wooden platform. Once their captive, Roger Swindon, (whose hands had been freed for the ascent) had been ushered into the cage, Curtis waved Nico and Rachel back across the platform, which he then raised, like a drawbridge, by cranking a wooden winching contraption.

"You'll be sorry for this," shouted the man from behind the wooden bars. "You're going to wish you'd never done this, mark my words! I'm not a man to be meddled with!"

"He'll be safe there," said Curtis, ignoring the man's shouts. "Never used it before, but I'm pretty sure it'll hold."

Roger hollered a few more threats at them, from across the gulf between the trees, before finally quieting down and lapsing into a pouting silence.

Atop another spiraling staircase, though still concealed within the mighty cedar's limbs, Rachel and Elsie's brother, along with the talking rat, had built an impressive structure—a kind of cottage with rough-hewn walls and open-air windows with conifer branch shutters. A stone fire pit had been built to one side, safely away from the host tree's trunk, and the remnants of an earlier fire were still smoldering, the little smoke there was flowing up through an opening that had been cut in the house's slatted roof. Curtis quickly walked to the fire and, pulling from a neatly stacked pile, began feeding new logs onto the embers. Soon, the renewed flames were warming the interior of the cozy tree house.

"It's not much," said Curtis shyly. "But it keeps you dry."

"I'd say," said Nico, who walked around the house, inspecting the dovetailed joints and the carefully knotted twine that held the beams together.

Elsie felt her face distort in a massive yawn; Ruthie asked their host, "Can I take a nap?"

A little bed, made of gathered moss, had been laid to one side of the fire pit, and Curtis offered this up to the young Unadoptable. He'd made a collection of similar moss tufts, just outside the door, and he gathered these together. Strewing them about the floor, he made a humble gesture. "This is the best I can do," he said. "Hope that's all right."

For Elsie, it was fine. As soon as she'd laid her head down on the green stuff, she found herself drifting into a deep and immediate slumber.

C H A P T E R   2 5

A Meal for the Marooned;
Intruders on the Perimeter!

The day bore down, harsh and brilliant, a blinding light rising over the flat, watery horizon to the east. Prue and Seamus lay huddled in the protection of a south-facing wall, and the light hit them as the rays of sun made a sharp angle against the flagstones and the ropes and the bones.

Hours passed, achingly slowly. The day ebbed into evening.

The two captives immersed themselves in an all-consuming silence.

Prue found herself in a kind of steely mediation, haunted by the premonition she'd had the night before that Alexandra, the Dowager Governess, had somehow returned. It wasn't something she could really put her finger on—it was as if the void left when Alexandra had been swallowed by the ivy had always stayed with her, a kind of notable, tangible *absence*. And now she'd felt that absence filled again. It felt different, for sure, but she was certain that the Dowager Governess had awakened and had returned in some form. She could only imagine how or why this had transpired—had it been the aim of the Synod? What kind of magic could possibly have brought back the spirit of a soul gone for these many long months?

Seamus, at her side, rubbed his eyes with his weathered hands. He, too, gazed out at the field of human and animal remains that stretched out before them and, like Prue, seemed to slowly and deliberately reconcile himself to their very sad fate. A flock of scavenging seagulls wheeled about in the air above them, perhaps excited by the new additions to this hopeless place and the promise of a fresh meal.

"Hi," he said, finally breaking the long silence between them. His voice was an aching creak.

"Hi," said Prue.

"Still get that feeling?"

She knew what he meant. "Yeah," she said. "Still got it."

The two of them lapsed back into silence, both of them wrapped in the sad, brutal realization of their current situation, which, charitably, could be called unfortunate. It seemed to Prue, for one, that everything that could've gone wrong, did go wrong—though the mind-bending set of terrible events that were now currently overshadowing the people of the Wood paled in comparison to her own, terrible circumstances: She was stuck on a rock in the middle of the ocean, wondering exactly how long she would survive before she became just another addition to the scattered refuse on the ruined fortress's flagstones.

"Hungry for dinner?" asked the bandit, attempting a smile.

"What, gnaw on some bones?"

From the pavers beneath them, Seamus picked up a healthy-sized chunk of stone, what had once been a piece of the broken wall, and weighed it in his hand. "Been a while since I was reduced to this," he said, feeling the knobby, heavy thing. "But I expect it'll come back to me." With some difficulty, he pushed himself up from his seat and began kicking the bones aside, clearing an area in the middle of the veranda. He then began searching the sky, watching the circling seagulls. He held the rock at an easy angle away from his body, a baseball pitcher loosening up on the mound.

Prue looked up to the sky, shielding her eyes from the sun, and guessed at the bandit's intentions. "Really?" she asked.

"Really," said Seamus.

"I'm not sure I'm *that* hungry."

"You will be," he said. "Might as well get our larder going.

We're gonna be here a while."

"I'm a vegetarian, you know," said Prue.

"A what?"

"Someone who doesn't eat meat. You don't have those in bandit-world, vegetarians?"

"Nope. Sounds awful." His eyes were still trained on the milling seabirds.

To be honest, ever since Prue had gained the extraordinary ability to confer with the plant world, she started to see her vegetarianism in the same stark light she saw meat eating; she'd had a revelation when she was young, having read *Charlotte's Web*, and had vowed to never touch animal matter again. But she'd never actually *spoken* to Wilbur, a kind of communication she'd shared with any number of her fellow organisms of the green, leafy variety. Still, one had to survive.

"Well," said Prue, "I'll pass."

"Suit yourself. We'll see how many days go by before you ditch the vegetablism and enjoy some lean"—he cocked his shoulder—"dreamy"—he flexed his wrist—"SEAGULL MEAT!" The rock launched from his hand and sailed up into the crowd of flying seagulls above their heads. It missed one of the large ones by mere inches, flying over the side of the ramparts and down into the churning ocean below. Seamus shook out his hand, smiling, and began to scout the ground for another projectile. "Out of practice," he explained to Prue.

Prue's eyes felt as if they'd developed a crust of salt, and it took some time, with her carefully rubbing them, before her vision was unblurred. She let her renewed gaze sweep their present living quarters. The castle had been the sort of structure one would expect to be built atop an inhospitable rock in the middle of the ocean: small, squarish, and, were it not for the fact that the entire roof had caved in long ago, it would've been completely devoid of natural light. A broken staircase was cut into the far corner of the structure, and it climbed a few, meandering flights before it, too, ended in a crumbled ruin.

A rock suddenly fell, with a loud crack, just inches from her fingers. She jerked her hand back and glared at Seamus, who was standing in the middle of the veranda, searching for another rock.

"Hey!" she shouted. "Watch it!"

"Oh," replied the bandit. "Sorry." He found another stone and began choosing his next target among a seagull flock, which seemed to be suddenly mindful of their predator; they were scattering now, cawing madly, flying just out of reach.

Momentarily defeated, Seamus put his hands on his hips and looked at Prue. "Buck up, lass," he said. "We'll get off this thing."

"How?"

"Time. Patience. Bandit-sense."

"Bandit-sense? How's that going to help us?"

"Nimble thinking. Stuff like that. Goes a long way. Been in worse scraps, myself."

Squinting up at Seamus in disbelief, Prue said, "Worse? Like, what?"

"Spent three days in a tree, whilst a hungry bear sat at the bottom."

"Doesn't really compare."

Seamus thought for a second before saying, "I got caught by the Mountain King, once, when I was trying to burgle his scepter—took it up on a bit of a gamble, actually. Brendan bet me I couldn't do it, and you know, a good bandit never passes up a wager. Got the scepter, so there's that."

"Why is that worse?"

"Fell in love with his daughter in the process. Tried to take her along. Didn't fare so well. A lot of extra weight. Got nabbed, spent a week dangling by my big toes in a cavern filled with poisonous spiders. Hence the name, Long Toe Seamus."

"Didn't know that you had that name."

"Doesn't come out much. Sore subject. But I cleared that scrape just fine."

"What happened to the princess?"

Seamus scratched at his beard and replied, "Funny you should ask: After I escaped, she ended up running away from her father—awful guy, the Mountain King—and finding me in the bandit camp. Nice woman, we married. Turns out bandit life wasn't to her liking, and she ended up going back to her father's fiefdom in the caverns below the Cathedral Mountains and overthrowing the Mountain King's regime with an army of rat soldiers. Good story, that. Miss her from time to time. I get the occasional letter. Gotta hand it to her, the woman made a really good borscht."

"That's heartening," said Prue lightly. "You ever been captured by a power-hungry religious sect and stranded on a deserted rock in the middle of the ocean? If so, how did you escape using your bandit-sense?"

Seamus shook his head at Prue's sarcastic tone. "Listen up, lass. You might be some chosen apostle for the Council Tree and a half-breed Outsider with the ability to chat with plant life, but you're a far sight removed from banditry. It's all about remaining limber, opening yourself up to the possibilities. And the like."

"I'm open," said Prue. "Look, I'm open." She held her palms out to the bandit.

"No. I'd say you're not. I'd say you're rather closed, actually, lassie. Time is our friend here. It's one resource we currently have a very lot of. Let's use that time wisely. We can start by cataloging our problems. Organization is the bandit's best ally."

"Is that a bandit saying?"

"Should be. Now, naysayer, Gloomy Gus, let's go down the list. First off, we have our fellow bandits, captured, assumed brainwashed."

"Infected by a parasitic fungi," added Prue.

Seamus cringed at the mention. He rubbed his nose. "Right," he said. "Assimilated into a religious sect of dubious morality. Correct?"

"Aye," said Prue in her best bandit voice.

"That's the spirit. Secondly, one of our team has experienced a, shall we say, *premonition* about the possible rise and return of the Dowager Governess, someone who was last seen making an evening meal for a patch of animated ivy. Correct?"

"Aye, aye, Cap'n," said Prue, getting into the spirit of the exchange.

"That's a pirate voice. There's a fine distinction between bandits and pirates, I'd have you know. Show a little respect."

"Sorry." And then: "Aye."

The bandit continued. "So that's two fairly dire predicaments. Before we begin managing the solutions to them, do you have anything else to add?"

"You forgot 'marooned on a rock in the middle of the ocean.'"

"Right, that. I figured that was, you know, assumed."

"Okay."

"Okay?"

"Okay."

The bandit smoothed his beard and began juggling the rock he held in his right hand. "Right. Now, a good bandit sizes up his obstacles and sees them for the trivial things they are, in the grand scheme of things." Prue was about to interject and challenge him on the "trivial" bit, but Seamus waved her away. "Stick with me here. Consider, for a moment, the vastness of the universe." He looked at Prue to make sure she was, in fact, envisioning this. "Consider the untold stretches of space, the unexplored and unknown lights that glint in the skies. The watching eyes of deities? Perhaps. Sand grains kicked into the heavens by the Great Sky Crab? There are those who believe that."

Again, Prue was set to interject and explain to Seamus what several generations of forest-living bandits had apparently failed to grasp, that those shining lights were, in fact, shining suns burning in far-off galaxies of their own, but it seemed a lot to put on him now, when he had such a head of steam going. "Go on," she said.

"Now, stand up. Come over here, in the middle of these flagstones."

Prue did as the bandit instructed, pushing herself up from her seated position against the ruined wall, and joined him in the center of the courtyard.

"Perspective is key. Imagine yourself one such celestial being, for whom human and animal existence, in its entirety, is one strand of hair on their knuckle. One such celestial being for whom time and its passing is such that a million years pass in the blinking of a single eyelid. Now, once again, let's, in our minds, catalog those few trivial events that transpire against us from the perspective of such a being. And how we and our struggles must appear to it. These flagstones, these bones. Our very bodies. The wheeling seabirds in the sky—how little they must appear! How infinitesimally small!"

Prue was really falling for this bit; she had her eyes closed and was gently swaying to Seamus's calming tone of voice. She let herself be lost in it, envisioning herself watching everything that had happened to her, all these tumultuous events at this perspective-transforming height.

"Very small . . ." A pause.

"Just, really, really small . . ." His voice trailed off. Then: "Though you have to admit, that's a pretty big bird."

Prue opened her eyes and saw, just on the horizon, amid a flock of swooping seagulls, a birdlike shape. At its present distance, it seemed to be roughly the same size as its neighboring birds, except for the fact that it was even farther off than the little shapes amid the flock; indeed, it appeared that it dwarfed its fellow seabirds by a good amount. As it drew closer it became clear that it was not just a *big* bird, but a *massive* bird, a gigantic bird, unlike Prue had ever seen before.

Or, actually, she had—once before.

"Is it . . . ?" she began, but stopped for fear of dashing her expectations. Instead, she grabbed Seamus by the hand and together they ran up the ruined staircase to the top of the ramparts. From here, it seemed, they could see to eternity. Clouds, lit red and pink by the setting sun, swept the distant horizon. The large, dark shape flew through the flock of seabirds and scattered them in a torrent of frightened cawing. Prue could now make out the little spikes at the top of the figure's silhouette: the horns of a great horned owl. It was, without a doubt, the Crown Prince of the Avian Principality, Owl Rex.

"See?" said Seamus, his voice steeped in disbelief. "See what a little bandit-sense gets you?"

The owl, its huge wings splayed, came up near the rock and lengthened his mighty trunk, his wings all mottled gray and white and his large black eyes wise beyond their years. His long body cast a wide shadow over Prue and Seamus as they backed away from the top of the fort's balustrade; they found themselves cowed by the bird's size and majesty, and not a little bit of fear was struck in both of their hearts at the sight of their rescuer.

When the giant bird made landfall on the top of the broken staircase, his weight set chunks of rock falling to the bone-strewn courtyard below. Settled, he shook his wings and curled them against his body, nicking something out of the corner of his shoulder with a quick peck of his beak. He then looked down at Prue and Seamus and smiled, if a bird could be said to do so.

"Hello, friends," he said.

"Owl!" shouted Prue. She let go of Seamus's hand and ran to the bird, wrapping her arms around his feathery chest.

The owl, returning the embrace, enfolded his wings around the small girl, enshrouding her completely. Seamus the bandit came up behind the two, giving a low bow.

"Hello, Seamus," said the owl. "I'm a little surprised to see you here."

"Very long story," replied Seamus. "One that I myself am just sort of clear on."

The owl seemed to frown then, and looked down at the girl in his wings. "We have much work to do," he said simply.

"Where have you been?" asked Prue, her face still burrowed in the bird's chest feathers. "I've been through so much. So much. And you were . . . gone."

"An unfortunate turn of events, I'll admit," said Owl Rex. "But I found I was needed elsewhere. I knew you could manage on your own."

The girl pulled away from their embrace and looked up into the owl's eyes. "You did? I'm not sure I have managed very well."

"Oh, you've done fine," said the owl reassuringly. "As fine as anyone, considering the circumstances. I got the occasional report, from some migrating bird here and there, while you were out adventuring. It seems to me you've handled things perfectly well." He looked around their present environment: the weathered flagstones, rife with bones, the courtyard below, the broken ramparts, the churning sea. "Just fine, I suppose, till now. Some kind geese alerted me to your imprisonment at the hand of the Synod, your conveyance to this forsaken place. Have to admit, this is a bit of a sticky one, isn't it?"

"Yeah," said Prue, feeling sheepish. "It is."

"No matter," said Owl. "That's precisely why I've returned. No doubt you felt the tremor last night. There are many, many things unfolding in the Wood at present. Some good, some extremely bad. Such that it doesn't quite behoove one as important as you to just be sitting here, moldering away, on this heap of rocks. You're needed, Prue McKeel." He looked over at the robed bandit and said, "And you too, Seamus, I suppose. Though I don't know that I've ever seen a bandit in such a strange getup. Robes don't necessarily lend themselves to forest crawling. If I'm not mistaken, I'd say that those were the robes of the Synod, the Mystics of the Blighted Tree."

"You'd be right, there, mate," said Seamus.

"Then things have taken quite a turn. No matter. For every action there is a counteraction. We may find that the domination of the Synod did not enjoy much time in the sun. A new era has begun, my friends, and if it is not directed properly, it may have dire consequences for the coming generations."

"Of the Wood?" asked Prue.

"And beyond. Even now, as we speak, the very ribbon of magic that separates the world of the Wood from the Outside is being challenged. The time of the First Trees is passing. A new One Tree is being born."

"What does that even mean?" asked Prue.

"No time," said the owl. "Suffice it to say, you're needed in South Wood. Immediately." He moved away from Prue, and, spreading his wings wide, he proffered his back to the two humans. "Get onboard. We have a long way to go."

The two gingerly climbed on the owl's back, Prue at the bird's neck and Seamus just behind her. The owl, surprisingly, seemed little encumbered by their weight. He crouched low on the pinnacle of the broken stairs and shook his wings out to their full span; Prue could feel Seamus's grip around her belly go suddenly taut. "Oof," she said.

"Can I tell you something?" asked the bandit as the owl cocked his head, as if waiting for the wind to shift.

"What?"

"Promise you won't tell anyone?"

"Sure."

"I'm afraid of heights."

Prue stifled a laugh. "Better close your eyes, then," she said. And just at that moment, the giant bird gave a heaving push and took flight from the ruin on the Crag, sending chunks of rock spiraling to the ocean water below, his two riders working desperately to stay astride. Prue heard the bandit behind her gasp loudly; she felt the sea wind rushing through her hair, and the sky opened up above her as the lonely rock where she'd been sentenced to live out her days grew smaller and smaller below her.

Though she'd done it now twice in her life, Prue could not escape the feeling of wonder while riding on the back of an airborne bird. Even Seamus had loosened up into the ride and had let go his grip on her midsection. The owl's long wings beat against the rising air currents, and he deftly steered them through the whipping air. A low bank of clouds had settled over the ground below them, like a thin layer of cotton batting, and they flew unseen in the lofty springlike sky.

They were to travel all night, the owl said. They would follow an ancient migration pattern that connected the ocean to the Wood. It had been used since the time of the Ancients, when spots of Woods Magic appeared everywhere, before the need to shore up their defenses against the encroaching tide of Outsiders. As if underscoring this claim, a group of squawking cormorants came buzzing up from beneath them, briefly flurried around their airspace before disappearing down below the bank of clouds.

The night overtook the day, and little stars revealed themselves in the dome of sky. Prue nuzzled up against the owl's feathery nape and drifted into sleep. Dawn was glimmering in the east by the time she was awoken by the owl's booming voice. "Not far now!" he shouted.

Prue's eyes blinked open and she scanned the ground below. How he could know where they were, Prue wasn't sure. The world beneath them looked like a tufted white blanket.

The owl shifted the angle of his right wing and the trio pitched sharply down and to the right; Prue heard the bandit behind her let out a little hoot. Within moments, they were skirting the layer of clouds, and Prue looked down to see her foot, hanging just below the owl's underbelly, disappear into fog. The world whited out for a moment, and then they reemerged on the underside of the clouds and saw the wide stretch of the Wood splayed out below them.

A Wood that, from this height, looked remarkably changed.

"What's happened?" shouted Prue.

The owl made no reply but instead swooped lower, and Prue saw the change that was occurring.

The ivy was laying claim to the forest.

Like a thick covering of moss besieging a mottled rock, so the ivy was consuming the woods. The plant seemed to expand from some central point, draping the surrounding forest in a heavy shroud of viny brown and green. There was nowhere on this patch of earth that Prue couldn't see the effects of the plant's ravaging. As they flew closer, she could actually see the stuff moving, stretching out and staking new territory in its march northward, topping the tall fir trees and spiderwebbing from treetop to treetop. What's more, Prue began to hear a sort of virulent hissing rising up from the vines.

"The ivy!" she shouted into Owl's ear. "It's happening!"

From where they were positioned, they could see the boundary demarcating the border between the lands of the Outsiders and the Woodians. Prue recognized the distant skyline of Portland's downtown; she saw the puffing smokestacks of the Industrial Wastes. She saw to her horror that the ivy seemed to have lapped up against the invisible line separating these two worlds, like plants in a terrarium pressing against the glass of their enclosure. It was clear that the Periphery Bind was the only thing holding the ivy back from claiming more than just the territory it had conquered in the Wood.

The owl circled a few times before angling in on a wide meadow overtaken by the plant. Within moments, his talons had touched the ground and his riders leapt from his back, taking in the scene.

"It's worse than I feared," said the owl, adjusting his footing on the strange surface.

"Where are we?" asked Prue. The landscape was, indeed, changed beyond recognition. The trees that marked the boundary of this clearing stood like shrouded ghosts, like covered furniture in some unused wing of a castle, rendered unidentifiable by the organism that smothered them. The ground below their feet heaved and shuddered under their weight; it seemed that they were not actually touching the ground, so thick was the layer of vines. A few lumps presented themselves here and there throughout the clearing, and some kind of mountainous pile of the stuff held the center: a towering hill of writhing ivy.

"South Wood," replied the owl. He lifted his wing and pointed at the gigantic lump of greenery that stood some yards from them. "Behold, the Mansion."

Prue gaped to see it, but she soon confirmed the owl's declaration: She could just make out the shapes of the building's two towers. The hissing was nearly deafening by now, and it took all her mental efforts to keep it at bay. Seamus, taking a few trial steps out into the new, living surface of the Mansion's estate, said, "Why isn't it covering us?"

"I expect it's being controlled from somewhere farther afield," said the owl. "It appears to be slightly dormant here, in the trough of the wave." He looked about him, at the strange, apocalyptic scene playing out before them. "Here, the damage has been done. The Verdant Empress marches northward."

"The Verdant Empress?" asked Prue. "What's that?"

"The reborn form of Alexandra. Born of ivy, she has taken the form of the plant itself."

"Isn't that what she'd set out to do before? With Mac?" A feeling of gloom had come over Prue, remembering the awful rite the crazed woman had attempted to complete.

"Oh, no," said the owl, his voice steeped in sadness. "That was a mere shadow of the power she now possesses. Her body was sacrificed to the ivy. She *is* the ivy now."

Seamus, some feet off, was inspecting a little lump in the greenery, about the size of a small chair. He'd just pulled aside a few handfuls of the plant that had encompassed the object when he let out a short scream.

"What is it?" shouted Prue, rushing to his side.

"Look!" said the bandit, sounding petrified.

She peered into the parted curtains of the ivy vines and saw, there beneath the veil of green and brown, a bit of auburn fur.

"It's someone!" she shouted as the two of them began desperately to pull the ivy aside. It clung, stubbornly, to itself, its woody tendrils locked together, and when they pulled, the plant only seemed to cinch tighter around its cocooned subject.

"It's stuck, the shifty stuff," said Seamus, releasing his grip on the vines. He stepped back and as he did so, the ivy collapsed across the small gap they'd made, once again transforming whatever object it surrounded into a lonely protuberance of green leaves and woody stalks.

"Hold up," said Prue, now focusing her mind to address the ever-present hissing, which sounded in her ears like she was standing in the middle of a circle of televisions, all playing static.

The plant life below their feet gave a sudden jerk, seemingly surprised to be spoken to. Prue knelt by the ivy-enshrouded figure and held up her hands; it was a useless gesture, but she found it helped concentrate her thoughts on the thing she was asking the plant. It hissed back at her, affrighted by her presence, before it slowly relented. The taut vines slackened and began to fall away, a horde of retreating snakes. Soon, the thing it had swallowed was revealed: a homely brown beaver, sleeping restfully on a park bench.

Seamus dove in as Prue let her arms fall to her side—she found that the communication had sapped a small part of her strength—and the bandit began gently shaking the beaver awake.

"Mm-hello?" said the animal, surprised to be grasped at the shoulders by the bearded, robed man.

"Wake up!" said Seamus.

"I'll do that on me own time, tanks very much," the beaver sputtered. "I'd just nodded off. No harm in that." He was wearing an overcoat, stained with oily smears; the remnants of a half-eaten meal were laid out, in stasis, on a napkin on his lap. He looked around, affronted, as if to say, *Can you believe the indignity?*

"You've been covered in ivy," said Owl Rex, approaching them from behind. "You've been frozen there for some time, it would appear. You've quite forgotten your dinner."

The beaver looked down at the food in his lap. He then looked out over the ivy-covered landscape, his little mouth falling open when he saw the hilly lump of green that was the Pittock Mansion. "Is that . . . ," he began.

Seamus nodded.

"Oh," said the beaver, suddenly reconciling himself to the situation. His face, just then, took a precipitous

fall as his memories seemed to return to him: "I remember now," he said.

"What?" prompted Prue, kneeling by his side. "What happened?"

"Ain't you . . . ," he said, seeing Prue. "Ain't you the Bicycle Maiden?"

Prue nodded. The beaver, dazed, looked up at Owl Rex. "And ain't you the Crown Prince o' the Avians?"

Owl bowed his head regally. The beaver shook his head in disbelief. "Well, I never," he said.

"And I'm the bandit Seamus," said Seamus, apparently feeling left out of the beaver's starstruck reverie.

"You don't look much like a bandit," said the beaver. "What's wi' the dress?"

"It's not a dress," Seamus countered, offended. "It's a robe. Long story."

The beaver looked down at the food on his lap and began speaking, slowly, haltingly. "I was just sittin' down to my lunch. My midnight lunch, that is. I'm a gas-lamp tender, ain't I? And I feel this crazy rumble, like a earthquake or some such. That's what happened." He paused, collecting his thoughts. "I had to grab me lunch, din't I, lest it spill about. Nearly threw me off the bench. Well, then I look up and see, in the gaslight, this figure just spiral up from the trees, yonder."

"A figure," repeated the owl. "What did it look like?"

"Couldn't see much, it being dark an' all. At least at first. But

I'm, like, frozen in place, right? Can't even lift my hands from my lunch. Then a couple more figures appear, giant like, just through the trees." The beaver shook his head, as if trying to dispel the image from his mind.

"Keep going," prompted Owl. "You're safe now."

The beaver's small black eyes seemed to be tearing up. "Awful things. I can only see their legs in the light of the gas lamps. Tall as any tree in the forest. Made o' ivy, they are. And that's when the vines came. Like a wash o' water, they came. Saw 'em come over the Mansion, there. Like an explosion. 'Fore I could get out of me stupor, though, they came over me and I promptly tuckered out, din't I? Must've put me straight to sleep."

While the beaver spoke, Prue found her attention diverted to the far treetops, imagining the horrible scene as the poor, distraught animal described it. What horrific shape had this disembodied woman taken in order to inspire such fear, to wreak so much ruin? The firs and the cedars, the hemlocks and the maples, all of them sported a writhing new growth of ivy vines, clinging to their topmost boughs and making their crowns sag under their weight. Everywhere she looked, she saw the telltale signs of the innocent, somnolent victims of the ivy's spread: squat mounds in the cloak of green that lay over the landscape.

"Quickly," spoke the owl. "To the Blighted Tree."

"Yes!" shouted Prue, remembering the parasite-infected bandits.

Just then, a loud noise diverted their attention to the mountain of ivy in the center of the meadow, the enshrouded shape of the Pittock Mansion. Some of the ivy had fallen away as one of the brick walls let loose a shower of debris, crashing to the ground; a broken hole was, for a moment, revealed in the building's facade before a new surge of ivy crept up and covered it. Prue shrieked to see the destruction.

"It'll tear down the whole building!" she shouted. She remembered, then, how she'd managed to make the ivy retreat from the sleeping beaver. "Maybe I can stop it!" she said.

"No, Prue," said the owl. "It is beyond even your powers. The Mansion is lost. Perhaps there will be time to save the Blighted Tree."

"The Blighted Tree?" asked Prue, nonplussed. "Why would we save that awful thing?"

"The fabric of the Woods is a complex weave of many different energies. All must be preserved. It is too much to discuss presently, when your powers are needed elsewhere." The owl proffered his back to Prue and Seamus, and they both climbed onboard. "Hold tight," he said before unfurling his vast wings and leaping into the sky.

Again, they were afforded a harrowing view of the devastation from the owl's back as he flew. The spread of the ivy was rampant; everywhere they looked they saw what appeared to be houses and buildings being torn apart by the infestation. Whole trees, sky tall and centuries old, were cracking and bending under the weight of the plant that was consuming them. The sounds of their breaking echoed through the misty air. Prue stifled a sob in her chest to see such desolation, to see the entire ancient forest being slowly swallowed by this greedy invader.

Soon, they were flying over the clearing where Prue had been abducted, those few days prior: the Blighted Meadow. There, as on the Mansion's grounds, the ivy was widespread, covering the entire area like a wriggling sheet. The owl, in midflight, shook his head sorrowfully as he taxied around the center of the clearing, saying, "It's too late!" in a voice loud enough to cut through the whipping wind.

"What's too late?" Prue shouted back.

"The Blighted Tree. It's been consumed."

Sure enough, as the owl settled down onto the ivy-strewn meadow and Prue and Seamus hopped from his back, they saw that the imposing tree, that ancient tree, which had demanded the attention of the clearing for centuries untold, was now nothing more than a small heap in the center of the meadow. Little lesser heaps dotted a circle around it, and Prue guessed these to be the meditating acolytes, put to sleep by the plant. While the great owl stood, seeming paralyzed by the scene, Prue rushed to the nearest ivy mound and began communing with the hissing plant, calling it away from its purpose.

LET, she thought.

She could make out the following word, issuing to her from the farthest depths of her hearing: *WHOOOOOO.*

LET GO, she thought. She could feel her energy peeling away, like she was treading heavy water.

She suddenly felt the ivy slacken; she reached out and began to pull its webbing apart to reveal a hooded, masked figure beneath. "Seamus!" she yelled over her shoulder. The bandit came running to her side. "Help me get this stuff off."

The two of them began yanking aside the figure's smothering shroud; the ivy yielded to their hands, seemingly under the trance of Prue's demands. Before long, they had the Caliph partially freed of the vines. Seamus grabbed the figure's cowl and threw it aside before carefully removing the silver mask, revealing the peacefully sleeping face of the bandit William.

"Willy!" shouted Seamus, his voice breaking with excitement. "Wake up there, lad!"

The bandit's eyelids fluttered, and he stirred in his sleep. His long yellow mustache twitched a little as he slowly woke. Once again conscious, he stared at Prue and Seamus blankly, as if they were perfect strangers. As if his eyes saw nothing. Just then, a look of fear overcame his face and he began struggling in his bonds, as his hands and legs were still confined by the ivy.

"Willy!" Seamus yelled again. "It's me, Seamus!"

But there was no shine of recognition in the bandit's eyes. That was when Prue heard the ticking noise. She reached out her hand and pressed it against Seamus's chest. "Hold up," she said. "There's more to do here."

Seamus, clearly distraught at his brother-in-arms's amnesia, stumbled backward while Prue held her palm up to William's face.

COME, she thought. She cleared her mind. She addressed the ticking noise. She addressed the organism inside William's skull.

The bandit sputtered, his bloodshot eyes thrown wide. He began to cough, and his hands struggled in their bonds. Prue continued to coax the weird life-form that had nested inside the bandit's nasal cavity; she cajoled it, rooted it out. It *ticked* louder, unhappy to be disturbed, while snot gushed from the nose of the bandit, who was by now buckled over in the throes of his dry heaves.

"It's all right there, laddie," soothed Seamus, at the bandit's side. "It's unpleasant, but you got to just let it out."

The hacking grew more intense, and Prue felt the parasite relinquish its power and fall under her command. Again, she felt her energy being sapped, and she fell back on her heels as William the bandit pitched forward and his retching came on again, renewed. From his right nostril bloomed the grayish-green stuff, and Seamus shot his hand out and grabbed it. His face contorted into a disgusted grimace as he eased the fungus and its web of connected hyphae, the meshy filaments that branched out from the central glob of the organism, out of his comrade's nose.

The ticking had grown deafening in Prue's mind, now that the Spongiform had been released from its host, and she could feel it longing to attach itself to another human. "Destroy it, Seamus," she managed.

Holding it out like it was a poisonous snake, Seamus backed away

447

from William's prone, coughing form and tossed it unceremoniously into the ivy. The ticking seemed to ebb in Prue's mind, though she was suddenly alerted to the sound emanating all around her. She scanned the horizon; identical lumps in the blanket of ivy gave away the location of more Caliphs, more ticking parasites.

"Let's get a fire going," she said. "I've got a lot of work ahead of me."

Meanwhile, William had lifted himself up from his knees and was pawing at his face, wiping away the remnant mucus that had smoothed the fungus's exit through his nostril. He looked around himself, dazed, until his eyes fell on Seamus.

"Seamus!" he said hoarsely. "What's happened? Where am I?"

"You're in South Wood, brother," replied Seamus. "You've been made a slave. But that's over now. It's all over now." The bandit's voice welled with emotion as he spoke; it was clear that Seamus heavily wore the burden of having brought this fate on the bandit band.

And so their early morning progressed, there under the mantle of cloud that hung low over the forest: Each mound of ivy was discovered to be hiding some slumbering person or animal within its mesh cocoon and they were each, in turn, freed and revived. Those who'd been given the Spongiform, the silver-masked Caliphs, were left confined up to their necks until Prue could make her way to them (her energy ebbing with every case) and coax the spidery fungus from their nostrils. With each one, a new bandit was unmasked and awakened. A new flurry of questions and celebrations and sad, guilty explanations from Seamus were shared among the reunited bandits at every turn. A dozen sleeping Caliphs had been roused and set to rights—some of them were local South Wood citizens, innocently caught up in the Synod's promised revival—before they arrived at the acolyte whose silver mask, once removed, revealed the sleeping face of Brendan, the Bandit King.

Once he'd been unslept and the fungus coughed up from his skull had been added to the blazing fire they'd started in the center of the meadow, he stood uneasily and, saying nothing, surveyed the crowd that was now surrounding him. Seamus rushed forward, seeing his long-lost sovereign, and threw himself at the Bandit King's feet.

"Oh, King," said Seamus, letting loose a torrent of sobs, "this is all my doing."

Brendan looked at his most uncertain, there in the center of the crowd. Prue had only ever seen him steadfast and regal, in his sylvan element, his forehead tattoo a totem to his strength. But now he looked muddled and confused as he stared down at the bandit who was prostrating himself before him.

"Rise," he said finally.

Seamus did as he was instructed, his head still bowed.

"What has happened?" asked the Bandit King. He held his hand briefly at his temple, massaging the skin.

"I was here, as an emissary," started Seamus.

Brendan nodded, as if to say, *This much I remember.*

"They took me in, the Synod," said Seamus. "The Mystics of the Blighted Tree. I don't remember much past that point. Just hazy recollections, really. I was fed that stuff—the Spongiform. It's a parasitic fungus; makes you do the will of the Blighted Tree and its disciples."

The Bandit King remained silent; his brow was placid and his eyes stayed fixed on his comrade. His hand fell to his side.

Seamus continued haltingly, "I came to the camp. Under the influence of that . . . stuff. I fed the rest of the camp the fungus, and you all fell in line." Seamus began to cry, big tears rolling down his nose and into the tuft of his brown beard. "We all marched back . . . here. And were made part of the Synod, doing the bidding of the tree." He sniffed a few times, collecting himself, ran his finger under his nose, and said, "I've failed the band. I've broken the oath. I will recuse myself from my brothers and sisters. If it be your will, I'll be a bandit no more."

Silence followed; Brendan searched the bowed head of his fallen brother for a moment before replying. "Seamus," he said, resting his arms on the man's shoulders. "I'd as soon let you leave the band as throw myself into the deepest pit of the Long Gap. You are no more at fault than any of us." He then surveyed his gathered subjects, his fellow bandit brethren, smiling, until his eyes fell on Prue.

Prue instinctively gave a little curtsy.

"Why is it that I'm not surprised to see you here, as well?" said the

Bandit King. "Prue of the Outside. It would seem that trouble follows you like campfire smoke."

He'd given her a wry smile, which Prue took as a hopeful sign that the bandit had returned to his old, sardonic self.

"Smoke follows beauty," replied Prue, smiling sheepishly. It was one of her dad's old saws, always hauled out during camping trips. Just then her vision swam and her knees gave out. The bandit Angus, who happened to be standing next to her, grabbed her arm and steadied her.

"Are you okay, lass?" he asked.

"Just a little . . . worn out, I guess," she replied. The work of freeing all the ivy's captives had been more exhausting than she'd anticipated.

Owl Rex walked through the crowd of the thirty-odd bandits and townsfolk; they all parted to let the giant bird by.

"Owl," said Brendan, acknowledging the Avian prince with a bow of his head. "What did you know of this?"

"Nothing, I assure you," was the reply. "I've been gone these many months, adventuring elsewhere. Suffice it to say, this is a once-in-a-lifetime cock-up, one that is unlikely to be put to rights anytime soon. We can but do our best. The Blighted Tree is no more. It has been torn apart by the Verdant Empress's wrath. She seems to be making good on her earlier threats."

"Who is this Verdant Empress?" asked the Bandit King. "She's no monarch I bow to."

"She is the living ivy itself, imbued with the spirit of the dead. Or near dead." The owl then turned to address the gathered crowd. "The woman you thought you slew on the field of battle, there on the ivy-strewn basilica during the Battle for the Plinth—she has returned. Indeed, she was never more than in hibernation, her spirit swallowed by the ivy itself. She has now come to finish her terrible rite and reduce the Wood to a desolation."

Brendan seemed to be regaining his strength, and he put in, angrily, "She'll not get far. Cover the Wood in ivy if she must, we'll still send her to the devil." His hand reached for a saber at his side that was not there. Instead, he clutched at the strange gray robes he wore and cursed.

The owl shook his head at the comment. "It's worse than that, much worse," he said. "The Blighted Tree has been torn down. This tree, standing for centuries, though much maligned by its detractors, has served a very important purpose. Along with the Ossuary Tree in Wildwood and the Council Tree of North Wood, it maintained the fabric of the Periphery Bind." The owl paused so as to let what he next said fall with the appropriate weight. "And without the Bind, the boundary between the Wood and the Outside is null."

"Null?" said Prue, suddenly panicked. "What do you mean, null?" She found a reserve of strength and pushed herself away from Angus's arm.

The owl turned to her and frowned. "Yes. Alexandra—the Verdant Empress—will move beyond the Periphery. Once she's done wreaking havoc on the Wood, she will consume the Outside as well."

While none of the individuals present, besides Prue, could truly envision what this statement suggested—none of them having ever set foot in the so-called Outside—it immediately conjured a very stark and terrifying picture for Prue. She found, while in the Wood, that she cared very little for the Outside; for its mundane realities and trivial concerns—but there was something in this, this suggestion that the boundary between the two worlds would be overrun, that made her almost protective of her home-world.

"Over here!" came a voice; they all looked to see one of the bandits standing some yards off, on the edge of the clearing. "Prue! You're needed!"

Rushing to where the bandit stood, they immediately saw the cause for concern: A small hut was in the process of being crushed under the weight of its thick mantle of ivy. Inside, a voice could be heard, crying for help.

"Esben!" shouted Prue, suddenly recognizing the growly timbre of the voice.

She threw her hands up to the surface of the structure and began coaxing away the ivy vines; the bandits fell in around her and started stripping the plant away once it had been controlled. The door was soon located; they were dismayed to find its latch was affixed with a heavy iron padlock.

"Hold tight there!" shouted Brendan as he turned to his fellow robed bandits, waving his hand. "One of you's got to have the key. Search your pockets, lads!"

The hut's strained framework wheezed as the ivy continued to constrict, bending the structure into a weird, oblong shape. Inside, something cracked. Esben let out a yell of surprise.

"We're going to get you out of there!" shouted Prue, her hands held to the living surface of the hut, willing the ivy to let up its pressure. The mass seemed too great; she was having a hard time communing with it all.

The bandits, almost comically, were it not for the gravity of the situation, were simultaneously patting the sides of their identical gray robes, searching for the key, before Brendan spoke up. "Look at that," he said, producing a brassy skeleton key from his pocket. "Had it all along." The lock undone, they threw open the door.

Inside, pressed up against the far wall, was a bear with two golden hooks for hands. He smiled sheepishly to see his rescuers. "Hi, there," he said. "Mind the ivy."

Indeed, the plant had made its way through the chinks in the hut's log walls and was busily crawling across the floor toward the bear. Prue leapt forward and, issuing a word of warning to the creeping plant in her mind, grabbed Esben by the hook. She rushed the bear through the door frame, squeezed as it was into a vexed rhombus, while the hut groaned and shivered around them.

Once they'd made the safety of the outside, Prue threw herself on

454

the bear, wrapping her arms around his massive midsection and only managing to cover half the distance. The bandits looked on, marveling at the sagging structure of the bear's former prison cell.

"And I thought it'd cave in just as we got him out," said Seamus.

"Only works that way in stories," said another bandit nearby, Gram.

Seamus gave one of the doorjamb posts a kick, and the entire structure blew to the ground in an eruption of noise, dust, and ivy. "There we go," said the bandit, satisfied.

Prue, momentarily jolted by the hut's collapse, turned back to Esben; she began busily pulling the last bits of clinging ivy from the bear's fur, motherlike, while she spoke. "I'm so sorry, Esben. I had no idea what was happening."

"They must've followed the badger," said Esben, still regaining his bearings. "They came at me quickly; I couldn't have escaped. Hooded things." He shivered then. "And then the ivy; it came on so fast. And the terrible crashing noises. I've been trapped in that cabin for who knows how long!"

"You're safe now," said Prue.

"Am I?" asked the bear, taking in the surroundings. Indeed, his environment had changed so drastically since he'd been taken prisoner that there was barely a resemblance remaining to that diverse forest he'd left when they had first locked him up.

"She's back, the Dowager Governess. Just in . . . some other form," said Prue. "She's taken control of the ivy."

"What does she plan on doing with it?" asked the bear, confused.

"She means to rend the very fabric of the Periphery Bind," answered Owl Rex. "She means to tear down the Trees of the Wood." The bird's head feathers were ruffled by a flurry of the wind and he looked southward, to the lowering banks of clouds on the horizon. "If it is her wish," he said, "she now rides for the Ossuary Tree, the second tree, to break it to its roots. Then, only a third tree will stand in her way."

"The Council Tree," breathed Prue. Her mind flashed on the peaceable folk of North Wood, on the chain of quiet Mystics, practicing their meditations around the gargantuan trunk of the great tree. "We have to go. We have to stop her."

"We can perhaps hold her back," said the owl gravely.

"But what of the girl's power?" put in Brendan. "She can control the ivy. Could she hold the tide at bay?"

The owl looked to Prue, frowning. "Even with your estimable powers, the Verdant Empress would overrun you."

"But the Mystics—if we rallied them, they could help. We could work together," said Prue.

"Perhaps . . . ," began the owl.

Just then, a thought occurred to Prue. "The cog," she said. "What about the cog?"

Owl Rex looked curiously at the girl. "Surely such a thing cannot help us now."

"But it's what the tree said—it said by reconstructing the mechanical boy, the true heir, it would unite the Wood. It would save it!" Prue's face became vexed, working out the intricacies of the plan. "I mean, if it knew what was happening all along—maybe it wasn't the Synod it meant to save itself from—but this Verdant Empress woman—Alexandra!" She turned to Esben and looked at him sharply. She understood, plainly, that perhaps her quest must, at some point, reach its stopping point. Its searcher must come to rest eventually, even if the desired outcome had not yet been achieved.

"We need you to start making the cog," she said.

The bear gulped, once, loudly. He held up his two hooks and said helplessly, "That woman robbed me of my tools. Without Carol, I'm not sure I can."

"You have to try," pressed Prue. She looked around her, surveying the gathered crowd. "Someone will need to be your hands."

Seamus, the bandit, stepped forward. He held out his knobby, weatherworn fingers. "I'm as good as any at molding a horseshoe or a hobnail," he said. "Not entirely sure what sort of cog needs be made, but I can give it a shot."

"Maybe," said the bear, somewhat unsteadily, his voice lacking the sort of steely pluck one typically expects at times such as these. He studied his prosthetic hands, uncertainly, in the wan light of the day before saying to the congregation of bandits, "We'll need a bigger fire, a hotter fire."

Just as the gathered bandits had all raised a collective "Aye!" and set about collecting what loose branches they could find from beneath the worming ivy, Esben the bear turned his solemn eyes to Prue and said plaintively, "I'll do my best."

"And that's all we could hope for," she replied, placing her hand on his arm.

Brendan the Bandit King stood apart, gauging the placement of the sun in the hazy sky. "She's got some time on us. If she's on to the Ossuary Tree, it won't be long before this Verdant Empress will cross the pass and into North Wood." He spat angrily at the writhing ground. "Us on foot, she'd long have laid the Council Tree to waste before we made Wildwood, even without all this damned ivy everywhere."

Owl Rex offered up a smile. "Then we will not travel on foot," he said, before unfurling his wings and leaping into the air. He wheeled about, some hundreds of feet above their heads, before spiraling upward and rending the air with the loudest birdcall many of the bandits and South Wooders assembled had ever had a chance to hear. It echoed through the still woods, among the ivy-crowned trees and the falling buildings and the sad, desolate landscape of this desecrated world: a resounding cry, a call to arms.

C H A P T E R   2 6

The Birth of Giants

The children had decided they'd spend the day at Bandit Hideout Deerskull Dragonfighter recuperating from their ordeal the night before, catching up on sleep and prepping for their long walk to South Wood, where they'd (hopefully) find Curtis's friend Prue and reunite Carol with his long-lost machinist counterpart. The kids passed the hours exploring the many walkways of the hideout while Curtis helpfully fitted his sister Elsie with a pair of handwoven moccasins—she'd been going it one-shoed since the duct-rats' escape from the stevedores in the security elevator shaft.

They were a trial pair he'd been working on in order to keep his hide-working skills up to snuff, and it was a great fortuity that they actually fit Elsie's small feet.

"Thanks, Bandit Curtis," said Elsie, wiggling her toes against the doeskin.

"Don't mention it," replied her brother, smiling.

Once night fell, however, Rachel found she couldn't sleep. She'd dozed a little that morning, when they'd first arrived at the hideout—though certainly not enough to replenish the amount of energy she'd expended, physically and emotionally, in her maiden saboteur action. She felt emboldened by everything that had taken place, and that night, after the salvaged dinner had been eaten and the wood-carved dishes had been cleaned and stowed, she sat with her palms to the crackling fire while the rest of the crowd, the five Unadoptables and Carol, all collapsed into a sardine-packed row and fell into dreamless sleep. All night she listened to the soughing of the tall trees as they were gently rocked in the dark's noisy breezes; she heard the hooting calls of owls and the cries of the night birds. She must've dozed off at some point; when she awoke, the air was warm and the light was bright through the stain of gray clouds in the sky; she'd lost track of the passing of time in this bizarre new world, and her head felt as heavy and confused as it had ever been. The other sleepers had long roused; their mossy cots were all empty.

Curtis walked into the hut and saw his sister wake and prop herself up by her elbows; he was carrying a handful of wineskins, dripping full with water. Setting them by the door, he picked up a nearby willow branch and stirred at the smoldering campfire.

"Morning," he said. "You slept well. It's getting on midday!"

"I think I was up most of the night," was her reply.

"Oh," he said, frowning. "Well, you'll get used to it. I didn't sleep much, either, when I first came here. Except for that first night, in the Governess's warren. But I had some blackberry wine to help with that." He smiled sheepishly before suddenly growing self-conscious of this admission. "It was sort of forced on me."

"Where's Nico?" asked Rachel, seeing the empty spot next to her pile of moss.

"He volunteered for lookout," said Curtis. He stirred the fire a little more before saying, "Seems like a nice guy."

"He is," said Rachel. "Though I don't know what he's thinking about all this."

"Seems to be taking it in stride. I guess the Industrial Wastes were kind of their own weird universe. This isn't that big of a change." He paused in his fire stirring and said, "It's good to see you guys again, Rach."

"You too, Curtis."

"How are Mom and Dad doing?"

"I guess okay, considering that they've been traumatized about you."

Curtis stiffened. "I didn't mean to cause anyone any grief."

461

"Well, that didn't really work out, did it? What did you expect?" She stared at her brother, waiting for his response.

Curtis shrugged defensively. "I don't know, Rach. I thought maybe you guys'd understand." He corrected himself before his sister had a chance to pounce. "I mean, if you'd only known what was happening. That I was wrapped up in this bigger thing. People *depended* on me, Rachel. And I figured that if you could see me, you would get it." He gestured to their surroundings. "I mean, look at all this. I *belong* here."

The fire crackled between them; Rachel didn't respond.

Curtis continued: "Not to say I didn't belong there, in the Outside. I love you guys, and there's really not a day that goes by I don't miss you and think about you. Mom and Dad and Elsie. Even you, though you were kind of a jerk to me, back home."

"What?"

"You were! There was a moment where we got along, but it was so long ago it's like it didn't even exist. I just remember old photos of us sitting together when I was, like, a baby. That's the last time I remember ever hanging out with you where you were nice to me."

Rachel felt her dander getting up. "Don't pin this on me. I'm not the reason you ran away from home."

"No," said Curtis, waving his hand in objection. "No. You weren't the reason. But it was a part of it. Like, all these little things building up. School was awful. Everyone had moved on from the stuff they'd loved as kids. All my friends had changed—since middle school began, it was like they were different people. I felt like they'd figured out something that was totally a mystery to me. Like, how to grow up. I just didn't get it. And then I found this place, and suddenly I could grow up—but in my own way, you know?"

"I guess so," said Rachel. "Couldn't you have done this out there?"

"Maybe. But I wasn't open to it. The stakes weren't high enough. Or something."

There was a pause between them as the fire snapped and flickered and the light of the day grew sharper as the sheen of clouds parted; it peered in through the open windows. Curtis was about to say something, perhaps something peaceable, to assuage his sister's anger, but he was interrupted by a very large crashing noise.

"What was that?" said Rachel suddenly.

Curtis leapt up and looked out one of the windows; the air was suddenly alive with the noise of frantic birdsong. "I don't know," he said. "Sounded like a tree falling."

It came again, the crashing. It sounded like someone had taken a particularly branchy tree and dropped it from a great height. Nico came rushing in through the door.

"Curtis!" he shouted. "You're going to want to see this."

Together, they rushed along a series of rickety bridges and up a staircase that spiraled the trunk of another cedar. From this vantage, they towered above the forest canopy and could see, seemingly, for miles. Nico scanned the vista; another crash sounded.

"There," he said, pointing his finger at a gap in the trees. "Please tell me what that is."

Curtis squinted, trying to make out what the saboteur had spotted; the forest was very thick here, in deepest Wildwood; something would have to be fairly big for one to spot it on the ground from their high vantage point. But then, just as he was about to question Nico once more, he saw it.

There, in the break between a circle of trees, was a tranquil meadow. Curtis could make it out plainly from their treetop. Another crash came, and Curtis saw the grassy soil of the meadow undulate as if it were a down comforter and someone had just given it a healthy shake. The source of this little quake soon presented itself: The thick and telephone-pole-tall leg of some bizarrely fashioned humanoid creature stepped out onto the grass of the meadow. Curtis gaped; soon, the rest of its body followed, and the creature was completely exposed in the center of the clearing, an awful smudge on this pastoral scene.

It was the ivy; and yet it was not the ivy. Rather, it was as if someone had taken a vast patch of the plant and, having molded it into the shape of the poor approximation of a human figure, fed it some monstrous fertilizer that let it grow to the size of a small building. And then, by some magic, imbued the creation with life. The ivy hung from the creature's frame like a shaggy coat and draped in long tendrils from its faceless head, like an overly hairy dog; it was a shambling, leafy hedge, come to life.

With every step the creature made, ivy took root and began to spread. Where trees stood in its way, it reached out its long, spindly arms and merely knocked them aside like traffic cones.

"Oh God," said Nico. "There's more."

Sure enough, just as soon as the ivy giant had lumbered across the meadow, another appeared on the edge of the clearing, great waves of ivy extending out from its every step. Another followed, close behind. Their footfalls and the ensuing tide of ivy crashed together, and soon whole trees were being swallowed by the leafy stuff; it clung to the trees' trunks and snaked up through the limbs until the shorter trees were all but swallowed whole, the wood aching and wheezing from the weight.

"Quick!" said Curtis, breaking from his trance, from the horror he'd felt to see such awesome, terrifying things waltz into his domain. "We've got to get everyone up."

"This isn't something that regularly happens, I take it," said Nico, breathlessly stepping away from the edge of the lookout post.

Curtis shot the man an annoyed glare. "No," he said flatly, before leaping down the staircase away from the platform.

"I don't know," said Nico. "Where I'm from animals don't talk, either." He quickly followed the bandit down the stairway.

When they arrived at the hut, all the children and Carol had gathered there and were in a state of frenzied activity. "What is that noise?" demanded Oz; Martha was holding Carol's arm protectively. She held back the branchy curtains and searched the view out of the window.

"I don't know," said Curtis. "Nothing I've ever seen before. Huge . . . huge things. Giants." His heart was rattling in his chest as he spoke. "Made of ivy, as far as I can tell."

"What do we do?" This was Elsie, her eyes wild. Suddenly, this tranquil forest world seemed not as safe as it once had.

Curtis looked down at his little sister, trying to tamp down his own fear. "I—" he faltered. "I don't know."

Another crashing noise sounded, this time closer. The walls of the little house shook and the tree swayed.

"Think of something," demanded Rachel, staring down her brother, hard.

Septimus the rat came scurrying into the room. "Curtis!" he shouted. "What are you doing? We've got intruders on the perimeter!"

Curtis looked at his sisters, blinked a few times, and then turned to the rat. "Right," he said, regaining his composure. "Where are they headed?"

"Toward the gully," said Septimus. "I heard Nico's call-out, went to go get a close-hand view."

"Are the traps set?"

"The ones in the gully are down, remember? We were working on them the other day."

"Damn," swore Curtis, before remembering his little sister. "I mean, shoot. Maybe . . ."

He felt every eye in the hut resting on him. The pressure suddenly felt overlarge, weighty. "You guys. Follow me," he said finally, pointing at Nico and Rachel. "Elsie and everyone else, stay put. Get to the crow's nest if you have to. As far as I can tell, only the shorter trees are being swallowed up. I think you're safe here."

"From the ivy?" asked Martha.

"These things—they're made of ivy. They're covering the forest. Every step sends out more shoots."

"What if they come at the hideout?" This was Elsie, her face lined with worry.

"We won't let them," answered Septimus.

Curtis gave them all a brief, determined look before he dashed out of the doorway and down the stairs toward the ground. Set into an empty knot in the tree a few steps down the stairs, a weathered chest had been placed; Curtis opened it and pulled out three scabbarded sabers and handed one each to his sister and Nico. The third, a pebble-pommeled sword, he saved for himself, strapping it to his waist.

"What's this?" asked Rachel.

"What's it look like?" responded Curtis.

Nico looped the belt around his black trousers and cinched it tight. Drawing the blade from its scabbard, he looked at the thing briefly before saying, "I think I can do this. *C'est facile.*"

Rachel, not as assured as her compatriot saboteur, fastened the sword around her waist and waited for her brother to lead on.

By the time they'd descended the ladder to the forest floor, the ivy was everywhere; it was flattening the low brush and teeming over the tree saplings, reducing what was once a vibrant, diverse-colored canvas into an ivy-strewn wasteland. What's more, Curtis found as his booted feet touched the ground that the stuff was moving, like a pit of writhing asps. It licked up his ankle as he made contact, trying to strangle his calf, and he kicked it away disgustedly.

"Careful!" he called out to Nico and Rachel, who were making their way down the ladder. "This stuff is really alive." His saber was withdrawn, and he held it poised as he stepped away from the tree. A vigorous tendril shot up his leg and his sword came flashing down, slicing the thing in half and sending it, withering, to the ground.

"What is this, Curtis?" called Rachel, high-stepping through the blanket of ivy. "Do you know what's happening?" Suddenly, a patch of ivy quivered at her step, and several shoots went climbing up her leg. She screamed, stumbling, and the ivy clung tenaciously.

"Rach!" shouted Curtis. "Your sword!"

Pinwheeling her arms, she managed to gain enough control to whip the saber from her side and catch the ivy vines by the base; lifting the blade up, she heard a satisfying rip as the plant went scattering and her legs were freed. Nico, seeing this, drew his sword as well and held it threateningly toward the blanket of ivy.

But Curtis's thoughts were elsewhere, drifting, as he made his way through the dense bracken. Like some shade of a memory, hailing

The ivy hung from the creature's frame like a shaggy coat and draped in long tendrils from its faceless head, like an overly hairy dog.

him from a long distance. It seemed like so long ago, and yet was only last fall: He'd been there, a proud member of the Wildwood Irregulars. They were fighting back wave after wave of the coyote army. To scuttle *her* plans.

The Dowager Governess.

And now, it would seem that somehow that terrible ceremony she'd sought to complete there, on the Plinth, had been achieved. By whose hand, he couldn't know. But it was clear, while the ivy lapped at his heels and he high-stepped headlong through the swallowed forest, that someone was certainly to blame for this enchantment.

He couldn't, however, have anticipated the horrors that the ivy could create: He rounded the felled stump of a large tree and had to leap back, his heart racing, when one of those ivy-built behemoths came charging down the hillside toward him. He waved his hand to Rachel and Nico, and they dove into cover behind him.

The thing was even more awesome from this perspective, here on the ground. Seeing it from the air had given it a toylike appearance; but from here, from below, the thing looked positively menacing. Thick curtains of ivy poured down from the crown of its head and all but covered its humanlike limbs, which, when they revealed themselves from within a thick screen of ivy, were seen to be rippling with viny sinews. The thing hadn't seen them, there concealed by the leveled stump, and the three of them watched slack-jawed while it slowly crashed its way through the forest; soon, two more appeared in its wake. One of them stopped and, letting its foot fall with a loud, crashing stomp, sent a tidal wave of ivy up an ancient hemlock, crowning it in vines until it was a sad, drooping thing, a Christmas tree over-decked with tinsel.

"Curtis," came a hissed voice. It was Septimus, just above them, hidden in the boughs of a tree. "They're moving toward Deerskull Dragonfighter."

Just as the rat said this, another crash sounded as one of the giants swung its heavy arm against a tree that had stood in its way; the tree's massive roots tipped up from the ground, sending a spray of dirt sky-ward, and it toppled to the forest floor.

Curtis thought quickly; diving out from behind the tree, he dashed toward the ivy giant, waving his saber wildly around his head.

He yelled something then, though he wouldn't later be able to remember what it was. Even Rachel and Nico, who were still cower-ing behind the tree trunk, couldn't be called upon to describe it later, so shocked were they to see this twelve-year-old boy go darting out into the path of possibly the most horrifying and grotesque spectacle they'd ever seen in their lives. All any of them really knew, at that moment, was that the ivy giants, all three of them, stopped what they were doing (which was stomping around, sending up rafts of ivy and knocking trees down) to stare at the small human with a look of seeming disbelief—though it couldn't be said that the giants had eyes—or even faces; their undulating green heads were totally fea-tureless, covered as they were in deep, shaggy tresses of vines.

Curtis made a few more prancing leaps, shouted something else, turned around, and started running.

One of the three giants lifted its bulky leg and let it fall, stomping out a flurry of ivy vines that shot toward the running boy; they hit the wall of trees Curtis had dived beyond and exploded upward into the branches. Rachel, seeing this, let out a little yelp. One of the giants, having evidently heard her exclamation, swiveled its weird head in her direction and began walking toward her and Nico.

"C'mon!" shouted Nico. He leapt from cover and, following Curtis's lead, did a little attention-grabbing dance before running toward the distant tree line. Rachel came swiftly behind, running as fast as she could through the thick stratum of ivy that covered everything. Soon, she'd made it beyond the trees and could see the golden fringe of Curtis's epaulets glinting in the breaking sun.

The giants' crashing steps sounded loudly behind them as the creatures gave pursuit.

"This way!" shouted Curtis, seeing that Nico and Rachel had followed him. They skittered across the forest floor while a wave of ivy followed them, a flurry of tendrils being sent out with every one of the giants' footfalls. Finally, Rachel saw Curtis reach a small glade and turn sharply to the left, diving behind a stand of sword ferns. She and Nico followed quickly after, rolling to a stop next to him.

"Heads down!" hissed Curtis, his own cheek kissing the cold scrub of the fern fronds. Rachel did as she was instructed; Nico watched the scene in the meadow play out.

The first giant came clambering past the line of trees and stopped, scanning the landscape for sign of its prey. The clutch of ivy at its large, clubbed feet seemed to pause as well, its waxy leaves swaying about like a many-headed hydra. It seemed momentarily baffled by the humans' disappearance, standing just on the outskirts of the clearing.

"C'mon," hissed Curtis. "Just . . . go!"

Rachel shot a curious look at her brother; his attention was fixed on the strange creature.

The giant, then, evidently seemed to make a guess as to which way they'd gone and it began to walk again, taking another lumbering step into the center of the glade. A loud, woody *click* sounded, and the giant flinched at the noise. No sooner had it done this than the greenery surrounding it seemed to peel back and a vast handwoven net, anchored by an unseen pulley in the trees, whipped up and neatly captured the creature's legs in its web. The behemoth toppled to the ground with a moan of surprise and anger; the ground tremored at its landfall. The trap gave a noisy complaint, as it was unable to lift the weight of its captive, but the giant seemed fairly ensnared regardless.

Curtis let out a little whoop and pumped his fist against his side, seeing the success of his well-laid trap. He looked at Rachel and Nico, saying, "Not bad, eh?"

The giant writhed in its bonds, letting out angered, rattling groans from its mouthless face. Nico and Rachel looked on with horror. Two more of the giants entered the clearing and, seeing their compatriot caught in the trap, began whipping about angrily, sending vines of ivy from the tips of their long, twiggy fingers.

And that was when Curtis saw her.

The ivy had rustled a little, the dormant ivy that sat in patches about the clearing and issued from the fists of the angry giants, before undulating alive, and the center of the clearing became awash in a kind of turbulent cyclone of writhing greenery, and then the center erupted and out of it grew a pillar of winding vines that, bizarrely, began to take the form of a very human-looking creature. A very human-looking woman.

Even though she was like a sculptor's replica of an original, the death mask produced by a handy plasterer, Curtis immediately recognized her. It was the same woman who'd taken him in and shown him the Wood in all its glory, when he'd first set foot in this strange place. The woman who'd first put a saber in his hand and given him his own uniform. The first person he'd ever truly known to be evil, and not in the way he'd been accustomed to, growing up in the Outside. She was not some idle felon, not some immoral crook; she was a woman who he'd seen become completely derailed by her own passions. He'd recognized it when he'd come across Prue's babbling baby brother in a crib surrounded by crows, with her there, complicit in the deed. He remembered her that way, standing amid those black, squawking things, and how her heart outshone even the dark birds in its opaque, bruised blackness.

But what he saw now was green.

Like the giants, her arms were ivy and her legs, splaying out from the ground, were ivy and her lithe torso was ivy. Her face was ivy, but the vines here began cinching closer together until features were constructed and two twin tufts of ivy vines grew from her head and draped down her neck, insinuating themselves together until they became the two braids that the woman had worn in life, so many months ago.

Curtis looked on and saw the writhing body of Alexandra, the Dowager Governess, re-formed from molten ivy.

He felt his sister's breath at his neck; he felt Nico's nervous, clutching hand at his shoulder. He wondered, then, if their horror at seeing this specter seemingly rise from the ether was as horrific to them as it was to him; they did not know the heart of this thing. Curtis had reckoned it immediately.

"No," he breathed quietly. "It can't be."

"What?" asked Rachel. "What is it?"

"Looks like a she," said Nico.

"We have to get out of here," replied Curtis in a whisper. In the clearing, this new, plantlike Alexandra had completed her transformation and was now standing and inspecting the damage wrought by Curtis's trap. She casually circled the collapsed net while the giant within had ceased his protestations and was lying dormant. The ivy-woman, some ten feet tall, did not so much walk as re-transform herself at every step, the ivy that made up her flesh and bones reconfiguring and re-entwining to give the illusion of walking.

Moving up to the netting, the ivy-made Alexandra reached one of her leafy hands out and touched the forehead of the captured giant, like a mother would the brow of a child or a cowering dog. Just as her fingers made contact with the giant's head, the ivy form dissipated and the netting collapsed in on itself, suddenly freed of its contents. The leaves and vines that had made up the giant's form simply fell apart, like a bubble bursting, and returned to the laden earth, to the swelling ivy at the plant-woman's feet.

Then, to the horror of the three onlookers, the woman raised her arms out and extended her fingers. The ivy below her hands ruptured and split, and suddenly two new forms began to rumble into shape. Before long, the budding shapes of two new ivy giants had been produced and were squirming into life. They started as little pupa, two burping embryos on the forest floor; they bawled and brayed in new life. Then, as the woman continued her conjuration, they found their footing and they sprouted new growth: Their arms and legs lengthened and found strength; a writhing crown of hair jetted from each of their heads. As stunted preadolescents, they were dwarfed by the other two, fully grown ivy giants. Soon, however, their spines straightened and they grew tall and strong, having achieved a kind of developmental adulthood in a matter of moments.

Nico said something, loudly, having finally broken the barriers of his own disbelief. "You have got to be kidding me," he said. Curtis tried to shush him, but it was too late; the plant-woman, Alexandra, had twisted her neck around and was staring with her baleful, hollow eyes in the direction of their hiding place. Her mouth gawped open; a horrible scream emitted from the dark space it made.

"GO!" shouted Curtis, and he thrust himself up from the ground. He could hear Nico and Rachel scramble behind him; he threw his hand out to his sister, who'd slipped on something in her desperation, and the two of them tore away from the scene in the clearing, not looking back. They didn't see Nico falter, strangely transfixed by the ivy-woman, but they heard him scream as a flood of ivy, sent by one of the giants' crushing footfalls, poured toward him.

They both looked around in time to see the man become swallowed in the wave, a wave that engulfed his black-clad, turtlenecked body in a short matter of seconds. His scream dissipated in the air and then he was gone.

"Nico!" yelled Rachel desperately. She hesitated momentarily, wanting to return to the small lump of ivy that remained where the saboteur had stood, but Curtis pulled her away.

"We have to go!" he shouted as the crest of ivy approached them. Rachel turned her attention away from her friend, the funny saboteur who'd become such a canny part of her world, and instead watched as the rolling ivy, having swallowed the man whole, galloped toward them. She let go of her brother's hand and started sprinting through the woods as fast as her legs could carry her.

Deluge!

The trees blew by her like mile markers on a highway; she threaded the obstacle course of the forest, following the practiced path of her brother, who leapt the fallen tree trunks and dodged the shrubbery with an exceptional skill. The sound of the ivy and the thundering steps of the giants only pushed her onward until the noise fell away behind them. She broke through a thicket of blackberry brambles and slid down a muddy embankment; when she looked up, Curtis was nowhere to be seen.

"Rach!" came a hissed voice.

Down the gully, Curtis was lying flat by a fallen tree. Rachel threw herself down the ravine, scrabbling along the incline madly, and took cover beside him. Just then, the trees above the gully broke open and five ivy giants came lumbering across the landscape, handily making the small gap with one stride. The little flurries of ivy exploded at their every step. Taking up the rear of the procession was the spectral woman, who paused momentarily at the far side of the embankment. Rachel sat against the fallen tree, her hand cupped over her mouth and her eyes streaming panicked tears. Curtis stared at his sister with his finger to his lips, willing her to fight the instinct to scream.

She stared at him, hard; together, they wished the world away.

Then the crashing footsteps began again and the ivy-woman was gone, leaving a trail of flowing green in her path. Only the sound of that creeping plant could be heard. Rachel let her hand fall from her mouth and said, "We have to go back for Nico!"

Curtis shook his head, cutting away a clutch of vines that had ensnared his knees while they'd crouched in hiding. "You saw what happened. He's gone, Rach."

Just then, a scream sounded, distantly, from some hollow of the forest. The two Mehlberg siblings recognized the sound immediately; they'd both heard that very scream as it changed from wailing infant to petulant tween in the privacy of their own home. It was, without a doubt, their sister Elsie.

"The fort!" cried Curtis, and they both leapt up, fighting back the snaking ivy, and ran in the direction of Deerskull Dragonfighter. The closer they got, the thicker the ivy grew; soon, they were wading through a knee-deep morass of the clinging stuff, their movements reduced to a slow-motion slog. They wielded their saber blades like machetes, cutting the stuff away as it clung to their pant legs and tangled around their waists. Elsie's screams persisted; soon, other voices joined in.

"HOLD ON!" shouted Curtis. He felt a jostling weight on his shoulder and looked to see Septimus, having leapt down from a low-hanging branch.

"The ivy!" said the rat. "It's taking over the fort!"

"We're trying to get there!" hollered Curtis, but with every step, the painful trudge became more and more difficult. Like the thickest mud, the stuff now clung to Curtis's boot heels stubbornly, and it required all his reserves of strength to take a single step. It seemed that the ivy left in the wake of the giants' footsteps continued to ensnare its surroundings in this web, and the world was being covered before Curtis's very eyes: The low-lying bushes were long gone; the saplings were bent, wilted heaps; the twiggy alders were swallowed whole and the big-leaf maples, already encrusted in moss, had grown a shaggy beard of vines. The tenacious plant was now claiming the farthest territory of the forest: It scaled the highest firs and cedars in its ineluctable conquest for the sky.

He knew the territory well enough; even under its current

transformation, Curtis could make out the large cedar tree that anchored the ladder to the fort. The bark of its trunk was completely enshrouded; even now the rigid, wide profile of the tree was being distorted by the ivy as layer upon layer of the plant was painted over it; the ivy clambered over itself to reach the higher boughs, like ants prostrating themselves at the base of some obstacle so its million-strong army could overcome it. He felt the vines making a vigorous assault up his lower back; he felt his steps falter. A vine snapped up and snagged the hilt of his sword, and he felt his arm held fast by the woody plant.

"Septimus!" he shouted. "Get help!"

"Help?" cried the rat, incredulous. "Where am I supposed to get help?"

"I don't know!" He heard Rachel holler; looking over his shoulder he saw his sister, waist-deep in the ivy mire, as a few vines snagged the strands of her hair and jerked her head backward. The rat, seeing this, jumped from Curtis's shoulder to a nearby tree and began scurrying up the ivy stalks, his small stature allowing him easy passage over the plant.

Up he went, his nimble legs darting away from any tendril that tried to ensnare them. Within moments, he'd reached the first platform on the tree; it was already completely blanketed. The railings dangled ivy like stalactites. The sounds of the shouting children could still be heard from higher up in the canopy. An ivy vine attacked his front foot; Septimus smacked it back admonishingly.

"Oh no, you don't," he sneered.

Looking for help, here in the depths of the woods, seemed like a fairly absurd task. Had he another moment, he would have suggested to Curtis that they were, in fact, the only real going concern when it came to help or assistance in Wildwood, and they seemed to be awfully busy at the moment. But appearances must be kept up, he decided, flying up the ivy-draped stairway to the main hut of the hideout. Here, the entire place had been consumed by the plant; he scrambled over to the gangway that led to the neighboring fir and, looking high into its branches, saw that everyone had congregated on the small shingle of space that was the fort's lookout station.

"Septimus!" shouted one of the children. "What do we do?"

Even though the crow's nest had been constructed within the highest limbs of the tallest fir tree within miles—the hideout's location had, in fact, been chosen for this very tree's particular qualities—the ivy was already snaking its way up the trunk, and its farthest tentacles were just touching the underside of the platform.

"Hold up!" shouted Septimus, rat-galloping across the bridge. "I'm coming!"

He scurried up the fir trunk, circling it as he went so as to avoid the most rapacious vines. When he made the platform, he was surprised to see that he'd beaten the ivy there—though it was fast approaching. On a simple, five-by-five wooden ledge stood six people. The platform had been built just ten feet shy of the very top of the tree, which itself stood some two hundred and fifty feet tall above the ground. The tree was hale and hearty, boasting some half dozen centuries on the earth, but its crown was swaying under the weight of its six (now seven) occupants like a particularly tall man undergoing a fainting spell. They were five children, a rat, and a blind old man, and they stood on the platform with their backs pressed to the tree's diminished trunk.

"Okay!" said Septimus, finding a postage-stamp-sized spot for himself. "I'm here."

The people on the platform shared uncertain glances.

"Where's Curtis?" asked Elsie.

"Down there, fighting ivy," said Septimus.

"We tried to save Roger," shouted Martha, pointing out at the nearby trees. "But we couldn't get to him in time." Everything was drowning in the ivy wave. The tree that held the weight of their captive's pen, several yards off, was completely enshrouded.

Septimus gulped. "Let's just hope it was quick and painless."

The wind picked up and buffeted the top of the tree like a rubbery antenna; wide-shouldered Harry gave a whimper and pressed his small back closer to the tree's trunk. The sound of the ivy, a kind of scratchy slither, was everywhere, like snakes moving through rustling leaves. They heard a shout from far below; Septimus reckoned it to be Curtis's voice. He peered over the edge of the platform and yelled, "Hang on there, Curtis!"

"What do we do?" asked Martha, her hand firmly grasped in Carol's.

"Get help," said Septimus. "That's what Curtis suggested."

"How do we do that?" This was Elsie.

Septimus chewed on his lower lip for a second before saying, "Shout?"

"That's sort of what we've been doing," said Ruthie.

Suddenly, a loud crack sounded. Some of the ivy had crept through a break in the platform's thin, hand-milled planks and had broken away a large chunk right below Oz's feet. He immediately lost his balance and pinwheeled out into the air.

"Oz!" shouted Ruthie. Just as he tipped off the edge, the girl managed to grasp hold of his hand. It was an impetuous move on Ruthie's part, one driven by the fierce love and dedication the two shared, but the very real facts of gravity and motion made it so that Ruthie joined Oz in his downward plummet.

Elsie screamed; Martha planted her feet. Harry jolted forward, his hand interlocked with Elsie's, and swung one thick arm in a quick swoop, snagging Ruthie by her black Chapeaux Noirs—issue pant leg. The momentum of the two children's fall was stopped, briefly, as the forward motion of the energy was distributed backward through Harry's arm to Elsie's hand; from there it was further absorbed by Martha, whose elbow was interlocked around Elsie's, and finally to

Carol, who, instinctively, had thrown his arms around the trunk of the tree while Martha looped her fingers into his hand-spun rope belt.

Septimus, now doubly certain of the very extreme lack of hope in their present circumstances, began running in quick, panicked circles on his small portion of the rickety platform. The ivy continued its steady crawl, unabated, and it began to lap over the edge of the shingle.

They were all screaming various shouts and epithets, a bond of adrenaline running through them. Except for Oz, at the end of the chain, hanging several hundred feet above the ground, who had promptly passed out cold.

Elsie felt like she was about to be torn in two; she could feel the ivy now, licking at her shoe soles. Terrified as she was of losing her footing, she could only watch as the stuff began its steady, untrammeled assault on her ankles and her calves. Septimus valiantly ran about, trying to swat off the encroaching vines, but soon it became too much. The platform was becoming overrun. The tree teetered under the strain of the ivy and the wind and the hanging chain of humans swinging from its crown.

Elsie looked at the ground; she looked at the sky and the scattering clouds. The long horizon laid itself out before her, and a kind of peaceful resolve descended as the pressure exerted between her left elbow and her right hand grew so great as to almost dissolve. There was nowhere to go now. There was nothing that could be done. *Why fight?* she thought. Her whole life, she realized, had led to this very point. Every choice, every decision she'd made revealed itself to her as a long chain, not unlike the one for which she was currently a link, one that led inextricably to her present circumstances. In this light, it was as if she'd been living this moment her entire life, as everything else: Every memory, every dream, was sublimated into this single, final moment in all its pitching, wheeling chaos.

So it did not surprise her to see Oz's pant leg finally tear—could they have really put so much faith in the seam-sewing handiwork of a bunch of subterranean-dwelling explosive experts?—and to watch the boy, his right leg comically bare, begin to fall. Some of the pressure on her arm vanished at that moment, though it couldn't be said to matter that much: The ivy was now entirely consuming her legs.

What was surprising, however, was the dark shape that suddenly flew beneath her vision, distorting the air between Ruthie's outstretched hand (torn pant shred firmly gripped) and Oz's spinning, falling shape. A flurry of wind and feathers.

Had it been a bird? But there was something else—had there been someone *riding* on the back of the bird?

There had, hadn't there?

However, she didn't have much chance to consider the implication of this bizarre vision when Ruthie, screaming, slipped from her grasp and another brownish shape dove in and stopped her from her free fall. The sudden loss of Ruthie's downward pull threw off the balance of the chain, and Elsie was nearly about to follow her fellow Unadoptables' trajectory when she felt something sharp pinch into the flesh at her shoulders and she was suddenly pulled upward, her feet torn free of their ivy webbing.

Her head bobbled on her neck and she looked down at her legs, a few strands of ivy still clinging to her shoes, as the world grew smaller below her and she rose into the air.

Fearfully, her heartbeat wailing in her eardrums, she looked upward and saw that she was being carried in the talons of an eagle.

What's more, as they rose above the highest treetops, the eagle fell into formation with a menagerie of avian creatures, small and large. Elsie saw, to her great surprise, that many of the bigger birds carried riders on their feathery backs.

"Els!" came a voice from just below her. She looked down to see her sister, Rachel, still shedding a thick coat of clinging ivy, in the claws of a massive egret in flight. Just behind her, his arms wrapped around the neck of a heron, rode their brother, Curtis, a look of absolute surprise written on his face.

Elsie felt the wind whistle in her ears; she felt the cool air assault her face. She glanced at the birds surrounding her: Astride their backs was an odd assortment of men, dressed in fraying gray robes. Each wore an untidy beard of his own; one of them, Elsie could see, had a truly intimidating tattoo etched on his forehead. She'd just noticed this detail when she heard an ecstatic shout from below her. It was Curtis.

"Brendan!" he yelled. "Jack! Bandits!"

Two of the men wheeled their mounts into a steep pitch and circled around to ride side by side with the boy. The air resounded with their merry laughter.

"Aye, hello there, young bandit-in-training," hollered Jack over the rushing wind.

Curtis, for his part, was stunned speechless. "Where . . . what . . . ," was all he could manage. Finally, he bowed his head against the back of his heron mount and said, "I can't tell you how happy I am to see you, whatever the situation."

"Us too, lad," said Brendan. Out of the looping cowl of fabric over his shoulders crawled a cowering rat.

"If only it didn't involve flying again," Septimus moaned.

They'd all been saved in the daring rescue, every last link in the chain that had threatened to topple from the treetop fort's lookout platform. The birds, hearing Curtis's and Rachel's screams, had dived down into the under-canopy and pulled them from their ivy snares. All of them were accounted for: Oz (just regaining consciousness, his surprise perhaps was the greatest), Ruthie, Martha, and Carol. Harry hugged the back of an eagle, marveling at the widening world below him. They all wore similar looks of wonder on their faces as the flock drew close and came into tight formation.

"But—where've you been all this time?" called Curtis.

"What?" shouted Brendan; the wind, having picked up at their new altitude, made conversing nearly impossible.

"I said—WHERE'VE YOU BEEN?"

Brendan spoke something into the ear of his eagle mount, and the bird gave a loud, marshaling cry. Just then, the flock banked downward, slowing. They were now above a portion of the Wood that had not yet been overrun by the ivy; a wide, grassy vale atop a hill in the midst of the trees presented itself, and the birds circled into a gentle landing on the soft down of the meadow.

Curtis leapt from his heron and ran straight to Brendan, as if to encircle him in a great bear hug. Remembering himself, he stopped short of the Bandit King and instead gave a low bow.

"King," he said. Looking up, with tears in his eyes, he said, "I've kept the band going. I've kept it strong. Me and Septimus. We were the Wildwood bandits. We built it all back." He faltered, his voice choked with emotion. "Till now."

The tattooed man put his hand on the boy's shoulder and smiled. "You've done well, Curtis," he said. "We can only be

thankful that you escaped the Synod's poison. The bandit creed was
kept with you."

"The Synod?" Curtis said, blinking.

"Religious sect," put in the bandit Jack, who'd dismounted his
eagle and had joined the two of them in the center of the clearing.
"They had us in their spell. Evil stuff. Seamus was the one who
brought it—he'd already been taken in by those devils."

"But the ivy is another matter," said Brendan.
"It did not come from these zealots,
but instead—"

Curtis interrupted. "No, I
know who's responsible. We
saw her."

"Her?" Brendan's eyebrow was arched.

"Alexandra," replied Curtis. "But not Alexandra. Like, a plant version of her."

The Bandit King nodded sagely. "Then what the owl says is true. She's returned to wreak her vengeance on the Wood. She's now on her way to North Wood, to bring down the Council Tree. We fly to the aid of the Mystics now, for the survival of the Wood."

Rachel, having dismounted her eagle with a bowing thank you, ran to Elsie, who had been gently deposited some feet away from her in the downy grass of the meadow. Running up on her, she practically tackled the girl, and Elsie laughed in her sister's uncharacteristically enthusiastic embrace.

"I'm okay, Rach," she said. "Can't breathe very well, though."

Rachel sheepishly released her grip on her sister. "All the scream-ing—I thought you'd, you know . . ." She paused, as if reckoning with the difficulty of the memory. "The ivy was all over me. I was done, for sure. Then these claws just grabbed my shoulders and I was in the air."

"And Nico?" asked Elsie, scanning the crowd. All seemed to be accounted for: Most of their crew were standing bemused in the meadow and sharing happy exchanges among one another. The sabo-teur, however, was nowhere to be seen.

Rachel shook her head. "He didn't make it," she said solemnly. "The ivy got him."

Elsie put her hand to her mouth, stifling a gasp. "No!"

One of the other riders, Curtis's fellow bandit as far as either Elsie or Rachel could reckon, had overheard them. He approached and gave a small bow before speaking, "I wouldn't be overconcerned for your friend," said the bandit, an older boy with a wispy mustache. He smelled like pinecones. "The ivy just sleeps 'em. He's like a caterpillar in a cocoon; should be fine once we get back to 'im."

"Oh," said Rachel, adjusting her composure to the new arrival. "Well, that's a relief."

"Name's Henry. And you are . . ."

"Rachel," she replied. "Mehlberg. And this is Elsie. We're Curtis's sisters."

The boy looked surprised. "Sisters? Aye, I heard he had sisters. Pleasant surprise. It's a family affair, I suppose, you Outsiders comin' in here."

Rachel smiled shyly; Elsie gave the bandit a polite curtsy and watched as the other bandits—young and old, men and women—all gravitated toward her brother. He was telling his incredible story: the fall into the Gap, his travels through the Underwood, his return to Wildwood, and his construction of Bandit Hideout Deerskull Dragonfighter. Septimus had crawled back to his preferred spot on Curtis's shoulder and was busily footnoting everything Curtis said with his own particular perspective.

"And that's when these guys showed up," Curtis explained to the enthralled crowd. "Completely random! And—you wouldn't believe it—but they had . . ." He paused here, suddenly remembering himself. "Prue!" he shouted loudly. "Where's Prue?"

"Yeah," said Septimus. "Where is she?"

"Flown on ahead, with Owl Rex and another gang of bandits," said Brendan. "The ones you see here stayed behind in South Wood, mustering arms, before we lit out. And a good thing we did; we weren't far when we heard your shouts. Turned around to investigate and lo and behold." He gestured out to the gathered children. "We found you lot—kids in a tree!" He paused for a second before saying, "And one old man. Who's he?"

"That . . ." Curtis found he could barely get the words out; in all the excitement of being reunited with his fellow bandits, he had quite forgotten about this other serendipitous discovery. "That—is Carol Grod!"

This information received a blank look from Brendan.

"That's the OTHER MAKER!" shouted Curtis. "The one we've been looking for!"

"That's him? The one who had his eyes out?"

"Yes!" shouted Curtis, waving Carol over to them. Martha, seeing the gesture, grabbed the old man by the hand and led him to where Curtis and Brendan were standing. "Meet Carol. Carol, meet Brendan the Bandit King."

"It's an honor," said Carol. "Thank you for swoopin in."

"This is the man," spoke Brendan, savoring his words. "This is the one who Prue's after? To make the thing?"

"The cog," corrected Carol, somewhat proudly. "The Möbius Cog, to be exact. One of my finest designs."

Brendan put his hand to his forehead and massaged his temple, his mouth slightly agape. "Then I expect we should get you to South Wood. They've already started work."

"Started work?" asked Curtis. "Who's started work?"

"The bear with the hooks," replied Brendan. "We left Seamus with him to be his hands. To be honest, though, unless this Moldiest Cog of yours is the sort of thing you'd shoe to a horse, I expect your services will be much needed."

Carol shook his head. "They won't get far. I suppose either one of us, me or Esben, could re-create the thing—but not without our hands or eyes. It is why Alexandra committed the atrocity she did."

"Well, it certainly did the trick," said Brendan, before putting his fingers to his lips and producing a loud whistle. "Brownfeather!"

One of the eagles walked to where he stood and bowed. "Yes, King?" he asked.

"Get this man to South Wood, as fast as your wings will carry him," instructed Brendan. He looked at Carol again, saying, "Can you manage the journey?"

"As long as I have a little help," said the blind man, nodding down to the girl at his side.

"Hello," said Brendan. "And you are?"

"Martha Song, Your Excellency," the girl with the goggles said. "At your service."

"Very well," said Brendan. "Fly, the two of you, to South Wood. Quickly. And may the Ancients grant you speed." He then turned to the rest of the assembled and spoke:

"The rest of you, mount up. We fly for North Wood, to the defense of the Council Tree. Every soul here, bandit or no, must be prepared to shed their blood for the cause. Our world—and the world beyond it—relies on our actions today. Our numbers may be small, but our courage needs must be the size of mountains.

"And as you fly, let the call go out to the surrounding country-side: The Wildwood Irregulars have marshaled again to set things to right. Birds: Those of you without riders, search the hollows and warrens of Wildwood. Find the areas untouched by the ivy's spread. Anyone willing to fight by our side will be welcomed; their efforts will not go unrewarded."

A flurry of smaller birds ascended into the air, a dizzying funnel, before exploding outward in all directions. The surrounding bandits shared a few fleeting words with their comrades before returning to their winged mounts and climbing astride. Oz and Ruthie climbed aboard a pelican that was offering its back, while Harry situated himself atop a bald eagle. Martha and Carol were already gone; the eagle Brownfeather and his two passengers were just now clearing the tops of the trees and disappearing toward the southern horizon. The young bandit Henry, with an undue amount of chivalry, bowed to Rachel and helped her astride his silver egret, before he, too, mounted up. She blushed beneath her black tresses and clasped her wrists at his belly as the egret bent its spindly legs and, with two hearty beats of its wings, lifted into the air.

Brendan watched all this activity proudly, a natural-born leader newly freed of his shackles. Just then, he felt a tug at the hem of his gray robe. He looked down to see it was Elsie Mehlberg, nine years old, smiling shyly up at him.

"Can I ride with you?" she asked self-consciously.

Without saying a word, Brendan reached down, picked the girl up by her waist—a feather's weight to the broad-shouldered bandit—and set her atop the back of a dappled golden eagle. Climbing aboard behind her, he gave the eagle a small whistle.

"All right then, Chester," he said.

"We ready?" responded the eagle.

The Bandit King said, "Let's fly."

C H A P T E R   2 8

Wildwood Irregulars,
Take Wing!

T hey'd soon passed the vanguard of the ivy tide; the wave had struck against the peaks and passes of the Cathedral Mountains, and like Hannibal crossing the Alps, it was charging mercilessly over the terrain as if the great mountain range was a small bump in the road. Prue saw it all from her vantage in the air: the sea of green coloring the world into one homogenous pattern like someone dragging a drab-colored paintbrush over a formerly vivid

496

canvas. Beyond the dividing line between the ivy and the uncovered forest, the patchwork fields of North Wood could be seen, drowsy in the afternoon light, untouched, untrammeled, and peacefully ignorant of the great invasion that was about to descend on them.

She rode a white heron named Oliver; Owl Rex led the flock of thirty birds. Other gray-robed bandits joined her in flight. Several South Wood citizens had volunteered as well. Once Brendan and the rest of the bandits reunited with them, carrying whatever weaponry they could scavenge, they would be a formidable force.

But who was their adversary? Could even the best-trained militia stand a chance against the awesome power of the ivy, harnessed by the reborn spirit of the Dowager Governess? Even now, the woman's awful handiwork was being done: Looking down at the world of the Wood, Prue saw that the borders between the provinces were being quickly erased. South Wood and the Avian Principality were effectively gone, their borders wiped away in the flood. Soon North Wood would be caught up in the deluge. The old divisions were disappearing.

It was all Wildwood now.

That's what Alexandra had wanted all along, wasn't it?

And there, just as her mind had touched on it, she saw the great expansive crown of the Council Tree itself, towering over its surrounding trees by magnitudes of greatness, standing resolute in the center of a great meadow. From this height, the sackcloth-clad

Mystics who surrounded its gnarled trunk were minuscule, little dots on a green field. As they drew closer, she saw that many of them were in the midst of their daily meditations. It surprised her to see them engaged thus: Surely the tree, in its omniscience, with its deep connection to the fabric that ran through the entire Wood—surely it had seen what had happened, what was coming, and would've long since alerted the Mystics to the danger they faced.

The flyers began their descent, veering low over the fields and the farms while astonished onlookers gaped at their progress. Somewhere, a bell was ringing. As they flew closer to the ground, Prue saw carriages being drawn up in front of the tiny farmhouses, filled with the accumulated belongings of the panicked residents. The winding roads that linked the plantations, one to another, were becoming clotted with these vehicles, all overflowing with the prized possessions—furniture and chests, framed portraits and pewter dishes—of a fleeing people.

"What are they doing?" Prue said, marveling at the activity. "They can't escape it!"

Banking sharply, the heron landed deftly on the grass of the great meadow, and Prue leapt from his back at the sight of two individuals she hadn't seen in a long while.

"Sterling!" she shouted. "Samuel!"

Indeed, there could be no mistake: Sterling the fox greeted her proudly in his bibbed jeans while Samuel the hare, colander jauntily flattening his long ears, stood at attention. They smiled, despite the circumstances, at seeing the girl.

"Hello there," said Sterling. "We got word from the swallow— that's the Alarum Bell you hear ringing. Wasted no time on that. But I can't figure for the life of me what the problem is here. Something about the ivy?"

"It's her!" said Prue. Sterling and Samuel had both been at the Battle for the Plinth, veterans of the Wildwood Irregulars—who *her* was needed no further explanation. "She's back! And she's got the ivy controlled."

A look of shock overcame the fox's face. He swiveled his head to look upon the circle of Mystics, still lost in meditation, gathered around the base of the mighty Council Tree. "But they've not given us any word," he said. "Seems like the tree would've alerted us long ago."

Samuel gestured with his thumb to the robed figures. "They've been like that for twelve hours now. Ever since last night, late." He paused, adding, "So."

Prue stared across the wide, grassy meadow at the Council Tree and its attendant Mystics, immobile and quiet. Just then, a wind picked up and a flurry of shapes, like static released from a freshly dried blanket, whipped up into the air from the green canopy of the tree and flew out across the clearing. One of the shapes traveled the distance to where Prue was standing with the hare and the fox and fell at their feet. It was a dead leaf.

Kneeling down, Prue picked up the leaf and studied it: It was brittle and ochre-colored, and a piece crumbled between her fingers at her touch, scattering to the earth. "What's this?" she murmured.

Sterling nodded knowingly. "It's been happening. Just a few months ago. The Mystics told us. Some kind of sickness, though no one seems to be able to tell what it is. Not the Mystics, leastways. They've been all mum about it."

"It's dying," put in Samuel. "The tree, dying. Can you believe it?"

"Where's the Elder Mystic?" asked Prue desperately. The idea that this ancient and wizened thing would be somehow expiring filled her heart with dread. "I have to speak to him." She remembered the odd young boy, the one who had conveyed the tree's wishes to her. He'd been Iphigenia's successor, by decree of the tree itself.

Sterling shook his head. "As far as I can tell, there ain't no head Mystic. One that came before, the young one, he disappeared not long ago."

"Disappeared?"

"Vanished. In Wildwood. He'd been to the Ossuary Tree, payin' respects. Never seen again."

"Strange." This came from Owl Rex, who'd just made a graceful landing on the meadow's surface. "Sterling. Samuel," he said, in greeting, and the two animals bowed to the Avian prince. The owl continued, "The Mystics must be warned. The Verdant

Empress—Alexandra Svik reborn—makes her way as we speak to break the tree to its very roots. She means to undo the Periphery Bind."

"Constabulary rules—not supposed to disturb the Mystics from their meditations," explained Sterling. "No matter the circumstances."

But Prue was already walking, briskly, toward the seated Mystics surrounding the tree. She'd reached out, inwardly, to the massive oak, insinuating her thoughts inside the cloudy noise she felt emanating from its gnarled and woody trunk. The tree, it was said, was unlike any other vegetal matter in the Wood; its ability to communicate with all of its fellow organisms predated organized language,

and so it spoke in symbols and sounds. These enigmatic voicings could only be unpacked by the Elder Mystic, someone who had spent enough time prostrate in meditation to the tree that a kind of sense could be made of the weird language.

To Prue, though, who received the tree's channeled images loud and clear as she walked toward it, the language was an obtuse and unknowable thing. It wasn't like the other plant life, not remotely, for whom cogent sentences could be constructed from their strange noises. Hearing the language of the Council Tree, she felt as if she'd opened some lofty tome about particle physics written in pidgin Mandarin. Something was being conveyed, that much was clear, but what, she couldn't know.

She arrived at the circle of Mystics. Looking down, she saw that each of them, all dressed in identical hemp robes, had their eyes open, their placid gazes fixed on the tree. Another rush of wind, just then, sent a flurry of ochre leaves down to the grass. Prue knew that the Mystics' meditation, as long as it was kept up, would be unbreakable. She walked on, toward the tree.

The trunk of the tree flowed down from its canopy like a torrent of thick syrup that had been frozen to the side of the bottle; it branched out from its base, and its roots bent and burrowed into the grassy soil of the meadow. A person could spend hours marveling over the patterns in play on one small section of the tree's wrinkled and aged trunk, over the many knots and divots that had etched themselves into the mighty oak's puckered bark. It was a giant among giants. And it was speaking to Prue. Or at least trying to.

As she walked closer, it became clearer and clearer that the tree was doing this: reaching out to her, drawing her in. She responded in kind; still the flurry of images and sounds in her head would not codify into anything resembling an understandable idea.

What? she thought.

There had been a pause, there, when she'd said the word, and it made the exchange at least somewhat resemble the brief quiet in conversation between two people as one speaker waits for the other. But the barrage of sounds that followed still did not make sense to Prue.

More leaves fell, and Prue felt a small cascade of the papery things alight on her shoulders. She took a deep breath and began to address the tree afresh.

Okay, she thought. *I don't understand you or what you're trying to say. But I'm doing my best. I've been following your directions all along. I've been going on faith. I've trusted the people around me, as best I can. But now this: You're dying?*

Noises; chattering; shapes.

Did you know this? I mean, this must've been happening all along! I can't help but feel like I've been let down. Like I've been misled. Is this part of the plan? Or have I not worked fast enough? Tell me!

Still: shushing; a rush of wind. Then, a quieting, like the stillness between gusts in a thunderstorm. And then: Prue saw.

What she saw was complex, disorderly. But, like making out the picture in between the lines of static on an old black-and-white television set, something emerged. She saw herself. But not the present version of herself: black bob, peacoat, Keds. Instead, she saw herself as an old woman, grayed hair and wrinkled brow, bent over some menial craft. Looking closer, she saw that she was knitting something. As the static cleared in the picture in her head, she was able to see closely that the thing was a cabled scarf and it seemed to stretch out from her clacking needles like a long, green path.

The image inverted, then, and had spun her around; she was now following this knitted path as it cut its way through a dense forest. She had the distinct sense that this path would lead on forever. However, the green scarf suddenly cut to her left and began a circuitous path that she soon realized was folding in upon itself. After having followed the curve of the scarf for a time, with each revolution growing shorter, she saw that the path let in on the center of a labyrinth; there, in the end point, was a single, glowing bud, nestled into the forest's loam like an egg in a nest. As she watched, the bud unfurled, revealing the tiniest sapling of a tree. Like a time-lapse film, she saw it grow three distinct limbs; at the end of each limb bloomed a single, green leaf.

That was when she was shaken out of the vision.

"Prue!" It was the voice of Sterling Fox. "Can you hear me?"

She blinked her eyes rapidly and turned to face the animal. "I saw something. The tree. It showed me."

"No time!" shouted the fox, his face lined with desperation. "The ivy! It's here!"

⚲

"Maybe it needed another few hits with the hammer," suggested Seamus.

The bear only stood, massaging his jaw with the back of his prosthetic hook.

The bandit cocked his head sideways and squinted his left eye, as if that would provide him a newer perspective. "I guess we coulda fired it a little longer. Just a little more fuel on the fire."

Still, the bear said nothing.

"Some gemstones? Maybe it needs something shiny. Something to dress it up a bit. You know, a little sparkle."

This time the bear responded. "It doesn't need sparkling. It doesn't need dressing up. It's a cog."

"Doesn't look like one," the bandit grumbled.

"No, it doesn't, does it?" said the bear, his hackles rising. He reached down and picked the thing up from the anvil, looping the point of his hook through its cavity, and held it out for the bandit to see. "It looks like a . . . I don't know . . . squashed metal insect."

And indeed, it did. The bandit by the bear's side could only nod at Esben's uncanny observation. However, their goal hadn't been to construct a squashed metal insect. It had been to create, with what tools and materials they could scavenge from a rapidly decomposing world, one of the most incredible and improbable machinations ever devised by man—or bear, for that matter: the Möbius Cog, a tri-sprocket oscillating monogear and the central component needed for a certain mechanical boy prince's life-giving functions. Had the cog's two inventors not been blinded and de-handed, respectively, they'd have been, without a doubt, on the short list for the South Wood Mechanical Fabrication Society's Gear of the Year.

(What the bear and the bandit couldn't know, however, was that the thing they'd created—this squashed insect—did have a purpose, albeit fairly arcane: When installed correctly, it turned the average household clothes dryer into a time machine that, when "wrinkle guard" was engaged, actually sent one's socks ten minutes into the future.)

"Start again," said the bear, and he threw the brass jumble into the dirt by the fire.

Seamus groaned and trudged back out into the surrounding forest in search of more fuel; Esben set the crucible back into the flames and began sorting through the drawerful of jewelry that had been salvaged from South Wood's collapsing houses and buildings. It was a sad lot: wedding rings, necklace chains, heart pendants. The trinkets' owners either volunteered the stuff, happy to be of service to such a grand gambit, or were sleeping beneath a mound of ivy and weren't necessarily available to not give consent. A few tearfully parted with the items, a nearby loved one consoling them as they gave away the locket their grandmother wore, the brass badge their father carried as a constable. And so it was with a heavy heart that Esben sacrificed these keepsakes to the smelter, all the while knowing that his reconstructing the Möbius Cog on his own was as likely as his building a living butterfly from some pipe cleaners and a ball of wax.

He selected another item: a circular pendant on a chain. Someone's name had been lovingly inscribed on the shiny brass. With a deep sigh, the bear dangled the chain from his hook and dropped it into the dimpled gray crucible.

He was so engrossed in his despair that he did not hear the approaching bird as it circled a few times above the pyre and landed some twenty feet off from where he was standing. He did not hear its two riders dismount and approach him, one helping the other walk across the difficult, viny terrain.

"Hello there, old friend," came a voice. It was a voice the bear recognized.

He turned and saw Carol Grod, his old partner and fellow machinist, standing in the midst of the wriggling ivy vines, holding the hand of a young black-haired girl. The bear sputtered a few times. He found he could barely speak. His knees buckled and he fell to the ground.

"What's he doing?" asked the old man, suddenly confused that his greeting had been given no response.

"He's kneeling on the ground and his mouth is moving, but he's not really saying anything," said the girl.

"But he's a bear, with hooks for hands?" asked Carol.

"Definitely," confirmed the girl.

Carol spoke to the air. "Esben, if it's really you and not some other bear with his paws removed, why don't you say somethin?"

The dam broke and Esben let loose a torrent of words: "Carol! Carol Grod! You're okay! You're safe!" He leapt up from his knees and threw his arms around the old man's neck.

"Hey there," said Carol. "Easy. I'm an old human, you remember. Made of more fragile stuff than you." The two then parted and Carol reached down for the bear's hands. Finding the metallic prosthetics, he said, "Oh, what she's done."

"I know, Carol, I know," said the bear. "And you—your eyes."

"These wooden ones suit me just fine these days." As if to show off the things, he raised his eyebrows and the wooden, painted orbs danced in their sockets.

And so the two friends stood, marveling at their sudden and unexpected reunion. They spoke over each other, trying to ferret out where the other had been all this time, wondering at what sweet horror the Mansion had visited upon them in their exile. They expressed sorrow and pity for each other's particular predicament, while insisting that their own had not been that bad; they'd managed as well as could be expected. In the end, though, they were each in agreement about the considerable serendipities at play that had brought them back together and the apparent gravity of their new task.

The bear was glowing. "You couldn't have come at a more opportune moment." He looked down at Martha and said, "And who are you?"

"Martha Song," replied the girl, not a little daunted to be speaking to a talking bear. "Mr. Bear, sir."

"You've got some goggles there," said Esben, pointing at the plastic pair perched on her forehead.

"Don't go anywhere without 'em," replied Martha.

"And today, they'll come in very handy," said the bear as he waved Carol and Martha to the roaring fire. "We've got some work to do."

"Where are you at with it?" asked Carol as Martha carefully navigated him through the ivy toward the fire pit. They'd constructed a kind of open kiln of salvaged bricks from the many dilapidated buildings of South Wood, each being slowly dismantled by the scourge of the ivy vines. An iron dowel held the crucible in place in the center of the pit's glowing coals.

"We've had two stabs at it so far," explained the bear. "Took a bit for me to remember exactly how it went—going totally off of memory here. I have no idea where the schematics ended up."

Carol tapped his forehead. "Got 'em right here. Ever since she took my eyes from me, those things've been burned in my brain. Spend days just sittin, lookin over those plans, seein ways to improve 'em. In my mind. A way to pass time, anyway."

"Well, that's good news, for once. And how are those fingers holding up?" asked the bear.

"As well as can be expected for an old man. How's the eyes on you?"

Esben blinked, rapidly, as if trying them out. "Pretty good shape, I'd say." He then reached down and grabbed one of their former attempts, the wiry insect-looking thing. "This is as close as we've come."

Taking the object in his hands, Carol rotated it a few times in his fingers before saying, "What's this, a phone-box widget? Some kind of dog's chew toy?"

Esben looked at Martha for explanation, startled by the old man's sardonic tone. The girl shrugged. "Well, no, but . . . ," stammered the bear, embarrassed.

"Oh, Esben. Oh, my boy. How the mighty have fallen." A grin was plastered on the old man's face. He felt at the object in his hands a little longer before saying, "Though if installed correctly, in a standard-issue clothes dryer . . ."

"Yes?" prompted Martha.

"Well, that's not going to help us any here," said Carol abruptly, before handing the thing back to Esben. "Back into the crucible with it."

And so it went, and the two machinists' labors began in earnest.

❧

They barely had time to brace themselves when the ivy wave came. It preceded the giants by several miles, having gained considerable steam over its long journey from the southern part of the Wood. It poured over the small huts and hovels and seeped into the furrows of the farmlands, covering everything in sight. The handcarts and flatbed trucks, hastily loaded with furniture, toppled in the wave while their owners were swallowed whole and put into a deep, seamless slumber. It crowned the tall trees and broke them in two; it dashed the constabulary and the Great Hall, splintering the ceiling beams and crushing the buildings to the ground as if they were made of tissue.

Prue stood just beyond the ring of immobile Mystics, all of them still fathoms deep in meditation, and steeled herself. She could see the rumbling ivy topping the trees from hundreds of yards off; it was only a matter of time until it reached the tree.

"We must stop it," she said, "at all costs."

Sterling had tried to rouse the Mystics, despite his instructions, but to no avail. While the robed figures' eyes remained wide open, fixed on the dying Council Tree, their faces belied no outward consciousness. Several bandits ran to Prue's side, brandishing what looked to be gardening implements.

"It's the best we could do," said one of the bandits, Ned. He was holding a pitchfork, about as menacingly as expected, considering the circumstances.

"Line up!" shouted Sterling as the crowd of Wildwood bandits and South Wood volunteers came into formation. They were joined by the few farmers and ranch hands who managed to escape the earlier waves of ivy and had run for the shelter of the tree. Together they made a line of about thirty humans and animals, bearing what looked like the cast-off pile of a tentative lynch mob.

"Once again," the fox side-mouthed to Prue, who was standing next to him, "not the finest fighting force the world has ever known."

But Prue's mind was being assaulted. The fox's voice sounded like a blur in her ears. She could *hear* the ivy coming on—it hissed in her mind like a fire hose on full blast—but she could also sense the approach of *her.*

Alexandra was part of the plant world now, and as such her presence outstripped her simple, corporeal frame. She was as much spirit as she was living organism, and her every thought rippled through the forest. The presence was becoming overpowering, and Prue found she had to concentrate very hard in order to keep it from bowling her over. She felt a nudge at her hip; she turned to see it was Samuel.

"You okay, Prue?" asked the hare.

"Yeah," she said. "It's just . . . a lot."

"It's coming!" shouted a voice from the sky; it was Owl Rex, soaring high above the assembled defenders.

White noise assaulted Prue as the ivy exploded through the ring of trees that surrounded the meadow. It paused in its forward momentum to gobble up these ancient arbors, crowning them in a matter of seconds and engulfing their leafy boughs in a thick, swarmy beard of vines. Then, satiated, it moved on to the individuals standing steadfast in the center of the meadow.

"What do we do?" asked a confused farmer, wielding a garden hoe.

"Just try to keep it back," instructed Sterling.

The ivy began its advance.

It flowed over the meadow's grass like water lapping up a smooth beach; it rippled and eddied against the little tufts of wood sorrel as it went, overcoming the grass like so much hair being dunked in a deep bath. It gathered speed, an advancing tide, and set itself to break on the hapless defenders that stood in its way. Prue, overcome, fell to her knees, her hands sinking into the earth. Sterling tried to help her to her feet, all the while keeping an eye on the coming wave, but it was no use. She was immobile.

The fox braced himself for the crash, the shock and concussion of this million-strong rush of angry, growing plant life splashing against their impotent weapons.

But it did not come.

Instead, the wave flattened itself against some invisible barrier, its brown underside revealed to the shocked figures who stood in the lee of the barrier's protection.

Prue lifted her head; she *commanded* the ivy. She found the strength, now, to deflect the ivy's angry hissing, and she pushed back with all her thoughts. A great wall had been constructed, seemingly from the air, and the ivy struck against it with the force of a tsunami. It erupted upward with all the force of its momentum as it tried to find the topmost edge of this invisible barrier.

"What's happening?" hissed the bandit Ned. He jabbed his pitchfork into the writhing wall of brown vines and was surprised to feel it snag some of the woody plant.

"I'm stopping it!" shouted Prue, her fists still planted in the earth. Great bulbs of sweat appeared at her brow, and she gritted her teeth against the onslaught.

All around them, the barrier made a perfect circle around the tree and around the meditating Mystics. Prue realized it wasn't her force alone that was creating this magic shield; the silent Mystics were helping too—she could feel their power channeling through her as she held back the wave of ivy and buffered the incredible sonic crush of hiss the plant was broadcasting to those few ears who could hear it.

"Cut it back!" shouted another voice—it was a farmer who, armed with a mowing scythe, had cut a huge chunk of the plant by the roots. A slag pile of vines had fallen at his feet, gray and dead.

The gathered defenders, the bandits and farmers, followed the man's example, but the ivy kept coming; for every yard of the plant they took out, more rushed in to take its place, lapping against the unseen wall.

The beating of wings sounded behind them; the birds, who had been circling the air above the tree, landed in the free space defended by the ragtag group, the circle of untouched meadow that surrounded the Council Tree. "To the air!" shouted Owl Rex, among them. The defenders, still brandishing their farming implements, backed uncertainly away from the embankment of ivy and climbed astride the large birds: They were herons, egrets, pelicans, and owls, and they took their riders with ease, bending low before unfurling their wings and, with a few swift steps, taking to the air. Prue stayed earthbound, channeling the meditations of the Mystics into the great barrier currently protecting the tree from being overrun.

Then came the crashing, explosive noises—like elephants' lumbering footfalls; Prue, caught behind the ever-rising bulkhead of ivy vines, couldn't see where the noises were coming from or who was creating them, but she felt a surge every time one of them sounded.

She could feel the tree behind her, still throwing her strange, disjointed images. What was it saying? She found it nearly impossible to split her attention between holding back the flood of ivy and trying to make sense of the tree's weird symbols that were appearing in her mind. Did it want her to hold the ivy back? There was something almost resigned about the communications. It was as if it wanted to be overrun, it wanted to be torn down.

Above her, she saw the whirling flock of giant birds as they dove down beyond the wall of ivy; they were attacking something, though she couldn't see what. The screams of the birds and the angered shouts of their riders rent the air. More crashes sounded; more heavy surges of the vines. Her strength was beginning to wane; she felt like she'd just sprinted a mile around a muddy track and her lungs were aching for reprieve. A glance behind her confirmed that the Mystics remained in their placid spot—each in a delicate lotus position, their gazes fixed on the central point of the Council Tree.

Suddenly, she felt something give. It was as if she'd been a part of a long line of grapplers on a tug-of-war course and her teammates had begun to fall away one by one. The ivy pushed forward, pressing its advantage against this new dip in resistance.

"No!" shouted Prue, calling over her shoulder to the Mystics. "Help me!"

But then the dam broke and the barrier fell away and the ivy cascaded down into the last defensible circle of grass on the meadow. Prue knelt down and held her arms out straight, *commanding* the ivy back, but she could only hold the scant few feet of ground that she occupied. Unable to break the field she'd created, the ivy formed into a giant funnel around her, a cyclone that rose and rose high into the air. The hissing noise was now enough to blot out all other sounds and all other thoughts, and she felt the numbing crush of gravity slowly reducing her power. The spinning cyclone shot higher and higher, and soon the blue-gray sky became an unreachable hole in the darkening vortex the ivy was creating around the girl.

"HOLD TIGHT!" shouted a voice; even amid the din of the ivy's swarming noise, Prue recognized the voice. It was the voice of an old friend.

She looked upward and saw a dazzling sight: a coat of brass buttons glinting in the dimming sunlight, the plunging form of a heron in free-dive. She saw Curtis Mehlberg, astride this white heron, threading the eye of the ivy cyclone. She felt his hand grasp her arm, and with what little energy she had, she managed to throw herself behind him onto the back of the bird, and the bird rose up as the spiraling funnel of ivy vines collapsed below them in a shower of tangling green leaves.

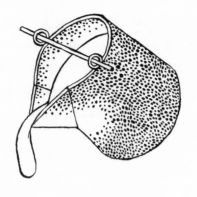

CHAPTER 29

The Body of a Prince;
The Battle for the Tree

The molds were carved from the broken husks of walnut trees, their cavities meticulously routed by Carol's nimble fingers as Esben gave him calm words of guidance. Seamus and Martha, working together, continually added wood to the fire while its heat poured ever farther out from the ring of the smithy. The ivy, which was so thick and pernicious that they had to keep their sabers at the ready, to cut the bolder tendrils before their ankles were ensnared, seemed to bow away from the heat of the flames, and soon a clear swath had been laid for the task at hand.

The two machinists bantered back and forth casually as they labored, two old friends deeply engaged in their true life's work.

"Not bad," said Esben, admiring the third mold they'd carved. "I wouldn't go so far as to say 'work of art,' but it's a work of something."

"Oh, I see how it is," replied Carol. "Easy comin from the guy who can't even pick his nose without runnin the risk of givin himself a lobotomy."

"Okay, I'll level with you," said the bear, smiling. "You actually haven't been carving out the molds—I've been doing that. You've just been making a series of ornamental toilet paper dispensers."

Carol let out an explosive laugh. "Here," he said. "Catch one." He tossed the finished mold in Esben's direction, giggling to hear the bear's hooks clack noisily together as he tried to catch the thing.

"Easy there," said Esben, who, after a few fumbling grasps, managed to have the thing spinning on his left hook. "You're dealing with a trained circus professional, you know."

"How fitting," said Carol.

With Esben guiding the way, Carol and Martha, together, lifted the crucible from the flames, their hands protected by thick gloves (and Martha's eyes shielded behind her plastic goggles). They poured the molten brass into the mold; after dousing it in a bucket of water,

Esben held the template in the fire until the cast burned away and the sprocket was revealed. The bear looped it onto his hook and studied it in the light of the fire.

"That'll do," he said.

"Damn right, it will," chided Carol. "Now we can keep sittin here, admirin our own armpits, or we can get back to work. Last I checked, we got two more to do."

Seamus, having dumped another load of logs onto the ever-growing pile by the fire, put in, "I hate to interrupt the repartee, gents, but if I'm not much mistaken, we'll need something to *put* this thing into eventually, right?"

Carol looked in his direction, miming shock. It was clear the old man was having the time of his life. "You haven't got the body yet?" He turned to Esben and said, "What, is he one of your fellow circus performers?"

"Carny, actually," said Esben. "Ran the ring toss."

"Ha, ha," said Seamus. "Seriously."

"Yes!" shouted Carol. "Get the automaton!"

The bandit gave a quick bow, gesturing to Martha to follow. The two of them began to make their way beyond the throw of the fire when Seamus stopped. "One thing," he said, turning around. "Where would I find it?"

Esben stopped the old man before he made another sardonic comment by saying, "The cemetery. There's a mausoleum."

"Right," said Seamus, remembering.

"And don't forget the teeth," added Esben.

"The teeth?" Seamus and Martha exchanged a confused glance.

"The whole thing is kaput without the teeth," said Carol. "The body must have its teeth."

"Got it," said Seamus.

"You know the way?" asked Martha as they began their trudge through the calf-deep ivy. The warmth and the light from the smithy's pyre ebbed away slowly.

"I think so," replied the bandit. "I was the emissary here, after all. Passed the place a few times. Most things don't much look like they did, though." The bandit was about to say something more when he suddenly shouted, "Watch it!" to Martha.

Martha tried to leap backward, but she found she was stuck; a particularly deep patch of ivy had caught her heel and was in the process of sending shoots up her leg. With a single deft motion, the bandit had drawn his saber and brought it down in a quick cutting motion, severing the vines from the plant.

"Thanks," said Martha, leaping away, freed, from where she'd stood.

"You better take this," said Seamus, pulling out a long dagger from his belt and handing it to her, hilt first.

They blazed a trail through the trees before arriving at what they assumed to be a road: Here even the ghost of a path could be made out through the blanket of ivy, like a mountain road after a heavy snowfall. After a few turns and intersections, blearily remembered by the bandit, they came to an ivy-draped metal gate. Once they'd cleared the vines away, the words SOUTH WOOD CEMETERY could be read there in tall, Gothic letters. The mausoleum of the deceased animatronic prince was not hard to locate; in the center of the cemetery, towering over every other ivy-blanketed tombstone and memorial, was a house-sized pile of writhing vines. Unlike the other crumbling buildings of the province, the structure, made of implacable granite, had proven impervious to the ivy. It wasn't long before they'd peeled

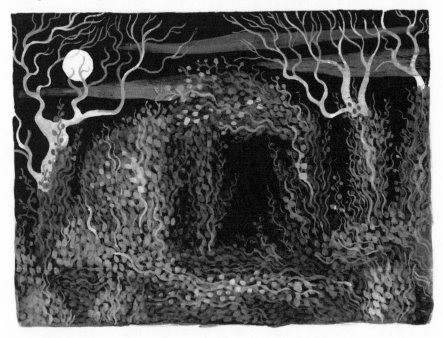

away the screen of vines to reveal the ornate iron door that guarded the entrance to Alexei's tomb.

Oddly enough, the door was slightly ajar, and several strands of ivy had made their way through the opening into the dark foyer of the tomb. Seamus quickly dispatched these invaders with his sword before slipping into the chamber; Martha followed. The darkness was pervasive. Martha lit a match and held it to the wick of the candle she'd brought, and the small glow dispelled some of the gloom.

"Ever been in a tomb before?" asked Seamus, making nervous conversation.

"No," said Martha. "You?"

"Nope. Guess there's a first time for everything."

"I'm experiencing a lot of firsts lately," replied the girl. She nodded quickly, making her goggles fall down over her eyes. "I have a question for you, actually."

"What's that?" asked the bandit.

"Are there ghosts? You know, in this world?"

The bandit guffawed a little, saying, "Nah. Children's stories. Campfire tales."

Martha paused a moment, chewing on this logic. "But there are, like, magic powers."

"Sure."

"And talking animals."

"Why wouldn't there be?"

"But ghosts don't exist."

"Kiddie talk, there."

"Okay," said Martha, thoroughly unconvinced.

They continued on, through the dust-steeped granite flagstones of the mausoleum's entry chamber. An opening at the end of the room let onto a larger chamber. There, the bandit and the girl found the sarcophagus bearing the body of Alexei.

"Whoa," said Seamus.

"Gross," said Martha.

"Nothing gross about it—he's a machine," said the bandit, walking up to the body and tapping his finger at the body's metallic cheek. Someone had cast aside the coffin's lid, somewhat unceremoniously. It lay in pieces on the floor. Martha appeared at Seamus's side, marveling at the strange corpse: its riveted joints and spring-loaded articulating fingers. The body had been dressed in a martial uniform, all gold brocading and brass buttons, stiff from years of quiet disuse. Martha moved to take a closer look at the boy's face. He'd been handsome, she decided, and his eyes were peacefully closed. Seamus reached his arm under the mechanical boy's midsection and lifted; the body gave a moaning creak, a rusty hinge long in need of a good oiling.

"Not too heavy, actually," said the bandit.

"The teeth!" exclaimed Martha.

Seamus looked up to the head of the coffin; Martha had pried the boy's mouth open and discovered an empty cavity.

"Gone?" asked the bandit.

"Gone," breathed Martha, craning her head around to get a better look into the automaton's mouth.

"Well, that's not helpful."

"What did they say? We need the teeth?"

"Doesn't work without the teeth."

Martha chewed on her lower lip. "Like, doesn't *work* doesn't work?"

"That's what they said."

"What do we do?"

"I guess we have to find out what happened to the teeth," said the bandit, his voice falling a little in despair. Finding the cemetery amid the ivy scourge was one thing: finding a dead boy's full set of teeth in a landscape rendered totally unrecognizable was quite another.

Just then, a distinctly young and feminine sob rang out. Seamus mistook the sound as having come from Martha, so intrusive was the darkness that surrounded them.

"Hey, it's all right," he said consolingly. "We'll figure it out. No need to cry."

"That wasn't me." She held the candle flame up to her face, which the dim light showed to be pale with terror.

"It wasn't?"

"No."

"Then who did it?" Seamus's voice trembled with fear as he spoke.

"It's all my fault!" sounded a disembodied voice, steeped in sobs. It came from the far corner of the tomb, and Martha and Seamus each gave out an eardrum-shattering scream, their bodies reflexively leaping into one another in a terrified embrace. They hadn't been there long when Seamus pulled himself from Martha's arms and ran, screaming, out of the chamber and back down the entry hall to the front door. Martha, frozen in her steps, whipped the candle around to face the specter.

"Who's there?" she called. "Spirit, name yourself!" She'd learned that line from ghost stories she'd been told by the older kids in the Unthank Home. It was always what the ghost hunters and the exorcists said when they bravely faced down some undead soul.

"I'm not a spirit," said the girl's voice. "I'm just a girl."

Martha walked tentatively forward, and the glow of the candle-light fell on a figure crouched against the far wall. She was a young girl, a little older than Martha, and she had long brown hair and sun-kissed skin. A garland of dead flowers was nested on her head, and her cheeks were streaked with dusty tears.

"Who are you?" asked Martha.

"I'm Zita," said the girl. "I'm the one who did all this."

☙

The heron, its two passengers gripping tightly to its feathers, corkscrewed into the air, and Prue's vision swam in her head. The wind, cool and brisk at this higher altitude, whipped at her coat and hair, and she looked down at the scene they were leaving on the ground below.

It was an awesome spectacle; it was a horrible spectacle.

The ivy had completely buried the great meadow in its tide; it had consumed the sitting Mystics and was now fully laying siege to the Council Tree, assaulting its giant, twisted trunk and climbing into its outstretched boughs, snaking over the leaves and limbs like deadly streamers.

She *listened* and heard the tree dying.

"No!" she moaned. "Curtis—put me down! I need to get to the tree!"

"No way!" shouted Curtis over the din of the battle. "We've lost a few already—we can't afford to lose you!"

"But we've already lost," was Prue's anguished reply.

"But we've got Carol! Carol Grod, the blind man! He's with Esben. They're making the cog!"

This news buoyed Prue's spirits considerably. She blathered a little, as overwhelmed by her present situation as she'd ever been. "But how? Where did you find him? And where have you been all this time?"

"Can we talk about this later?" It was Septimus the rat, sitting at Curtis's shoulder. He pointed a single spindly finger at the ground below them.

There was no need for further explanation; Prue looked away from the Council Tree and saw, for the first time, the ivy giants. There were seven of them now, and they were falling into position in a circle around the tree. Their heads were each obscured by a long, tangled mop of ivy, and their gargantuan legs sent waves of vines out into the meadow with their every crashing footstep. The air was filled with a flurry of massive birds, each one carrying a mounted rider, who dive-bombed the ivy giants, harrying their movements with swift attacks to their arms and heads. The bandits who'd stayed behind to muster arms had arrived; they attacked the ivy giants with swords and muskets, their every attack receiving great, throaty cheers from the farmers, who were still armed with garden tools and farming implements. Still, those carrying scythes and shears managed to cut away large chunks of ivy that made up the giants' bodies; with every attack the birds' talons took away even more, dropping the dead vines to the covered meadow below.

Watching the whole thing with a cold, measured grace was the Verdant Empress herself. Prue knew her as soon as she laid eyes on her. Even though Alexandra's body stretched yards above her height as a living human and her flesh seemed to be made of the ivy itself, there was no doubt that this was the woman who'd abducted Prue's baby brother and attempted to sacrifice him on the Plinth, those many months before. The same woman who'd raised an army of coyotes to wreak havoc on Wildwood; who'd plotted, in her despair over the death of her son, to reduce the entire Wood to nothing.

And it appeared she was succeeding.

She stood some yards off from the action, callously watching it transpire, her attention fixed, as the Mystics' had been, on the Council Tree itself. She was watching the brutal efficiency of her dark handiwork.

"Bring me low!" shouted Curtis to the heron, and the bird dove swiftly down from its heights to graze the neck of one of the ivy giants. As they passed, Curtis gave an impassioned yell and swung his saber, cutting away a huge lock of the giant's ivy tresses. The creature lowed in anger and swung one of its trunklike arms in the direction of the bird, but the heron's swiftness outmatched the lumbering movements of the giant, and they were soon flown to safe airspace.

"There's no use!" shouted Prue, her eyes still intent on Alexandra herself. With every chunk the flying fighters took out of the ivy giants' hides, the woman simply raised her arms and more ivy climbed from the meadow's surface to graft itself onto the giants' wounds. "They're made out of the ivy! It keeps just growing back."

"Then we go for the queen!" shouted Curtis, and the heron, marking the boy's words, banked sharply to the left and carried them, in all swiftness, toward the Verdant Empress.

She watched them come, this tall, green, reborn form of Alexandra. Her dark, empty eyes narrowed to see them approach.

She lifted her arm, a supplicating gesture, a greeting between old friends; vines shot out of her fingers and ensnared the talons of the heron.

The bird cried loudly and they began to plummet; Prue, thinking quickly, *commanded* and the ivy fell away. The heron regained its bearings, and they looped around the back of the Verdant Empress in a tight, dizzying circle.

"Watch her fingers!" shouted Curtis as he leaned away from the bird's torso, his saber extended.

The Verdant Empress whipped around to confront them, and no sooner had she done so than Curtis's saber came bearing down and struck her in the shoulder. She let out a scream of anguish as the limb fell away, the bundled stalks of its musculature rending at the shoulder joint, and was dashed to the ground in a shower of deadfall.

They hadn't had much time to enjoy the afterglow of their successful attack, however, when Prue tapped on Curtis's back and pointed her finger in the direction of the angered creature. She had bent low and a new clutch of ivy vines had clambered up her legs from the meadow's floor, binding itself at her shoulder to grow a new limb.

"Oh," said Septimus, seeing Prue's gesture. "Well, that's going to be a trick, isn't it?"

But a new enemy had been dispatched; waving her newly sprouted arm over the thick blanket of ivy in the meadow, the Verdant Empress made a conjuration and little smooth lumps began to emerge from the bracken, looking every bit like eggs made from ivy vines. Prue watched with horror as these ovoid bunches began to shake and break open, revealing distinctly birdlike shapes within. They opened their viny wings, just babies in their nests, and raised their ivy beaks to the sky. Their growth was then spurred as their little bodies gathered more of the plant, and soon they were each as big as any of the large birds that were currently thwarting the ivy giants' advance in the meadow. They sprang into the air, scores of them, and giving a terrible cry, lit into the flying corps of bandits and farmers with flashing talons and gnashing beaks.

One such ivy bird flew for Prue and Curtis, and the heron deftly dodged a grab the thing made for her neck. Gliding sideways, she quickly outflew the fledgling creature and circled around for another attack on the Verdant Empress.

"They're fast!" shouted the heron.

Just then, they heard a scream from below them; Sterling Fox, astride an egret, was engaged in a full airborne tussle with one of the ivy birds; the egret had reared up and was tearing at his spectral foe's underside with his talons. Sterling was holding on to the egret's neck desperately, swinging his pruning shears impotently at their attacker.

"Hold tight!" shouted Septimus. He looked back at Prue, gave her a quick wink, and leapt from Curtis's shoulder.

They watched him fall headlong into the ivy bird, his quick fingers grasping hold deep into the viny innards of the thing. Then, with the tenacity only a rat could muster, he began laying into the creature with his teeth. It let out a hollow, woody cry and fell away from Sterling's egret, but not before Septimus had jumped from its rapidly decomposing body and onto the fox's shoulder.

Curtis let out a heroic whoop at the rat's clever action before turning his attention back to the Verdant Empress, raging at the edge of the circle of giants.

"See if you can't get us closer to the woman!" shouted Curtis to the heron.

Suddenly, Prue felt two sharp pincers stab into her shoulders; she jerked her head upward to see that one of the ivy birds had dropped down on them from above and had clamped its talons on her back. She screamed and tried to evaporate the specter, like she had the tendrils the Verdant Empress had shot from her fingers, but her mind grew confused. The heron had banked sharply in an effort to lose the attacker, having heard her rider's call, and it sent Prue's mind spinning in vertigo; she couldn't muster the focus to dissipate the animated ivy. She felt her body lift from the back of the heron; the ivy bird was intent on carrying her away!

"Hold up there, lass!" came a voice. Suddenly, the talons were torn from her shoulders, taking a good portion of her peacoat with them, and she dropped heavily back onto the heron. Looking up, she saw that her attacker was being carried, its claws grasping at thin air, by a very large eagle. On the eagle's back rode Brendan the Bandit King; a young girl who looked very much like Curtis's younger sister

Elsie was clutching his midsection with one arm and wielding a small saber with the other.

"Mind your flanks there, lass," he called again. "A good bandit always does!" And then he had veered off, his eagle pitching sharply away to do another flyby at one of the giants. Prue thought to ask Curtis if that had been, in fact, his sister, but the chaos of the moment did not allow such trivial questions.

The incredible aerial battle waged on. The ivy birds crashed headlong into the avian defenders—the reborn Wildwood Irregulars—who held their ground with courage and resolve. The sky was alive with their zipping and plunging; the birds and their riders quickly learned that an eagle's talons, properly applied, could tear these ivy creations to shreds, and the vines were soon decorating the air like so much confetti at the New Year's stroke of midnight. It wasn't long, however, before the Verdant Empress, seemingly unassailable, would raise her hands and more such hatchlings would birth from the very ground.

But Prue's attention remained on the Council Tree. She saw that the Irregulars, for all their smarts and bravery on the aerial battlefield, could not hold back the ivy from consuming the ancient tree. It was now completely enveloped, as more waves, one after another, piled onto the last. The shape of the tree—the huge trunk, the wide canopy—was now totally lost. The thing had become unrecognizable, just another lump of teeming ivy in a world covered in the virulent plant.

With another wave, another push, the ivy began to tear the tree down.

A massive *crack* rent the air and Prue felt it in her chest, like a piercing needle. Through bleary, bloodshot eyes, she saw this massive, Paleolithic thing, this king among flora, this towering giant among the oldest, wisest trees: She saw it cracked mightily in two. The noise was explosive; it demanded the attention of every warring bird and rider in the vale. They all saw it, they all heard it—but only Prue truly *heard* the tree fall and die.

She heard the tree give a relinquishing sigh. She felt it lapse, then, into silence.

She also felt something snap, though she couldn't know what. Her understanding of the thing that broke when the Council Tree cracked in two and fell was nil; even the oldest of the Woodians were ignorant of the inner workings of the spell that was woven into the trees, the thing that created a boundary between the Wood and the Outside. But at the moment when the ivy pulled the Council Tree down to the ground, the last anchor of the Periphery Bind was broken.

The ivy was loosed upon the open world.

The Reluctant Resurrectee

S he'd kept the teeth; she'd kept each of the items the Verdant Empress had asked her to retrieve. She'd rescued them from the floor of the ruined house after the spirit had been awakened, and she'd carried them with her when she sprinted for the safety of the boy's mausoleum, the only place she knew would be spared the ravages of the ivy. The items were there in her pocket, in the pocket of her gray robe, and she held them out to show everyone gathered in the ivy-strewn meadow. An eagle feather, a white pebble, and yes: a full set of teeth. As Zita told the story, they all listened slack-jawed.

Seamus, having recovered from his earlier fright, briefly raged at the girl for what she'd done, showering her with recriminations as if she was a misbehaving schoolchild, which she was, to a certain degree. As for Carol and Esben, they remained strangely silent during the retelling, understanding that Zita's actions were just one part of an intricate web that was being woven before them. The girl wept a little in the telling and Martha gravitated to her side, resting a consoling hand on her shoulder.

"It's okay," said Martha. "What's done is done."

"I just . . . ," simpered Zita. "I just wanted to make things right. For someone." She looked through her tear-blurred eyes at each of the individuals in the meadow: the old blind man, the bear, the bandit, and the little girl with the goggles. "It's like, so much had gone wrong, you know? I mean, with me. It's like—can't I just fix things for someone, anyway? Like, relieve someone's pain. That's all I wanted to do, I swear."

When she was done, the crowd remained in silence. Finally, Carol motioned to Martha, who walked to his side. Setting his hand on the back of the girl's neck, he walked forward to Zita and said, "I understand your pain, child. We all have experienced loss. All of us. You've done what you could. And now, you truly do have an opportunity to set things to rights." He held out his knobby, weathered hand, its palm open. "Let's have those teeth, then."

She set them, the boy's teeth, in his hand, and the old man closed his fingers around them. He then had Martha walk him back to the fire, where he reached into a small groove in a rock and produced something shiny and spinning. He turned to Martha and smiled.

"Hold out your hand," he said.

She did as he instructed, and the old man set the completed Möbius Cog in her palm.

It was a beautiful thing; all shining brass, its three concentric rings, wrapped one into the other, spun fluidly around a kind of glowing core. How two beings had managed to construct such an incredible thing was well beyond Martha's ken, but she knew it was a thing of beauty.

"It's . . . ," she managed. "It's wonderful."

"Ain't it?"

Esben appeared in their huddle around the cog, and he smiled at his creation. "An improvement over the first, I'd say," he put in. "We made some extra embellishments."

"And now, the final test," said Carol.

The boy's chassis, all shining brass and metal, lay naked by the fire, stripped of its regal uniform. They'd built an operating table for him, made of the salvaged boards from the collapsed hut at the edge of the meadow, and this was where he was laid, like a statue on top of an ornamental sarcophagus. Martha guided Carol to the boy's side; Esben stood opposite him. Seamus and Zita stood quietly at the boy's feet, watching the transpiring surgery in a hushed trance.

"Screwdriver," said Carol.

Esben, with a little difficulty, pinched the handle of a small flat-head screwdriver between his hooks and handed it across the table. He then guided the blind man's hands to the first of the four screws that were set in the corners of a shiny, square plate in the automaton's chest. Each one came out fluidly, and Martha caught them in her hands as they rolled out of their holes.

"Oil," said Carol. Martha, holding a small oiling can, dutifully applied a few drops of the stuff to the two hinges that sat inlaid by the machine's rib cage.

The plate was folded open. Inside, the boy's innards could be seen by everyone present: a landscape of myriad cogs and sprockets, the workings of the most complex grandfather clock ever imagined.

In the center of the boy's chest, amid the stationary workings, was a small, round, and very empty cavity, the size of a tennis ball.

"Cog," said Carol. Martha handed the Möbius Cog to Carol. The thing glowed and whirred in his hand. With a little guidance from Esben, he found the empty spot in the boy's chest and gently set the cog in place.

It slipped into the opening with a snug *click*, and the glow began to expand. It cast a warm illumination onto the cold metal of the surrounding gears. The miraculous orb's three rings started spinning faster and the purring whir grew louder and soon the mechanics of the boy's chest began to slowly shift into movement.

"Close it up!" instructed Carol, having heard the sound of the boy's gears working, and the door in his chest was closed and its screws replaced. The whir of the cog became muffled behind the metal plate, but still discernible. Both Carol and Esben stood back, waiting.

Nothing was happening.

And then: The boy's eyes fluttered open.

The crowd surrounding the table gave an audible gasp to see the machine come to life. The little blue irises in the boy's opaline eyes flickered side to side, taking in this new onslaught of vision. His mouth rasped open; the hinges moaned.

"More oil!" Carol cried. "He's trying to speak!"

Martha flew to the machine's head and daubed grease on its mouth hinges. The eyes watched Martha carefully as she did this. A moment passed before the boy tried the mechanics of his mouth again; he clacked his jaws together a few times before issuing the first word of his newly remade life.

"Why?" he asked.

<hr/>

It was an odd picture, to be sure: the massive wall of ivy growing up on the edge of the Impassable Wilderness, seemingly contained by some invisible force field, but most Portlanders didn't think much of it. They'd become so accustomed to ignoring this strange and inhospitable stretch of land on the border of their city that this phenomenon mostly went unnoted. The ivy had sprung up early that morning, growing larger and larger as it lapped against this transparent wall, but nothing much else had happened, so it was assumed to be relatively benign. In fact, by the following afternoon, it had been all but forgotten, and most Portlanders went about their day as they normally would.

"What's that, Daddy?" asked one particularly precocious toddler, sitting in the back of her parents' station wagon on the way home from day care. They were driving along the Willamette Bluffs and were afforded a good view of this forbidden no-man's-land and its bizarre transformation.

"What, honey?"

The child was pointing to the squirming, wiggling ivy wall, just on the other side of the river, which by now had completely curtained off the typical view of the I.W.'s many tall and imposing trees. "All that plant," managed the toddler, with what few words she had to describe a three-hundred-foot-tall screen of positively menacing-looking ivy vines.

The child's father, who's name was Foom (for reasons too strange and complicated to unpack here), simply said, "Oh, that's nothing."

"Is it mad?" pressed the child.

The girl's father laughed. "You say the funniest things sometimes. I'll have to remember to put that up on SocialFace later."

"Will it get us?"

"Comedy gold," was all her father said, and that was that. By the time the Periphery Bind, the magic ribbon that, for millennia untold, had kept the Outside safe from the impositions of the Impassable Wilderness (and vice versa, depending on your perspective), dissipated with its quick snap, the child in question was sitting on the floor of her room and removing the head from her Intrepid Tina doll while her father was in the living room, merrily broadcasting his daughter's childish bon mot for the world to mindlessly skim. The ivy had built up so much force, pressing against the barrier, that when it was unleashed it was like some pent-up Mesozoic lake that had, after centuries, been finally made free to swamp the world in a flood that would transform the immediate landscape for centuries more to come.

The citizens of the Outside did not know what hit them. Literally.

When the Bind broke and the wall of ivy exploded forward, the first to be consumed was the Industrial Wastes. The milling horde of stevedores, carefully picking through the debris of the collapsed Titan Tower, were caught unawares; they'd just unearthed the toupee of their beloved leader, Brad Wigman, and were preparing to sanctify it as a relic for a religion of their own future devising, when the tide of ivy crashed through the gravel roads and alleyways of the Wastes like muddy water through a sluice box and poured over them with the force of a tsunami. They were, each of them, frozen in place as the magic coursing through the ivy pitched them into a deep, untroubled sleep. Soon, the chemical silos and web of piping of this forbidden land was covered as if with a furry green tea cozy and the ivy moved on, splashing into the water of the Willamette River.

The rampaging plant bridged the water handily, rumbling into the current, and soon made landfall on the far side. It captured trucks that were idling by the wharves and fishermen as they quietly bobbed their lures from old wooden docks. It gave shape to the Ghost Bridge, that mighty structure that spanned the banks of the Willamette only when its bell was rung; the ivy, being shot through with enchantment, was unaffected by the bridge's nonexistence, and so those Outsiders who happened to be gazing out at the river in that particular direction for a moment saw the vision of a gorgeous suspension bridge being seemingly knitted out of thin air by vines of ivy—that is, before they succumbed to the wave of the plant too, and then all memory of the vision was erased in their dreamy slumber.

And then it moved on; it went farther afield. It swept along the placid avenues of the neighborhoods that bordered the Impassable Wilderness, up in the hills, and it poured over the cars navigating the looping streets, freezing the traffic in its widespread green cocoon. The power of the Verdant Empress and her thrall over the ivy was such now that those who were unlucky enough to be swallowed were instantaneously slept; reactions were limited to the following fleeting thought, which, oddly enough, was entertained by nearly every Portlander just moments before the wave of ivy overtook them: "What should I have for dinner? That's strange; it looks like some big green carpet is just about to . . ."

Gaining steam as it covered more territory, the ivy fell in torrents on the downtown, climbing the tallest buildings and filling the lowest basements. Unsuspecting citizens, perched over their coffees, had scarce opportunity to dash off a witty riposte about the coming vegetal deluge on their phones when they were consumed and frozen in stasis, tossed haphazardly into some strange dream. Cats and dogs, swallowed. Bicyclists, swept up. Laundromats, fire stations: blanketed. Parks and schools, civic administrative buildings and carefully restored Craftsman houses in the gridded streets of the East Side—nothing was spared.

The flood covered everything; everything was placed in a fathoms-deep sleep.

Prue looked out on the devastation from the back of an airborne heron and wept.

⚘

"Well, that's a difficult question," said Esben, in reply to the first query to come from the mechanical boy's reborn consciousness. "Like, in what sense?"

The boy, Alexei, the mechanical boy prince, the heir apparent to the Pittock Mansion, pushed himself up on his elbows as each joint whined noisily from years of disuse; Martha kindly doused each complaining hinge with the oil can as he shifted. He swiveled his head

543

on his neck, a telescoping metal conduit, and surveyed his new surroundings. He looked at the bear, the boy's face still betraying no
sign of understanding or emotion. "Why did you do this?"

"Do what?" asked the bear.

His eyes, while still being the cold eyes of a machine, caught the
bear's gaze and fixed him with a look of intense betrayal. "Why did
you do this to me?"

The bear, clearly out of his depth, stepped back from the table,
abashed. Carol moved forward. "We're your makers, Alexei," he
said. "We made you." He motioned to Esben, though he'd only
managed to indicate the air beside the bear, who helpfully stepped
sideways so as to meet the old man's gesture.

"You did this?" asked the boy. His voice was calm and soft; the
slightest tinge of an echo was the only thing to suggest that the sound
had originated from a metal container. Otherwise, it sounded like a
boy's voice.

Esben nodded.

"Then you can unmake me," said Alexei.

"But . . . ," stammered Esben, surprised. "We went through a lot
of trouble. And not just us, but . . . a lot of people."

"No one asked me," said the boy matter-of-factly.

"Well, no. But—" said Esben, but Carol interrupted.

"You're alive, Alexei! Again! Smell the air. Feel the ground
beneath you," said the old man, the emotion rising in his voice. He

stamped his feet a few times against the soft turf of the ivy bed, as if to illustrate.

The boy marked the change that had overtaken the landscape. "What's happened?"

"Your mother," replied Esben. "She's, well, she's gone a little crazy."

"My mother?" Alexei processed the word slowly, as if having to reconstruct the reality he'd previously lived piece by piece. "My mother."

"She's become a part of the ivy. It's a little messy," said Carol.

"But not only that—there was a kind of prophecy involved. You were meant to come back and, well, set things to rights." Saying this, Esben made quick, uncertain eye contact with Seamus and Martha. He was clearly winging it; none of them had foreseen the mechanical boy taking his revival so poorly. "I think I'm getting that all right. You'd have to talk to Prue to get all the details."

The boy on the table only looked blankly at the individuals surrounding him; they all squirmed a little in his gaze.

"Thing is," put in Seamus, affecting a quiet and polite tack, "we kind of have to get a move on if we want to stop her. She's already pretty far gone. And we're supposed to meet up with the rest of the gang in North Wood. So we should probably . . ." Here he made a kind of sweeping motion with his hands toward the northern edge of the meadow.

A silence settled over the gathering. Finally, Alexei said, "Can I have a moment?"

"Oh sure, sure," replied Esben.

"Just not, you know, too long," put in Seamus. Everyone's glare at the bandit seemed to out-wither one another's. Martha inked the automaton's knee and ankle joints with oil, and he threw his legs over the side of the table and, pushing away from his seat, took his first tentative steps. He looked down at his metallic body, all rivets and plating, and said:

"Could I get some clothes in the meantime?"

They all rushed to retrieve his regal uniform, which Martha had folded neatly and laid in a pile at the base of the table. It resembled a strange coronation, this dressing of the Governor-Regent apparent, but soon he was back in his princely costume. He gave a curt nod to his dressers before walking some yards off to an ivy-covered rock, and there he sat, his chin in his hands.

He sat there for a long time.

The rest of the group remained at a polite distance, over by the dimming fire, while the ivy churned around them. They didn't speak much to one another; occasionally, one of them would glance in the direction of the pensive prince, who, for the most part, remained completely still, staring out at the empty meadow and the far line of ivy-smothered trees. Now a vine of ivy made an attempt for his knee; now he wiped it back with a flick of his mechanical fingers.

Time passed; the sun continued its downward migration. Still, the mechanical boy sat in his place on the rock, his chin resting on his hands.

"You'd think," said Seamus, the first one to speak for a time, "that after all that time being, you know, dead, he'd be a little happier."

"I imagine it's complicated," said Esben.

The bandit looked up in the sky, at the lowering angle of the sun, and said, "I expect we'll be needed soon."

"What's he supposed to do, anyway?" asked Martha.

"Search me," said the bandit. "Something Prue concocted."

"It was decreed by the Council Tree," said Esben. "That the true heir be reconstructed." He looked at Carol and frowned. "We did that much, despite the odds. Don't know what else we should do."

"Let me go talk to him," said Seamus. "I've had some experience cooling the heels of some of the younger bandits when they get in a

state. I'll slap some sense into him and we can be on our way."

The bandit began to stand up, despite the unanimous calls for him to not do this, when Zita, who'd been silent up to now, spoke. "I'll talk to him."

"You?" said Seamus. "Not likely. This is all very simple. I'll just—"

"Seamus, sit down," said Carol firmly. The bandit eyed the blind man for a few moments before doing as he'd been directed. "Let the girl go."

Zita flattened the front of her white dress—she'd long ago ditched her father's Synodal gray robe—and stood. Taking a deep breath, she walked over to where the mechanical boy sat. She paused briefly by his side before sitting down on the ground beside his rock perch.

"Hi," she said.

The boy didn't respond.

"I'm Zita. I live near here." She waved a hand, meaning to point out the direction of her neighborhood, but quickly realized that the landscape had been so transformed as to make it impossible to know which way her house was. "Or somewhere."

Still no response; the boy's eyes were fixed on the distant trees.

"I was the May Queen," said Zita, at a loss for how to proceed. "That was pretty cool. I wore my crown today." She pulled the thing from her head and studied it. "Seen better days, I guess."

The boy glanced at the garland in her lap; it was the first sign of his attentiveness, and she tried to capitalize on it. "So, this is all kind of my fault. Bringing your mother back and all. I didn't know that this other stuff was happening, all this stuff about rebuilding the cog and reviving you. I haven't even met the girl who was making it all happen. Her name's Prue. Sounds like a nice girl. She's from the Outside." She paused then, trying to find her way forward.

"I guess I'm saying that I can't really know how you feel, but I know you're upset. I mean, they said you removed the cog yourself, the first time. I can't imagine, really, what you're going through. And I think it sort of sucks that you were brought back to life the first time and you didn't want it. But you have to understand where she was coming from. Your mother, I mean. She lost you. That's so huge. And she had a chance to bring you back. What person wouldn't do that? What person who loved another person so much wouldn't do that?"

She found she was beginning to cry as she spoke. She fought back the tears, saying, "My mom died. Kind of out of nowhere. She was, like, there one day and gone the next. And I would've given anything to have her back. Anything. And when I met this spirit, your mother, and she was so *desperate*, you know? And it was like she'd experienced the same sort of loss as I had. We were kindred. I had to do what I did. In a weird way, I was bringing back my mom."

The tears were flowing now. "I get the feeling she's not back 'cause she wants to be. Like you. I think she's angry, like you. And I might be going out on a limb here saying this, but I think she might be angry at herself. For doing what she did. And all she wants is to be forgiven. And you need to be that person to forgive her."

"Why?" asked Alexei, an echo of his first declaration.

"Because she was freaked out. And she lost you. And she's human." She paused, then, before saying, "Or she was."

The mechanical boy prince processed all this for several silent minutes. Zita was about to stand and walk away, her mission failed, when he spoke again. "If I do this, if I go to her, will you send me back?"

"What, like, take the cog out again?"

"Yes. Take it out. Destroy it. Unmake me."

"If that's what you want," said Zita, though she knew she was out of her depth here. It just felt like the right response.

The boy heaved a long, rattling sigh and stared back out at the strange new world he found himself living in.

Wildwood Regina

Their defense had been repelled; the tree had been toppled and the Periphery Bind broken. They all watched from their winged heights and despaired to see the Verdant Empress mount the fallen husk of the Council Tree and revel in her victory, her arms outstretched; she was not unlike a tree herself, with her branchy arms made from vines of ivy. From her new perch, she commanded her soldiers like a conductor beating out the time of a kinetic symphony.

Undaunted, the Wildwood Irregulars lit into their enchanted

enemies with as much vigor as their energies would allow.

The gray afternoon gave way to evening; the great battle waged on.

The ivy giants, emboldened by their creator's success, fought off the Irregulars' aerial bombardments with increasing skill. Prue, through her tear-blurred eyes, saw each of their fellow Irregulars go down in a shower of vines, thrown from the fingers of Alexandra, battered by one of the giants' fists or caught in the gripping talons of the ivy birds.

They heard Brendan's call, followed by a scream of the little girl behind him; they'd been snagged by the ivy and were going down. The plant had wrapped itself around the bird's wing feathers and cinched tight like barbed wire; the bird had immediately lost control and plummeted in a deep spin into the layers-thick tangle of ivy on the ground.

They fell like meteorites: tangled bales of ivy falling from the sky.

"No!" she heard Curtis shout, seeing the Bandit King plummet. One of the ivy birds, its mouth open in full gape, came crashing toward them and exploded in a flurry of ivy, covering the heron from beak to talon in a mesh of vines. Prue felt her stomach drop out as the heron abruptly lost its glide and began crashing toward the earth.

"Hold on!" Curtis shouted, and Prue held tight to his torso.

The ground came rushing toward them, full force, and they fell headlong into the sea of ivy.

The stuff was so thick and ingrown, here at ground zero of the invasion, that it was not unlike being buffeted about in a surging ocean. Prue, separating from Curtis and the heron in the fall, plunged deep into the plant; her vision went blank for a moment before she opened her eyes and saw that she was submerged in the green sea. She held her breath and waved her arms; her feet couldn't touch the ground. Kicking frantically, she found she could actually swim through the stuff, and she fought hard to get to the surface, gasping for air as she did so. The vines grabbed at her ankles and snagged in her hair; she screamed and shook, treading through the deep growth, trying to keep her chin above the ivy ocean's surface. She felt herself moved along by the rush of the ivy; a kind of spiraling mountain was being created around the broken heap that had been the Council Tree, where the Verdant Empress stood, her feet now two solid columns of ivy, her long braids lashing in the wind.

Prue saw Curtis just a few yards off, struggling to stay above the surface as well.

"Curtis!" she screamed. "Stay moving!"

"I can't!" he shouted back. "It's pulling me down!"

Using all her inner strength, she *commanded* the ivy and made a kind of channel between the two of them; she swam over to her friend and grabbed his hand as the motion of the vortex continued to grow in speed and strength. The channel she'd created was soon overcome with new vines, and Prue felt them crawling over her shoulder, pulling her down. She looked to the center of the mountain, where Alexandra stood, her long green arms whipping about her as she stirred the great maelstrom of ivy around and around, faster and faster.

"Children!" Alexandra called over the deafening hiss of the ivy, the first words they'd heard the specter issue. Her voice was both cold and radiant. "Come! Come to me!"

They were being pulled inward in the maelstrom, closer and closer to the source and the center; the speed of the whirlpool now was nearly dizzying.

Prue looked to Curtis, her hand still locked in his.

"Just go down, Curtis!" she shouted. "We'll just go to sleep!"

"Sleep?" Curtis yelled back.

"We'll sleep. Maybe forever. Don't be afraid!"

"I'm afraid, Prue!"

"I know. I know. But—just relax. It'll all be over soon."

She felt her friend's grip relax in her hand; she felt his fingers slip from hers. She saw his head dip under the surface of the ivy sea. She watched him go down.

Prue then turned her head to the Verdant Empress, kicking and *commanding* all the while, her every muscle attuned to staying afloat just a little longer. She felt the ivy surge forward in its circular motion toward the broken Council Tree; she could sense that the Verdant Empress was drawing her closer.

Come, said Alexandra, now speaking directly to Prue's mind, through the language of the plant world. *Do not fight. Join me.*

NO! Prue's mind responded. *LET ME GO!*

But still she was pulled forward. She saw Alexandra reach out her spindly arms; she watched them, all shoots and tendrils, stretch inhumanly out from her long body. The fingers beckoned her. Prue was pulled forward, no longer in control; she felt the ivy embrace her.

She felt a long sleep begin to overcome her.

And then it all stopped.

She didn't know how long she'd been there, suspended in the ivy. It could have been five minutes; it might've been fifteen years. But Prue felt the world fall out from beneath her; the spiraling force of the ivy had come to an abrupt stop. The vines that had entwined her arms and legs, that had twisted themselves into the strands of her hair, all let go. She was dropped, and her feet felt the hard surface of the grassy meadow itself. She collapsed in a ball, drained of her strength. Opening her eyes, she saw that a long passage had been drawn in the ivy bed—a canyon of the churning vines—leading straight up to the hewn tree and the Verdant Empress herself.

Prue lifted her head from the ground and saw that Alexandra had frozen, a being in suspended animation, her gaze fixed on some point just over Prue's shoulder. Following the spectral woman's gaze, Prue turned and saw a monarchal figure, a boy dressed in a smart uniform, step down from the back of a golden eagle some yards behind where Prue lay crumpled. A girl had ridden with him; she stepped down as well, the hem of her white dress grazing the tips of the meadow's grass, newly freed from the scourge of ivy. As the boy walked closer,

Prue could see that his flesh vibrantly caught and reflected the inter-mittent rays of the dimming sun like a bright, light mirror. She could see that he was a machine, this boy, made of steely brass.

"Alexei," she whispered, bowed by awe.

The boy heard her; he approached and offered his hand. She took it, feeling the cold grip of his metallic fingers press into her palm. He helped her to her feet, which she regained with some difficulty. Her knees wobbled; she stared at the boy intensely, marveling at the pristine whiteness of his eyes, the immaculate smoothness of his skin. But the boy didn't tarry long with Prue; instead, his attention was returned to the spirit at the end of the long channel of ivy.

Seeing the boy, the ivy spirit let out a heartrending moan.

Alexei approached. The girl in the white dress walked beside him.

"Hello, Mother," he said, and the Verdant Empress flinched to hear his voice.

"What have they done?" The voice issued from deep inside the towering figure; it seemed to flow from the river of ivy around her.

"They've brought me home," replied Alexei.

"I brought you," said the boy's mother quietly. "I gave you life."

"I know," said the boy. "And I forgive you."

Then the Verdant Empress's temper was dissolved, and her long arms retracted. Her body seemed to shrink as the ivy vines that had built up her columns of legs and the intractable trunk of her torso seemed to fall away. She was no longer the imposing, enraged thing that had razed her surroundings with every step, every conjuration. Now she seemed almost human.

Alexei continued his approach; Zita the May Queen walked with him, her hand clasped in his, two kindred spirits on a promenade: she in her white dress and garland of dead flowers, he in his brocaded uniform, cloaked in the dust of a tomb. The moat of dry land ended at the stump of the Council Tree, where the ivy had flowed out from his mother's feet. This was where Zita stopped and let go of the mechanical boy's hand; Alexei took a first uncertain step on this hill of ivy, then another. He ascended the pedestal Alexandra had made of the ancient tree and stopped at the apex, standing mere feet away from the Verdant Empress.

Alexandra held out her arms; her son stepped into them and laid his head, softly, on his mother's chest.

Her ivy arms, now slim and small, closed and she wrapped her son in a long embrace, bowing her head so that her lips graced the metallic smoothness of his brow with a tender kiss.

And, at that very moment, when the kiss was laid on the boy's head, and the mother's arms were firmly wrapped around her child as they'd been when she'd first held him, when she'd first cradled him as a baby, when she'd held him as a child crying over some lost bauble, when she'd held him as a boy when a fever had come on strong, when she'd held him as a young man in the full throat of summer, and when the horse had thrown him and he lay motionless on the flagstones and she'd held him then—at that very moment, the ivy ceased its endless writhings and lapsed into immobility and fell quiet.

Then: the arms that had enwrapped the boy turned to what they had previously been: just a gathered and bound bunch of ivy stalks, and the form of the Verdant Empress fell away and was returned to the ground, to the ether.

For Prue, it was as if the very air had been returned to her lungs. The two walls of ivy on either side of the clear strip of grass leading to the stump of the tree settled and compressed, flattening to the ground like downy feathers after a particularly ferocious pillow fight. The plant collapsed into the canyon the Verdant Empress had created, and Prue was swamped by the torrent.

STOP! she called instinctively, and found that the ivy responded very well; it was no longer under the powerful enchantment of the Verdant Empress and so had reverted to its normal suggestible self. Truly, were you to poll any Woodian Mystic (or anyone else, for that matter, with the ability to communicate with plant life), you'd find that ivy, under normal circumstances, is the easiest thing to persuade to your control. Soon, Prue had called away the languid vines and had a small stretch of ground emptied. She heard a voice call to her, a familiar voice, a boy's voice.

"Curtis!" she yelled, batting away the ocean of ivy. "Are you okay?"

"Yeah!" came his voice, some yards off. "What happened?"

"She's gone!" shouted Prue. Peeling apart a curtain of the plant, she found her friend, busily cutting through the thick jungle with his saber.

"Gone?"

"Alexei came, Curtis. He got here just in time. He went to her. I don't know what he said, or what she said, but she just disappeared. Like that!" She found she had tears in her eyes as she spoke. "The tree was right—we were right! We needed to bring him back to save everything. I just never in a million years expected it to turn out this way."

Curtis had a giant grin on his face by the time he'd pulled himself from the vines and stood in the open ground that Prue had managed to clear. They fell into a hug, the two friends, and laughed loudly.

"Where were you, the whole time?" asked Prue between fits of relieved laughter.

"Oh, I was around," he said, still smiling.

"Alexei!" shouted Prue, suddenly remembering. "Let's go find him!"

They fought through the jumble of ivy, Prue clearing the way as she went. Soon they arrived at the foot of the Council Tree's stump; they stepped clear of the vines as they climbed to the top of the mound. There, they found Alexei standing, staring at the ivy-strewn ground where the reborn form of his mother had only recently stood. By his side was the girl in the white dress. She saw Prue and Curtis approach and smiled, saying, "Are you Prue?"

Prue nodded. "I am. Who are you?"

"I'm Zita. I'm the one who made all this happen." She seemed abashed then, and she looked quietly at her feet.

"You're not," said Prue. "This was all in the making, a long time ago." She felt the solid wood of the Council Tree's stump below her shoes. "You had as much control over these events as a leaf does in the time of its falling." She smiled and added, "Someone really special told me that once."

They both looked up at the mechanical boy, who stood silent at the top of the mound. Prue gave Zita a quick nod before walking the few steps to stand at Alexei's side.

"Hi," she said. "I'm Prue."

"I know," said Alexei. His voice, brittle and metallic, was tinged with sorrow.

"Thank you. Thanks for coming back."

"I didn't make the choice."

"Sometimes we don't make the choice," said Prue quietly. "Sometimes, I guess, the choice is made for us."

The mechanical boy prince took a long, rattling breath and exhaled out into the clear air around him. "It's bracing," he said finally. "Breathing. I'd forgotten."

"I can imagine," said Prue.

They stood there for a time, quietly, before Alexei spoke again. "I suppose we'll have to do something about this ivy," he said.

Prue looked out at the horizon; as far as she could see, the ivy was everywhere, settling into silent, dormant pools. Nothing had been spared.

"I can do it," said Prue. "I need to know something, though."

"What's that?" asked Alexei.

"Will you stay? They need someone. The people of the Wood. Everything will need to be rebuilt. They'll need someone to lead them in that. To show the way. I was that person for a bit, I guess. But I think my time is done."

The mechanical boy stared out into the middle distance. His fingers opened and closed at his side as he thought. Zita had climbed the tree to stand beside them; she, too, awaited the boy's response.

"I don't know," said Alexei. "I didn't ask for this fate. I was gone from here. And now I'm back." He looked at Zita, then, and spoke. "I asked her to take the cog out, once I'd done what had been asked of me. But now I'm not sure. I'm not sure."

"Take some time," suggested Zita, grasping the boy by his hand and holding it like a longtime friend. "Think about it. Breathe the air. Then make a decision. I'll do the thing, the thing you asked. But Prue's right. We need you."

Prue gave a low bow to the heir apparent, Alexei, and stepped away, leaving Zita and the boy alone at the top of the mound. Curtis was waiting at the bottom of the slope; Septimus had crawled himself free of the ivy and had found his spot back on the boy's shoulder.

"What now?" asked Curtis.

"I've got work to do," was Prue's reply. She smiled warmly at her old friend before saying, "And then . . ."

"And then what?" Curtis looked at her with a deeply puzzled expression.

"I don't know. Something the tree wanted me to do. I guess it's been a part of this whole thing."

"What do you mean?"

"You'll see, Curtis," said Prue. "You'll see."

She laid her hand briefly on the boy's shoulder, before turning and hiking to the top of the ivy-laden stump of the Council Tree.

She stood on the fallen husk of the tree and threw her hands out to the ivy, taking the position of a hardy fisherman in the midst of a cascading spray, miles out to sea, pulling in the trolling nets. She grabbed fistfuls of ivy and with her arms and her mind began pulling it back like a blanket from a bed, like a magician pulling the shroud from a glass box and revealing the disappeared woman.

It pulled back from its farthest remove first, where it had just touched the trees and grasses of the far farmlands on the outskirts of the city of Portland. It moved quickly, sweeping back from the territory it had amassed in its initial wave of devastation. It pulled back from the streets and alleyways; it uncovered the cars on the interstates and receded from the heights of the tallest skyscrapers and unwound from the lowly parking garages. It revealed the figures of businessmen, eating their lunches on park benches. It unveiled sweethearts, walking hand in hand on busy sidewalks; it released the coffee drinkers and the book browsers and the line cooks and the bicyclists and the bag boys and the counter girls—it released them all from their sleep and they woke with a start, wondering at the strange and deep reverie that had just overcome them.

All the while, from her spot on the trunk of the giant dead tree, Prue *pulled*.

The plant withdrew from the locks and wharves on the Willamette River; it forded the water and quickly retraced the steps of its rampaging invasion across the Industrial Wastes. It shored up against the wild woodland of the Impassable Wilderness and retreated into the dark of the trees there. It was pulled down from the tall trees, though many had already succumbed to its crushing force. It ebbed, like a tide going out to sea, across the lush green landscape it had covered, unveiling a thriving world of tree saplings and the green shoots of newborn plants. It fell away from the unsuspecting denizens of South Wood, and they shook themselves free of their dreamy slumber. It freed the nests of birds in the Avian Principality; it swept across the wilds of the central province of this land and scaled the high peaks of the Cathedral Mountains. Finally, the receding tide of ivy rolled across the farm plots and village squares of North Wood and arrived at the edge of the great meadow itself.

Prue, from the center of the clearing, continued to draw it in. As the surplus piled at her feet, she willed it to be swallowed into the ground.

The ivy flowed across the meadow and loosed itself from the bodies of the sleeping Wildwood Irregulars. They awoke and blinked their eyes, these farmers and bandits and birds, and stared into the glimmering sunset, the glowing moonrise. Elsie was lying flat on her back and enjoying a pleasant dream in which she'd been having a tea party with the actual Intrepid Tina; they'd just sat down and the woman in the pith helmet was telling her that she'd done a good job, a real fine job, and that Elsie was a shining example for her fellow Intrepid Girlz—a model for all the qualities that the group held sanctified: bravery, kindness, and pluck.

Not far from her was her sister, Rachel, who was standing in the midst of the freed grass of the meadow and staring at her hands. She looked up and saw her sister and smiled, as if to say, *What is all this, what do you know* . . .

But the ivy didn't stop there; it continued to pull away, and finally the last strands were swallowed back to the mound in the center of the clearing and disappeared into a small hole in the broken wood of the Council Tree's split trunk. Prue swayed there, her hands still extended, still *speaking* to the ivy until the last leaf had disappeared; and then she collapsed.

Alexandra held out her arms; her son stepped into them
and laid his head, softly, on his mother's chest.

The meadow was full of waking sleepers, all rubbing their eyes as if they'd just woken from some centuries-long slumber. They were foxes and hares and humans and birds; some wore gray robes, some bib overalls. Many carried implements of war; some held the simplest gardening tools. There were children among them and they all flocked to one another, sharing stories of daring that were each more incredible than the last. They'd fought off the attacks of the ivy giants, they said; they'd dodged the blitzing birds and scored a few hits themselves with the sabers and spears they'd been given.

Alexei, having descended the pedestal of the tree, stood some feet off, taking in the air of the living world, this world he'd been brought back into. Zita walked to join him. They stood quietly in the meadow while the figures of the Wildwood Irregulars, all around them, emerged from their sleep.

The Mystics, too, had awoken to the new reality that faced them: The Council Tree, the totem of their practice, had been split in two and now lay collapsed on the floor of the meadow, its great leafy canopy splayed out across the ground. The ivy had caught them in deep meditation, seated in lotus position, and they'd remained there throughout the entire battle. They now stood, slowly, unsteadily, and took in the scene playing out before them.

Prue lay immobile on the top of the broken tree. Curtis, seeing his friend fall after the ivy had been completely contained, scrambled up the trunk and knelt by her side.

He called her name; she didn't respond. Her face was quiet and still but her cheeks still blossomed with color; when he laid his ear on her chest, he could hear the frantic beat of her heart.

"C'mon, Prue," he whispered. "Hold on, there."

He slipped his arms beneath her waist and stood, her slack body draped between his elbows. This way, he slowly stepped down from the top of the broken tree, following the long path made by one of the enormous roots. Arriving at the meadow's grass, he saw that the Mystics were there to meet him.

"She's not well," he said. "She's not conscious."

Wordlessly, one of the Mystics, an older woman, reached her arms out to Curtis. He transferred Prue's limp body to the woman's arms, and she laid the girl down on the soft turf of the clearing's floor.

"We know what has to be done," said the Mystic.

The Mystics carried the girl deep into the forest, far from the old bastions of civilization. They crossed the Cathedral Mountains and wound their way down into the wooded wilds of the old middle province. They traveled for days; the bandit band followed close behind, cantering their horses. They'd insisted on accompanying the Mystics, for fear of newly formed marauders in the woods, emboldened by the sudden change in the landscape and power structure—though in truth, the Mystics needed no entourage; they'd made this pilgrimage yearly and had long resolved themselves to the dangers of the journey. It had been decided, long ago, that whatever events might befall them and thwart their path, it was intended by the fabric of the forest and was thus to be accepted as part of the natural plan of the Wood.

In the middle of the forest, not far from the smashed trunk of the Ossuary Tree, a path had been cut into the greenery of the forest floor. Arriving here, the Mystics fell into a line and began following the path, which led in a circuitous route through the trees. It flowed like a circle; with each revolution, the path moved farther inward until the followers of the path found themselves walking a spiral.

In the center of the spiral was a sapling tree. Three branches sprouted from its tiny trunk; two of the branches sported a single leaf. The third branch was naked.

The Mystic in the lead of the procession carried the unconscious girl: the black-haired girl who had pulled in the ivy, who had brought the makers together, who had united the Wood and brought a new peace. The Bicycle Maiden, Wildwood Regina.

The woman Mystic laid Prue's body at the foot of the young tree. Slipping her arms from beneath the girl's waist, she stepped away and waited.

The ground churned beneath the girl momentarily, before silently opening up and swallowing the girl's body whole into the loamy ground.

A few of the bandits had followed the Mystics on their circuitous route along the spiral labyrinth; they sat hidden in the trees, some yards off. Despite their typically steely composure, each of the bandits fought tears at the sight of the girl's succumbing; one boy wept openly watching his old friend and partner disappear.

Then: Something shook. The forest itself seemed to heave a long breath.

Everyone's attention was drawn to the newly formed tree in the center of the spiral. They watched as the third branch, the naked branch, of the sapling suddenly sprouted a new, green leaf.

CHAPTER 3 2

Wildwood Imperium

The borders had been erased and the civilized enclaves pulled down; buildings that had stood for centuries had been laid to rubble. The tree's grand prophecy had come true: A new era had been ushered in.

It was all Wildwood now.

※

The birds flew out from their nests and made homes in new parts of the forest, now free of the burdens of boundaries. The farmers of old North Wood set about rebuilding their demolished homes and plowing up their fields, ruined by the invasion of the ivy. It was summer now, after all, and the planting had to get done. Already, the weather had improved mightily and the Mystics were promising a banner year for the harvest. Whatever they'd lost in the deluge of ivy, they were sure to regain in time.

The bandits returned to the fort built by their younger members, Curtis and Septimus, and set about rebuilding the structures and staircases so that a new cadre of bandits could call the place home. Oddly enough, when the ivy had been peeled away from the holding pen, the bandits were surprised to see that its captive had disappeared; apparently, when the viny plant had crowned the tree, the bars of the pen had been bowed apart enough to allow easy escape. They searched the nearby perimeter for Roger Swindon, the villainous bureaucrat-turned-Caliph, but they never found him. Some months later, a bandit ranger team returned to camp with a torn gray robe. It had been found rudely discarded at the opening of an abandoned coyote warren. Its owner was nowhere to be seen. One thing was clear: They had likely not seen the last of the old villain.

The Wildwood bandits' numbers had winnowed considerably during the long winter, and they'd lost several good members in the battle for the Council Tree. It was suggested that some outreach wouldn't hurt; waylaid coachmen would now be given the opportunity, after a holdup had transpired, to abandon their servile post and join the illustrious Wildwood bandits.

Elsie and Rachel, who'd stuck by their brother's side after the ivy had been dissolved, approached the Bandit King with a suggestion.

"You're looking for recruits?" asked Rachel.

Brendan only raised an eyebrow to the girl. "Yes, but we won't just take anyone."

"I'm not talking about just *anyone*."

"They'll need to be hard," said the Bandit King, putting on his gruffest voice. "And brave."

"They're both of those things," assured Rachel.

"And crafty."

"Crafty in spades," said Rachel.

"And willing to live long months in sordid conditions. And work well with others."

"Check," said Rachel. "And check. Sometimes."

The Bandit King paused and eyed this Mehlberg sibling carefully. "Where would you find such a fount of solid bandit material?"

A reconnaissance party was dispatched beyond the borders of Wildwood to the Industrial Wastes. There, in an abandoned warehouse in a forgotten quadrant of this wasteland, the surviving members of the Unadoptables remained, forging a life for themselves amid the wreckage. They needed very little persuading; the promise of a life in the forests seemed a desirable alternative to their present circumstances. They arrived at the border of the Impassable Wilderness and linked hands with the half-breed girls, Elsie and Rachel

Mehlberg, and ventured beyond the Periphery Bind, their former place of captivity, into the strange land.

In time, they would grow to be great bandits, bandits of renown. They had many further adventures alongside their new companions; one of the Unadoptables even grew to succeed Brendan in the title of Bandit King, but that was to come much, much later. In the short term, they were simply happy to have found a home together, far from the world that had abandoned them.

A new Periphery Bind was conjured; it sprouted from the stripling bark of the One Tree and the world, again, was protected from the many dangers of the Impassable Wilderness (or vice versa, depending on your perspective)—not that any Outsider could have noticed the difference. The invasion and subsequent retraction of the blanket of ivy did not receive an ounce of regard from the population beyond the boundaries of the I.W., and the people of that world continued on with their quiet and very mundane lives.

The elder Mehlbergs, Lydia and David, arrived home from their jet-setting romp around the world, disappointed in their failure to find their missing son. When the cab deposited them at the front stoop of their North Portland home, they were surprised to see that the dining room light was on.

"Did we leave that thing on the whole time?" said David.

But no: Inside the house, sitting at the dining room table, stacks-deep in a cutthroat game of gin rummy, were none other than all three of their children: Elsie, Rachel, and, yes, Curtis. Curtis the missing boy. He wore, strangely, a uniform that looked like it had leapt from the pages of *War and Peace*, all epaulets and gilded sleeves. They dropped their luggage with a *bam* and ran, hollering, to wrap the boy in the most tender tackle that the two middle-aged parents could have managed.

The story the three children told their parents, when they'd become settled and the shock of seeing their beautiful boy returned had somewhat ebbed, was fantastic beyond words, and it was a testament to the imaginations of Lydia and David Mehlberg that it was not only believed, but promised to be kept as a secret. They were chagrined to learn that Curtis would need to return to this world—he'd taken an oath, after all—but they were understanding of the importance of his role among his bandit brethren.

They could come and visit any time. They were half-breeds as well, after all.

⁂

Alexei chose to stay and to stay alive.

He'd seen the devastation his mother had wrought on his native land, and despite his misgivings about his being a mechanical re-creation of his former, living self, he felt like he had an obligation to the people of his country. The boy's return was met with excitement and celebration from all quarters; it was unanimously agreed that Alexei should ascend the throne and be given the title that the Ancients used for their reigning monarchs.

He was named Wildwood Emperor and was crowned with a salal wreath, as the Ancients had done.

A great party was given at the site of the old Council Tree in celebration of Alexei's coronation. It took place not long after the ivy had been dispelled, and invitations were sent out far and wide by hawk and sparrow. Owl Rex and his retinue of eagles arrived in full military regalia. Rarely had the people of the Wood seen those grumpy raptors let go their austere expressions and enjoy themselves; once the second cask of poppy beer had been uncorked, the old generals were regaling the crowd with stories of harrowing battles and singing the old songs from their flying corps.

The Wildwood bandits arrived by horseback. It was generally agreed among the partygoers that they proved to be the best dancers of the crowd, there under the pinprick stars and the paper lanterns that showered the wide meadow with light. Several dancers, having chosen a bandit for a partner, seemed not to notice that their purses grew lighter with every turn around the sawdust-covered dance floor.

Elsie and Rachel returned to the Wood for the party; many a dancer fought for a chance to take a turn around the floor with one of the two black-haired sisters, and Rachel had barely escaped the grasp of one particularly persistent farmhand to get a sip of cordial when she felt a tap at her shoulder.

"May I have this dance?" asked a voice.

She was about to demur politely, when she turned and saw it was none other than the saboteur Nico, having been discovered in the wreckage of Bandit Hideout Deerskull Dragonfighter not long after the bandits had returned. He'd ditched his black uniform for the mismatched costume of a Wildwood bandit, which he admittedly wore with considerable panache. Rachel threw her arms over his shoulders and gripped him in a tight squeeze. "I thought we'd lost you!" she shouted.

"*Moi?*" he asked, affronted. "*C'est impossible.*" He then took a step back, bowed deeply, and proffered his hand.

She took it, smiling, and the two danced off onto the floor while the band whipped up a rousing reel.

A dais had been erected at the far side of the room; several local craftsmen had come together and designed a magnificent throne, in honor of the returned mechanical boy prince, the newly crowned Wildwood Emperor, and this was where Alexei abashedly sat while well-wishers and congregants brought flowers and benefactions to the savior of their land. He accepted their gifts with embarrassment, squirming uncomfortably under all the blushing attention. Not long into the party, he saw Zita come into the light of one of the paper lanterns and he stood up, gesturing her over.

She came up to the dais and bowed.

"Don't bow," said Alexei. "Please."

"Sorry, Your Majesty," she said.

"And don't call me that. It's me who should be referring to you that way, May Queen."

Zita blushed at the mention.

"Will you sit with me?" asked the boy, patting at a small chair that had been set beside the opulent throne. "It's awfully lonely up here."

Zita smiled and gave a low curtsy. "If Your Majesty wishes," she said. She ignored the glare the boy gave her as she crossed in front of the throne and took her place at his side. Together they watched the whistling, wheeling party as it played out before them, while the paper lanterns cast dancing shadows on the wooden floor and the band played merrily under a sky filled with stars.

☙

But that is not the end of the story.

There is more.

In a leafy borough of Portland called St. Johns, there lived a man and a woman and their young child.

And though they were blessed with a family, they were heartbroken over the loss of their daughter, a girl of twelve short summers who'd disappeared earlier in the spring. They carried their grief bravely, however, because they knew that their daughter had become a great power in a distant and dangerous land and perhaps had died in the defense of this land. They'd known of her exploits from her telling; they'd met talking birds and a sentient bear with hooks for hands. They knew that whatever had happened to their daughter, she had lived a good life and had persevered bravely for a downtrodden people.

But still, this did not dispel their grief.

A shadow was cast over their lives. They struggled to regain a feeling of normalcy and poured all their love into their young son, Mac, and watched him grow happily into a toddler; they marveled over his first sentences and his first stumbling steps. They remembered their daughter when she had done the same, those years before, though sometimes this would make their loss come back afresh.

Then one day, while mowing the lawn, the father saw something growing amid the freshly cut grass. In a small circle of earth, the sprout of a tree had grown. Getting down on his hands and knees, the father pulled back the grass and made a little bed of dirt for the small green shoot. A seed must've taken, he decided, blown by some neighbor's tree. He felt connected to the tiny sprout for some reason, and so he became the tree's staunch steward.

He watered it meticulously and kept the weeds from infringing on the small circle of turf he'd carved away. He fed it compost; he built a small fence around it to keep the deer from chewing at its fledgling limbs. Perhaps it was because of his insistent caretaking, perhaps it was because of magics beyond his ken: The tree grew at an alarming rate.

Each day the father would walk out onto the back porch of his simple house and see that the tree had grown several feet during

the night. His wife and his son soon joined him in his careful minding of the strange tree, and together they would replace its compost and feed its roots with water and fertilizer. The tree continued to grow quickly; soon it was the size of a juvenile sapling, and from its trunk grew many long, healthy limbs, sporting an array of waxy green leaves.

One night, as the father lay asleep in his bed with his wife by his side, he felt something tug at his blanket. He opened his eyes to see it was his young son, having woken up in the night.

"Daddy," said the boy. "Come see!"

They both, the husband and wife, followed the child down the stairs and through the kitchen and out onto the back porch, where they saw that the tree, the tree they had so meticulously watered and cared for these many weeks, was gone.

In its place, in the small circle of dirt and compost where the tree had been, was their daughter.

"PROOOO!" shouted her brother, getting her name right for the first time.

They ran to her and threw their arms around her and bathed her in kisses; she smiled blearily at them, having undergone some incredible journey, and happily returned their embraces. They walked together, this overjoyed, reunited family, and returned to the shelter of their house's kitchen where their daughter, once she'd recovered from her reverie, told them an incredible story about a land in upheaval, about the strange cult that gained control over it; she told them about a ship that took her to a faraway rock in the ocean, where she thought she'd die—until the great bird prince rescued her and returned her to a land overcome by a reborn spirit, made of ivy, bent on the destruction of this land, and how only the return of the spirit's son, the heir to the kingdom, would stop the devastation. She described the heartbreaking reunion of these two, mother and child, and how the ivy was pulled away and the boy became the emperor of this strange land.

The girl's mother listened to the story attentively; her brother barraged her with questions; and her father, shaking his head and smiling at the incredible tale, only said, "Who's up for some hot chocolate?"

And, indeed, they all were.

The End

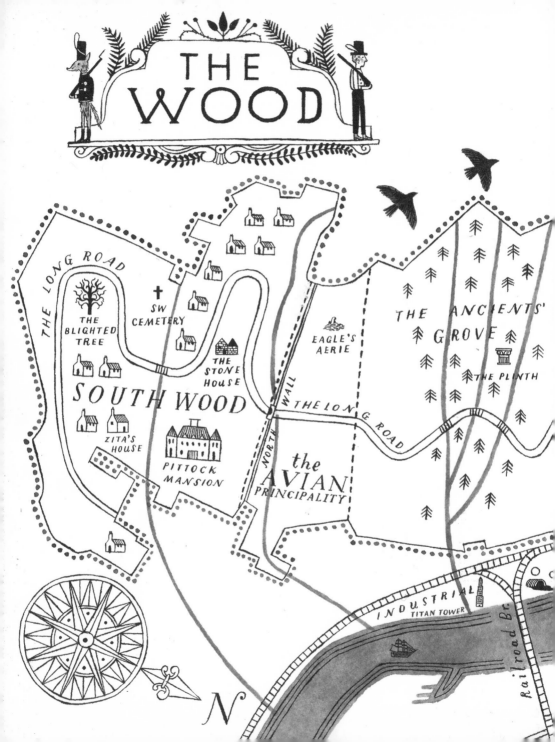